I0590230

# HER DARK GRACE

## RAE VALTERA

A WRAITHMARKED NOVEL

First published in the United States of America March 2025 by Lake Country Press & Reviews.

Cataloging-in-Publication Data is on file with the Library of Congress.

ISBN Print 979-8-9922275-0-5

Ebook 979-8-9922275-1-2

Author website: https://www.raevaltera.com/

Editor: Tara Sexton

Cover Artist: Lain Valentine

Cover Design: Rae Valtera

Formatting: Juliet Bridges

Lake Country Press
Publishing & Reviews

*To the religion who told me my existence was wrong—*
*thank you for the content*

# CONTENTS

# AFFINITY GLOSSARY

 **RA**
FIRE & VISIONS

 **VA**
WATER & HEALING

 **TA**
EARTH & SHAPESHIFTING

 **SA**
AIR & GLAMOURS

# A Letter from the Author

Hello reader. As much as I want to say rage and storm, I must warn you that lightning strikes in the most unusual places. And so, I am here to tell you to take caution before diving into this tome.

Her Dark Grace is a book about many things but at its core, it is a book about trauma. And while I did not want to include real life phobias into the novel, you will find parallels to them within the text. In addition, this book contains the following content warning: infanticide, chronic pain, suicidal ideation and attempt, torture, whipping, assassination, character death(side), alcoholism, religious trauma, genocide, institutionalized mental illness, prejudice, infertility, and explicit sexual content.

So dear reader, if you have decided to surge ahead and join the storm, then inside you will find a woman, who above all else, loves. As brutal as her story is there is one thing I want you to take from Eirlys. It is her capacity to find love in the most heinous of times and horrid of places.

But also, she never forgives because she will never forget. She will ravage the land and grow something new in the chaos.

If you proceed, I invite you to take my hand and hers, and rage with us.

# CHAPTER ONE

## EIRLYS

The chill of desperation clung to Eirlys like the beaded rain lingering on her skin. Despite her affinity for water, the now retreating storm had made her vigil miserable, but she hated to go home empty handed. She ignored the cramp starting in her calf, too stubborn to give up, until three shadowed figures finally appeared on the horizon.

Wind-swept waves lapped against the shore and muffled their angry shouts. One of the women—dark-haired and golden-skinned—gestured frantically, holding tight to the bundle in her arms.

A Skath infant.

The reason Eirlys had waited in the cold and dark for hours beside a cairn of boulders. The very same rocks where, twenty-seven years ago, her mother left her to die. No one in Kygem came to the Barrenlands for any reason other than to abandon their supposedly evil child to the cruel, harsh elements.

The shifting wind drew Eirlys's thoughts away from the past and into the increasingly dangerous present. As the clouds

1

drifted away from the silver ringed moon, illuminating the landscape in its hazy lavender light, the overcast night suddenly became clear and bright. Losing the much-needed cover of darkness, Eirlys swore under her breath.

The group came closer, stopping short of the arid soil, not yet brave enough to step into the Barrenlands. Their footfalls were quiet in the grass on the north side of the border, while Eirlys knelt in the still damp dirt beneath her. The moonlight lit up the features of the two women, the dark-haired one with the infant and another with light hair and pale skin. Their companion was taller, with broad shoulders, though his face was obscured by the deep purple hood he wore. A proselyte—one of the priests of the Ancients, the so-called gods of the north. They often administered the last rites to the children left to die.

These days, when she wasn't guarding the prince, Eirlys ventured north in hopes of saving those infants. More often than not, she'd wait long into the night and trek home with nothing to show for her efforts. The worst was when she was too late—an abandoned infant taken by dehydration or abandoned in the dead of winter, bearing frozen blank stares.

The terrain was unforgiving, wracked by the wind and rain and dust—the lifeless ground, a stretch of dull, gray nothingness and scattered rocks. A stark contrast to the lush coastal plain just beyond Kygem's borders. The only building in the area was the massive guard tower, standing sentinel in the swaying green grass.

Which was why Eirlys stayed hidden, coming only at night. If she was discovered, she would never hesitate to strike a Kygemian down, but it'd be harder to save the Skath she was here for if she started leaving bodies strewn about the land—especially if she started killing proselytes.

Perhaps next time she would dye her hair a different color.

The blonde roots and bright blue tips did nothing to help her blend into her surroundings.

If only she was a Ta, possessing the ability to shapeshift, like the rough-scaled lizard on the rock in front of her with an all too knowing gaze. It made for the perfect camouflage since it was one of the few animals to naturally travel the land bridge. The lizard skittered across the boulder's surface, moving back and forth, tail flickering restlessly. It reminded Eirlys of the way her adoptive mother's braid swung when she was angry or annoyed. Some things never changed, no matter which shape Lita took. Her mother looked at her now, lizard eyes blinking with impatience.

Eirlys and the not-exactly-a-lizard tensed as the pale skinned woman wrenched the baby from the dark-haired mother's arms. The blonde stomped into the Barrenlands, followed by the proselyte who spared a glance back at the grieving mother letting out a high-pitched keening. Eirlys ducked further behind her hiding spot, finding a small crack between the rocks to keep an eye on the situation.

The other woman teetered on the edge of the border, biting her lip before plunging into the mud, screaming, "Mekita!"

The child let out a wail when Mekita placed the babe on the barren soil. Whether it was the child's cries or something else, the dark-haired mother reached for her infant.

"Don't touch him, Sayiv!" Mekita yelled, grabbing her arm.

Sayiv whipped around to face her partner. "We can't just leave him here. He is our son!"

Mekita's laugh was malicious and full of ire before she turned to the proselyte—who had not yet interfered with the argument—as if begging him to explain it.

The proselyte stepped forward, reaching out to grasp Sayiv's shoulder. "That thing is not a child; it is not your son. It is an abomination and must be sent to the void to be cleansed."

Eirlys seethed. Her hands clenched into fists, so she didn't grab the dagger strapped to her thigh. No matter how many times she heard Kygem's views on her magic, it never got better. They would slaughter her right where she hid, all because she was Skath.

Well, they'd try.

Eirlys's magic reacted to her rage and pulled in the shadows around her, deepening the Wraithmark on her face. The line from temple to temple crossed over her eyes as dark as the star-strewn sky. Eirlys cursed, willing her pulse to slow and her magic to fade.

She shook her head, the anger swirling through her mind. How could such a small detail as a strip of darkness or light mean the difference between death and life? Why did Kygemians care whether someone drew their power from the light or the shadows created by light? Two sides of the same coin. Dark and Light. Skath and Klara. And that small little infant would die for that difference if Eirlys wasn't there to interfere on his behalf.

Sayiv shrugged off the proselyte's hand.

Mekita scoffed. "If you want to go to Kestrya and live among the vermin who don't know evil when they see it, be my guest. Cross the Barrenlands. I won't stop you, Sayiv."

The mother choked out a cry and at her stuttering breath, the unpleasant burn of tears caught Eirlys off guard. So few people were willing to cross the Barrenlands, to curse themselves. Better to leave their child to die than to risk the consequences waiting in the dusty soil.

The Ancients, those northern false gods, knew exactly what they were doing when they cursed these lands. As a part of the Skath Treaty, written to end the war, the strip of land connecting the southern islands to the northern continent was gutted of life and magic, leaving the land and sea as barren as the name. Anyone who crossed was left infertile and stripped of some of their magic.

If someone wanted to leave Kygem, they had to cross and curse themselves alongside their infant. But a cursed life was better than no life. Eirlys had yet to find a way to keep the curse from the infants she saved.

"Mekita, please!" Sayiv was screaming now.

"Enough. Let Price do his duty so we can go home." Mekita turned, stomping away from the child and her partner. The proselyte remained.

"Price, he will starve out here," Sayiv said to him. She pulled out a small ceremonial dagger, just the right size to pierce an infant's chest. Was that what Eirlys had survived? "Can you do it instead? Give him a clean death at least?"

Kygemian cowards were willing to sacrifice their infants, but so few of them had the guts to do the killing. They would rather their children suffer. Eirlys touched the tiny scar on her chest. It was a habit she couldn't seem to break. But no matter what her birth mother intended, Eirlys had survived to grow up in the southern realm of Kestrya where her magic wasn't persecuted by religious sacrifice.

Price reached for the dagger, cupping it gently in his hands. "I came here to administer the rites and support you, cousin. I will take care of the child."

*Take care of*—like the infant was nothing more than a problem to be solved.

Sayiv threw her arms around the proselyte and he held her tight for a brief moment. "Go. You should not be witness to this."

Sayiv gave the child one last look before she ran back through the grass.

Eirlys let out a soft curse. Maybe she could knock the proselyte out and grab the baby, but he was facing her direction.

She needed to distract him or stay hidden and pray he was a coward who wouldn't actually do the killing.

*Please let him be a coward.*

The proselyte lowered himself to the ground and adjusted the swaddle around the infant. He was gentle, like he truly cared for him. The tiny boy was wrapped in a handmade knitted blanket. On the light green fabric, little suns in butter yellow wool shone with the love his parents had put into each stitch. Now it was abandoned alongside the child with only his would-be murderer standing over him.

"High Grace of the Ancients." His prayer started soft, voice accented with a sort of twang. "By your light, as your proselyte, I beseech you to take him into your arms. Send his spirit into the void, let him reconvene with the wraith and cleanse his spirit of this evil. And Ancients, hear my plea. If you find this sacrifice worthy and the penance fulfilled, may you send him back to his mothers, cured of his affliction and free from the torments of evil. Hallowed by the light."

"Mom, go," Eirlys whispered, fearing that any moment he would kill the infant. Eirlys might be able to heal most wounds, but she could not heal the dead.

A bright light flashed around the lizard, hopefully hidden by the boulders. A small rodent-like creature darted out from the rocks, drawing the proselyte's attention.

Eirlys snuck around the boulders, on the balls of her feet. The mud was soft and quieted her footsteps and with the waves and wind, she wouldn't be heard. But would she be fast enough? Just as she was approaching, the proselyte started to turn. Lita chirped, running at the man. Price turned back to the rodent, his head cocked under the hood.

When she was within arms-reach, Eirlys stopped breathing. This close, she could see the proselyte's stitching on his cloak and the child's large, round eyes staring up at her. Eirlys lunged for the infant, her fingertips barely caressing the blanket when a blade sliced across her wrist. She drew back, hissing at the sting. Her Wraithmark bled across her face as her magic pulled in the shadows around her to heal the wound, knitting muscle and skin in a rush of cool, gentle magic, like that of a trickling stream.

The proselyte sucked in a breath. He advanced on her, stepping over the child. Eirlys scrambled backward, not out of fear but needing room to maneuver. Price lowered his hood. Jet black hair was tied into a bun, showing off prominent eyes and angular cheekbones. He was striking, nothing at all like some of the proselytes she had seen before. And there was something deadly in his gaze—Price was no average proselyte.

The cloak fell to the ground, revealing white leather armor and a sword strapped to his hilt on his hip. Eirlys palmed her two daggers. If she kept him distracted, Lita could grab the child.

Price reached for his sword, but Eirlys wasn't going to let him get that far. She attacked. Quicker than she expected, his blade was in his hand, blocking her dagger. His opposing hand hit her wrist, knocking her second blow askew. She parried, sliding the dagger blade down the length of the sword, and bringing it up to gut him. But he stepped back, Wraithmark glaringly bright in the soft moonlight. Flames danced along his fist, and he pulled his hand back to strike. She pulled on her magic, creating a shield of ice and snow but the flames never touched it.

Her mother hissed a curse, and Eirlys dropped her shield in a splash of water.

Lita, no longer in the shape of any animal, knelt in the mud, cradling a blistered and raw arm while Price held the child against his chest, backing up, backing toward Kygem. If he managed to cross the border, she and the baby were fucked.

Eirlys ran past Lita, ignoring her mother's shouts. Price's boots touched the grass before she made it to the border. Eirlys stuttered to a stop in the lifeless mud, her shoes just close enough for the blades of grass to whisper across the tips. In another heartbeat, Lita's presence was soft and warm behind Eirlys. After sheathing her daggers, Eirlys reached for her mother's hand, quickly healing the burn. A flash of pain seared through Eirlys's forearm—the price of her healing magic.

The proselyte made a disgusted noise at the sight of her Wraithmark. But before he could flee, Eirlys begged in flawless Kygemish. "Please, he doesn't have to die. I'll take him back. He'll be Devoid, but he doesn't have to die. Tell the mothers that you did it. They don't have to know."

The shock of her speaking his language only lasted a moment. "My Gods will know," he growled.

"They offer a choice, right?" Eirlys asked, grasping at anything, something to convince a religious man to betray his beliefs. "Cross the Barrenlands to become Devoid or die. I am offering him that choice."

"He will never be purified in the light," Price said, his fingers flexing around the infant.

It was Lita who spoke next. "He will not be reborn in the light but if your gods are right, his spirit will be cleansed in the void after his death. What is the harm in letting him live?"

"My cousins deserve to have their son brought back, pure and clean."

Eirlys gritted her teeth. Was there any point arguing with a man such as this? If she wanted to save the baby, she would have to take one agonizing step forward and fight him off without somehow harming the infant. Eirlys didn't want to take that risk, so she needed something that would appeal to his beliefs.

8

When the solution came to her, she didn't ruminate on it. She was never one for thinking things through.

"I am not Devoid," Eirlys said. "If I was, trust me, I would have wrenched the child from your dead hands."

Price's eyes narrowed, darkening in fear. "What is your point?" he said, voice low in warning. He could easily have shouted for backup, yet he stood engaging with her. Perhaps Sayiv and Mekita didn't want their families to know about the child. According to Lita, many people in the north pretended to have stillborns rather than admit their child was Skath.

"Eirlys, no, let's go. It's over," Lita urged in Kestryan, pulling on Eirlys's arm.

Eirlys planted her feet. "We are so close. He's right there."

"You can't cross the line!"

"I can't just leave him," Eirlys screamed. "That man will surely kill him now!"

Lita tightened her jaw, a hardness appearing in her eyes. "Think about August."

It was a low blow. Eirlys had spent the last three years advancing to the rank of Captain in the prince's elite protectors: the Shadow Guard. If the curse ruined her magic, she might lose her position or worse, put August in danger. But would August want a guard who left an infant to die? Would he love her knowing she'd rather protect herself? She was certain she could not live with herself if she left now. And it wasn't like children were in her and August's future. His mother made that perfectly clear—Eirlys would never be queen, would never marry August. Eirlys would watch on the sidelines, ever his protector, ever his sword and shield.

Never his.

But Eirlys would give up so much more than her fertility and the purity of her magic to continue to save infants from Kygem's theological tyranny.

A soft sorrow fell over Lita's expression before she bit her lip. In her eyes laid all the words that were too tired, too worn out by years of sneaking to the border. How Lita was sorry the north hated Eirlys, how she wished she could protect her from it all, how she knew Eirlys would endure worse to save as many Skath infants as possible.

Eirlys straightened her shoulders and ignored the ache in her heart. "I'll cross the border and curse myself. Two Skaths will be cursed today. That should be enough to appease your gods and your twisted beliefs."

Surprise flitted across Price's features. "Why do you care so much?" he asked. "It's one infant of thousands."

Eirlys offered one small bit of truth. "So was I."

Price looked between her and Lita. "You managed to get her out without cursing her. That is impressive."

Lita stiffened. "Don't worry. I didn't do anything but curse my own soul."

On the contrary, Price appeared to be amused, bordering on curious, and it made Eirlys's skin crawl. She went to open her mouth, but Price looked up to the sky, like he was praying. She itched to scream at him, to call him all the names she could think of, to cross the border and drive her daggers into his chest. How many lives had he taken? How many children had he prayed over to come back in his idea of purity? As if her magic was something evil instead of merely different.

"I accept your sacrifice in this matter," Price said. Adjusting the infant to one side, Price sheathed his sword and raised one gloved hand to his forehead, then to the sky. "Absolve me, Ancient Ones. Take the sacrifice of this woman and child and know that it is done in your name."

Eirlys wanted to vomit—she was not here to sacrifice for the Ancients or their perverse faith. But if she was able to bring the infant home, then let this man lie to himself.

Price knelt on the ground and placed the baby on the grass. He stared down at the child, swaddled in the blanket. One tiny hand reached up and Price flinched away. Then he backed up a few steps, and she realized the man's eyes were blue, bright and alert.

"His mothers named him Ronan," he said.

Ignoring her thunderous heartbeat and bracing herself for the pain, Eirlys stepped into Kygem. Shocks, bolts of searing lightning, threatened to seize her muscles. She bit down on her tongue, blood coating her mouth, the metallic taste flooding her senses. Though every step was agony, she would not stop, would not let this be in vain. Then the child was in front of her, and she knelt to scoop him up in her arms.

When she stood, Price jumped back from her, hand flexing near the hilt of his sword. Did he see his death in her eyes? Or perhaps her determination to save as many infants as possible? Perhaps he didn't think she was capable of sacrifice, but that was all she had ever known.

For a moment, she wanted to console Price. To let him know that his cousin's child would grow up safe and happy. In the end, she clenched her jaw shut. He might have let him go, but it was not without a cost.

He could strike them both down in a single blow. With her hands full of the child and the aftermath of the curse, she wasn't sure she could fight him off. Then he relaxed and with one last look at the child and her, walked away.

She watched the muscles of his shoulders tighten. Why would he turn his back on his enemy—one he just cursed? Maybe he had a death wish but Eirlys was in no mood to grant it.

"Let's go, Ronan," Eirlys whispered to the child, bounding back towards the Barrenlands.

Lita waited for her at the border. Eirlys knew she would

have crossed. She would have sacrificed her magic for Eirlys, but they needed it now more than ever. In a flash of light, a bay mare stood where Lita had been a moment ago. Using one of the boulders scattered across the land, Eirlys swung herself onto the horse's back. Together, they galloped away.

As Eirlys fled the realm of her birth with Lita once again, this time holding an infant she saved, she did not regret the choice to cross. Not when the little one in her arms smiled up at her with those deep blue eyes, finally quiet. Finally safe.

So, she ignored the tears flowing down her face and the still blooming pain of the curse's shocks. She knew she would return to fight again—it wasn't as if Kygem could take anymore away from her.

As if there was anything she wasn't willing to give.

# CHAPTER TWO

## EIRLYS

"Heal me."

Rory pulled up the sleeve of his guard uniform, revealing the smooth expanse of his forearm. Before Eirlys could protest, Rory's dagger was in his hand, and a bright red line of blood welled from the cut made across his pale skin. He should've healed instantly as a Va, which meant he was keeping his magic at bay to test her.

"What the fuck is wrong with you?" Eirlys asked, jumping up from the bed.

As soon as she and Lita had arrived in Virva, Kestrya's capital city and her home, Lita let it 'slip' to one of Eirlys's friends that she'd crossed the demarcation line. Despite her protests, they'd rushed a Va healer to her house, restricting her to bed. After hours of poking and prodding and examinations, she was finally alone in the room with her best friend, another member of the Shadow Guard. The rest of their squad clustered in the hall, taking turns pacing past her open door. Eirlys shot them an annoyed look before turning back to Rory.

His usual smile was absent, replaced by a deepening scowl. He held out his arm, the blood beginning to gather along his arm and drip down his wrist. "Heal me," he repeated, blue eyes all steel.

Eirlys rolled her eyes. "No need to bleed out on my floor to prove a point." She reached forward, grasping his arm and trying her best to hide the shaking.

This was the moment of truth—the moment she would discover what toll the Barrenlands had extracted from her spirit. She hadn't dared to use her magic yet, too terrified to reveal the true cost of saving Ronan.

She sucked in a breath, holding it tightly in her lungs. If this didn't work, Eirlys wondered who she would become. Not the right-hand guardian of the prince, surely. Would they remove her from the Shadow Guard, strip her of her rank? What use would she be to August if she couldn't heal him anymore?

The already crushing weight of her decision nearly floored her as her chest tightened painfully.

*Devoid.*

By the Goddess, she hated that word. Not because it now belonged to her but because it made it seem like the void, the place where all spirits returned to, was no longer accessible. If she couldn't enter the void, she could not be welcomed into the Valley by her goddess, Zoasis. Eirlys still held faith in Zoasis, but if she was denied access because of her choice in this life, she would claw her way there, if she had to.

Rory's blood flowed over her fingers, staining them crimson, pulling her back to herself. Releasing a slow breath, she let her natural instincts guide her as she reached for her magic. The shadows in the corners of the bedroom, dimly lit by the remnants of dusk streaming through the windows and the candles flickering on her nightstand, gathered to her. Eirlys's Wraithmark darkened.

Cool wraith wove through Rory's body, guided by Eirlys until the wound flashed, bright and searing on her arm. She barely registered the transfer; she had mended her fellow Shadow Guards so many times, she often could ignore the way their pain seeped under her skin as she healed them. The gash knitted back together, leaving Rory's arm smooth and perfect, save for the blood still coating his skin.

It worked. Her magic still fucking worked.

Her relief was short-lived. Rory pulled back, blue eyes shrewd as he inspected the smooth skin he'd cut into moments before. Then he flipped the dagger, holding it by the blade, and offered it hilt-first to Eirlys.

"Your turn."

Eirlys snorted, grabbing the blade, and made quick work of slicing her arm. Even small Va children could heal their own wounds. The magic was an innate part of their powers, flowing as effortlessly as a stream trickling between moss and stone.

From the sting, she'd cut too deep. But the spirit within her rose to the surface, like a mirror of herself inside her body, ready to heal. Yet the blood continued to seep. Nothing happened.

Rory made a noise in the back of his throat, fear and disbelief mingling in the sound. "Here," he said, reaching for her. His Wraithmark, dark like ink, spread across his face.

"No," she said, stubborn as always. "Maybe it's just not innate anymore, like healing another person."

He frowned but stepped back, magic still called to the ready.

Eirlys searched for the slash in her arm. She felt it, both as pain and as a spirit, sensing the need for healing. She gathered her magic and in what should have been a meager flash of magic, she healed herself.

Except it went completely wrong. The spirit turned in on itself, a writhing uncontrollable thing. Eirlys couldn't get a handle on her own soul. Instead, the magic twisted, the wraith tainted and split apart. The small cut on her arm exploded in blood, muscle, and skin, exposing a stark white bone underneath the ruined mess of mangled flesh.

"Fucking shit!" Rory screamed.

Eirlys stared in shock and disbelief at her arm, horrified that her magic betrayed her in such a way. Her healing magic, the one thing she relied on when fighting an enemy, had been stripped from her. The tears streaming down her face were not from the pain, which she barely noticed as Rory patched her up, but from something deeper that was now broken inside of her. The loss of a magic that for nearly three decades had been as much a part of her as her limbs or the beating of her now ragged heart.

"Eirlys?" He said her name like a question.

How the fuck was she? Confusion warred inside her. She would never, could never, regret becoming Devoid, not when doing so saved Ronan. But that did nothing to temper the growing anger.

Rory stepped closer and she had to turn away. Wiping the tears from her face only served to temporarily remove them. They returned with a vengeance. She stumbled forward, knocking into her vanity, her hands catching the mirror as it nearly fell over.

Before she comprehended what she'd done, her knuckles were bloody, and shards of glass rained onto the floor. Her reflection still stared back at her through the cracks as if mocking her broken powers. She gripped the frame and threw the entire mirror to the ground. Then she turned to her cosmetics, slamming bottles against the wall. Flashes of red—fresh blood and makeup—stained her clothes, the floors, and the walls.

When Rory tried to grab her, she shoved him back. Her magic exploded from her fists, biting cold pushing through his shirt. He hissed away from the pain. But in a moment, his Wraithmark deepened and the burn from the cold was healing. She hated herself for thinking it, for acting on it, but she wanted him to hurt. She wanted him to bleed as his still working Va magic darkened across his face. She punched at him, over and over again, the icy magic freezing over her hands. He merely blocked her. He did not try to stop her, did not try to fight back. Through each slash and freeze and cut, he let her rage.

Eventually, she slowed. Tears tracked down Rory's cheeks and he looked like she felt— utterly devastated.

No marks marred his skin; he was healed, perfect and unblemished. She slid to her knees, covering her face, as if she could shut out the world, Rory's pitying eyes, and the mangled remains of her magic in her own body.

As she knelt in the chaos, there was a gust of wind, a cloak of comfort around her. August's glamour bathed her in sweet blackness, the illusion of serenity, of night and stars, of warm blankets and forehead kisses. It was a darkness of peace and serenity, conjured by the brightest of Klara magic.

His power smelled like home, a sea on the verge of a storm. Soft wind kissed her cheeks, drying her tears. And when Prince August of Kestrya, the man she loved, pulled her into his arms, she clung to him, so solid and real beneath her fingertips.

"I'm so sorry," she sobbed.

"I never want to hear you apologize for saving anyone."

That, of course, made her cry harder.

His next words whispered soft and deadly against her hair.

"I will destroy them for this. It is time that Kygem's reign of terror is finally challenged."

She stilled against him, the wind surrounding them whipping in more frantic patterns. Her calm and steady August trembled, but not from fear. His rage was so rare she barely knew his face without a smile; anger was more her thing. Normally, he exuded the serene grace of royalty. The last time he lost it was when he held his dead baby sister in his arms after the assassination. Even then, Eirlys had been the one to rage, to kill, to enact their revenge.

"Eirlys?" he asked when she didn't answer, pushing her back to study her face.

It took her a moment to speak. They were so close, their noses nearly touching, and all she wanted to do was fall into his gray eyes, now darkened into a brewing storm. The planes of his face were sharp, cutting through her sorrow like knives —his mouth turned down in a frown she never wanted to see there again. Her August was all light and serenity, easy joy; this new expression promised retribution against Kygem—for what they did to the Skath and what they'd done to her.

So Eirlys breathed in his sea-soaked scent, taking strength from his resilience, the love for her that poured off him like rain across the desert, promising something better on the other side of the storm. "You can destroy them. So long as when the time comes and you want to light that match, I get to be there to stoke the flames."

A soft laugh escaped his lips, sending a shudder through her as it huffed against her skin. In some ways, the laugh promised violence—but it was the kind of violence Eirlys longed for, retribution and revenge.

"I'd never dream of taking on Kygem without you. You've always been the one making the killing blow."

Eirlys thought about her newly broken magic. Could she

still fight when the edge she had was now gone? It wasn't as if the rest of the Shadow Guard, save for Rory, could heal themselves. They learned to fight wounded and hurt. And despite her healing magic, Eirlys was no stranger to pain. Even now, her knuckles bleeding and a small sting on her cheek where a rebound of glass must've sliced her, she barely noticed it.

"Promise me?" she asked again.

She knelt before him, covered in blood, surrounded by broken pieces of glass that may as well have been her spirit. He gathered her face in his hands, those stormy eyes intent and sure beneath the bright Wraithmark.

"Eirlys Resier, even if it costs me my last breath, I will see Kygem either freed or rubble and dust. And by the Goddess, her lover and the four daughters, you will be at my side when it collapses."

When August dropped his magic and pulled Eirlys up from the floor, she rose with renewed purpose. A promise in her heart and from her lover's mouth.

Kygem would be stopped.

# CHAPTER THREE

## AUGUST

They had done it. He had done it. The blood didn't coat his hands, but they would be forever stained by his choice.

August tried not to think too hard about the assassination while he made his way to the royal study. Three months ago, Eirlys returned to him cursed, Devoid. And while she worked through her condition with the help of a therapist and intense training with the Shadow Guard, August refused to stand by idly. He was done being the passive prince of an altruistic queen.

Perhaps that would all change today—was already changing, he thought. Elation and something close to anxiety set his limbs buzzing, his mind a whirlwind. The note folded neatly in his trouser pocket carried a weight far greater than he could bear alone.

Nyala Galinis gestured for him to enter, her dark features revealing nothing. She gave a small bow before following him through the door. August tried not to bristle at the bow—he hated such formalities. Nyala and his mother were lovers. She'd raised him alongside the Queen and King, but Nyala was always distant, if not a little harsh. August loved her all the same, but he knew better than to show it.

"Good, you got my missive," his mother said when he entered the room. The note, short and to the point, only included the news itself, and a demand that August come to his mother's study at once.

She was battle-dressed in tight black pants and a deep blue tunic cinched at the shoulder, finished with a wide black belt. She wore her greaves, but now that the worry of immediate danger had passed, her breastplate sat at her feet. Her hair, a deep red like dried blood, darker than August's own reddish-brown curls, was in its usual severe bun, but today fine strays dared to break loose around her forehead. The news from Kygem had rattled them all, even more so that their trusted contact hadn't been the one to send it.

He nodded to his father as a way of greeting. The king was dressed similarly, although his armor remained in place. Unlike the queen, he appeared relaxed, staring out the open window facing the sea. No Kygemian ships lined the horizon —a good sign, surely, that they were not about to be attacked.

August hesitated, unsure where he wanted to start. "Is it true? The queen and king of Kygem are dead?"

Redna dipped her chin. "Yes, but we have a problem. Emzelhal is the one who sent the message."

"Evrit's son?" August tried to remember the child that the assassin, Evrit, took with him to Kygem. But this plan was twenty-seven years in the making and August was three at its conception. He still did not understand how his parents managed to get Evrit and a child into Kygem, nor how they survived this long as both were Skath. Whatever happened twenty-seven years ago was a blessing by their Goddess, a miracle.

It was August's idea to use their spy to assassinate the king and queen. His plan to take out the entire royal family was inspired by the constant attacks on his own life. Seed chaos in Kygem, rattle the north, before sending in Kestryan troops. Then let Eirlys enact her own revenge.

Even though he'd proposed the plot, the shock of its success reverberated through the castle. Everyone was on high alert, unsure what Kygem would do in retaliation, or if the murder could be traced back to the Kestryan royal family.

"Is Evrit dead?" August traced the lines of his nails against the pad of his thumb. He wouldn't mourn the loss of Evrit and he wondered if that made him a bad person, a bad prince.

Redna delicately shrugged. "Emzelhal does not know. He merely knows his father went into the castle to kill the queen and her husband. Though, he mentioned Evrit may have strayed from the plan."

August ground his teeth together. The spy never liked taking orders from the queen, much less her young, inexperienced son, but August made it clear how important it was to destabilize the north's power structure. It was their one chance to hit Kygem where it hurt, a blow that might keep them from recovering in the war August wanted to start. But the assassination had failed in one thing—the heir still lived.

"Either way, Kygem forces did manage to catch Evrit before he enacted the entire plan," his father commented. "It seems we will have to contend with another queen. Our sources say she is not yet twenty."

The age of majority in Kestrya was twenty, but even then, August was barely considered an adult to his people at almost thirty. When one lived for centuries, what was three decades?

"That might work anyway. She won't have the knowledge or skill to wage a war."

"She doesn't need knowledge or skill," Nyala said, speaking up for the first time. "Those Ancients of theirs are five millennia old and have fought plenty of wars against us."

"What can twelve Naevni do against our Wraiths?" August asked.

"How many Naevni are in your little group?" Nyala asked, those umber eyes turning fierce. "A hundred?"

"Almost," August said. Seventy-nine Naevni stood in his army, a unit called the Wraiths.

"I'd say you need ten to one odds to beat the Ancients, on our best day and their worst."

Nyala's advice was too valuable to discount. As the royal advisor, Nyala also held the position of public relations liaison. However, before she found her way into August's mother's heart, she had trained with the southern Naevni, the Necromancers. They seceded from Kestrya over five thousand years ago; however, trade still flourished between the two nations. Legends claimed their leader was once a part of the Ancients, the supposed gods the north worshiped. If Nyala knew the Ancients' true strength, this plan might indeed fail.

"So, we wait again? Another what, century?" August slammed his fist on the table. "Five thousand years we have watched Kygem kill their children, sending their sons and daughters over the Barrenlands and making them Devoid. We have sat back and done nothing. Eirlys has done more for this country—for the northern Skath—than this pathetic excuse of a royal family has in centuries."

"The Skath Treaty keeps us at peace," King Samlet said, far too calmly. His blond hair glowed with the afternoon sun, haloing his head.

"Father, we are not at peace. We should not want to be at

peace. Not while infants die and mothers mourn and fathers run away with their children, cursing them to a life of infertility and corrupted magic, to a life as a refugee."

"We agree, August," Redna said, her voice strained. "Which is why we approved the assassination. It would give us an advantage in a war. But are you so interested now that it has partially failed? When it means putting our people at high risk for the chance to save another realm?"

August stared at the table, at the map. To the north, Kygem was a crescent shaped northern continent, with its vast plains, cliff shores and snow-covered mountains. So much continuous land. His own home, Kestrya, was a conglomerate of islands, and one strip of land connected his realm to the northern continent. The Barrenlands, as they were now nicknamed, was formally known as the Span of Tenniris. The isthmus between the realms was their only land connection.

Three months ago, he'd realized it wasn't enough to take the Skath in. Kneeling on the floor with a sobbing Eirlys in his arms, surrounded by the evidence of her shattered magic and loss, he knew they needed to go farther, do more. And now, as he stood in this room looking at his mother's resignation and his father's relaxed pose, none of the people surrounding him were willing to take the risk.

"We should table this discussion," Redna said. "I know you are eager to prove yourself, my son. But let us sit on the information, see what Kygem does and how much power they retain. Queen Aydra will not be crowned until the mourning period is over. We have time."

Time was the one thing August felt slipping away from him. Ever since he held his dying baby sister in his arms, he knew time was running out. In his nightmares, her cold body reminded him she only got five years to live. Even among immortals, among royals, time was not guaranteed.

Not in this cruel world.

"Go get ready," Redna said. "I know Eirlys is eager to see the little one and I think you both could use some happiness. You should spend some time living, not brooding over war."

August watched his mother go to Nyala, seeking comfort in her oldest friend and consort. His father still gazed out the window. They'd seen the destruction battles between the two realms caused.

But they did not have to watch as the woman they loved came back to them in pieces. Perhaps then, they would have torn apart the world for her.

# CHAPTER FOUR

EIRLYS

**B**aby Ronan's little fist gripped Eirlys's hair with a strength only small children possessed. Gently, she untangled his chubby fingers, then spent the next minute trying to make sure every blonde and blue strand was truly gone from the boy's hands.

"You're so good with him," Nik said, sitting down beside Eirlys.

She propped Ronan up on her knee, facing away from her, partly to protect the rest of her hair and partly to give him a view of the pub where his adoption party was taking place.

"Plenty of experience," Eirlys said. She spent time volunteering with Devoid children and their families before her incident. She wasn't ready to go back just yet, but Ronan held a special place in her heart. Plus, one of her fellow Shadow Guards was giving him a home.

She looked over at Nik. The always stoic soldier had melted away into a gentle father. The way his hair was a few days past its usual strict cutting schedule, showing off his crimped curls.

26

Dark stubble along his jaw meant he skipped shaving that morning. All for a child neither he nor his wife were prepared for but whole-heartedly loved.

They took in Ronan mere days after Eirlys returned to the city, but the paperwork took a bit longer. However, today Nik was officially a father—though as he put it, he became one the moment he held Ronan in his arms.

"You'll help me explain it all when he's older right? What happened to him, how to come to terms with it?" Nik asked, reaching for Ronan's hand. The boy gripped his finger and threw his head back so fast, Eirlys barely avoided losing a few teeth.

Though Eirlys never said the words out loud, she found that with time, she was grateful for the proselyte who had given up Ronan. Maybe there was a little bit of good in that man despite his evident hatred. He could have called down the entire army of Kygem upon them and yet, he let them walk away. Cursed, but alive.

"Of course," she said, but frowned. "I do think it was different for me. My aunt loved me enough to save me and raise me on her own. His... well, I'm a stranger to him."

"You won't be, right Auntie Lissie?"

Eirlys spluttered hearing her childhood nickname combined with the word Auntie.

"I mean, Eirlys is a bit of a mouthful for a child," Nik teased.

She rolled her eyes. Ronan started bouncing on her knee and she realized why. Nik's wife was making her way over to them, with wide eyes and a bright smile. Nik was the only one in the Shadow Guard who was married. He met Aliah in school, and they were practically engaged then. It wasn't hard to see why either. Perpetually happy, Aliah brought out the best in their solemn Nik.

"How's my big boy?" she asked, reaching for Ronan.

"If you pick him up, you best be bringing him to me," Basil said from across the room, both teasing and utterly serious.

Aliah rolled her eyes. "They have been at our house nearly every day this week. Might as well make them up a bed in Ronan's room."

Eirlys passed Aliah her son. "Is that why their glasses are broken?" she asked.

Nik laughed. "Yep. Ronan is in a grabby phase. He'll grow out of it."

"In like two years," Eirlys muttered.

Nik gave her a gentle shove, and they watched Aliah take Ronan over to Basil and Caden. Looking back, Caden signed for Eirlys to join them. The Shadow Guard picked up sign language from the late princess, who'd been deaf, but continued to use the signals even after her death. It was their way of honoring her memory.

Before Eirlys could shake her head or sign back, Nik spoke.

"Where's August?" There was a pause, then Nik's expression became suggestive. "And Rory?"

Eirlys tried to hide the smile on her face. It wasn't hard to figure out what was going on between the three of them—her, August, and Rory weren't really hiding it either—but they hadn't said anything yet. Mostly because it was too new, and Rory and Eirlys were still figuring out their feelings for each other. They were best friends and, yes, the sex was phenomenal, but that didn't have to equal much else. In any case, it didn't really matter. Eirlys was the happiest she had been in years.

"August got called away as we were leaving but he should be here soon. Rory stayed behind to guard him."

Nik nodded. "They wouldn't miss this right?"

Eirlys touched Nik's hand. "Not for the world. Ronan will be the most well-guarded, spoiled child with all of us."

The door opened and the smell of fresh baked bread wafted through the pub. Eirlys breathed deep before getting up, already knowing who it was.

"Tell your mom I miss her cooking," Nik said.

Things were finally improving between Eirlys and her mother, but they still weren't great. Lita hadn't fully forgiven her for crossing the border, for making herself Devoid and nullifying what she had done all those years ago to keep them from the curse's effects. Eirlys didn't think Lita would miss this, but she was still relieved to see her here, stumbling under the weight of too many presents.

"Careful, Mom," Eirlys said, grabbing a package from the top of the pile before it toppled to the ground.

Lita peeked around the stack she was carrying. "Oh good. I'm glad that didn't drop. His Kato is in there."

"Why did *you* get him his Kato?" Eirlys asked.

Kato's were normally given by the grandparents of the child three days after birth. Supposedly, this was long enough for the mother's spirit to disengage completely from the child's so that they could receive their affinity from the void. Inside the Kato lay a purified piece of magic. But the outside, the Kato itself, was unique to every individual, each piece of glass carefully sculpted into a symbol. Eirlys wondered what shape Ronan's would take.

Eirlys's own Kato, made by Queen Redna of all people, was a scene of a mountain with a river flowing between slopes. Though the entire piece was beautiful, she never truly felt connected to any bits of serenity. She was more of a raging storm than a peaceful river.

"Well, Aliah's parents are both deceased and Nik's parents... " Lita caught Eirlys's gaze before looking away.

"Wow," Eirlys breathed. She never thought that Nik's parents would hold on to their prejudice that much. They abhorred Eirlys and her Kygemian blood. It had nothing to do with Skath or Klara magic. Nik was as Skath as Eirlys was, the entire Shadow Guard was. But they more or less wanted Kygemians to stay out of Kestrya. They believed the whole refugee program was a strain on the realm and its resources.

"They are designating me honorary grandma, I guess."

Eirlys chuckled. It made sense. Lita and Eirlys's place abutted the castle grounds in what used to be the old servants' quarters. At first, it was easy for the Shadow Guard to crash there between shifts, especially after doubles. Lita would cook for them or wash their clothes and eventually became an honorary mother for a group of misfits with undying dedication to their prince. Even after Nik married, he tried to stop by for dinner at least once a week. Or that was how it was before Eirlys saved Ronan. Maybe this could heal those fractures.

Lita finally put down the gifts, set out her baked goods, and before she could even fully turn around, Eirlys threw her arms around her.

"Thank you, Mom," Eirlys whispered as the burning in her throat caught her unawares. "No kid deserves a better grandmother."

Lita patted Eirlys's back. "He might not be my blood, but he is of my heart. Nik is like my son, and you saved Ronan after all."

Lita's eyes flickered over the room, landing on the corner where Basil had managed to wrangle Ronan away from Aliah. They tossed the child a little into the air, and the baby came down giggling hard enough to fill the room with a bell-like sound, bringing a smile to everyone's lips. The creases around Lita's mouth softened, and when she looked back at Eirlys, the slightest of silver lined her eyes. "I've been thinking a lot about what happened at the border. I didn't save you just to keep you sheltered forever. I saved you because it was the right thing to do, just as you saving that little boy was. I forgive you, my daughter. I was angry but not for the reasons you think."

"Why, then? If this wasn't about me becoming Devoid?" Eirlys asked.

Lita gripped her shoulders and looked into her eyes. "I just worry that one day you are going to give up every last bit of yourself. That you will destroy yourself to make the world a better place, but you won't be around to see it."

Eirlys flinched. In truth, she never thought she would make it to the other end, never saw herself as part of the picture when she imagined the Skath free from the north's blades. Why was she needed in a world of harmony? She was meant to fight, to shield, to rage against the world. She found peace in violence, in purpose, in action. She honestly didn't know who she was without it, without her cause.

Before she could reply, August and Rory walked in. She looked between her mother and her boys.

Lita sighed, but it was one of understanding. "Go. Take whatever happiness life gives you, Eirlys."

She kissed her mom on the cheek and went to join in the celebration.

Ronan, to everyone's delight, was VaSkath, like Aliah, Eirlys, and Rory. They spent a good portion of the evening manipulating water in front of the baby. He took to it easily, grabbing water from the air and flinging it across the room with shrieks of joy. Most of the guests ended up partly wet before he passed out in his mother's arms.

Aliah decided to take him home, but when Nik rose to follow, August requested that his Shadow Guards remain behind. Ever the understanding wife, Aliah merely smiled, kissed Nik, and bid the rest of them farewell.

"Is anyone else here?" August asked. His tone set Eirlys on edge, her nerves buzzing.

"Mom is," Galen said, nodding to Lita, who gathered the remaining gifts to be delivered to Nik's house.

"She doesn't count," Caden said as she plopped into a chair beside Eirlys.

Though Lita was not a trained fighter, she was privy to more information about the movement of the Shadow Guard and royal politics than most. It was hard to keep stopping the conversation when she kept drinks filled and bellies full.

August only nodded curtly.

"We have received news from Kygem. Though an announcement will be made public shortly, this news brings a potential new threat to my family."

Eirlys stiffened and wasn't the only one. The entire guard sat rapt with attention, shoulders tight, all senses on high alert.

"As all of you know, I have decided that my reign will not be an idle one. While my mother has made great strides to ensure the safety of the refugees in this country, she has only dealt with the symptoms. There is a festering wound in the north, and it must be cauterized."

"Hear, hear!" Basil said, toasting the air with their ale. Light green eyes twinkled behind their glasses, and Eirlys worried they were too drunk.

That didn't stop her from lifting her own glass, but she did not drink, focusing intently on her prince.

"Today, we have received news that will allow us to take advantage of the north's fragile state." August paused. Out of the corner of her eye, Eirlys saw Lita standing off to the side. She rarely paid apt attention to the conversations, though Eirlys suspected she took in every word. There was something new about the way she clung to August's words. It sent an unusual shiver down Eirlys's spine.

"The queen and king of Kygem were assassinated sometime within the last fortnight."

Before the cheering and hollering of the guards got too loud, August raised his hand. "Our work is not complete. An heir is ready to step in and she will have support from her gods. But this provides us an opportunity, a chance to sow discord in the north—a chance to weaken them."

August looked around the room, catching the eyes of his guards. Not one of them disapproved. Who could? While the loss of a life should never be taken for granted, Eirlys and her guards planned to use their deaths to start the freeing of Kygem.

"Are you okay?" August asked, his eyes catching on someone in the back. He stepped forward, concern tightening his features.

Eirlys whipped her head around—Lita was hunched over, a hand pressing into her chest, and it seemed like she couldn't breathe. August made it there before her. With a gentle grip, he helped Lita into a standing position.

Venom laced her eyes as she looked up into his, turning the bright green into something deadly. Eirlys stepped back, shocked by the hatred raging in her normally loving mother's gaze. "What have you done?" she spat in August's face. "Do you have any idea what this means?"

"Mom, stop." Eirlys placed a hand on August's shoulder to reassure him. "I know they were your queen and king for most of your life, but surely you cannot still feel sympathy for them."

Lita shook her head. "It's not about that." She gulped in a few breaths, each one as shaky as the last. "Fuck, I thought we had more time."

Her mother pulled her attention towards Eirlys. The icy, slick feeling of anxiety and fear crawled over Eirlys's skin.

"Mom." One word, one pleading sound to make this terror go away.

"I need to talk to you alone," she said.

Eirlys glanced around but the faces of her guards and her prince were already hardened into resolution. She wasn't getting away from them.

"I don't think that's possible."

"Fine," Lita snapped. "They will all know soon enough."

"Lita, why don't you sit?" August suggested but she pushed him off.

She paced back and forth, her thumb nail in her mouth. A very old habit Eirlys barely remembered from her childhood. "Goddess, where do I begin?"

After another few moments, Eirlys grew restless. Unable to keep the words in, she blurted, "Just spit it out."

Lita stopped. She was on the verge of crying. "You will all hate me," she said. Sinking into the nearest chair, she covered her face with her hands, as if she couldn't look Eirlys in the eye. Somewhere deep in her bones, Eirlys knew her mother's next words would bring nothing but pain. Though she was confused and terrified and dread pooled in her gut, Eirlys knelt beside her mother and put a hand on her knee. Lita gasped in a shaky breath, and finally let the words slip out, each one a small dagger falling from her tongue to slice through everything Eirlys knew. "My real name is Lita Pendry. I am the younger sister of Queen Ambrosia Pendry, the woman who was assassinated."

Eirlys froze. Her fingers numbed, her brain a fuzz of disbelief. Queasiness followed, chomping at her guts, her throat, the back of her tongue. Her hand fell away from Lita's knee, and though her feet were numb, she rose and stumbled away.

"Eirlys is Ambrosia's eldest daughter."

Eirlys's spine collided with a table, and she reached back to grip at something solid as the world shifted beneath her. She wanted to beg her mom to stop. To stop talking, to stop where the next line would go. Eirlys prayed to her goddess to take it all back. To wake her up from this nightmare. But there was no taking it back. There was no sleep to wake up from. Not even her nightmares could imagine something so cruel. The truth crashed upon her, and she could not escape from the reality of her life splintering into tiny, tiny pieces.

"Eirlys will be the next Queen of Kygem."

# CHAPTER FIVE

EIRLYS

August was shouting.

Lita was pleading.

Eirlys was falling.

The world tilted. For a moment, it felt like she was upside down. Like the world was trying to shake her off. This fraud, this monster, that somehow had always been her. Traitor and scum. Fucking Kygemian royalty.

She was one of *them*.

Nausea rushed in with a vengeance. She stumbled back, her knees hitting the bench this time—she sat, bent over, breathing with her head between her legs.

The voices finally made their way over the rush of blood in her ears.

"How could you not tell us?" August asked.

"I was protecting her. I didn't expect you to assassinate her goddess-cursed parents!"

"Fuck!" August kicked a nearby chair, sending it skittering across the floor. "They'll kill her on sight."

Caden's voice, not small but soft, said, "Lita, if what you said all this time was true, then they believe you and Eirlys are dead. They will have no reason to look for you two, right?"

August groaned.

"I wish it were that easy," Lita responded. "Unfortunately, there is magical binding on the crown traced through the lineage. They cannot crown a new queen while Eirlys still lives. They will find out she's alive."

"So run," Rory suggested. That made Eirlys pop her head up. There was no fear or hatred on his face, only genuine concern. "Get out of here. Head south."

"If the Necromancers won't take you in, there are unincorporated lands. You can hunt and forage," Nik suggested.

The idea of being on the run, of never being able to sleep with both eyes closed, forever looking over her shoulder, settled inharmoniously with everything Eirlys ever wanted to achieve.

"We just don't know enough information," August said. "I'm not about to send Eirlys away when we don't know what Kygem is planning. We are a large realm with lots of islands; they won't find her easily."

August reached for Eirlys, and she went into his arms. Something about the way he still held her, knowing who she was, made everything about to come worth it. He would not abandon her or even Lita. But Eirlys was not going to wait around for Kygem to make their move. No, August was right— they needed information.

"This is by far the most irrational, reckless, terrible plan you have ever come up with," August whispered behind her.

His voice hissed over her skin, sending shivers down her limbs.

"Yeah, well, it's the best one we've got," she said back, not bothering to lower her voice.

August cringed. "I think you'll be lucky not to get murdered right away."

Eirlys laughed, a little too sarcastically. "Well then, everyone's problem is solved. She'll be happy—she's been dying to get rid of me for years."

Before August could sputter a reply, she nodded at Lita standing beside her.

"Ready?" Eirlys asked.

Lita shook her head but started walking forward, entering the royal study.

Like always, Queen Redna's rich, dark hair was in its austere bun, not a single strand daring to fall out of place while she sat very poised and very still in a small green reading chair. A book lay discarded across her lap, and she looked over at her husband, seated at the fine mahogany desk near the wall.

"Well, hello ladies," King Samlet said. "How can we help you?"

Lita opened her mouth and Eirlys thought she was relieved to finally be telling the truth after three decades.

Neither the queen nor king spoke the entire time Lita explained. Redna's cheeks were flushed with anger, but she kept quiet. Her eyes darted to her son, whose hand was now intertwined with Eirlys's while Lita finished her story.

"That's quite a tale but one I entirely believe. You benefit nothing by telling me this, yet you stand to lose a great deal." Redna sighed, steepling her hands and touching the tips of her pointer fingers to her lips. Her attention shifted solely on Eirlys, who swallowed. "It could only have been your plan to come to me. That loyalty and honesty can be quite charming.

Explain to me what you think I can or would want to do for you."

August's fingers squeezed her hand reassuringly.

"Your Majesty, we have no intel on Kygem. On what is happening. We don't know if they have figured out that I'm still alive. I think, by using me or Lita, you can use your Ra powers to See them."

Samlet made a noise in the back of his throat, impressed or alarmed—Eirlys couldn't tell. "That is an idea."

Redna shot him a look. "What do you expect to gain from using my powers like this?"

"We just need information. If they don't know about me, we wait. We bide our time. If they do know, then we need to act fast."

"So, you'll run?" Redna asked.

"No, Your Majesty. We will lure them in, and I will be the bait."

Considering she hadn't told her mother or her lover that this was her actual plan, they both reacted minimally. August's hand spasmed against her palm and Lita lost a bit of coloring in her cheeks. She'd pay for that later but for now, she had bigger worries on her mind.

"I take it your precious little Shadow Guard will agree to this plan," Queen Redna asked.

Eirlys ignored the jab. "Yes."

Redna sighed. "Meet me in the solarium in fifteen minutes. Just you, Eirlys."

"Mother," August started but Eirlys shook her head.

"Yes, of course, Your Majesty."

The hurt on Lita and August's face threatened to tear at her resolve but she kept her back straight and her chest high. She ignored the fact she hated visions with a passion. And Redna knew it too. It was why Eirlys thought she would agree. She normally would never go to a Ra for help, not unless she was truly desperate. And they were so far past that point, Eirlys wasn't sure if there was anything she wouldn't do now.

The solarium did not contain any lights. During the day, the southern-angled sun pierced the windows, alighting the room with a golden glow and baking warmth. Orchids, hibiscus, and begonias were planted around the room, their mixture of floral and dirt scent lingering in the air. Ferns and palms nearly covered one of the west-facing windows, providing shade for a few of the plants that preferred a little less light.

Redna, for all her poise and grace, didn't look like a queen at the moment. Her simple white dress brought out the deep tones of her skin while she sat on the floor. In front of her unlit incense lay at the ready. Though she was nearing a hundred-twenty-five years of age, she didn't look any older than Eirlys. Still, most of the time, Eirlys felt their age difference. That was gone at this moment. Redna could have been twenty-five, seated with her legs folded on the intricately tiled floor, praying to her goddess. Eirlys finally saw the woman beneath the crown. The version of Redna Samlet had fallen in love with and who made it her life goal to redefine the refugee program was sitting across from her.

"How long has it been since you've been Read?"

Eirlys swallowed. "Years."

Redna nodded and gestured for Eirlys to sit. She complied, crossing her legs.

"Redna?" She purposely didn't use her title.

Redna peeked one eye open. "Yes?" Her question was filled with curiosity.

"Will me being Devoid affect this at all?"

After closing her eyes, Redna paused. She was quiet for a while. "I don't believe so. While the void is harder for you to access, you are not harder for the void to access. Your spirit belongs there, in the end at least. We never have problems with Naevni moving anyone through the void when they shimmer, Devoid or not."

Eirlys sighed in relief.

"Did Lita ever tell you what your parents look like?"

"No," Eirlys said. Lita had always been tightlipped about her parents. Now Eirlys knew why.

"That's fine. It would only be marginally helpful anyway."

Redna's Wraithmark flared bright across her face. She touched her finger to the tip of the incense to light it, the elemental side of her Ra abilities conjuring a spark. The smell of cinnamon, cloves, and something odd, like burning wood mixed with pure alcohol came from the smoke. Redna's own magic leaned into that char smell, laced with a hint of an apple grove on an autumn day.

"Give me your hand." Eirlys placed her hand in Redna's. "Close your eyes and remember to breathe."

Eirlys barely had a chance to obey before the pull of the void sucked her in. Flashes of images streamed across her vision. The Barrenlands and a man. Eirlys sucked in a breath. It was the proselyte. Eirlys had barely spared him a passing thought since she left and brought Ronan home. The vision followed Price across the land, back to a group of soldiers. No wonder he was skilled with a blade—a guardian as well as a priest. Time passed strangely, focusing on moments and then... an entourage of royals appeared.

A woman with hair the color of Lita's stood beside a person whose deep black skin matched their intense onyx eyes. Price greeted them both with enthusiasm and familiarity.

"Brisa, it has been far too long. What can I do for the royal family?"

Eirlys sucked in a breath outside of the vision. Perhaps her goddess had truly forsaken her. Her luck had finally run out that the person who cursed her was on a first name basis with the goddess-cursed royal family of the north.

Before the brown-haired woman could speak, another voice came from around the carriage. The woman was short, her thick, wavy, strawberry-blonde hair billowing in the sea breeze. A round face, round lips, and large eyes gave the impression of sweetness. She would have been beautiful except for the sneer on her face.

"I want you to tell us the identity of the woman who you let steal an infant," she said.

Price's brown skin paled before he bowed his head, something he hadn't done for the first woman. "Princess Aydra, a pleasure."

Aydra did not seem like she gave a fuck about Price's reverence. "Answer me."

"I don't know," Price said. "It was dark. She was dressed like a guardian, fought like one." His breath caught. "She spoke Kygemian and did say she was originally from Kygem but I didn't think anything of it. Another woman was there but I did not recognize her. What is this about?"

"Price," Brisa said, stepping forward. "Someone assassinated our parents and they claim that Princess Eirlys is alive."

"May Gyda deliver them to the Valley. Oh, Brisa, I'm so—"

Brisa raised her hand, cutting off Price's condolences. "I wish we had time to mourn. But right now, we need all the information about that woman." Her voice did not waiver, even though her eyes were limned with silver.

"What does that have to do with her?" Price asked.

Aydra snapped her fingers, and a servant appeared, carrying a photo album. "Did the other woman look like this?"

Price stared down at the glamoured image and the vision shifted to look with him. Eirlys nearly pulled herself out, panic surging through her veins. In the portrait stood Lita, dressed in a silver velvet dress, a small tiara placed on her head. Beside her was another woman and Eirlys knew, just knew, this was the woman who had birthed her. The stranger had waves of golden-brown hair and amber eyes. Though her coloring was different, Eirlys saw the phantom of her own features reflected back. Her face was kind and joyful, the image leaving a melancholy ache in Eirlys's core.

"Who is that?" Price asked, pointing to the picture of Lita.

Brisa stiffened. "Our aunt, the one who supposedly killed herself. Princess Lita."

Eirlys didn't think it was possible for the proselyte to grow paler but at the mention of her name, all the color flushed from his face. He teetered on his feet.

"That is what the other woman called her. They spoke in Kestryan but I remember that name. It didn't occur to me that she would be the same Lita. I've heard of her in passing but I thought she did something terrible to be struck from the family portraits."

In annoyance, Brisa closed the book and the servant stepped away. "Mother used to say it was because she was ashamed of the royal family. That Lita took her own life so soon after Eirlys's supposed death was why she couldn't stand to see her sister's face. Apparently, Eirlys was a Skath infant." There was bitterness to her words.

Price grabbed Brisa's hand as if begging her for forgiveness. "Brisa, I made her cross. She wasn't Devoid and that was the payment for letting her take Ronan. I thought... I prayed that if

I cursed them both, it would be better than killing one Skath. What have I done?"

Before Brisa was able to offer any comfort to the proselyte, Aydra spoke up. "Lita was there. And if she is still alive, then she probably took Eirlys."

"We don't know that."

"Don't be dense, Brisa. This cannot be a coincidence. You heard what the assassin said. Lita and Eirlys are both alive." She looked over at Price. "Oh, get a grip. Go see your goddess, and next time you see a Skath, drive that sword you love so much through its heart."

Brisa gave Price a grimaced smile, but the dark-skinned guardian walked over to him and placed their arms around him. They whispered something in Price's ear and strode off.

"Well, what do you think? Is it worth it to contact the Kestryan Royalty to see if they can locate our aunt and sister?" Brisa asked.

Aydra smirked. Then she looked up. Like she was staring right through the vision. Right at Eirlys and Redna.

"I don't think we need to go that far," Aydra said. "It seems they have come looking for us."

Eirlys reeled back but the magic kept her locked in place.

"Hello, sister."

# CHAPTER SIX

## AUGUST

August's shoulder slammed into the door of the Solarium, nearly ripping it from its hinges. Nothing in existence could have kept him from the room once Eirlys screamed. The humid air rushed past him as he hurried to her side and pulled her free of his mother's grasp.

"Eirlys." He tapped her face gently.

She jolted awake, prepared to fight whatever danger they had Seen. Then she focused on him, and said, "They are coming. They are coming for me."

Those goddess-cursed northern bastards. They would not get their hands on her. She belonged to him, to Kestrya, to the Shadow Guards. Whatever desperation shown on his face made her reach for him and he helped her to sit. But she teetered for a moment and groaned, grinding the heels of her palms into her eyes.

"Redna?" Lita asked, shaking his mother.

August checked with Eirlys. "I'm fine." She smiled at him,

though it was small and tinged with worry. "Make sure she's okay."

Lita moved over to allow August to approach.

"Mother?" August smoothed his hand over her cheek. Her Wraithmark still glowed brilliantly on her face, and she was whispering, frantic and low. He leaned down to try to hear what she was saying but with a strangled gasp, she awoke. She still appeared dazed, like the vision hadn't quite let her go.

"Mother?" August asked again.

"The Kygemian Princess is strong," Redna said.

August scoffed. "She is a teenager; you are over one hundred years old. She is not *that* strong."

Redna let out a shaky laugh. "She's pissed. Her parents are dead, and her birthright belongs to a Skath."

Eirlys made a noise in the back of her throat. "That's fine with me. Either she can surrender and I'll let her keep that wretched crown, or I'll wear it out of sheer spite."

"Over my dead body," August growled. Anger like he had only felt once before coursed through him, icing his veins. His magic flickered on his face. Only Eirlys's worry kept him from exploding out in a torrent of wind.

"I don't think they will want a Skath on the throne. It's merely a bluff I can use if the plan goes awry." August glanced at her, and something steeled in her gaze, hiding her shaking and straightening her spine. He should have known better than to think she wouldn't be okay. Eirlys never backed down from a fight and was never afraid to do what she believed needed to be done.

August nodded before turning back to Redna. "When will they be here?"

Redna's power flashed across her eyes. "They want to prepare. They plan to scout the areas, but it won't be more than a week."

The resolute look on Eirlys's face scared August. She was too eager for this battle, too eager to sacrifice herself for the cause. If Eirlys had her way, August had seven days. A plan clicked into place as he took in her raised chin. He needed to make her fall so back in love with Kestrya that she would never want to leave.

The royal agora—an octagon shaped open space laid with off-white stone tiles—shimmered in the midday heat. A forest of cypress and poplars followed the gated road to the Karakos palace, which perched atop a rocky outcrop, just visible over the trees. On the opposite side of the square, roads between blue-roofed buildings painted white to stave off the heat fed into the market, where guardians patrolled making sure no SaCarriages entered the busy square. On hot days such as this one, the scent of the sea carried over the land, salty and humid.

Festivities were well under way, and performers set up their entertainment around the fountain in the center. A glamoured dragon, displaying lapis lazuli scales and flecks of gold, took to the sky. It danced on the wind, and when its mouth opened, the glamour nearly felt real as lightning shot out, crackling across the blue expanse above.

The aroma of baking bread and freshly caught seafood filled the air. August stopped at one of the stalls and bought a plateful of oysters topped with a spicy tomato paste. It was Eirlys's favorite, but the scowl on her face as he returned to Rory and her did not bode well for August.

"You love these," August said, wafting the smell in her direction as they dodged children running underfoot and adults pushing through the busy crowd.

"This is ridiculous," Eirlys spluttered, ignoring the oysters. "August, I cannot believe you agreed to this."

She gestured wildly at the gathering people.

"Kygem has taken too much from me, from us. I was not going to let them ruin today."

As luck would have it, and August did believe it was luck— the day before the Kygemians were due was August's birthday. Which meant that he got to convince his guards, and most importantly Eirlys, to spend the day with him. To pretend that tomorrow would not change the course of their futures forever.

It might have been easier if he believed it himself.

Years ago, before his siblings had been brutally slaughtered, August might have been able to believe that tomorrow would not bring despair. But life had shown him just how cruel it could be.

"Even you are worried," Eirlys said, reaching for the plate.

August smiled. "I am, but I'm not going to let that get in my way."

Eirlys slurped down an oyster. "I would never dream of something as serious as the north making their way to the city right now getting in your way."

The smile slipped from August's face. "I didn't mean... "

Eirlys held up her finger. "I only meant that you see the good side of everything, and I need that. I need someone to be optimistic."

Rory reached over Eirlys's shoulder to snag an oyster. With a soldier's quickness, she smacked his hand away. "Get your own," she snarled.

Rory looked at August, a hurt expression on his face.

"I don't know what you expected," August said but he went back and bought Rory his own plate. He watched his lovers try to steal oysters and the coveted sauce from each other, bickering like an old married couple.

Suddenly, he was being hoisted in the air. He almost drew on his magic but Caden's disastrously loud laugh underneath him made him relax.

"It's tradition, my prince," Galen said from underneath August's shoulders.

"Come on, not this year," August begged.

"It's your thirtieth, too," Nik warned.

August started to worry just how bad this was going to be when he was launched in the air. If he wanted to, he could pull on his magic and avoid the somehow still chilly fountain he was thrown into every year, but he didn't. Breathing deep, he enjoyed every second of laughter echoing between his guards from below. He landed with a splash. As he sputtered to the surface, the roar of the crowd nearly deafened him.

Before he could even stand, Eirlys and Rory joined him in the water. Their magic permeated the air, the scent of rain on a parched desert mixed with citrus and fresh streams. Together, they lifted August onto a throne of ice, supported by columns of water. He looked over at his people, cheering and shouting birthday wishes at him. His Shadow Guard celebrated, shit-eating grins plastered on their faces. And below him, his lovers were laughing and whooping, Eirlys's voice bright and cheerful.

As the sun began its descent, performers scattered to the square and set music twisting through the agora. August pulled both Eirlys and Rory into a slow dance. They passed Nik and Aliah holding baby Ronan between them. He waved, boldly using both fists. A pang of guilt shot through August. By tomorrow night, Nik would be locked in a battle against Kygem, all because he wouldn't let Eirlys go. He'd fight for her but how much was he willing to sacrifice to keep her by his side? He tried to remember that Nik and the rest of the Shadow Guard were completely willing to fight for her, too.

"August?" Eirlys asked, something like sorrow etched on her face, but before he could ask about it, the tune to the song changed and she stepped away. The odd look vanished, replaced with a smirk. That expression could only mean one thing, and August backed hastily away from the dancing before his lovers could rope him in.

"Not joining us for the next one?" Rory asked, all innocence.

August let out a snort. "No, thanks. I don't want to look like a fool on my birthday."

Rory gave him a wink and grabbed Eirlys's hand. As the thrumming beat of the tempo heightened, skirts lifted to reveal feet pounding in time with the drums. The song was not about the upper body, but the tapping of shoes and keeping the rhythm. Eirlys and Rory didn't try to beat out the crowd—their competition was each other, a game of who could keep the beat the longest as the tempo raced on, faster and faster. Her eyes locked onto Rory as the two faced off. Sweat gleamed off their skin and they shared matching grins. The look of complete and total elation on Eirlys's face made August's heart soar.

Eirlys loved her people, her culture. She loved to dance, to lose herself in the music, to lose herself with him and the others she cared for. She loved so openly and freely, and it made him love her more. At that moment, no matter what blood ran in her veins, she belonged here; she belonged to him and to Kestrya. She may have been born Kygemian, but Eirlys was Kestryan to her core.

Eventually the sweat-covered Shadow Guard made their way to refreshments. Cooled white wine, bright and acidic, washed down any remaining thirst. Even Eirlys, always cautious and alert, went back for a second glass, soaking in the last bit of normalcy before everything changed. August winked at her, and she stuck out her tongue, which resulted in Caden flicking said tongue. Eirlys looked so offended when she closed her mouth that the entire Shadow Guard laughed until tears were pooling in their eyes.

"Come on," Rory said, slinging his arm around August. "Let's go to the beach. I bet the water is so nice right now."

"I agree. Besides, any more alcohol and we'll be useless tomorrow," Eirlys said. At her words, everyone fell into a somber silence. She lifted her glass to the lavender moon and said, "Take whatever happiness life gives you."

Her voice broke on the last word, but no one stopped to comment. The toast was repeated across the line. August tipped his glass back, letting it soothe any lingering tightness in his own throat. He planned to make as many memories tonight as possible. He was going to take his happiness and cling to it with a child's stubbornness.

August and Rory led the way through the agora, dodging the revelers. They bobbed and weaved, their group shuffling amorphously through the crowd.

"Sorry," Eirlys said to someone from behind them. At her following gasp, Rory and August turned, magic at the ready across their faces.

She halted, her wrist in the hand of a Seer, one of the Ra's who performed for festivals. A blood red scarf wrapped around her head and her Wraithmark shone brightly. Only the whites of her eyes were visible. Eirlys tried uselessly to snatch her hand away.

"I don't want to be Read," she said, but there was no conviction in her voice. As if she realized when August did that this was not a con, not a Ra simply seeking their money. No one was brave enough to touch the Captain of the Shadow Guard, much less try to use magic on her.

"You know they are coming," the Ra said.

Eirlys pulled on her magic.

"She's a civilian," August reminded her.

"Then get her off of me," Eirlys said through gritted teeth.

But when August stepped forward, the Ra let go, blinking away her Wraithmark.

"Didn't mean to bump into you, Captain," she said.

Eirlys's magic faded from her face but before she could even respond, the Ra was making her way through the crowd. August rushed toward Eirlys.

"Are you okay? You're trembling."

She shook herself out and cracked her neck. "It's fine. That was just... weird."

They barely took another step before three other Ra appeared out of the cracks in the crowd. The trio surrounded them, pressing Eirlys into August's chest as she sought to escape their eerie gazes, two blazing with Klara light, one darkening with Skath shadows. They walked in a circle, keeping Eirlys and the Shadow Guard in the center. They never took their eyes from Eirlys.

"Okay," Eirlys said. "This is scaring me."

If Eirlys was scared, August was sure it was terrifying everyone else.

One of the Ra darted forward, grabbing Eirlys by the arm. She gasped. Through sheer will alone, August watched her not send her fist into his face. He pulled her close and her eyes went wide. The guards went into motion, but she held her hand out to stop them.

The Ra rose onto his toes to whisper in Eirlys's ear. His lips moved but August couldn't make out the sound. He worried if he pulled on his power that the Ra would assume he was attacking them.

Then Eirlys's eyes rolled back in her head, and she collapsed.

August caught her, Rory a second behind him. Like she was having a nightmare, Eirlys jerked as he lowered her to the ground.

"What in the void is wrong with you?" August yelled, though logic and rational reasoning told him this was beyond their control. Their magic had taken over, either through the will of the Goddess or some act of fate.

The three Ra surrounded Eirlys once again.

In a haunting tone, reminiscent of the void itself, they repeated one phrase.

"They are coming."

"They are coming."

*They are coming.*

# CHAPTER SEVEN

## EIRLYS

E irlys hated nothing more than she hated visions. Truly fucking hated them. Even though she knew they were coming eventually, she wanted more time. But she was out of that and then some. The ship was approaching, and she needed to get out of the agora and away from August.

She opened her eyes to find the worried faces of her lovers. The Ra must have dispersed afterwards as planned.

"Are you alright?" August asked.

Eirlys gripped her temples. "My head is pounding." She didn't even have to pretend. Her head truly ached.

Rory placed his hand over hers. "I don't sense anything, but internal ailments aren't really my specialty."

"Why don't we take her to another Va?" Caden suggested, pushing through the concerned Shadow Guards.

Everyone agreed and seemed to be ready to join her like a bunch of busybodies.

"Please, not everyone needs to make a fuss." Not only could Eirlys not imagine a worse scene than her and six other people showing up for a headache, but she had no intentions of going to another healer. She eyed Caden.

"That wasn't a typical Ra vision," Basil said.

Eirlys waved them off. "I know. I know. Look, why don't Caden and I head to the healer? You five go test the waters. We'll be there shortly."

August grabbed her arm, worry tensing his fingers to the point of bruising. "I don't want to leave you alone."

Eirlys reached for his face, tracing the line of his jaw, memorizing the feel of it. She would never forget the color of his eyes, or the way his mouth quirked up. "Do you know how much I love you?"

His face softened, though the crease in his forehead remained. "Only about half as much as I love you."

"You can't divide infinity," she said, as she always did. She kissed him, gentle and soft. Her throat burned, and she wasn't a good enough actor to keep the pain fully off her face. "We have enough to worry about tomorrow, my love. Go and enjoy the beach. I will be there shortly." The lie was sour and sharp in her mouth.

He nodded, touching his forehead to hers. "Come back to me quickly."

For a moment, she was sure he figured it out. But then he kissed her nose and pulled back—a big grin spread across his face. He clapped Rory on the shoulder. "Come on," he said. "Maybe we can sneak away for a moment."

Eirlys chuckled, but she heard it catch.

Rory stared at her, the corners of his mouth turning down in a frown.

"What?" she asked.

"Nothing," he said quickly. He leaned down, planting a kiss on her brow. "Go get your head checked out. Hopefully, those Ra won't ruin our night."

Nik, Galen, and Basil followed Rory and August, signing their goodbyes. Caden stood, quiet and somber by her side.

"I should have said goodbye to them," Eirlys whispered.

"You already made Rory suspicious."

Unable to hold back the tears, she let them slide down her cheeks. "Thank you, Caden. For doing this."

Caden only nodded. "Come on, Captain. You have a ship to catch."

On the way to the royal docks, Eirlys wondered if she was making a huge mistake. It had to be a mistake in some way, but she didn't know how else to handle Kygem and the truth she couldn't deny.

Eirlys was a queen. Sure, it was of the realm that wanted to see her dead. But the crown offered power and a chance for the one thing she'd always dreamed of. More than a home, and August, and a place in Kestrya. More than the beautiful life she'd made here.

For so long she had been running. Every infant in her arms meant a race back to Kestrya. Even as a baby, Eirlys fled from Kygem. So many mothers and fathers ran from the north. They escaped, they fled, they ran away—away from the cruelty. Even Redna, who wanted to do as much for the refugees as possible, only made it easier to run. She offered them refuge but not change. A place to go but not a place to call home.

And Eirlys was tired of running. With the crown of Kygem on her brow, she could change the fate of the Skath from inside the north itself.

So, after the vision, she'd gone to talk to Redna alone. And together, they devised this plan. Redna sent the Kygemian convoy an invitation and safe passage to shore. However, Eirlys could not do everything alone. August or Rory would never let her go but Caden, though they were friends—best friends—was the only one who understood what Eirlys stood to gain, what she could accomplish in Kygem.

And what she was trying to protect in Kestrya. Her friends would die for her, fight until their last breath to keep her in the south. Eirlys was not worth dying over. Not to mention the guilt if anything happened to them: to Nik, leaving Ronan and Aliyah alone, to Basil and their goofy nonchalance about the world, or Galen and who knew how many lovers he'd leave behind. Or Caden, who taught her how to fight in a dress and use the correct silverware. And Rory, who had been with her since nearly the beginning. And August, who shouldn't be allowed anywhere near Kygem but who would find a way to join the fight anyway.

Caden ducked into the forest near the castle. She came out holding a bag and handed it to Eirlys. "Your daggers are tucked into the false bottom. It's padded so hopefully they won't notice."

Eirlys nodded. "Perfect. I assume the rest is just clothes."

"Mostly. I did put your Kato in there too."

Eirlys made a face and Caden laughed, clasping her arms. Eirlys's throat tightened as Caden shook her head, mahogany hair brushing over each shoulder. "I know you think you are a raging sea, but I think a mountain river works for you. You might wander, carving your way through the rocks and trees, but just around the bend are raging rapids or a torrential waterfall. The river can be even more dangerous than the sea because some people might not be able to see the danger that lies ahead."

She took Caden's face in her hands. "I'll keep that in mind. By the time I'm done, Kygem won't know what hit them."

Caden scrunched her nose at Eirlys, and they both laughed. "Let's go."

By the time they got to the docks, their friends would be

starting to get worried. Eirlys needed to be on that ship before they decided to come looking for her. Hopefully, the docks would be the last place they'd expect.

Caden hugged Eirlys, brief but tight. "Remember, even in the bitter north, to take whatever happiness life gives you." Before Eirlys let the sorrow bursting in her chest free, Caden stood straight. "No tears. Don't let them see how much they have taken, how much you have given up. Let them think this is a dream come true."

Never show the enemy any weakness. Eirlys held tight in her mind and steeled her spine.

"Then get out of here, guardian. There is a prince who is probably cliff diving right now."

And with that Caden blessed her with one more smile and was gone, fading back into the night like a wraith.

Redna waited for her at the edge of the water, facing the sea. Eirlys walked up beside her. "They should be coming around the shore shortly."

"Thank you," Eirlys said.

Though neither looked at the other, they were eye to eye, queen to queen. Both had spent their lives protecting August and saving Skath. Redna didn't like Eirlys—she never really had. Eirlys felt much the same about her. But surprisingly, Eirlys didn't hold it against her. The Queen of Kestrya had suffered a lot in her life, and she held onto every little bit of happiness she was granted—from her husband, to her lover, and to August and her realm. Eirlys was too reckless, too chaotic, and that threatened her way of life.

"I should have treated you better," Redna said.

The ship rounded the shore, sailing beneath the shadow of the castle cast by the moon.

"It doesn't matter, Redna."

"Perhaps. I cannot change what has been done but this

choice you are making," she took a shuddering breath, "I don't know anyone who would have the guts to even try it."

For the first time since the Ra had told her that the plan was happening tonight, she was finally nervous. With sweaty palms and a thunderous heart, she worried the side of her cheek.

"Maybe I'm not brave but just really, really foolish."

Redna shrugged. "No one who has ever changed the world was first said to be wise."

Finally, the ship dropped anchor, the gangplank thudded to the dockside, and Kygemian royalty stepped foot onto Kestryan soil for the first time in millennia.

The two princesses Eirlys and Redna had seen in the vision were preceded by the same dark-skinned guardian, and— Eirlys blanched. An Ancient, one of the false gods of the north, had personally come to deal with the Skath heir.

These "gods" were the ones responsible for the law that sentenced Eirlys to death as an infant. These were the gods who sentenced all the Skath to die, the gods her mother whispered about in hushed tones as if they could hear her all the way from Kygem. The goddess standing before her in flowing ivory robes, trimmed in scarlet, haunted Eirlys's nightmares. Especially the one where she was trapped in the Barrenlands, and her faceless mother was aiming a dagger at her chest, right where the small, puckered scar lay over her heart. An Ancient always appeared displaying a gory, blood red Wraithmark and pushed the dagger in.

"Well, this is quite the surprise," the Ancient said in Kygemish to her subjects.

Eirlys found her tongue, unglued it from the roof of her mouth, and, with only the temerity of someone who was about to leave everything behind, said, "I'd say. I didn't realize that I was worthy of a god, but as your queen, I welcome the honor you have bestowed upon me."

Redna's mouth dropped open with an audible pop, followed by a tense moment of silence. Then the night was shattered by the sound of a Naevni piercing the air. Their power was the scream of losing a loved one mixed with the howling of wind through a broken window.

Jagged fractures of light crisscrossed in front of the Ancient, like she was walking through a broken mirror. Shimmering, one of the deadliest abilities of the Naevni, took them instantly from one place to another, using the void to travel the plane of existence. She appeared before Eirlys, her hand whipping out to grab Eirlys's throat.

"Let me go," Eirlys coughed out. The strength in the woman's hand caught her off guard. She was sure this goddess, false or not, could crush a rock into dust by squeezing her fist around it.

"Cosyn." A voice came not from the docks but behind Eirlys. A voice that still held the northern accent even after twenty-seven years of living in Kestrya. A voice that reminded Eirlys no matter how old she was, her mother could always use that tone on her, and she would comply.

Lita's footsteps clapped on the dock boards.

"Now, I have been gone for a long time, but I still know the law fairly well. You cannot kill Eirlys while the crown falls to her. So, put down my daughter unless you want the entire nation of Kygem to know you don't believe in your own laws."

Cosyn's eerie white eyes narrowed at Lita. The ship's crew had gathered to watch, sailors and guardians alike.

Lita fell in beside Eirlys and leaned a bit forward. "Unless you plan on killing everyone here, I suggest you let her go." Her mother stared down a god and effectively scolded her like a child.

"She'd better watch her tongue," Cosyn said, dropping her hand. "And you should watch your back, Lita. Stealing the child, raising her in secret; you should be executed where you stand."

Eirlys reached for her own throat. Only for show did she call on her magic. Cosyn's face twisted in disgust as the onyx Skath magic spread across her temples, but Eirlys still pretended to heal her throat, though she could feel the bruises starting to form already. Shit. Kygem could not know that she couldn't heal herself.

"You have obviously never raised a child," Lita said in Kestryan. She wrapped one arm around Eirlys's shoulder. "Are you alright?" she asked in the same language.

"Sure, splendid. Just nearly got my throat torn out by a goddess." Then Eirlys realized Lita stood beside her, not leaving. "Go, Mom."

Lita rolled her eyes. "Absolutely not."

"Mom, please." Eirlys begged now, alarm rattling through her. This was not part of the plan, and she could not let Lita return to Kygem. Who knew what they might do to her?

But Lita would not be swayed.

"No," she said firmly. "I will not let you go to the north alone."

"An Ancient just threatened to execute you."

"Cosyn's had a stick up her ass for millennia."

Eirlys shook her head, glad the conversation couldn't be understood by the still seething goddess a few feet away. "I don't know why but I didn't realize you had met the Ancients before."

"We have a lot of catching up to do."

In truth, Eirlys hadn't really let herself think about her mother's confession. The fact that she had lied for decades about Eirlys's and her own past. There had been too much to do, too many secret goodbyes to say. Besides, how could Eirlys be mad that Lita lied when her entire plan was to leave her mother behind in Kestrya?

The brown-haired woman eyed Redna before taking a deep breath and walking toward the queen. Briar? Bella? Eirlys couldn't remember her name.

"My name is Brisa Pendry, Princess of Kygem. This is Deryn Olisa, one of our guardians."

"Redna Karakos."

Brisa went to open her mouth, but Redna cut her off.

"Is there a reason you are talking to me and not the person you have invaded my lands to retrieve?" Redna did not give the princesses much attention, seeming like she wanted this interaction finished.

The princess closed her mouth. As if it hurt her to do so, she looked at Eirlys.

"Hello," she said.

Eirlys resisted the urge to roll her eyes. What were they expecting her to do? Grow a second head and start spewing scalding water out of her mouth?

"Stop talking to it," Aydra said from behind her sister. Eirlys remembered *her*. She shuddered. This woman, still practically a child, haunted Eirlys's dreams.

"Aydra," Brisa's tone warned.

"No. You keep acting like that thing is related to us. If that assassin hadn't told the realm about her... " Aydra sneered. There was the look of disgust and hatred Eirlys had seen on the faces of the parents of the infants she'd saved. "We would have just killed her and been done with it."

Eirlys swallowed. She assumed that was their plan from the beginning; though like Lita, she knew the law of the north.

"We can still make a deal," Aydra said, now seeming to deem her worth the breath. Her voice was mockingly sweet.

"What kind of deal?" Maybe, just maybe Eirlys could stay here. She could leverage her crown for protection for the Skath, to remove the curse of the Barrenlands.

"Abdicate the throne and remain here, safe in your little"— Aydra gestured to the surrounding land, wrinkling her nose— "sweltering realm."

"And what can you offer me in return? I give up the crown and... ?"

"You get to live," Aydra snarled.

"No," Eirlys said, calmly. If she'd cared about her own life, she would have never taken this risk. Her own life was worth far less than the fate of the northern realm and the Skath that were born there.

Everyone around them stood tense. Brisa and Deryn were watching, eyes wary, hands on weapons. Redna, off to the side, kept flexing her fingers. Deciding whether or not to defend Eirlys? Or whether to burn the dock, the ship and all of her problems away in one fell swoop?

Eirlys walked towards her sister—the word still a foreign concept to her. She gazed down at Aydra and those amber eyes blazed with fury and revulsion. "Here are my terms. I will surrender the crown to you if, and only if, we draft a new treaty here and now. The Skath in the north will no longer be persecuted. If you don't want them, fine. We will set up a system in which we will take them across the Barrenlands. Your gods will undo the curse of the isthmus as well so there is no danger to those willing to help."

Apparently, Eirlys had a knack for surprising the gods. Cosyn quite literally looked speechless.

Aydra merely blinked at Eirlys like she had indeed grown two heads. And though she wasn't sure, Eirlys thought she saw Brisa smile, for just a moment.

"Those are completely ridiculous demands," Aydra finally spat out.

"That's a no then," Eirlys said. "Fine, I'll have to do it myself." She turned to Brisa. "If you don't mind, I think we best be on our way."

Brisa nodded. "Yes, um, please, come aboard."

Lita took a step forward. Eirlys stepped between her mother and the gangplank. "No."

"Lita has much to answer for... "

"I don't care. She stays here."

A rarely angry person, Lita's rage was plain on her face. Cheeks ruddy, eyes mere slits. "I made my choice years ago, no matter the consequences. You don't get to make this choice for me now."

Eirlys stifled a cry, wanting to throw a tantrum like a child. Only a mother could bring that out in a fully grown adult. Lita strode past Eirlys, walking onto the ship first and leaving Eirlys staring at Redna at the end of the dock. She raised her hand and Redna returned the gesture. Her face glowed with pride.

Then Eirlys boarded the ship. The anchor was being pulled. Between one breath and the next, the ship lurched from the dock. She stood at the railing, a goddess to her back, a pissed off princess to her right. Aydra seemed to be boiling from the inside.

Brisa and Deryn were working the ropes and Eirlys was impressed. Kygem wasn't known for its naval forces, being one gigantic land mass rather than Kestrya's island nation.

It was on the railing, staring back at the home Eirlys had given up, that she noticed the rustling of leaves. Spit out from the dark of the forest, August burst onto the moonlit pier. He stared at the ship; his eyes focused on her. He ran to the dock, past his mother who shrunk back into the shadows. He didn't notice her. His feet pounded loudly on the wood, and when he made it to the end, he called on his magic.

"Stop," she breathed, chest tightening and throat burning and heart breaking. "Let me go."

Maybe he heard her. Maybe he hadn't planned on launching himself into the air to catch the ship like she thought. It was just the kind of reckless thing he would do.

But the light shining from his face sputtered out as he raised his hand, leaving only the moon to highlight the tear tracks streaking his cheeks. An air current rippled past her, the last remnants of his fading magic and his wrenching grief, trailing his voice with it. "I love you."

She opened her mouth to whisper back into the wind, but someone yanked her shoulder, spinning her around. Face to face with a gap-toothed man, Eirlys tamped down her disgust. He reeked of vomit and piss and brine.

"Let's get you to your quarters, your Highness."

Eirlys shrugged her bag high on her shoulder and followed him. She did not look back at August. She did not turn to see if the rest of them appeared. She had said her goodbyes today, in laughter and in dance, in joy and in mirth. She gave them the best last day she could have.

The man led Eirlys and Lita down below deck. Lita frowned but Eirlys didn't care. She wasn't here to be queen of Kygem to get the best rooms. She was here to make Kygem pay for all they had done but most importantly, to keep any more Skath from facing the blade.

"I need to search you and I'll need to take this," the man said, grabbing at Eirlys's bag.

"Be my guest," she said. She would have done the same to anyone entering her realm but that didn't make her happy about it. She shoved it toward him, hard. He huffed and barely maintained his balance.

"Get out of my sight," he sneered, slamming the door.

It locked.

Eirlys hadn't been searched. Not that she was able to stash much on her person, but she had the essentials.

The room they were in was dark, the only light coming from a porthole. Eirlys felt around the wall for a Ra glass but there were none to be found.

"Here," Lita said, lighting a lantern with a set of matches instead of the normal Ra crystals.

"A bit archaic." Eirlys used the light to examine the room. It was mostly storage, some dried goods, a barrel that sloshed with liquid. Extra rope coiled in the corner like a sleeping snake. Fabric to patch the sails was stuffed into a crate.

"At least we have blankets to lay on if we need it."

Lita did not think that was funny.

Eirlys ignored her and went to the porthole. Maybe she could see how far from the shore they were. Instead, she caught sight of a bag—her bag—landing in the sea.

"Mother fucker, my daggers were in there." Eirlys rolled her eyes. Trying to throw a Va's goods overboard was pointless, not to mention just plain rude.

Eirlys went to pull on her magic—she could easily lift the bag back onto the ship. She imagined their faces when her sloppy wet bag landed back on the deck. But nothing happened. A gnawing black ache emerged inside her. What in the void was going on? The last time she had felt this she'd been in basic training during her conscription...

It dawned on her then. Obsidian. The only material capable of stripping an immortal from their powers.

"Mom," Eirlys said. "Try drawing on your magic."

Lita frowned. Then her eyes widened. No Wraithmark appeared.

"Curse them!"

She'd been such a goddess-cursed fool. Too blinded by grief and resignation to see what was happening the moment they stepped onto this fucking ship.

Eirlys pulled a dagger from her boot. Eirlys stabbed the tip into the floorboards, prying up the wood. The first piece only gave way to the structure plank. Metal met wood and she opened a hole big enough to see below. The black shiny material of obsidian winked at her, mocking her for thinking she could make it to Kygem. They cared nothing for honor, for their own laws, except to ensure Skath infants died.

"Eirlys." Lita's voice came out a little too concerned for Eirlys's liking.

She looked up and her stomach lunged for her throat. Smoke was billowing through a small hole in the ceiling. Lita started choking. Eirlys grabbed her mom's hand and yanked her to the floor.

"Help me break the obsidian." She thought of the porthole, but with the smoke bearing down on them, that option was lost. If they could get a big enough hole in the floor to fit through, it might allow access to the void again. The whole room must have been lined, but it couldn't be that thick or it would unbalance the ship.

Eirlys and Lita scrambled to the gap in the floor. They pulled the boards up, ignoring torn nails, but the harder they worked, the more they breathed. Eirlys could feel the smoke clinging to her lungs, suffocating her. No matter how hard Eirlys hit the obsidian it wouldn't budge. Her skin and knuckles cracked, the bones in the heels of her palms splintered until blood started splattering into her face with every punch.

"Fuck," she said, sitting back. Her hand was a ruined mess and every breath seared in her chest.

"Go to the barrel," Eirlys commanded Lita. "Soak your shirt in whatever liquid and cover your mouth."

Lita did as instructed. Eirlys ran to the door, propriety and pride left behind on the shore. If they couldn't use magic to break free, there was only one option left. She screamed for help, banging on the door. Her shattered knuckles screamed in agony and when she couldn't take the pain any longer, she kicked the door. Above deck, she could hear fighting. Someone was yelling. Then a loud thunk shuddered against the door. Eirlys stepped back and took in another lungful of smoke.

The door opened. Brisa coughed into the smoke, pulling her shirt over her mouth. "Oh gods," she breathed as Eirlys's body finally gave out.

She heard Lita shouting her name. Someone grabbed her by the arm. By the time she was lifted out of the smoke-filled room, sweet oblivion was pulling her under.

# Chapter Eight

## Price

Sweat dripped down Price's spine, its descent creeping along with unnerving slowness. He exhaled out of his nose, keeping his mind on even, deep breaths. In and out, in and out. A muscle in his back contracted as the bead passed over it, and he rolled his neck in a slow, even circle, willing the discomfort away.

Hunger gnawed at him; he tried to ignore it, but his empty stomach made it hard to meditate in the wretched heat of the temple. He had taken one look at his breakfast and couldn't put the fork to his mouth. Not yet, not until he was absolved by his goddess.

*Focus.*

He closed his eyes and tried to count his heartbeats.

Suddenly, the feeling became worse, more torturous. His throat filled with bile and nausea crept up the back of his tongue.

*Breathe, Gods curse me, just breathe!*

But nothing worked. Every nerve began to fray, his patience wearing as thin as the edge of a blade.

Giving up, he pulled on his magic, absorbing the light from the shiny white marble all around him. Though he didn't even open his eyes, his spirit could sense the magic, the cutting brightness searing the ground and baking the air.

Fire licked over his skin, fervid and fierce, lapping up every single bead of sweat from his body. The flames were so carefully controlled that his clothes remained intact, drier now, but not a scorch mark or singe on them.

As it always did, the pain flared, burning hotter than his magic. Agony seared through his nerves. His head exploded with it, and he fell back onto the small blanket he had placed for his mediation.

He groaned and placed the crook of his arm over his eyes. The idiot Va didn't have any clue how to help him.

*Meditating will help clear your mind. If you get angry or frustrated, breathe in and out. Like this.*

As if deep breathing was some secret technique.

This Va was the last in a line of healers appointed to help him. To fix him. Nothing ever worked–well, almost nothing. Obsidian always took the pain away, but he hated being without his magic more than he hated what it did to him. He shouldn't feel that way, as it was a gift from his Gods, but the pain.

Some days he wondered if it was all worth it—if his life, his magic, was worth the cost. His parents didn't pay the price for what happened to their son. Price did, every day.

As his power began to recede, his muscles relaxed. His body was never truly devoid of pain, but he'd learned to tolerate a certain degree, which allowed him to put it out of his mind.

With a sigh, Price heaved himself off the ground. It wouldn't do well for him to be caught on the ground if his goddess decided to show up. He couldn't even fathom the amount of trouble he was in. Would they strip him of his proselytehood? Force him out of the guardians? After all they had done to keep him alive, he had betrayed them.

What possessed him to allow that woman to take the child? To let her go? Her pleas were nothing he hadn't heard before. Parents often came to him, begging to be an exception to the tenets of their religion. He spent his adult life guiding the lost back to the light and somehow, he had succumbed to the darkness of one woman's desperate cries.

Eirlys. His fucking queen he had forced to become Devoid and let her go with his cousin's child. At least he knew he would only be punished for letting Ronan live. Even the Ancients had a tenet against killing the queen. He had overhead arguments about what to do with her. Maybe he shouldn't have stayed his sword. He'd thought about driving it through both of them, ending the two of them right where they stood. Was his ignorance enough to be absolved from that sin? He didn't know and the scripture was not helping in this matter. So, he traveled to his patron goddess's temple.

Nym's vast Hall made of white and tan quartzite was the most unique temple of the Ancients. The diamond recesses were stacked in reducing numbers from the bottom to the top and above each diamond were windows. It was a testament to the Goddess of Perseverance that her temple lasted the longest without need of repairs or replacements. The building was nearing five thousand years old and still withstood the test of time.

"Proselyte," someone called to him.

Price was grateful he had sat up as an acolyte ran to him. He recognized the face but could not remember the man's name.

"Hallowed by the light," Price said, touching two fingers to his temples.

"As foretold through Sight," the acolyte said, repeating the gesture. He then checked to make sure they were alone before leaning close. "Did you hear about the princess?"

No one in the entire realm missed the announcement even if Price had been told personally. The brutal assassination of their queen and king and the shame revealed through it. Princess Eirlys, the supposed stillborn first child of the queen, was alive. And worse, she was Skath. For Price, it was even worse that he already met her.

The man still waited on his answer, so Price said, "Of course."

"I know the Codex states there is only a certain time before one can make a sacrifice. But surely, a sacrifice is better than allowing a Skath to wear the crown."

Price swallowed. If only he hadn't just read the Codex, looking for some clue as to what they were supposed to do now. But the scripture was clear in this matter at least. "Acolyte, your words go against the very axioms of our religion. We do not kill outright. We merely allow the spirit to reconvene in the void, to be brought back as a Klara through reincarnation."

"But surely, our laws will not allow her to live?" the acolyte said, appalled. "She is a Skath, Proselyte."

"I am aware of the princess's affliction." Price held his hand up, stopping the conversation. It bordered on the impious. "And despite it, there is little we can do now. The Maxim is clear. Redeliverance, by reincarnation, must be performed before the spirit takes root in a child."

The timing of redeliverance was unclear but theorists held the belief that any time before a year of age was acceptable, any time after two years of age would be wasteful, and the time in between, required divine prophecy. Although no one would be punished for sacrificing a Skath over that age, it effectively became murder according to the gods. And for the Acolyte to want to murder the future queen, the thirteenth goddess of their pantheon, was sacrilegious.

"There will be time to discuss scripture in the coming months, Acolyte but for now, trust in our gods. They will know what to do." He said it with more conviction than he felt. Price fished a tithe out of his pocket. "Can you take this to the chalice?"

A small piece of Price's magic lay within the glass. Typically, he gave on worship days but today, he needed a bit extra.

The acolyte accepted the tithe and headed off, but not without a backwards glance.

Price let out a long breath before turning his attention to the altar in the back of the Hall. He sat on the ground, prostrate, waiting for his goddess to appear.

She came in a swirling, howling sound. Price kept his eyes on the ground, palms facing the sky until the tip of her glass staff touched his hand.

"My dearest Price," Nym said.

Price rose and smiled at his goddess with her skin of russet amber and thick wavy hair. The stories say her eyes, five millennia ago, were as deep and velvety as the leather she still wore and her hair as black as the night sky. Her leathers were not of this time, but tied together with sinew, and dyed indigo and ochre. She and her twin were one of the few gods to not appear in the traditional robes.

"Ancient Nym," Price said. Then he was at a loss for words. He should weep at her feet to be absolved but for what? Which part of his sins did he even begin to confess and lay down before him?

"I know you are hurting, my precious one," she said. Her

hand reached out and stroked his cheek. He leaned into her touch, grateful she talked first.

"Tell me how to make it better. How do I earn your forgiveness?" he whispered into her palm.

Nym brushed her fingers over his lips before drawing her hand back. It had been years since they had been intimate, but it still crossed his mind from time to time. The feel of her, the way he was able to worship her with his body.

"I have spoken to my siblings about your misdeeds. Your ignorance on the matter is understandable. No one knew about the princess and the law is clear in this matter. Not even us gods can harm her as our laws state. However, you let her take the child."

"You haven't told Sayiv or Mekita? Let them not know the worst of me."

It was hard to read the face of a five-thousand-year old being but Price had learned the subtle ways in which Nym's face changed. His goddess pitied him, and he never felt lower than he did in that moment.

"We will not divulge that information," Nym said curtly before she softened. "I think I have a way that you can earn forgiveness."

"Anything," Price said. He'd beg at her feet for the rest of his life. He would administer the last rites to every Skath born in the north, he would drive the dagger in himself for the chance at redemption.

"Her Grace will need to be trained in the ways of the Ancients, but she will also need to be guarded. We have heard many unsavory rumors and if we can make it so that one of our own, a proselyte, was protecting her, it might make others reluctant to harm her."

Price frowned. He was getting off too easy and he knew it. "That is all?"

Nym *hmmed*, her finger tapping her jaw. "Well no. We want information on her as well. Especially between her and her mother. If you can help us gather any information on Kestrya that would be delightful. However, what we need most of all, is to know if she is worth saving. Such as we once saved you."

"That practice has been forbidden," Price said, as if his goddess did not know their own laws. He snapped his mouth shut and Nym cocked her head at him. He had never been anything but devoted and loyal to his goddess and the pantheon she stood alongside. But the princess, the mention of his own alteration made his nerves raw and his mind blur in panic. He tried again. "I was a mere infant when you saved me."

"You were and by the grace of our late queen, she allowed you to live and sent your parents to us."

"And I have been blessed since," Price said, if only to appease his goddess because that wasn't what he meant.

He didn't know what was wrong with him, but he shook any negativity away. He was being tasked by the gods and no greater honor could be bestowed upon him.

Nym moved on as if nothing happened. "It would not be undesirable if the princess got to know you. To see you like a friend and confidant so she may one day realize her Skath magic is a burden, a malady to be cleansed. But we must request one more favor. It would be to our great benefit if Her Grace remains unaware of your previous affliction."

Price bowed his head in acquiescence. Even if something about these penances made him feel uncomfortable.

"Price," Nym said. He cast his eyes up at her, keeping his head still bowed. "We are counting on you. For the life you now have and for the magic that flows in your veins, we have never asked you for anything."

Perhaps she was right, and they never asked for anything.

But the words rang false, as if every day of his life, he wasn't required to be grateful. He was grateful, he reminded himself.

"We ask this of you now as we enter uncharted times. Be our constant, our faithful. You'll find her at the Pendry castle."

Without giving Price the time to question her, Nym stepped through the void, the shattering reality cracking behind her before she disappeared.

Fuck. As if this whole thing wasn't conflicting enough, he was now being charged with the new queen's safety, as well as her conversion to a religion that hated the very magic in her veins. And if he failed, he could wander the void forever, without finding paradise—trapped in the endless expanse, forever lost for his misdeeds in this life.

He needed to get there quickly if he was to succeed. Even his fellow proselytes were tempted to kill the queen—those in line for the crown would not be as easily persuaded to stay their hand.

But as he walked out of the temple of the very gods he worshiped his whole life, the pain struck across his nerves like a warning, the lightning before the thunderous boom. He was supposed to hate her for being Skath but treat her like a deity because she was to be his queen. How could he lead a woman from the path of darkness when shadows of doubt were slinking across his mind?

# Chapter Nine

## Eirlys

Years of guardian training kept Eirlys sharp, especially during sleep. So only pure exhaustion kept her from becoming aware of the scents, the acrid air, the dust and mildew smell of a room long forgotten, floating through her sleep-clouded mind. Hazily, she grabbed the blanket and pulled it over her shoulder, turning to fluff her pillow. Something strange and piercing tugged at her palm, pulling her from her half sleep with a start.

She blinked, staring at the foreign white ceiling, ribbed with redwood beams jutting out in an octangular shape. Her heartbeat quickened as she eyed the Pendry crest, a silver triquetra knot, seated above.

In the center of the knot was a swirling pattern illustrating the Va's healing and water magic. Each point lay the symbols of the remaining magical affinities. A triangle surrounding an eye for the Ra who had the Sight and ability to summon fire. For its use of the earth and of shapeshifting the body, a square with a circle in the middle stood for the Ta. Last, a circle in a circle for the Sa's control over crafting glamours and the very air around them.

As she analyzed the crest, and its meaning, memories of the past few days slammed into her. Kygem. She was in Kygem and, from the looks of it, brought straight to their castle, right into the lair of her enemies. Except she wasn't their enemy any longer, was she? She was one of them. And her sister tried to have her murdered before she could even step foot on her homeland.

Any sense of family ties or honor Eirlys may have conceded to the princess of Kygem was thoroughly snuffed out. Princess Aydra had to be one who sent the smoke flooding in—the surprise in Brisa's expression when she'd opened the door on the ship conveyed her ignorance to the plot, at least. Eirlys covered her eyes, trying to shut out the light and the heartache and the sight of the stupid Pendry crest above her.

Lita. Oh Goddess, was she even alive? Eirlys sat straight up in bed, scanning the room. She wasn't here but that didn't mean anything. She was still alive when Eirlys passed out. There was nothing she could do in bed.

Frustrated, Eirlys took stock of the room, letting the soldier in her try to find any weak points to be exploited.

It was circular, a tower. A plush black bear skin rug adorned the light gray stone floor underneath the bed. Four posters reached from the bed to a few inches under the ceiling and beautiful, heavy, royal blue curtains fell from each post. The stone walls were bare, like the chamber sat unoccupied for centuries. Perhaps there was an old servant stairwell or other escape long forgotten, or the locks would be rusted enough for her to break. The room gave off a forlorn, melancholy feel, empty and forgotten. The roaring fireplace lined with ornamental white marble only cast shadows of doubt on the walls.

At last, she noticed the round spike of obsidian penetrating through her left palm. Fear coated her throat. Blood crusted around the black rock and a dull ache spread up her arm. From the slight numbness and unresponsiveness in her hand, whoever inserted it made sure there would be damage. Eirlys would need a healer if she removed the spike on her own. With her inability to heal, she would lose use of the hand if left alone for too long. And she had no way of knowing how long they planned to keep her in here. At least someone healed her scraped skin and any damage the smoke caused her lungs. Small mercies, she supposed.

The bedroom wasn't a dungeon, but without magic, it might as well have been.

She tried to remind herself that she chose this, to come here and accept the crown. That she knew the dangers involved but even still, Eirlys rose, seeking her escape. The door to her right matched the wood of the beams and two floor to ceiling windows adorned the wall to her left. Eirlys examined the closest window, which turned out to be a glass door opening onto a small balcony. She tried the handle—locked. The mechanism appeared new. Eirlys rolled her eyes.

Through the glass, an unfamiliar city glowed in the dark. The lights twinkled, narrow and long and tall, nestled in the dip of a valley. A hint of a river stretched on the right side of the jumble of buildings and ship masts cut across the moon's reflection on the water where they were docked along the bank. She must have been high above the city on a hill or mountain, or the castle would be the tallest she'd ever seen. August's own balcony wasn't this high, and the Karakos castle sat atop a rocky outcrop.

August.

His name tore through her mind and heart faster than an arrow and sharper than steel. Breath fled from her lungs. He had barely let her go, and with all her heart she wished she could have abdicated right then and there, renouncing a heritage she'd never wanted, and stayed by his side in Kestrya, where she belonged. The slinking doubts in her mind crept with claws across her thoughts.

Before she succumbed to her grief and any lingering feelings of indecision, Eirlys stomped toward another doorway and found what she was looking for. A bathroom. It seemed stocked, but the only towels were loose threaded.

Back into the room, she opened another door and found a massive closet of clothes. She stopped her tirade for a second and wondered if they were for her. Were they Lita's or perhaps, Ambrosia's? There were dresses ranging from formal to casual, a few sets of pants and skirts for casual wear.

Out of spite and anger, she chose the fanciest linen dress she could find. She didn't have a knife, or magic—yet—so she stepped on one corner and yanked upward. Then used her teeth to tear strips of the fabric off. She tried to ignore the flowers delicately woven into the dress. Snowdrops. Like her name.

Strips in hand, she grabbed a leather belt, went back to the bathroom and turned on the water. She placed the belt in her mouth, biting down. Not wanting to lose her nerve, she pressed on the obsidian with all her might, not stopping until she was sure was going to pass out. Her teeth ached against the belt, but she didn't cry out. Blood pooled from her hand. She cleared it away with the water, pushing on it again. Pain radiated up her arm as the spike pushed against tendons and nerves.

She couldn't fucking stop now, so she let out one cry, ignored the tears on her face and shoved against the back of the obsidian.

It fell to the floor in a spray of blood.

But her magic flooded back into her veins. She shoved her

hand under the water, nearly blacking out from the pain. Once clean, she started shoving the strips of cloth into the wound, like staunching the bleeding of an arrow puncture. Though she couldn't heal herself, she was able to slow the flow of blood. Too much and she might throw a clot.

Finally, she took the last pieces of linen and wrapped her hand. The pain was nearly unbearable. Even with her magic, she was too vulnerable right now. All she wanted to do was lie on the floor and fall into her exhaustion. Instead, she drank water straight from the tap, wiped the sweat from her face and cleaned up every drop of blood. The obsidian spike lay heavy in her pocket.

Let them come for her now.

Some brief amount of a time later, where the pain subsided into a throb, the lock to the door clicked and every nerve went taut. Eirlys backed away, slow and deliberate. Closing her fists gingerly, she braced for a fight.

"Her royal highness, Princess Aydra Pendry," the attendant announced.

Eirlys's good fist clenched around the cursed obsidian spike. She dove forward before catching sight of the bolt in a crossbow, drawn, and pointed at her. She stopped and backed away from the door. The guardian motioned for Aydra to come in.

The woman was barely more than a child. Her eyes were bright brown, like ambers resting in a fire, her body soft, full of curves, busty. Eirlys also recognized her own features in her young sister's face.

"Hello," she said. She eyed the bowman, then Eirlys, wary as a mouse in a snake's den.

She should be. Eirlys glared at her; heat flushed her face. Only the crossbow held her back. She was fast, but not loaded crossbow fast even with her magic practically humming.

"What do you want?" Eirlys asked.

"I'm only here to persuade you to abdicate the throne," Aydra said.

Eirlys blinked. "Absolutely not."

"Why must you make this hard for me? Why the fuck do you even care about the snot-nosed Skath infants? You have your life. A good one from what it seemed."

"Are you kidding me?" Eirlys didn't even know where to begin explaining her feelings when the person she talked to lacked all compassion and empathy.

"You and Lita could go back, where she would be safe." Aydra's eyes twinkled.

"What do you mean 'safe'?" Eirlys said through gritted teeth. The bowman still trained the crossbow on her.

"Well, you see, we can't touch you, or so the Gods say. But the traitorous princess who stole the heir and raised her in secret? We can touch her," Aydra said.

"Lay one finger, one single flame of magic on my mother and even the void won't be able to put your spirit back together again."

"All you have to do is abdicate," Aydra said sweetly.

Eirlys's first reaction was to cling stubbornly to the crown. To the reason she'd left. But Lita was supposed to be safe at home, not here to be used as a pawn against her. Fuck.

If Aydra was the only one standing in her way, then there were options. How pissed would the gods be if she killed her younger sister? Enough to enact revenge on her mother? For a moment, Eirlys couldn't breathe. Not Lita. She tried so hard to keep everyone out of harm's way, to only put the danger on herself and she failed.

And Eirlys didn't much appreciate failing.

"So, I don't abdicate the throne and what? You kill Lita.

Then what?" Eirlys was grasping at straws, but what other choice did she have?

"Hmm, I guess that is a good point," Aydra said. Fire flashed from the girl's hand—Eirlys dove to the left, not willing to reveal she had her magic back just yet. "I suppose, if neither of you are alive"—another jet of flames shot toward Eirlys, searing into her shoulder—"then I don't have a problem anymore."

The room blazed hot and stifling. That was enough. Her magic swelled through her veins, and Aydra's fire met a swirling storm of water and ice. Steam billowed through the room, the air a mix of vapor and smoke.

The man wielding the crossbow could not be seen through the inferno, but Aydra stood in a stark outline still near the door. She coated her skin in ice, exhaustion wearing down on her quickly. But she ran towards the girls and jabbed the obsidian into Aydra's neck, spinning her around to block the bowman as the fire died in a whoosh. The gaping hole in Eirlys's hand made it hard to maintain her grip but she ignored the pain once more.

Aydra gagged under the pressure of both the spike and Eirlys's hand. She hadn't come close to her jugular, but blood still ran down the princess's dress. Her goal had only been to stop Aydra's Ra magic and use her body as a shield. The man sighted on the struggling women before lowering his weapon.

"Now, Your Majesty," Eirlys whispered, harsh and hot in Aydra's ear, "we can talk."

Aydra struggled and Eirlys pressed her hand deeper, causing Aydra to cry out. The bowman ran out of the room, probably for reinforcements.

"Yes, I much prefer this manner of conversation. Let's get some questions answered, shall we?" Eirlys didn't wait for a response. "Why were you next in line for the throne?"

"Brisa abdicated," Aydra choked out.

Interesting enough for Eirlys to file away for later.

"How does the crown work?"

"One of our ancestors cursed it. If someone were to try and take it by force, the crown would take a piece of their spirit."

"Like the Barrenlands?"

Aydra nodded. "Gods, please."

"Not so tough now, are you, little girl? Let me tell you something. I don't want the fucking throne. I don't want to rule this savage realm who would have rather seen me dead than with a crown on my head. But we don't always get what we want, and I'll throw myself into the void before I bow to a queen as cruel as you."

Aydra sputtered, trying to get words out, when the smell of roses and molten metal preceded Princess Brisa. She froze, startled at the sight of Eirlys, feral and wild. The bowman came in behind her.

"Get out," she snapped to the guard.

He didn't move, just eyed the princess. Though she'd obviously changed, her skin still smelled metallic, like a freshly bellowed forge. A growl echoed from Brisa's throat, the low rumble of a lioness, and her eyes shifted to an icy gray with vertical pupils as her magic spread across her face. The guardian wisely darted from the room.

Brisa eyed the black obsidian before her mouth twisted in a smile.

"Spiking her with obsidian proved to be a bad idea, huh?"

Aydra jerked, struggling to get out of Eirlys's hold, but Eirlys pressed her hand deeper into Aydra's throat. The princess coughed, choking.

"I would suggest not killing her," Brisa said to Eirlys, stepping forward, hands up. "I understand why you want to, but

Lita is alive, and you are alive. Killing Aydra will only upset the delicate balance."

"I don't give a fuck about the delicate balance. She threatened my mother. She nearly burnt down the room."

Brisa did a cursory glance of the room. "Curses, Aydra. What the fuck is wrong with you? Are you so far gone that you would murder a woman in her room the way our parents were slaughtered in their beds?"

"She's fucking crazy. That Skath magic has twisted her into a monster. She ripped out her obsidian. Should have made her drink it. Drown her in it."

Eirlys jerked backwards, letting go of her sister. "You attacked me, and you—"

But Eirlys was at a loss for words. No matter what she said or did, she would always be seen as a Skath. And while she was no less Skath here than in Kestrya, in Kygem all they saw was a monster.

"Go grab Isbeil and get healed," Brisa told her sister. "Unless you want Eirlys to do it."

Aydra stared between the two of them, hand on her throat. She glared daggers at Eirlys and left. But this fight between the two of them was far from over.

Eirlys turned her attention back to Brisa and was shocked at how similar they looked. Brisa shared Lita's chestnut brown hair the way Eirlys and Lita shared their eye color. They all had the same nose, the same chin and mouth. If Brisa was wearing heels, they were the same height. Eirlys met Brisa's eyes, a mix between green and brown, flecked with speckles of gold, like the sun filtering to the forest floor. A smudge of metal dust stained her nose. A small iron crown sat atop her head. Her velvet green dress stretched across her biceps and clung to her hips and stomach oddly, as if the garment were made for a thinner person.

"Was Aydra right?" Eirlys asked. "Is my mother a prisoner?"

Brisa swallowed. "Unfortunately, yes. But she was given her old room here in the castle."

Eirlys nodded. "I told her to stay home. I told her not to come."

"She raised you?" Brisa asked.

"As her own. Though I always knew she was technically my aunt."

Brisa glanced back towards the door. "Where did you learn to fight like that?"

"In Kestrya." Her tone was bitter and sharp. She wasn't about to give Kygem anything to use against August.

"You can trust me," Brisa said.

Eirlys laughed, bitter and small. "No, I really fucking can't."

Eirlys went to rub her face, but Aydra's blood coated her palm. Instead, she wiped the back of her hand across her forehead. Her hand was cramping fiercely, sweat and nausea making it hard to maintain focus. But before she could ask Brisa to fetch a Va, the piercing sound of the Naevni flooded the room.

Three women stepped through the shattered reality from the void. One with braided brown hair was wearing light blue robes. Eirlys recognized another Va at once, but she could not focus on her. Not when the goddess demanded all the attention in the room.

Her stark white hair waved over her shoulders, cascading past her hips. Unlike Eirlys's, this hair was devoid of all color. The eyes focusing on Eirlys were light gray, so close to white, as if she didn't have irises. Her white robes were hemmed in blood-red, matching the Wraithmark fading across the woman's eyes. Eirlys struggled to breathe and wondered how the Va could stand to be so close to her.

The goddess held a chain in her left hand; a transparent golden spirit of the dead, a Kenos, stood at the other end. The chain was attached to a manacle around the Kenos' throat. The spirit woman stared wide-eyed at Eirlys. A scar extended from the top of her left eye to her cheek bone and a smattering of burn scars across her left cheek. Spirits in the void lost all worldly injuries unless the injury marred the soul. This woman's wounds did not mark her death. Somehow, she survived her injuries to heal, to scar and then to die. How did she end up chained to one of the Ancients?

The Ancient pulled on the chain and the Kenos ripped her gaze away from Eirlys.

"Well," the Ancient said, pulling Eirlys's attention back to her. "What in the void am I supposed to do with you?"

# CHAPTER TEN

## EIRLYS

"I sbeil, Brisa, why don't you show our new Dark Grace how to properly prostrate herself?" the Ancient commanded coldly.

The Va, whom Eirlys assumed must be Isbeil, collapsed to the ground. Her legs crossed underneath her body, and her arms extended with her palms facing upward. "Oh, reverent Gyda," Isbeil recited.

Brisa followed suit, though she did not say anything. Perhaps because she was a princess.

As Gyda pulled an ornamental glass staff from her robes and tapped Isbeil's right hand, then Brisa's, Eirlys's mind reeled. Twelve 'gods' formed the pantheon of Kygem's religion, the Council of the Ancients. Eirlys didn't remember the hierarchy of all the gods, having only vaguely paid attention to her mother's teachings; but Gyda, she remembered that name. If Zoasis was Kestrya's main goddess, Gyda was Kygem's.

As Isbeil rose, Gyda turned her attention back to Eirlys, who took a shaky step forward. Her whole body rejected the movement, but she sat crossed legged on the floor, her palms facing upwards. She closed her eyes against the need to rage at the indignity, but this was not the being to cross, not now. Silently, she prayed to Zoasis for strength as she revered a false goddess. Gyda's glass staff tapped Eirlys's hand. The pressure lifted, and Eirlys struggled to not gulp air in droves while she got to her feet.

"Princess, I must speak with your sister alone," the goddess said, directing the words at Brisa. Eirlys didn't bother to acknowledge the concerned look Brisa threw her way before she exited the room, instinct telling her to keep eyes on the Ancient in front of her. An enemy.

Once Brisa was gone, the goddess cocked her head like an eagle waiting to strike its prey. When she spoke, her voice thundered through Eirlys's mind. "Isbeil will heal you. They have told me of your affliction."

Although Eirlys was sure the goddess meant her lack of ability to heal her own body from being Devoid, Eirlys did not miss the note of disgust. When Eirlys didn't move or speak, the goddess's face grew hard.

Gyda motioned to Isbeil, who gestured for Eirlys to sit at the table. Eirlys took her seat and held out her hand for Isbeil to inspect.

Isbeil's fingers probed the muscle surrounding the gaping hole. Eirlys hissed in pain.

"You might be scarred, but there will be no lasting damage," the healer said.

Eirlys frowned, biting her tongue. Though another scar annoyed her, the wrath of a goddess for talking back was, likely, much worse. Her throat ached from the memory of the other Ancient's anger at the dock. She'd been defiant there, but they were not in Kestrya any longer. Gyda watched them closely, and Eirlys's fear bubbled up inside her, twisting her gut. Isbeil pulled water to heal the wound, the magic soft and cool on Eirlys's skin. The aching burn on her shoulder faded, as did the agony in her hand. Too bad nothing could be done for the burnt ends of her hair.

"Thank you," Eirlys said, examining her smooth palm. The back of her hand showed a small, puckered scar, barely noticeable.

"I would like to examine you later. We do not have Devoid here, but we might be able to help."

Eirlys gnashed her teeth together. If there was a cure, a way to remove the curse, Kestrya would have figured it out ages ago.

"Thank you. I appreciate the offer, but there is no way to restore the spirit."

Isbeil pursed her lips. "Perhaps we have far more advanced magic."

Eirlys blinked at her, completely insulted but far too aware of the Ancient watching her every action. With a hard swallow, Eirlys agreed. And Redna said Eirlys would never learn to control her temper.

Isbeil smiled and stood. Gyda waved her hand and Isbeil vanished from the room. Eirlys gasped. The Naevni roamed the void, transporting themselves and others on the physical plane from one location to the next in a matter of seconds. She'd never seen one do it without touching the other person. Gyda merely shoved Isbeil into the void, and the casual display of her immense power raised goosebumps on Eirlys's arms.

"Draw your magic," Gyda said.

Eirlys refused, though whether it was stubbornness or fear, she did not know. Gyda merely smiled and her Wraithmark flashed red across her face. The room once again filled with unbearable pressure. Eirlys gasped for breath again as her lungs tried to expand against the force. The pressure released.

"Draw your magic," Gyda repeated.

Trembling, Eirlys closed her eyes and breathed in. Deep and wondrous magic flooded her system. Her fingers curled inward forming two balls of water above her palms. She opened her eyes, and Gyda's face was contorted in anger. The goddess blinked, and it was gone.

"A Skath queen," Gyda said, not bothering to hide the disgust in her words. "Aydra told me you will not abdicate."

Eirlys merely nodded. She released her magic, the water dissipating into the air.

"Do you know I have spent my days figuring out what to do with you?"

"Why not kill me?" Eirlys asked, a hint of that curling, fiery ember rising within her.

*Good job,* she thought to herself the moment the words left her mouth. *Give her ideas.*

"It crossed my mind," Gyda mused. "You know I tried, once."

Gyda's eyes flashed to Eirlys's chest, where a small scar stood out against her skin. Eirlys traced the raised shape, so familiar to her. Her heart thundered under the puckered skin, her body reacting before her mind understood. She always thought her mother tried to kill her—to know it was this goddess was even more terrifying. Her throat tightened and she fought back the urge to scream every curse she knew into the void.

"How did you survive?" Gyda asked.

Eirlys shook her head. "I don't know. I obviously don't remember."

Gyda mused for a moment. "Lita says when she found you, the wound was shallow. But I know I bled you dry."

Eirlys shuddered under Gyda's slightly widened gaze as if she were a puzzle to be solved. It was one thing to know someone tried to kill her; it was another to hear it from the would-be murderer's mouth. "So, what now?"

"The whole realm knows of your existence, thanks to the Skath assassin who murdered your parents."

Eirlys bristled. Aydra had said something similar. But if August sent the man who killed her parents, why would he tell them that Eirlys was alive?

"What will *you* do with me?" she asked.

"My current intent is to keep you alive. There have already been two attempted sieges on locations where the people think we are keeping you. No one suspects the castle... yet. But it's only a matter of time before an attendant breaks their oath of silence or slips up."

"I thought regicide was illegal," Eirlys said.

Gyda smiled again. Eirlys noticed her smile never reached her eyes, as if a puppeteer pulled the strings on the corners of her mouth.

"There are fates worse than death. For now, you are to be protected while we discuss the matters at hand. One Skath does not frighten me—but the people do not understand how inconsequential you are to this realm. They think you are dangerous, but they don't see how insignificant your rule would be. You will live and you will die. The reign of the Skath queen will be a distant memory by the time I care to reflect upon it."

"However," the goddess said, annoyance sharpening her tone, "if the citizens don't accept you, well, that creates a problem *I* shall have to deal with. The Council will be in touch."

A howling sound echoed in the chamber and Gyda vanished. Visceral anger had clung to goddess's words, sharper and more malicious than Eirlys's own self-righteous fury.

Eirlys trembled as tears filled her eyes. Fear clung to her

throat, and she scratched at it, clawing away the feeling inside her. Obsidian was nothing compared to complete powerlessness overwhelming her thoughts. What good was one woman against twelve immensely powerful beings? Gods or not, the Ancients were giants among ants. Immortals weren't even worthy of being acknowledged; a few people squished wouldn't even register as the scum on their shoes.

She had promised to bring Kygem to its knees, but gods held the realm in their very palms.

When the morning light streamed through Eirlys's windows, Brisa returned.

"Come here," she said, voice soft.

She unlocked the balcony door and led Eirlys to the stone balustrade. Directly below her balcony lay a small patch of grass, neatly trimmed and vibrant in the summer sun. The circular yard was set about with marble benches, planters of roses, peonies, and azaleas. Before the forest took over, finely pruned fruit trees, cherries, bright green apples, and pears hung plump on the branches. It was all perfectly stunning, but the woman in the middle of the yard drew Eirlys's attention. Her hands clenched the banister, leaning over as fast as she dared, her fear of heights completely forgotten.

Lita walked with delicate steps, her fingers bushing over the various plants. There was a wonder to her movements, a nostalgia emanating from her.

Eirlys looked at Brisa in shock, who held a finger to her lips.

She whispered, "I couldn't get approval for you to see her in person. This was the next best thing."

It was the best thing. To watch her mother walking around,

alive, and healthy, back in a place she so obviously thought of as home. Lita wore a soft, silver dress, complemented by a delicate bracelet and matching necklace. She took a seat at one of the benches and glanced up, giving Eirlys a small smile. But she didn't focus on Eirlys for long, most likely to not alert anyone that they were being allowed to see each other.

After what seemed like only a few seconds, a guardian came and led Lita back towards the vast walls of the castle. Eirlys's heart sank watching her leave, but at least her mother was alright and being treated with some compassion.

The sunlight bathed the distant city in golds and yellows and the mountains surrounding it were all craggy cliffs interspersed with evergreens. The castle was settled on the southwest side of the valley's cliff face; the river ran northwest, parallel to the range.

Brisa brought her back inside, locking the door again before leaving with a promise to send up some refreshments. Maybe she had misjudged the woman yesterday.

Eirlys headed to the washroom, needing to at least splash water on her face. Eirlys tried not to stare at herself in the mirror, but the glance she caught frightened her more than she cared to admit. Pale and clammy, her blonde hair was plastered to her face, the blue too vivid, too happy. Her eyes, though bright in color, were wide in horror.

The door opened, and Eirlys brandished the soap dish in her hand. A stocky man in an attendant's uniform came in carrying a hot towel and water on a tray. When he set it on the polished blue marble countertop, it only shook for a brief second.

He sketched a jerky half bow, said, "Refreshments are on their way, madam," as politely as he could manage, and nearly sprinted from the room.

Though tainted with prejudice, the towel was pleasantly warm when she placed it on her neck.

A shrill cry came from the hallways. Eirlys ran out, magic at the ready. The door was cracked open.

"Please, for the love of the gods, don't make me go in there," a woman was screaming.

"Please miss," another voice, deeper and soothing.

"Did you see Princess Aydra? She was coated in blood, saying the Skath in there will kill anyone who dares to enter the room."

"Don't be a child. Do your job," the man said.

Eirlys dropped her magic and sat quickly at the small two-chair table. The attendant pushed the door open.

When she caught sight of Eirlys, the woman's eyes widened in terror and she moved forward, shuffling her feet as if every step brought her closer to death. Eirlys watched her briefly before she sighed and got up, startling the woman, then moved to the far side of the chamber, near the bathroom door with her arms crossed. The woman set the tea down and glanced at Eirlys. Eirlys smiled her thanks and to her surprise the woman smiled back before realizing what she had done and ran out of the room once again.

The woman's sobs made the tea so bitter that Eirlys barely enjoyed it. She was alone here. Completely and utterly alone, with only the weight of a crown she didn't know how to use and the storm raging in her blood to keep her company.

# CHAPTER ELEVEN

## PRICE

"Lord Price."

Deryn, Price's oldest friend and once commander, grabbed him in a hug. Their smile was bright against their dark lips and Price realized how much he missed them. He relished in their hug before pulling back.

"By the Gods, it is good to see you." Price clapped their shoulders.

"It is, but I wish it was under better circumstances."

Price wasn't even sure if Deryn meant the death of the queen and king, the fact that their princess was a Skath hidden from them for three decades, or Price's own transgression and his assignment here.

"We have a room prepared for you in the Quarters. Dress quickly." Deryn handed him a key, a number inscribed on the top. It reminded him of being back in the barracks. "Meet Brisa and I at the bottom of the Heir's tower."

"Hallowed by the light," Price said.

They clasped Price on the shoulder but remained silent. Then Deryn gave Price a small shove in the right direction.

Price tried to shake off the uneasy feeling of meeting an old friend who did not seem the same. Deryn had been Price's guiding light in the early days in the guardians and was the one who suggested becoming a proselyte. Back then, Price didn't have faith. All he had was a burning anger at the world for the pain he suffered. In more ways than one, Deryn had saved him. He was far too reckless, constantly getting into fights, and he railed against the gods, his parents, even the queen who had been the one to help his parents. He was never going to be Ra enough, never going to be Klara enough, never going to be good enough. Then one day, he was at the bottom of a bottle of something far too strong when he first considered it... the way to never have to feel again. It was because of this that Deryn pleaded with the Gods to take him in.

And he found a place where he belonged in the Congregation of the Ancients. The Goddess of Perseverance took a liking to him, and he honored her with his patronage. Persevere and he would someday walk into the Valley, into a place of paradise where his soul would be remade, whole and well. It was this that kept him faithful throughout the years. He needed to be free of the pain, to know that one day, it would end but first he needed to atone or spend his afterlife wandering the void searching for the broken pieces of his spirit.

He was surprised to see the white armor of the guardians laid out for him instead of his proselyte attire. He clutched at his purple robes. For a long time, he wanted to pretend that he was a better proselyte than a fighter, but the truth was, he was more skilled at ending lives than guiding them. Besides, the princess needed a bodyguard, first and foremost. He couldn't cleanse her spirit if she died. So, he dropped his proselyte robes into the laundry chute. They would be taken back to one of the Halls in the city.

He bathed thoroughly and quickly, then sat in front of the mirror and plaited three braids back from either of his temples, pulling the top of his hair up, keeping the long black tresses out of his face. He finished off the guardian style with two braids starting behind his ears. He glanced in the mirror for a second, ensuring everything was exact. Unnerved by the look in his eyes, triumphant and more confident than he had felt in years, he got up to dress.

Kygem guardians wore white and silver with the purple insignia of Kygem. The ivory leather tunic consisted of square patches knotted together and worn over a linen white shirt fitted under leather bracers and light gray pants tucked into calf-high boots.

While he dressed, an odd feeling coursed through him, a mix of slick regret and a fiery longing, as if he was losing the one purpose that kept him grounded for so long. He reminded himself it wasn't the robes that made him a proselyte. Maybe his purpose, his true purpose, would be to guide the new princess to the path of light. If he kept her alive long enough to do so.

Although doing so caused him immense pain and guilt, he tried to remember what she had been like that night. Grimy was the first thing that came to mind but even caked in mud and dirt, she'd been fierce and strong. A Va, he remembered suddenly. The Pendry line had not seen a Va born into their household in five thousand years, since the first warrior queen.

With a sigh, he got up and met Brisa and Deryn at the entrance to the tower. He remembered the early days of roaming the castle when he and Brisa used to hide from their lessons, giggling under the empty bed frame. Queen Ambrosia never failed to find them, having already dismissed their tutors.

"I'm glad to see you," Brisa said. Her clothes were disheveled, and he noticed a spot of blood on her cheek.

"What happened?"

Brisa's eyes turned pale, her Wraithmark flashing across her face before receding back into her skin. "How close were you and Aydra?"

Price shook his head. "Not close."

Apparently, that was the answer she needed to hear. "Aydra tried to kill Eirlys twice already. Once on the ship getting here and then after she arrived."

"She's an acolyte," Price exclaimed. But he knew that Aydra was merely training to be a proselyte because her mother wanted her to, not because she did. Even at a young age she was power hungry for the crown the moment Brisa abdicated.

"Yeah, well, acolyte or not, she thinks Eirlys is dangerous." Brisa glanced up at the spiral staircase. "Is she?"

And how could he deny what he saw? She was more than just a good fighter; she was a natural.

"Yes," Price said.

"Good," Brisa said with a sigh. "She is going to need to be ruthless to have any chance of staying here. If she wants the crown."

"So, she won't abdicate," Price guessed.

"No, not to Aydra at least."

With the way Eirlys fought for one infant, Price wondered if she would ever give up the crown for anything less than the destruction of their gods and religion. Fuck. How was he supposed to lead this woman into the light when she spent all her life surrounded by the darkness? How was he supposed to look her in the eye and preach that her magic was evil? Fuck if he knew.

"Want me to go with you?" Brisa asked.

"Or me," Deryn added.

Price shook his head. "No, let me do this alone."

He took the stairs two at a time and braced himself for the wrath he knew would be coming his way.

A key hung on the outside of the door. Curse them all—they had locked her in. She may not have worn a crown yet, but she was their queen, their thirteenth goddess by all rights. No matter her power draw, she did not deserve to be treated like a prisoner.

Before he opened the door, he steadied himself, plastering a smile onto his face. He turned the lock and pushed the door open.

Princess Eirlys stood with her back to the door. Her hair was a light blonde color like her father's had been. He hadn't been sure the first time, but he had noticed the color on the tips. Blue. Almost the same color as his eyes. She wore a pair of black slacks and sleeveless cream tunic. Her arms were crossed, and she did not greet him.

"Your Grace," he called, unsure if he should enter the room. Something made him desperately want to, but he planted his feet, one hand gripping the edge of the doorway.

She turned and cursed in Kestryan, a string of words he didn't know but could easily guess the meaning.

"What the fuck are you doing here?" she said, switching to Kygemish with a sneer snaking its way across her face.

He noticed her accent more now. Although she spoke Kygemish, her vowels flowed longer, and her consonants were soft, less guttural than he was used to hearing. More like his own southern Karavesh accent.

He swallowed. Well, she hadn't immediately gutted him so that was a good sign.

"The Ancients"—he didn't miss the way her brows

furrowed at their name—"assigned me as your personal guardian and proselyte to help guide you in your journey to the light."

Her eyes, a viridian to rival the finest emeralds, narrowed at him, accessing him. Something lurched inside of him. His magic nearly flared, and the pain rushed through his nerves, burning with cold flames.

"Everyone thinks I'm a monster, all because I'm Skath. Do you?"

So, she was already starting with philosophical questions. "I think your magic has a sway over you. It can make a good person do bad things, but I don't think you are inherently a monster."

Though she used no magic at all, her anger roiled across her face as dark as a summer storm. But she did not move towards him. She was holding back. Was she giving him a chance? "And the infants you murder?" she snarled.

Gods, he wanted to deny it. He almost did, almost let himself tell her he'd never done the deed because it was true. Ronan would have been the first. Typically, he administered last rites and let the parents choose the manner of the sacrifice. But if he denied that he never sacrificed an infant, it would be as good as admitting he never wanted to. Admitting he didn't fully believe in the religion that had saved him. Being strong for Sayiv had been a near thing. Truthfully, if Eirlys hadn't revealed herself as a Skath, he would have handed him over... and that was a truth he couldn't look at too closely.

"It is not what they are, but what they will become."

Her bitter laugh sent chills down his spine.

"Oh, you are just completely wrapped around their little finger, aren't you?"

She stepped towards him as if expecting him to do something. Flinch or flee perhaps. There was a wariness to her that made him uncomfortable. What outweighed the other, her being a Skath or her being his queen?

Since he was bound to protect her, the Ancients obviously thought it was the latter, so he would as well.

He stepped forward, carelessly and without regard to her obvious discomfort and knelt in front of her. She studied him but did not pull away. Then he grabbed her hand.

On the surface, calluses met calluses, two warrior hands clasping each other. But the moment her skin touched his, everything in him relaxed, his magic, his spirit. The pain disappeared. Gone, completely and utterly gone. He could breathe as if he didn't know what breathing had been like before. Air came in with a peaceful coolness. His heart, though beating fast, was steady and life giving rather than chugging along, desperate for relief.

Price would never be the same again.

He never wanted to let go of her. He never wanted to touch her again. How was it possible a Skath had brought him to his knees both literally and figuratively? The core part of his religion was to purify, to cleanse the Skath of their magic. And yet, her touch brought him closer to paradise than he ever thought possible. A forest fire tore through his mind, burning his beliefs faster than he could quell the flames.

She frowned. He was gripping her hand far too tightly and he let go.

The pain erupted back in him with a fury of disbelief. Two people raged within him. The one who wanted to go to her, to touch her, to never stop, and the other wanted to run, run far away, and drown in obsidian bliss until he was nothing.

"Eirlys Pendry," he said, her name a bit breathless on his lips. If he stopped now, he would not take this assignment. By the Gods, she would freak out if he told her. If she knew. He was probably freaking her out now. And he wasn't exactly at liberty to explain anyway. He took a deep breath and blew out through his mouth and barreled on despite the anger flashing across her face. "I swear by the Ancients to be your sword and shield. From this day on until I no longer draw breath, or you release me from your service, I will protect you, Your Grace. Hallowed by the light."

Then he reached for her hand again. She let him gently take it and though he didn't need to close his eyes for this part, he relished in the feel of it because he would not touch her ever again if he could help it. He kissed the back of her hand, sealing his vow.

When he let go, he stood and she drew away from him.

Eirlys clasped her hands in front of her. "So, what exactly should I expect from my conversion?"

Price chose to ignore the bitterness in her voice.

"Well, it'll be mostly theology. Though, I am a proselyte and a Ra, I've never had a vision or even the whispering of a prophecy."

This confession of his shortcomings seemed to cause her to relax. "Good, I hate prophecies, visions, the whole creepy looking into the future thing."

Price frowned. "Our religion is based on the gift of Sight. You will lead our people through certain rituals based on visions. I'd suggest getting used to it."

Eirlys cringed, before she straightened her shoulders, standing taller, defiant. "If sitting through a bunch of bullshit visions helps me win over the people and the gods, I'll do what I must."

By the Gods, this blasphemous woman was going to be the death of him. He touched his forehead with his two fingers and brought them up, beseeching his gods to absolve her tongue.

"I made you uncomfortable." A breathy embarrassed laugh escaped her. "I apologize. It's been a rough day."

He smiled, slightly chastened by his outburst. "Don't be bothered. We can learn from each other."

She stared at him aghast. "You want to learn about my religion, about Kestrya?"

"If that's okay. I'm fascinated by your religion, actually. As a proselyte, I have my beliefs, but I am curious to hear about yours."

Her fingers trailed the seam of her pants. "Alright, I can share my religion with you and perhaps we can find common ground?"

"I'll take you up on that offer, Princess Eirlys."

Her eyes went wide at his remark. Guilt rushed through him again. She was their future queen, their thirteenth god by the Codex, and yet she hadn't even been addressed properly enough to be used to it.

"For tonight, you should get some rest. I'll be right outside the door and only lock it if I must leave."

She grabbed his hand as he turned around, and blessed sweet relief coursed through him. He jerked, separating their touching skin, and promised himself to find a pair of gloves to wear around her.

"Sorry," she said, hurt finding its way into her face.

He yearned to explain it all to her but was bound by his Goddess. Where would he even begin anyway? His duty was to protect her, to prepare her. But his true purpose here was to gain her trust so when the Gods demanded her sacrifice, she would be willing. If only the void would swallow him up. He'd remain there until the end of time to avoid this assignment, to avoid her, to avoid betraying her trust.

"Can you leave the door open, please?" she asked.

He lifted his hand as if to touch her. Gods, he wanted to touch her. But he stopped himself, letting his hand fall to his side. "If you need anything, please ask."

He walked outside the room, leaving the door open. Brisa must have instructed for a decently comfortable chair to be placed in the hall. Beats the floor. He might be able to catch a few hours of sleep in it. He listened to her moving around, the sliding of fabric on skin then the ruffling of her bed.

She sighed, and Price turned in his chair to look at her. Her eyes held something in them, appraisal and a heat Price found hard to ignore. But she said nothing else and closed her eyes, sliding further into the pillows and blanket.

"Sleep well, Your Grace," he said.

# Chapter Twelve

## Eirlys

S he did not sleep well.

   She tossed and turned all night, and when she woke, her muscles throbbed. She expected an attendant to bring food in, but once she dressed and exited her bathroom, Price was sitting at the little table with two bowls of porridge and a pot of tea.

Eirlys paused in the doorway, skeptical of this strange new man. His behavior from the night before, on top of him bringing her breakfast, made her wary. He hadn't looked up and she took the opportunity to study him closely.

His flawless complexion reminded her of the pale brown beaches surrounding Virva. His jet-black hair was held back with a tie in a messy jagged bun, the two braids from yesterday present behind his ears. His eyes still stunned her; as her eyes were the brightest green, his were the brightest blue, cerulean pools in prominent, angular eyes. His nose had been broken and not set or healed properly and yet it added to his beauty rather than detracted from it.

"I don't bite," he said, those brilliant eyes flicking up to watch her. Again, there was that soldier's gaze, that constant need to watch and know the world around him—embedded in his bone, just as it was in hers.

She leaned with her arms crossed against the door frame. Yesterday, she had been taken aback, between the Ancient's visit and then seeing him. Of all the Goddess cursed people, why him? Zoasis had a wicked sense of humor.

So today, she was furious. "No, you just would have killed me for being Skath before you knew who I was. How am I supposed to trust you?"

"Then why did you decide to trust me last night?" Price asked.

Eirlys scoffed. "Goddess, you won't even deny it, will you?"

"And lie to you?"

Every single nerve went off then. So, she had been right. He did think about killing her even after she became Devoid. How close had he been? And did that matter now that she had his oath? If he'd been any other person, not a proselyte, she might not have accepted that, but a religious man takes his vows seriously.

Price's face became serious. "Tell me, Your Grace. Did you not have the same thought about me?"

Well, he had her there. "Of course I did. If it was between you and the baby, Ronan was making it home."

Price stopped smiling, his expression turning downcast. Then, like he couldn't help himself, he whispered, so quietly she barely heard him across the room, "Is he okay?"

"Why the fuck do you care?" she snarled.

Price stiffened. "You are right. I shouldn't care."

Eirlys blinked, surprised by his choice of words. He *shouldn't* care but he did. Instead of blowing through the storm however, it only fueled the tumultuous feelings inside of her.

For a moment, she was distracted by the way his teeth grazed his bottom lip as he stared down at his teacup. "I'm trying to help you. I need to help you. You will need friends here, allies. You can't afford to push me away."

"How exactly do you plan on helping me, proselyte?" Eirlys yelled, finally relieved to have someone to be angry towards. Eirlys didn't want help from baby killers. But most of her plan hinged on being able to destabilize the governing body, not realizing the governing body meant gods and goddesses she had no power to overthrow or destroy. This man was no god, no false deity. She exploded on him in a rage she'd kept contained for days. "I've single handedly rescued infants your realm deems worthy of death for years. I have seen what you worship, and I am not impressed. How can I trust a man who believes I should have died at birth? Who would have struck me down simply for the color of my Wraithmark?"

She strode forward and Price rose from his chair, but she was beyond caring, beyond scared. Fear had turned into something deadly and reactive. The shadows leapt to her face, her normally cold magic searing her veins. She wanted him frightened, to hate her, to prove to her that his religion was something she would never believe in. That he was the monster, not her. But his eyes traced the Wraithmark on her face and he didn't move even when she approached him, invading his space.

"Am I a monster?" she snarled. "Do you fear this?"

"Stop," he begged. "If it is my life you want, I'll gladly lay it down for you. If the only way to absolve myself in your eyes is my death, it is yours."

And that brought her up short. The laugh which escaped her was choked and bitter. "How the fuck can you help me if you are dead?"

He reached for her then and that was the first time she

noticed him wearing gloves, white leather like the rest of his uniform. Eirlys tried to hide her flinch, but his hand fell just as the whisper of his touch reached her temple, as if he was reaching for the very thing that made her Skath.

She breathed in deeply, trying to calm herself.

"Your Grace," Price said, and she met his eyes. "I don't fear you the way you think I do. I am terrified of you because I think, in the end, you could best me. But this—" His gloved hand reached out slowly, gauging her reaction. When she didn't move away or react, he stroked the Wraithmark on her face. She stopped breathing entirely. "It does not frighten me."

The last remnants of her anger succumbed to his touch. Her magic faded. Did she imagine the look of disappointment on his face?

Hunger gnawed at her suddenly, her stomach growling. The tension in the room softened but did not go away entirely. "Let's eat."

Price gestured for her to sit and they both sunk into the chairs. "Cream? Sugar?" he asked as he picked up the teakettle.

His eyes crinkled when he smiled.

"Just sugar, please," she said.

Price dipped a spoonful of sugar into the glass and handed it back to her. She took a sip, savoring the warmth before she reached for her porridge and tossed in a few pieces of sausage, eating well for the first time in days. They quietly ate until she was satiated. Leaning back, she sipped her tea again though it was now cold. Without thinking, she drew on her power and warmed the liquid.

Price stared at the Wraithmark spilling like ink on snow across her temples, a look of confusion on his face.

"What?" she asked, feeling the shadows fade from her face.

"Why are you doing this? Why not just abdicate and go back home?"

She studied her tea for a second, watching the small dregs swirl at the bottom. "What if I can change things here? What if I can prove that the Skath have been misjudged, blamed for an act over five thousand years old?"

Price swallowed audibly. "You mean change The Skath Treaty? It was in works long before the Beast King murdered his brother and his family."

Eirlys shrugged. "But what if?"

"Those are not just our laws; they are the tenets of our religion founded before The Skath Treaty. It isn't as simple as one Skath being a good person."

Carefully placing the teacup back on the table, Eirlys leaned forward and looked Price right in his stunning eyes. Her fingers were a hair's breadth away from grazing his gloves. "I think it is that simple. Am I evil? Right now, if I didn't have my magic, would you call me evil?"

He avoided her gaze, staring at his gloved hands as if they held the answers. When she realized he wasn't looking at his hands, but hers, she waited.

"What do you want me to say?" Price said.

"I want you to look me in the eye and tell me you want Kygem to remain as it is. Look at me and tell me I should have died."

He picked up his cup and sloshed some tea over the side. He set it down, frowning. "You want me to say I despise our laws?"

"Do you?"

"It is not my place to question the law of our gods. I follow them and my religion, Your Grace." Then he seemed to gather himself and finally met her eyes, determination set the lines of his face. "Besides, you act as if we don't allow them a choice."

The snicker that left her mouth came out harsh, scraping her throat. He frustrated her to no end, and she barely knew him. He had his faith and his gods, but Eirlys had her lived experience. Maybe she should be trying to persuade him she believed but she wasn't there yet if she could ever be persuaded to lie in the first place.

"A choice? Tell me, Price." She spat his name as if it were laced with venom. "What choice is it exactly? Murder a child —" When Price opened his mouth to speak, Eirlys raised a hand. "I know what you believe about the spirit, but trust me, as I sit here a full-grown adult, when I say I don't give a fuck about your semantics."

He slumped back into his chair, lips tight.

She took that as a sign to continue. "Only a fool would believe that traveling across the Barrenlands is something everyone can do. If you are not prepared, if you don't have the money or the means, there are no options. Since it is illegal to help anyone cross to Kestrya, only the rich or the lucky make it. So, tell me again, what choice are your gods offering? For many it is a death sentence either way. And even if they do manage to cross into Kestrya, it is a cursed life for both parent and child."

"But Kestrya welcomes the Skath with open arms," Price countered.

Eirlys threw up her hands, knocking the table and sending the dinnerware clattering against the wood. "It isn't about being Skath. Kygemians aren't always treated well. Some people don't care but others, well, they were complicit in the sacrifice of how many Skath infants until their own? It is hard to look someone in the eye and know they are willing to sit back and watch the killing of innocent children."

She watched the realization dawn on his face. Good, let him feel guilty. Let him question what happened to Ronan again because they both knew if Eirlys hadn't been there, Price would have not hesitated to do his gods duty, to sacrifice an infant.

"You hate us all," he whispered.

Eirlys shook her head. The anger slowly left her, waves of the dizzying red emotion leaving her exhausted. "I don't. You think that my mother and I haven't had this conversation over and over again? She lived here for decades, preaching the same bullshit. I used to ask her all the time why it took until I was born for her to change her mind. And all the other parents who cross the line did the same thing until their own child."

"How often are people crossing?" Price asked.

Eirlys took a moment, wondering why he cared. Would he proselytize to those attempting to cross?

"Maybe a dozen or so a year. Then whatever I could save, which wasn't a lot." A handful on a good year... nothing on the years that made her go home and weep for every infant she had failed. She would not fail them now. If she could not convince Kygem to dissolve The Skath Treaty, then maybe she could scrub it from existence.

They sat in tense quiet, where their breaths were too loud.

"Ronan is a Va, you know," Eirlys said, not being able to handle the pressure growing between them. "He's getting big. My friend adopted him. He and his wife are raising him. A little family of Skath. How horrifying, right?"

But Price didn't look horrified. His lips barely turned up at the corners but there, plainly on his face, was relief and something close to delight.

"Thank you, Your Grace."

Eirlys sat back, tracing her finger around the rim of her cup. If Price could be convinced that her magic was no different than his, if she could sway a proselyte to be on her side, her pleas to the gods might be heard. If a man of faith could see that the Skath were not evil, then maybe there was hope for this realm after all.

In a world pitted against her, Eirlys needed him as much as she was loathed to admit it.

"Call me Eirlys," she said softly.

"If you wish, Eirlys."

By the time a small lunch arrived, Eirlys worried Price was tired of her questions, but he answered every single one without complaint. From the age of her sisters—Aydra was a mere nineteen, while Brisa turned twenty-six that summer—to the Council of Ancients who were composed of the twelve gods and kept Kenos as their personal servants. She avoided the more explosive topics by keeping to basic facts she absolutely needed to know.

Price might be a proselyte of the religion that once sentenced her to death, but he was also a wealth of knowledge she would be a fool to not use. Even if he rebuked her offer to heal him or even examine him after he appeared to be in pain. It was like gnats were continuously gnawing at his skin. She tried to tell herself that if her magic was so abhorrent to him, he wouldn't be sitting here talking to her or guarding her, but it crushed something inside of her. She was used to being different, but not hated.

Eirlys trailed the whorls of the wood pattern on the table while she thought about how in the void she was going to convince twelve gods to change their entire doctrine when she couldn't even get the man who was sworn to protect her to let her use her magic on him.

Muffled voices outside the door drew her attention away from her storm-ridden mind. Someone stomped up the stairs followed by the sound of pursuit, then what Eirlys assumed was a person being shoved into the wall. The door wasn't locked since Price was inside; for the first time, Eirlys wished it was.

Price rose from his seat. "Don't move."

Eirlys had zero intention of staying put in a room which was effectively a trap. She rose, ignoring Price's groan.

"Give me a weapon," Eirlys whispered.

"Do you have a death wish?" he hissed. "A Skath with a weapon, even if you are the future queen, would be a sure-fire way to ensure whoever killed you did it first and asked questions later."

Eirlys gritted her teeth.

The door burst open. Brisa's cheeks were flushed, her hair haphazardly pulled into a ponytail. "Get Eirlys to the throne room. Now," she commanded.

Whether it was Brisa's tone or the fact that Price and Eirlys were both soldiers trained to respond to imminent threats without question, they both immediately followed Brisa from the room.

The hall stairwell descended or ascended, circling the outside of the tower. Realizing this was her first time out of her plush prison since she arrived, Eirlys peeked out of the windows to catch a glimpse of her new home. In the middle of summer, the trees' evergreen needles were deep emerald-black, shadowing the earth. She caught sight of the city between the leaves and parts of the grounds.

At the bottom, the tower led into a long wide hallway where a guard sporting a black eye sneered at Eirlys when she passed. The rumble of a growl escaped her sister's throat, and the guard backed off.

They'd passed a few doors when a crack vibrated through the hall. The sound of a whip hitting flesh, the thwack of leather tearing skin. Eirlys remembered the time she'd been at the dangerous end of the weapon, the whip wrapping around her hand, slicing into her palm until stark white bone appeared where the skin of her knuckles had once been. The woman's breathless thank you after Eirlys stopped her punishment made all that pain worth it.

Kestrya outlawed whipping centuries ago, but a few places still lingered on the barbaric tradition. During her conscription, she was sent to some of the more heinous places Kestrya had to offer. Though she wanted to, she had never turned the whips on the users.

The din grew louder, the grunts of the victim finally audible when they entered the large entrance hall. Citizens lined up, waiting at the door. Their eyes tore into Eirlys, and Price tensed, the muscles in his shoulders bunching. Eirlys made eye contact with each of them, refusing to show fear. She was their rightful queen, and she would not yield to their hostility.

Beyond the door, a vaulted ceiling rose three stories high with balconies on either side. A large dais stood in front of her, and mounted upon it was a large, gilded chair. Eirlys stopped. This must be the throne room. *Her* throne sat straight ahead.

A dignified seat of white marble loomed beneath an impressively decorated archway, while the windows directly behind them showed a vast mountainous landscape. The throne was adjoined by three large, but far less ornate, seats for those aiding the queen. Fixed on the front legs, one on each side, was a blade of obsidian and a blade of glass, each handle covered with red leather. White velvet pillows embellished the seat. She half expected the crown or scepter to be there, too. But this was not a coronation.

Price gripped Eirlys's elbow, begging her not to move from his side, as she took in the scene. Guardians surrounded them with bows at the ready, in a circle following the pattern of the royal purple runner flowing down and around the dais. Aydra stood to the left, arms neatly folded, the silver banners behind her a backdrop too beautiful for the small, cruel smile on her face. Before her, a brunette woman's arms were stretched upwards, attached to a whipping pole. She was shirtless, the pale skin of her exposed, back marred by bloody, gleaming flesh.

The whip lay on a pedestal, blood dripping onto the violet runner.

"Don't leave my side," Price said.

"I don't understand," Eirlys said, trying to figure out who the woman was and why she was here.

Her mind refused to believe what she was seeing, trying to protect her from the horror. Seeing her, stripped and being whipped like an animal, was more than Eirlys could bear. Her limbs went numb, her brain all fuzz and haziness. She'd know this woman anywhere.

"Mom," Eirlys breathed, voice cracking.

Eirlys wrenched her arm free from Price's increasingly hard grasp and rushed toward Lita. An arrow missed Eirlys by inches, whirring passed her cheek, close enough to feel the whisper of the air being sliced. She snarled, jumping to the side and scanned the archers. She was about to draw her magic when Price rushed to her side and grabbed her again.

"Are you daft?" Price yelled, though Eirlys wasn't sure if it was directed at her or her would-be killer though he looked furiously down at her.

She tried to tear away from his grip again when Aydra flashed in front of Eirlys. "No one is to interfere with the traitor's punishment."

Only the archers kept Eirlys from ripping Aydra's throat out. Instead, she thought of her former queen and the air of haughtiness which never failed to make Eirlys flinch even when it wasn't directed at her. "And what trial has convicted her? Who sentenced her to this punishment? Surely not your queen or gods."

Eirlys worried she wouldn't sound regal enough or Price's presence would be a show of weakness, but Aydra shifted on her feet, not meeting Eirlys's gaze.

Eirlys wanted to throttle her—claw her nails down her face until she bled and turn the whip on Aydra's back. But in the back of her mind, she heard the whispers that clung to her existence here in Kygem—*monster*—and held her temper in.

The black-skinned guardian who'd been on the ship sprinted into the room from behind the dais. The tall immortal's features were harsh but handsome: a strong jaw, smooth, full lips, and a straight nose. Their hair was cropped short, forming a black halo around their head. Eirlys recalled hearing their name, Deryn. Brisa raised her eyebrows and Deryn shook their head.

"Get her down," the guardian commanded, snapping their fingers at the archers.

Aydra snarled when the guardians stepped forward. "You do not command them over me, Deryn. I pass judgment." But her voice was shrill, begging to be obeyed rather than commanding it.

If her mother hadn't been strapped to the pole, back bloody and barely conscious, Eirlys might have felt pity for her. *Might have.*

Deryn ignored Aydra and approached Eirlys who tensed, swallowing hard. She took a small step back into Price's grasp. He stiffened at her closeness but kept his position.

"I will not harm you, Your Grace," Deryn said. Their voice was warm, rich, and soothing. A voice that commanded great honor and respect while also knowing how to tame a wild beast or in this case, a feral daughter.

Brisa appeared on Eirlys's other side, placing a hand on her shoulder in solidarity. Price's warm fingers pressed against her back, reassuring her.

Deryn faced Aydra. "You are no queen. You are a spoiled princess who didn't get her way. You command no one here."

Before Aydra could utter a word, Deryn faced the archers. "Unless your queen, who stands with me, says otherwise, Aydra does not command you. If I find out a single person has taken orders from her or anyone else who is not a commanding officer, I will see to it personally that said person is discharged and disgraced from the service."

The guardians shuffled, many putting arrows back in their quivers.

With the threat of being shot gone, Eirlys took her chance and lunged at Aydra, gripping the shorter woman, and tossed her into the archers who had to catch her. Despite wanting nothing more than to tear into the bitch, her priority was her mother. She rounded the pillar and lifted Lita's face who blinked and tried to smile through her gag. Eirlys wrenched the leather from her mouth while Deryn unchained Lita and helped the woman off the whipping post.

"Lay her here," Eirlys said.

Brisa knelt beside Eirlys and grabbed her hands. "If you use your magic here, you might undo all the good Deryn just did for you."

"Do you have a Va on hand then?" Eirlys asked, looking around the room.

Brisa bit her lip. The archers surrounding them would not help Lita. Eirlys knew this in her bones and so did her sister.

Without meaning to, she caught Price's blue eyes and the look of determination there. "Do it," he said. His magic flickered to life on his face, the sword in his hand lighting with flames, daring any of the surrounding immortals to try him.

Eirlys snatched her hands away from Brisa's grip and took a deep breath. On her exhale, she released her magic. Hisses and curses fill the hall around her, but she blocked them out. Water pulled between her hands and over Lita's back, covering the wounds. Preparing herself for the pain, she healed the slashes, feeling every one of them on her own back. Between one breath and the next, the pain receded, and Lita's back was a perfect slate of ivory. Eirlys used her power to fling the remaining blood across the room, aiming for the archers to coat them in their shame.

Lita groaned and propped herself onto her hands and knees. Someone wrapped a shawl around her bare torso.

The soft carpet cushioned Eirlys when she leaned back, trying to breathe. She scanned the guardians and the crowd of citizens peering into the doorway. Fear sharpened to pure hatred in their eyes, a stark reminder that she was Skath. She was the lost princess, their soon to be queen, and they despised her. If given the chance, any one of them would kill her.

Panic like Eirlys had never known coursed through her body in slick, pulsating waves. One of the archers reached for an arrow and fueled the fear within her. Eirlys's power exploded from her as bowstrings creaked.

Throwing a cover of snow and ice behind her, she bolted.

# CHAPTER THIRTEEN

EIRLYS

A string of curses sounded behind her, followed by a soft murmur. She sprinted through the halls and found the heavy ornate white oak doors. Not bothering to pause, she pushed them open. Shards of the city peeked through the branches of dark pines and bright birch, but Eirlys left them all behind. She ran until her chest ached, until the way wound from pebbled pathways to trampled trails. The smell of the forest surrounded her, drowning her like the oppressive weight of this nightmare.

Oh Goddess, did she leave Lita behind with strangers? With people who just had her whipped?

Getting her breath under control, Eirlys turned but she saw nothing to indicate the road back to the castle. A twig cracked and Eirlys spun, sending a chunk of ice soaring through the trees, her inky Wraithmark prominent on her face.

"That's her!" someone shouted, and Eirlys ran again.

She sprinted through the trees. Her lungs screamed in denial as she pushed on further. She whipped below a branch, then over a fallen log before the ground disappeared. A steep hill plummeted toward a creek. She failed to catch herself, tumbling over her head and skittering to a stop halfway down. Scrabbling to her feet, she sprinted for the creek. The water, even in the dead of summer, was icy. If her affinity had been any other, it would have set her teeth chattering. Instead, she rushed into the depths, where she pulled on her magic and waited.

At least a dozen people crested the hill and Eirlys blanched. The throne room had been a constrictor, crushing her until she couldn't breathe. She'd escaped its hold only to find herself in a pit of vipers, poised and venomous, ready to strike.

She was going to die. This was it. The odds were never great, but now, here, she would die in this creek. Sparing her potentially last thoughts on her loved ones, she hoped her mother would be pardoned if the problem—Eirlys—was no longer in the picture.

And August. By the Goddess, she hoped he would be okay. He and Rory had each other, at least.

She didn't wait for them to get close. With her magic singing through the creek, she lifted her arms and attached tendrils of water to her like tentacles. She swung and pushed her magic, sending the arm to the nearest immortal. The blonde woman reared up the earth and shielded herself. Eirlys swung her other arm, freezing the water and slamming it on a Ra man. Pain radiated from her shoulder as the weight of the ice tore a muscle, causing her to let go. Water spilled down the hill.

"Gonna stand in water all day, Skath?" one of them asked.

Eirlys shrugged and spun, sending a chunk of ice toward the speaker. She tried to catch it, but the cracking sound preceded her scream. She fell to her knees, staring at her broken hands.

"You bitch!" a man screamed at her as if he hadn't ambushed her, with the intent to kill. He rushed her, wielding dual blades.

The whistle of arrows preceded the two shafts striking his chest and he collapsed.

Price, Brisa, and Deryn—who nocked another arrow—appeared at the crest of the hill.

"By the order of your gods, you will not harm her," Brisa commanded.

Eirlys rolled her eyes. They knew their laws; they thought she was the exception, and even if not, she wore no crown. She was nothing to these people but a Skath on their land, a blight to be wiped out.

"She's nothing to us," one of the women said, echoing Eirlys's thoughts.

Another man continued. "If she dies, the true queen can rule."

Bitterness lanced through Eirlys, leaving the taste of bile in her throat.

"If she dies, you forfeit your life," Price said. "Don't think I don't recognize you, Ilias. Or you, Olena. A lord and a lady, shaming our bloodline. Your uncle is Jasper Inwood, right? How would he feel about the way you're disrespecting his great grandmother's laws? Queen Erie implemented the binding on the crown after watching her family murdered, her cousins hunted, and their children slaughtered. She fought against this behavior."

Ilias and Olena stopped, their Wraithmarks fading.

"Let's go," Olena said to her brother.

As they turned away, the leaves around the hollow whispered with the sound of another arrow being loosed.

Price shouted, "No!"

Wind tore around Eirlys to protect her, but the shot hit,

tearing between her ribs and her arm. The impact knocked her into the water and Brisa charged, two battle axes in her hand. Eirlys gawked at her sister. She pounced, human legs no longer under her but massive strong paws of a mountain lion. As soon as she hit the dirt on the other side of the creek, the rocks grabbed the Sa with the bow and arrow. Panicked, he tried to fire at Brisa. A roar of anger came from behind Eirlys, and Deryn's wind blasted through the air again, sending the arrow into the dirt instead of her heart. Before Eirlys took another breath, Brisa's two axes cleaved the man's head from his shoulders.

The remaining parties ran off, leaving the two dead men and the woman, who still sobbed over her broken hands on the hill.

Eirlys regarded Brisa—breath coming hard, inhuman eyes shining bright—and realized that was the second time Brisa had saved her life.

Eirlys lowered her shaking body into the bath, chamomile and lavender scenting the room. As the tension left her body, her tears mixed with the soapy water. They were tears of relief and anxiety, of joy and fear; the tears of her confusion, her helplessness, and her loss. Her hands trembled in front of her.

In under a week, she had gone from being one of the most feared legends in Kestrya to... this. From being so resolute in her purpose to not even sure if she would live to see the next day. Not even her crown had protected her as promised. She longed for her mother's touch and comforting words, the feeling of safety only a parent can bring their child. Tonight, she felt like that again, small, and vulnerable, trying to traverse a world she didn't yet understand.

"Eirlys?" Brisa's soft voice rang from the doorway. "May I come in?"

"Yes."

Eirlys wiped her face with the hot water and turned toward her sister.

Sisters. Siblings.

How strange that she never thought of her birth parents having children after her. Both realms prided themselves on their children because immortals did not conceive easily. And with five thousand years of crossing the Barrenlands, Devoid refugees could not contribute to Kestrya's population. While Kygem's birth rates doubled Kestrya's, their sacrificial infanticide stifled theirs.

"Can I tell you a story?" Brisa asked, sitting beside the tub on the floor. The top of her head was barely visible.

"Of course," Eirlys said, her curiosity piqued.

Brisa sighed and ran her hands through her hair. "I want to tell you why I abdicated the throne."

Eirlys froze, her attention on Brisa's every word.

"First, you need to consider what it's like having a dead older sister, the true queen as they called you, the stillborn who everyone mourned for. They held me to imagined standards, a romanticized version of who you would have grown up to be. The people, even our parents, had this ideal version of you. Your name was whispered in the streets like a prayer. You were dead, and I was your shadow."

Eirlys had never given her potential family much thought, but Brisa had to live with the weight of knowing her dead older sister would always be better than her. It surprised Eirlys that Brisa didn't hate her more than Aydra.

"I understand now why they were so insistent on me

learning the Skath Law to its core. Why they pushed it so hard. Because of you. If they could produce a Skath, then so could I. Of course, they didn't tell us any of this. As future queen, my education focused on laws, politics and because my mother was incapable of lifting a sword, she made sure I trained in combat."

Brisa paused. "I'm sure you know, but being queen, even a future queen, means meeting many people, a lot of traveling. I loved talking to our people, encouraging them to be good citizens, to promote our realm for what I thought was good.

"As I neared twenty, my mother started talking about marriage. I thought of marrying, being pregnant, and birthing a child to watch her face darken. To have gone through all that pain only to watch as they ripped my child from my arms. The thought twisted my stomach so much. I knew then I would not have children. The risk seemed too great. When I told Mother before my twenty-first birthday, she was, of course, shocked, but she understood. Now I see she knew too well where my thoughts had gone. What she had to do with you was not something she would wish on her daughters. She suggested I abdicate the throne to Aydra. I thought we had decades more, not mere years. I agreed and it was done. I don't regret it, not for a second. I regret never telling the realm why, though. Maybe if I had…"

"You couldn't have." Eirlys placed her hand on the side of the tub and Brisa grabbed it. "As you saw, I was close to the royal family in Kestrya. I understand what someone must sacrifice for the good of the realms. I've disagreed plenty with the Kestryan queen, but I understood why she needed to do things she did."

"I didn't stay in the castle. I left. Moved to Alby with Deryn. I became a blacksmith and I'm blessed good at it, too. I only moved back in when—" Her voice hitched. Brisa shook her head. "I wanted you to know, today aside, there are more of us on your side than Aydra or the Ancients will have you believe and well—" Brisa stopped.

Eirlys sat up and studied her sister, still seated on the floor.

Brisa caught her eyes and half smiled. "Well, the world might be changing. And more than a few people want it to."

Two Kygemian princesses—two different paths. Brisa and Lita had defied their realm, their religion, for their own personal morals. They both wanted a different world, a better north. But one thing Eirlys hadn't considered before stepping on that ship, even if she could change the north, was the north worth saving?

# Chapter Fourteen

## August

The sea spray settled on his skin, as heavy as the guilt settling into his spirit.

August braced against the railing of the vessel, the land barely visible on the horizon. The familiar cerulean sea should have felt like home, but all he could think of was her. Goddess, he had let them take her. He had let her leave.

The thought swirled in with the million others, piling on his shame. The dead look in Rory's eyes, a new coldness settling between them. It wasn't that she brought or held them together—it was losing her, mourning her that took precedent. Between him and Rory and the grief felt by the entire Shadow Guard, there was not yet room for more. Not yet, August promised himself. Perhaps, in time, when the bruises faded from under Rory's eyes and the jagged wounds in both of their hearts scarred over.

His mother did not understand, did not grieve as he did. He snorted to himself—he never should have expected anything less. Neither his father nor the council would go against the queen. So, August left in the dead of night with his Shadows beside him and a crew under his command. They did not question the prince, but they all gave him sidelong glances. No one, not Nyala or the Goddesses and their four daughters, could have stopped the revelation from spreading. Eirlys, the now ex-lover of the prince of Kestrya, was about to become queen of Kygem.

August feared she would die before she got the chance.

Either way, he couldn't sleep, he barely ate, and at Rory's suggestion, August needed to do something even if it failed. Nyala outright refused to help him contact Emzelhal or even peek in on Eirlys in Kygem. He was without a lead and he hated it. So, he was making his way to the Wraiths. On the bright side, as the only heir, Redna could only punish him to a certain extent when he returned.

Dressed in a white cotton shirt and deep red breeches, no one would have known August was the prince, except for his Shadow Guard. Each one of them, Rory, Caden, Nik, Basil, and Galen, wore their gray uniforms. They were shadows, Kenos, specters on the deck. They did not help the crew. They merely watched the skies and seas and him. Always him.

He removed his bridge coat when the boat docked, trying to ignore the five sets of eyes clinging to his back. He was more than grateful to the five of them, especially now. It wasn't just the absence of Eirlys, although without her the guard felt incomplete. But at some point, Kygem was going to find out he ordered the assassination. And that storm could break before they got wind of it.

The general of the Wraiths stood with her hands clasped behind her back. Sarit wore a simple one-sleeved chiton, cut short in the newest fashion, and trousers. She shared the same olive skin tone as August, common among Kestryans, but her hair was the more usual black. She looked normal. She looked young. She was neither of those things.

The Wraith general was nearing four hundred years old, the oldest Naevni on the continent. Unlike many of her kind, she had not defected to the Necromancers, finding their practices bordering on the heretical. Instead, she commanded the greatest force August could put together. Their secret weapon, for which Kygem would never be able to prepare. If he didn't blow it now.

"Prince August," Sarit said, giving a small bow of her head.

"I've told you, August is fine," he said.

She smiled before turning serious. August's insides jumbled, his blood running cold.

"I must insist you will not find what you are looking for here."

Curse his mother and Nyala.

"At least let me talk to them," August pleaded.

"I cannot deny you, my liege, but be forewarned Nyala visited while you traveled and said the consequences would be severe."

August wanted to rage, to yell until his throat was raw, but he had been raised a prince. He tamped down every ounce of boiling anger and breathed.

"Thank you, but I still have to try."

Sarit merely turned her back to him and led the way through the cobbled pathways. No one asked if he wanted a SaCarriage. No one asked if he was tired. A few of his guards remained quiet at his back, while others leapt from neighboring rooftops, scanning ahead, before they jumped down to meet the group as they entered a new block.

Seventy-nine Naevni lived in this part of the city. They trained, they practiced, and they hid their powers when outside of the area. Now they gathered in the small agora.

A small dais was set to one side, but August ignored it. He pulled on his magic, the light from the sun fueling his power, and soared above the crowd. Curses flowed from his guards, and Basil took to the air behind him. August hovered over the bubbling fountain in the center as Basil landed below him.

The Wraiths turned towards him. He needed to make every word count. He let his power flow, touching the air around the square, feeling for the edges. He amplified his voice but made sure to cut off the sound before it escaped the area.

"I know you have been told about the situation. The Captain of my Shadow Guard is no less than the current heir to the Kygemian throne. This news is not what is important to me. Eirlys dedicated her life to Kestrya, to me. She fought and bled for our realm. We should not be so willing to let her succumb to whatever the north has in store for her."

"I heard she chose to go." August could not see the speaker. Others in the square muttered in agreement.

"Yes, because she believed she had no other choice," August said. "But she has a choice. We have given the Kygemian Skath the choice to live here, free and loved. We are not Kestryan because we were born here. We are Kestryan because we believe the Skath are no different than Klara or Naevni. That the infants they slaughter daily deserve a chance to live. Eirlys deserved, and still deserves, that chance."

The eerily quiet crowd stared at August.

"What are you asking of us?" This time, August saw the man who spoke standing close to the fountain.

"To help me bring her and her mother home."

"You want a war?" someone else said.

"War is coming, regardless," August said. "We cannot avoid it. We have sat idle for too long and watched Kygem mock our religion, our goddesses. We have watched them kill children, destroy the future of parents. War is inevitable."

Murmuring skittered through the crowd.

"You ask us to not only risk our lives, but yours, my prince, when we have been explicitly told not to aid you."

August smiled at the man. "My mother has been through a lot. She lost her own family when she was young, and the death of two of her children has blinded her to the actions we need to take. I will not be bound by my siblings' death, forced to live in the shadows of their demise because of fear. I will be the prince you need, the future king who will not let our neighbors continue to terrorize their own, with or without my mother's blessing."

The charged quiet weighed on both the crowd and August. He tried to breathe, to wait it out. He let the words settle and almost gave up when someone finally spoke.

"I'll do it."

A woman near the middle of the crowd raised her hand. Others parted for her to walk toward the prince. She had rich brown skin and large, expressive eyes. A flash of familiarity coursed through August, but he couldn't place her.

"I trained with Eirlys for the royal guard. I helped you and her escape when your family was attacked."

August blinked at the woman. The attack on the agora, the screaming, Eirlys torn between Amalthea and August. In the end, it didn't matter, Eirlys had no choice. She saved his life by getting him to the closest Naevni and they shimmered out of the burning Royal Agora to spend the winter in the southern courts. The Naevni who saved them had the person's same brown skin and eyes, but she had transitioned into the woman before him.

"I remember you," August said. "But I am sorry, I do not know what you would like to be called."

She graced him with a gorgeous smile. "Thank you. My name is Vara, my liege."

"Vara," August said, committing the woman's name to memory. He lowered himself to the ground to greet her. "Shall we discuss this in more private quarters?"

Vara agreed. The crowd parted for them again, a few whispered in harsh tones while others pulled back in disappointment. Only a handful praised Vara while she led them to her small apartment.

"What do you need from me? I assume you have a plan, and we aren't blazing in with just the Shadow Guard and me?"

August chuckled, remembering how much he had enjoyed being around her in those months after the attack. "No. There is a man. His name is Emzelhal, the son of the man who had been spying for us for almost thirty years. Find him. I need to talk to him, but if he cannot get away, I need news of Eirlys. To know she still lives. Lita too."

"As you wish, my prince."

Vara threw on a cloak, fastening the loop. She threw the hood over her head and grasped August's hand. She placed a small glass orb in it, golden swirling wraith glowing within.

"I'll be back, but if you need me, contact me with this." She faced the Shadow Guard. "It'll help me find you if I can touch you."

Each of the guards held out their hand and Vara pulled on her power, the sound of the void almost deafening in the small apartment.

"Thank you and be patient, my prince. I'll find this man as fast as I can and return."

She almost stepped through the void before August grabbed her hand. "Take this," he said, placing a small bag of money in her hand. "Whatever you need."

Vara pocketed the bag and her Wraithmark flashed a brilliant red. She stepped through the void and was gone.

Galen managed to acquire a room in a nearby inn. The

reality of the last few weeks started to weigh on August as they walked into the room. Another place that wasn't home, another bed without her in it. Another Goddess-cursed day of waiting and not acting. He wanted to act and yet, the idea of taking one more step, one more breath was beyond his ability.

Caden stepped up to him, her copper eyes filled with tears. "I'm sorry."

He stared at her confused, his grief forgotten for a moment. "Whatever for?"

"If I hadn't helped her fool everyone, she might still be here. We'd know she's alive."

"We don't know that she's dead," Rory practically snarled. He refused to believe Eirlys was dead.

"They haven't announced her as queen though, or even as heir," Galen said, worrying his bottom lip.

August ignored the back and forth. He wrapped Caden in a hug, breathing in the salt laced scent of hair. "When Eirlys makes up her mind, when she wants to do something, there is no stopping her."

Caden sobbed into his shirt. He held her until her guilt and pain subsided into something less volatile. "We cannot hide our grief from each other," August said.

Rory put one arm around August, leaning his head to rest on the man's shoulder. "That goes for you, too."

So, August let go. Tearless sobs escaped his throat. August let himself feel. He let himself be. Not a prince, not a warrior, not a general. He was a man who lost the love of his life. Although she was gone, August was not alone. He had friends and they loved him. At that moment, he needed them more than he realized.

# CHAPTER FIFTEEN

## EIRLYS

Eirlys bolted upright in bed. The balcony door was open, the curtains swaying in the wind. Price stood outlined against the night, flaming sword in hand as he stared over the stone railing. An illogical need coursed through her, wanting to pull him back from the edge. When had she become worried for his safety? Over the last few weeks, she'd become used to his presence—his ever-vigilant watch at her door never faltered, despite the utter boredom he must have felt.

"Void it!" he cursed.

Eirlys scrambled out of bed and went to the door. The nights were still mild, but the breeze carried a chill, signaling the early start of autumn. "What happened?"

His magic was still bright on his face when he shook his head, frustrated. "You were talking in your sleep. You've been talking all night but then I heard you whimper before you screamed. I rushed in and a Sa was floating above you. I charged him but he dove off the gods' cursed balcony."

Her heart stuttered, coming to life again and beating faster than hummingbird wings. "What did he look like?"

"Cropped dark hair," Price said.

She couldn't rule out August, and she wouldn't put it past the fool to try and 'rescue' her.

"I think he was a Skath." He didn't look at her when he said it, instead staring out at the moonless starry night.

She stared at her open balcony. Despite being stifled in her room for weeks, she no longer felt any desire to go outside. Eirlys wrapped her arms around herself, clutching onto anything, utterly vulnerable and stepped back from the cool air.

Price followed her inside, his eyes finally moving from assessing the situation to Eirlys before staring at the floor with flushed cheeks.

Modesty was not something Eirlys ever considered—nudity was as natural as the magic in her veins. Tonight, she had fallen asleep in a loose shirt and her undergarments, which Price seemed to think was worse than if she'd been stark naked, based on the color filling his face.

"I should get dressed," Eirlys said, leaving Price and his darkening eyes alone.

She dressed in black pants, thigh-high supple leather boots and a cream, form-fitting sleeveless top embroidered with lace. She wished for her weapons, her belt, something besides her marginalized magic. It took her shaking hands dropping the lace twice before she realized her whole body was trembling. Panic would do her no good and yet its claws were already deep within her.

Though she had been adjusting to life in the castle—well, her rooms—she hadn't done much in the way of learning. Price kept trying but she was being a stubborn fool about it and didn't see the need to learn about Kygem's realm or religion when she planned on tearing it down anyway. Not that she told him that.

When she left the closet, he stood in front of the fireplace. His magic glowed on his face while he lit a fire. The flames were stunning blue, like his eyes, like her hair.

Eirlys was grateful for the gesture and the warmth and she wasted no time sitting. She curled her knees into her chest, wrapping her arms around her legs and let the heat seep into her bones, chilled from fear.

"I sent a message to Brisa and Deryn. They should be here shortly."

When she didn't say anything, he frowned, turning away from the fire and casting his face in shadow. Oddly, it suited him. He leaned against the wall, facing her, like he was waiting for her to talk, or break.

"I've never been more scared," she whispered.

"I can imagine," Price said.

"No." She chewed on her lip. "No, you can't."

He frowned.

"I've spent most of my life glowering down the point of a sword or the flicker of a flame. I crossed the Barrenlands more times than I can count, always knowing that I might meet my end there. Die in the same place my mother wanted me to." Indeed, the very man she now attempted to seek comfort from had crossed steel with her.

"Sounds like you were tempting fate," Price said, trying to make a joke.

Eirlys gave him a small smile though she was far from amused. She sighed. "I have looked death in its ugly, ruinous face, and I have survived when so many people have wanted me dead.

"I have a scar on my chest from where Gyda stabbed me when I was a baby. Your goddess tried to kill me. You tried to kill me." Price flinched but did not, could not, deny it. "Goddess, my own people and my own sister are trying to kill me. And who knows what that man wanted, but it didn't seem friendly. So, not only are Kygemian's trying to kill me, but there is someone out there who can infiltrate my locked balcony. Price, I don't have weapons. I am terrified to use my magic."

A strange mix of emotions crossed his face, like a battle raged in his mind. Suddenly, he pushed away from the wall and came to stand in front of her.

He gestured to the spot beside her. "May I?"

From the moment he entered her room, she'd wondered what sick twist of fate placed the man who wanted her dead as her guard, her protector. And despite his deeply flawed beliefs, he was kind and gentle and sweet. He was so fucking loyal that it made her devotion to August look like mere duty.

And this wasn't even the most vulnerable she'd been with him. She slept with his ever-watching gaze on her, never feeling trapped, but safe. She knew how to recognize the shelter in a storm, rather than seeing the confines of the walls. So, she nodded.

He folded his long legs under himself, briefly leaving a tense space between them. Then, hesitantly, his arm wrapped around her, his gloved hand squeezing her shoulder. That gentle touch broke whatever control she was keeping on her emotions. Fear welled up in her throat, a sob breaking free. Without consciously deciding to, she leaned into his chest, letting her tears stain his shirt.

Eventually, the tears slowed until she was nothing but a dried-out husk being kept together by Price's grip. She felt his words across her hair. "I am here. I will protect you the way you would have protected your prince."

"Why?" she asked.

He chuckled, breathy, chest moving under her. In a move

both familiar and startling, Price leaned his head against Eirlys's. "I guess I'm like you in a way. I was... sick as a baby. I was my parents' only chance to have a child. They didn't want to lose me. My parents went to your mother, real mother," Price cleared his throat. "She helped, made me better. And if the last thing I can do with my life is protect her daughter, then that's what I'll do."

"Is that why you're still in pain? From the illness you had?"

Price went still, muscles rigid.

"Oh!" Brisa's exclamation had Price and Eirlys spinning to face her, a tangle of limbs and embarrassment. Finally free of each other, they both stood.

Deryn occupied the doorway behind Brisa.

"Are you alright?" Brisa said, approaching Eirlys.

No, no she wasn't okay. "Yeah," she said, not fooling anyone.

"What did the Council say?" Price asked.

"You saw the Council tonight?" Eirlys tried not to feel completely left out and failed.

"We went immediately after receiving Price's message. The Ancients were... "

"Fucking useless," Deryn said. "We are on our own in finding this man."

Eirlys snorted. "They were probably wishing he threw me from the balcony. Brisa, you don't think Aydra would be working with a Skath?"

"No," Brisa said after a pregnant pause. "No. She wouldn't do it even if it meant the crown was hers and it brought back our parents."

The answer did not make Eirlys feel any better. If the man wasn't working with someone in the castle, maybe he worked with someone who had infiltrated the castle before—who knew that this room was kept empty for years.

Price waved his hand in front of Eirlys's face. "What are you thinking about so hard?"

"It seems awfully coincidental that two separate groups infiltrated the castle without anyone knowing." Brisa frowned. Eirlys took a deep breath. "What if this man was also with the assassin? If he already knew how to get in?"

Price rubbed his face. "Shit. And it's not like the assassin is talking."

Eirlys whirled on him. "He's still fucking alive?"

The room stilled with acquiescence.

Her mind was a chaotic swirl of thoughts. The idea that a man who assassinated royalty had been allowed to live was incomprehensible. Eirlys had wasted no time killing Lex for what he had done to Amalthea or what he planned to do with August. She hadn't been quick or efficient. The feel of her blade sinking into his chest over and over again still haunted her because of how much she enjoyed it.

"Where is he?" Her voice was as cold as her magic when it punctuated the air, the ground around her frosting over.

Brisa and Price glanced at each other. "He's at Night Stone. A prison in the north only accessible through the Gods," Brisa explained.

Deryn reached out and touched Eirlys's arm, making her jump and drop her magic. Casual touch between them was becoming normal and she still wasn't sure if she was grateful or put off by the idea.

"He refuses to speak," Brisa explained.

Eirlys interlaced her fingers together, took a deep breath and pushed out her hands, cracking her knuckles.

"Let me try."

Ancient Olga, Goddess of Truth, walked into Eirlys's room from the void, the air around her fracturing. The sneer on her face was the first thing Eirlys saw. Like every Ancient, Olga had bone white hair and eyes. Her hair, stick straight, was cut in a hard line at her chin and across her brow, setting her angular face in sharp relief. Her skin nearly matched Price's, a warm sandy beige. Karaveshian, for sure, if it was even called that five thousand years ago when Olga sprang from the earth. Or however goddesses, no matter how false, came into being.

Eirlys pressed her lips into a tight line. Her frustration at the north for not having any portals was only tempered by the fact that she could not tell anyone, even her allies, that Kestrya was filled with Naevni. Enough that they powered portals across the realm. It was an expensive form of travel, but it was convenient and easy. Instead, Eirlys would have to be taken to Night Stone by the very creatures she promised to destroy. But she had to focus on one thing at a time. For now, she needed to survive and that meant finding out what the assassin knew.

Aydra appeared by Olga's side, and Eirlys stifled the groan in her throat.

"Brisa has requested for you to be allowed to see the assassin. She made a convincing case that your"—Olga looked Eirlys up and down, disgust plain on her face—"*talents* may be of some use."

As usual, Aydra shot Eirlys a sickly-sweet grin. Brisa, Deryn, and Price waited off to the side—they adamantly refused to let her go alone.

The goddess continued. "But make no mistake, every word, every movement will be watched. Any hint of remorse or camaraderie—"

Eirlys's teeth gnashed together as white-hot rage filled her blood. Olga paused.

"I have nothing in common with that assassin." The lie fell

easily from her lips before she realized her mistake. Olga noticed as well. The assassin and Eirlys shared a power draw. Being Skath alone in a realm full of Klara was enough to make anyone nervous.

"Yes, well, we will see." Olga pursed her lips and reached out to Eirlys.

Gooseflesh crawled over her body, tightening her scalp, and sending cold shivers through her. Placing her hand in Olga's, she found blue eyes monitoring her. Disappointment marred Price's gorgeous face. Was it because she was terrified of Olga or the task she was about to perform?

A few moments later, Eirlys clung to Olga, one hand tightening on the strap over her shoulder. The void rushed by before spilling them out into a sea-wrecked coast. Eirlys inhaled, but the tangy, salty air was muted by the north's cool climate, barely tingling her senses.

On the cliff loomed Night Stone Prison. Thirteen massive, square towers surrounded the fortress in an almost perfect circle, connected by fortified, thick walls. Circular, glassless windows studded the towers, big enough to let out an arm and nothing more. The gleaming dark of the walls reflected light, like a diamond of the deepest black. Obsidian—the entire cursed thing was made from obsidian. No one's magic would work inside the beast.

The looming structure made Eirlys feel small and insignificant. At least her mother wasn't being kept here. They could have kept her in this place, magicless, defenseless, *alone*. Eirlys shook her head. No place should have made her feel grateful to the infant killers she now had to rule over.

Price and Deryn glanced at the Night Stone prison, their mouths in matching tight lines. Aydra wrapped her arms around herself while Brisa swallowed before squaring her shoulders.

"This way," Olga said and led the group inside.

Power leached away once Eirlys crossed the threshold. Although it was futile, she tried anyway to pull on her magic. Nothing happened. The darkness swam around her and burrowed into her bones. RaGlass lined the walls, and the gray light cast from it lent everything a hollow, flat glow. It reminded Eirlys of the Barrenlands. The oppressive gray where if she thought about it long, she'd be drowned in its never-ending dullness.

Olga stopped near what Eirlys assumed was the center of the prison. The rounded outer wall showed no door, but Olga placed a small glass key into the wall. The obsidian seemed to absorb into itself, creating an arched doorway before them.

Still circular, the room's walls, floors, and ceiling were carved from obsidian. Its shiny, glassy surface reflected the shadow-selves of those who entered, staring at them from six different directions. In the center, plain metal bars encircled a cage. There was no keyhole or door. The bars entered the floor and connected in an arch over their occupant's head.

Eirlys slung her bag to the ground in front of the bars, out of reach if he dared try for one of the instruments inside. She'd had to make do with what could be found in the castle, but her time in the royal guard taught her lessons she wished she'd never had to learn. How to empathize with her captives, how to pretend she thought their actions were well placed and honorable. Things that made her vomit her guts out afterwards.

As she took in her parents' assassin, her stomach clenched. It looked as if someone had tortured him, but Eirlys knew the moment she voiced her plan aloud that no one had deigned to stoop so low. Even the two guardians balked at the idea of letting Eirlys use her persuasive skills.

And it was Price's disappointment that cut deeper. She

needed allies, but in truth, she wanted the proselyte to like her, to show him that the source of her magic wasn't the evil thing he had been taught to believe. What if today, to find out the information they needed, she'd undo all the progress they had been making? What if today all three of her allies started to look at her like everyone else in the castle did?

The man who killed the queen and king might have once been attractive—not striking—but plainly handsome. The kind of handsome one settles down with, finds comfort and peace in. It had all been melted away. His scalp, face, and parts of his chest were covered in scars, healed jagged pieces of flesh connected all wrong. Burnt. The marks of a raging inferno of flames that no Va could withstand the transfer to heal.

"Who did this?" Eirlys asked, keeping her voice flat.

"Aydra after we found him in the city," Brisa said. "We had to obsidian her to make her stop."

So Aydra could torture the man near to death in the middle of the city out of rage and sorrow and still be seen as the rightful heir, but Eirlys suggesting some mild persuasive techniques had her allies looking at her like she was something vile.

Eirlys swallowed down the injustice. "You needed him alive. Why? He told you everything, right?"

"Obviously not, or we wouldn't be here," Olga said.

A flash of blue eyes, the color of a crystal-clear sky, met her own under melted lids.

"Hello," he said, cocking his head to the side. His voice was so normal, so calm and smooth. It was jarring considering the state of his skin.

His mouth twisted terribly as a mockery of a smile appeared on his mangled lips. "Oh, you are a beauty. I'm sorry you had to meet me like this." The assassin gestured an arm downward. His hand was in pristine condition until halfway up his forearm. "I'm Evrit."

"I am here to ask you some questions," Eirlys said.

The man shot a look toward the bag. "There will be no need for your special skills here."

"You'll answer my questions?" Eirlys normally needed rapport with her captives before they willingly answered anything.

Evrit eyed her audience. "I'll answer questions, but only for you. Alone."

"I don't think that will be possible."

"No?" Evrit merely shrugged and sat in his cell. He was humming a tune popular in Kestrya though it was decades old.

Eirlys turned her pleading eyes on Brisa and Deryn.

"We are not leaving," Aydra said.

"Eirlys," Brisa said her name with the sorrow of someone already defeated.

So, she turned to look at the proselyte and one of the gods he worshiped. "Price, Olga, I beseech you. Let me talk to him alone. If not for the sake of my soul, then for the sake of closure and knowledge."

Olga looked ready to burst, to drag Eirlys away from this place but then Price folded himself onto the ground prostrate.

Eirlys wanted to yank him up, suddenly finding herself fiercely protective of the man who was sworn to protect her. It took every ounce of self-control to keep her from jumping between Price's prone body and Olga's white-hot glare.

"Ancient Olga, Goddess of Truth, please know by my words and my oath that I trust her. Even if you cannot, trust me. I will stay by her side, if the assassin will allow it."

Olga glanced up and behind Eirlys's shoulder. Eirlys risked looking back and saw Evrit's amused expression. He eyed Price before nodding.

"A future queen cannot be left alone. I understand. The proselyte may stay."

Olga leaned and pressed her hand on Price's shoulder, then whispered something in his ear. His back tensed for the briefest moment.

Then Olga strode away, the rest of them following the goddess out of ear shot. Price remained seated on the floor and Eirlys realized he was praying, the words muffled by his position before he stood and faced her.

Over the past couple of weeks, Eirlys had seen Price as a warrior, a protector. She didn't forget but it was easy to overlook that he was a proselyte, sworn to the gods as much as he was to her. The truth left a bitter taste in her mouth, and she wondered if she could truly trust him.

"What do you want to know?" Evrit asked.

Before she faced her parents' murderer, she had to decide what questions to ask and what questions she needed to avoid. She could not implicate August or mention that Evrit wasn't working on his own. She also had her mother to think about. If she fucked this up, they didn't have to punish Eirlys; they had Lita. Even if she trusted Price with her life, she wasn't about to trust him with her mother's.

"You crossed the border twenty-seven years ago?"

"Yes. Got lucky, too. We had been planning to cross for years and when my wife died, well, there was nothing left for me in Kestrya."

Eirlys frowned. That was more information than requested, which meant there was something there to distract Eirlys. She ignored the bit about his dead wife and his plans. If Price caught onto the "we", it was possible to implicate the realm of Kestrya rather than a rogue assassin.

"Did you cross with anyone?"

"Multiple people. They were all gathered around the spot

where the princess pretended to kill herself. I merely joined them on the way back."

He gave her that horrific grin again and she clenched her jaw.

"Did you bring someone with you from Kestrya?"

Evrit flashed to his feet, hands circling the bars. Although she did not step back, every instinct screamed at her to do so. He was her height, but the platform of the cage made him taller, and he looked down at her.

"What makes you think there is someone else with me?"

Not a no, so she was getting closer. If she was going to be queen, if she was going to rule, then she had to trust her instincts.

"A man infiltrated my room and jumped off my balcony. Higher than I have known anyone to survive. Who was he?"

Evrit blew out through his nose, in a short huff. "I taught him better than to get caught."

Eirlys reached her hand toward the man, touching the back of his hand lightly. A noise of discontent sounded behind her. "Who is he?"

With a disgusted huff, Evrit pulled his hand away. "Emzelhal will finish what I started, I swear to the goddess and her lover. Nothing you can do will stop him."

Eirlys paused. "Emzelhal?"

"Tell me, Eirlys. Why do they still stand? Why is *he* still alive?" His eyes flicking to Price, then back to her. "And I have heard rumors of the prince's guard captain, fierce and strong. You can defend yourself better than he can. And yet, you look to him for assistance, look to them like they command you. I put you on this throne to destroy it, not to bow to the gods and lust after one of their corrupt priests."

"I chose to take the throne for the sake of the Skath," Eirlys protested, ignoring the rest of his words. She wanted to gauge Price's reaction but didn't dare look away from the assassin.

"Take your tactics elsewhere." Evrit stepped back from the bars. "I have no desire to talk to a traitor of her own kind."

Already stretched thin, Eirlys lost her patience and grabbed Evrit by the neck. She yanked him forward, slamming his head into the bars. Blood splattered across her face, warm and coppery. She gripped his throat tighter, and he spit on her. She breathed into her nose, feeling blood and saliva slide down her cheek, and tried not to vomit.

A warm presence flitted behind her back, the ghost of his fingers pressed against her spine.

With one hand, she flicked the blood onto the floor.

"Price, I'm fine. I can handle this." His protectiveness wasn't helping the situation.

He didn't move, but Eirlys couldn't focus on him.

"I don't know what your motives are. If you have a partner out there, they will find me much harder to kill than my parents."

Eirlys released her grip and Evrit stumbled back.

"Let's go," she said to Price, walking back toward her waiting crowd.

"Look at me, child," Evrit said. Hands clenched into fists, Eirlys faced him. He lifted his body from the floor. "I sacrificed my son's fertility and magic, making him Devoid. I raised him in secret for this entire plan, sacrificed my own life to get you here. What have you sacrificed for the Skath? A cushy job in the castle protecting the prince of a line that has been too much of a coward to free the north. Decades of work to watch my prized queen succumb to Kygem in a matter of weeks."

Eirlys lunged for the bars and Evrit backed out of her reach. Rage spilled from her, her arms reaching for him, face pressed against the bars like a feral beast.

"You want to talk about sacrifice! I was loved, I was happy in Kestrya. You have no idea what I have sacrificed to be here. What I have given up to save the Skath."

Price grabbed her around the waist and wrenched her away from the cell.

Evrit leaned back against the bars and crossed his arms. "What are you going to do, Eirlys? You have taken the crown but not the responsibility."

His derision hit all the right nerves. This had been his plan. A Skath Queen, on the throne of Kygem, and Evrit and his son, Emzelhal, orchestrated it all. The choice Eirlys made, to go to the north, to take the crown, had never really been a choice after all.

She shoved away Price and faced Evrit. "You fancy yourself the hero, but you have taken your life to ruin mine. I hope a hole in the hallowed Kygemian ground is worth it. When I finish what I came here to do, without your help, your name will be as forgotten as your bones in your grave."

Then she walked away, leaving both Evrit and Price to pick up their jaws from the floor.

When Olga returned them to the castle, the goddess took Price to the side. Eirlys watched with trepidation as they talked in rushed whispers. The void cracked around and Olga was gone, but not before Eirlys caught the smirk on her face. She couldn't be sure, but she was certain she had not said anything that would betray her true purpose here.

Price walked behind her up the stairs to her tower and she couldn't help but ask him, "What did Olga want?"

"You know what she wants," he said, sounding tired and worn out. "It is no secret that I was assigned to you for more than one purpose."

Her footsteps faltered and she tripped. Price was there in an instant, picking her up off the floor.

"Four Daughters, why would you tell me that?" She searched his face, looking for some trick.

"Because you are too smart to not have realized. And tonight, I saw a woman who is desperate for change. You will do anything for that, and I am terrified of how far you will go to achieve it. I want to help you, not hinder you. I won't give the gods anything to condemn you. But if you picked a fight with them, or they with you—"

He stopped and reached down to touch the scrape from where she fell. His hand flexed hard; fingers splayed. Not to get away, but an involuntary reaction to her touch. She hissed at the sting but let silence fall between them.

"I fear you will destroy yourself to get to them and I wonder if you won't just happen to kill one of them in the process."

"If I don't have to kill them, I won't."

Price shook his head. "Don't lie to me. If given the chance, you would slaughter them. Evrit was right to question why you haven't burned this castle to the ground yet. You should for all we have done to you."

Eirlys clamped her mouth shut. She would not admit it to him. What if Olga had told him to reveal himself to gain her trust? The worst part was that she *wanted* to fall into his blue eyes and lay her faith in his tortured hands.

It was the only thing she could do to break their contact, jerking back from those hands and wrapping her arms around herself. The games of this realm and this throne were deadly and putting her trust in the wrong person meant not only her death, but the death of the people she'd come here to protect.

Eirlys turned her back on him, not bothering to change out of her bloody clothes as she crawled into bed. Price started to head to the door and gods, fuck it all, Eirlys betrayed herself by grabbing at his bare hand, briefly touching before pulling back.

"Wait. Can you stay with me? In here?" Her voice quavered and Goddess, she hated it, she didn't have the strength to bear it all alone. "Just until I fall asleep?"

Price swallowed hard and sat on the side of the bed, back tense.

"I don't bite you know," Eirlys murmured, bringing up one of their first mornings together.

"Now, I don't believe that for a second," he teased, but kicked off his shoes and leaned against the headboard.

Carefully wrapping the blanket around her, she created a barrier between her and Price. Eirlys didn't miss the look of relief on his face, or surprise when she scooted close enough to lay her head on his lap. He smelled of woodsmoke. Every fire in the castle was lit with RaGlass, its purple crystals twinkling in her fireplace ready for cooler days. She hadn't smelled woodsmoke since her time in the guardians when they spiked them with obsidian and sent them into the woods. It reminded her of times when she and Rory laid under the stars, gazing at the gold and blue galaxy streaking across the sky and the smell of her clothes when she returned to August's arms.

Gently, shyly, Price ran his hands through her hair, and she fell asleep to the rhythmic feel of his fingers.

# Chapter Sixteen

## Eirlys

A shudder of the bed jostled Eirlys partially awake, and she almost yelled at August for being obnoxious. Reality pounded in on her like a hammer, brutal and swift, and she opened her eyes to her room in the castle. She reached for the crumpled spot where Price had laid and hopefully slept. Still warm with the heat of his body, her touch brought his scent from the sheets, woodsmoke and autumn air.

Had it only been a couple of weeks since he came into her service? She tried to count back the days, but everything was muddled, one moment bleeding into another. In her dazed state, she'd invited a stranger into her bed, a Kygemian who worshiped their abhorrent gods and should have wanted to put a dagger through her heart. She hated this realm—she should have hated him, and he her. He couldn't even stand her touch. But though they disagreed, something had fundamentally changed last night.

The man who was invading her every thought walked in her room.

Her mother stepped in behind him.

All propriety was lost as Eirlys raced from her bed. She collided with Lita, her arms holding her tight. She ignored the tears on her face, burying her head into the crook of Lita's neck, where she was safe and home. She opened her eyes for a moment when Price cleared his throat.

"I was able to convince them to let you see her for one hour," he said.

Eirlys lifted her chin, placing it on Lita's shoulder, not willing to let her mother go yet.

"Thank you," she mouthed.

Price took his leave and for the first time, he locked the door from the outside. Eirlys assumed her treatment was worse than Lita's, but the woman had been whipped and was clearly more of a prisoner than Eirlys if they needed to lock her in.

Eirlys pulled back, assessing her. She seemed healthy with a nice color to her skin and her eyes were bright. She may have been a tad thinner, but nothing definitive.

"Are you okay?" she asked in Kestryan.

"Truly, I am," Lita responded in the same language. "They haven't touched me since the throne room. On the contrary, I am fed, walked, and allowed to see the sun."

"Mom, dogs get that kind of treatment."

Lita shrugged. "I'm not in Night Stone." Eirlys shuddered at the mention of that horrible place. "I know you are okay. That is what matters to me."

Those facts were not all that mattered to Eirlys. But Lita did not look bothered, and Eirlys couldn't stand to argue with her. Not if they only had an hour.

Lita walked the perimeter. "The garden below used to be a pool, some centuries ago. I guess they filled it in when no more Va were to be born to the Pendry's."

Eirlys watched her mother warily. "Why are you telling me this?"

Lita sighed. "Because I don't want to die and leave you with unanswered questions. I owe you the truths I hid from you, the ones you begged me to know growing up."

Eirlys rushed to her mother's side, grabbing her hand. "Mom, what are you talking about? You aren't going to die."

Lita gave a sad smile. "Yes, I am. I don't know how long they will wait, but it will happen. The moment they locked me up, I knew I didn't have much longer in this world. I only wish I had more time with you."

"Don't talk like that," she insisted.

"I want to prepare you. For my death. For this realm." Lita pulled her hand from Eirlys's to grip her face, forcing her to look into Lita's eyes, the eyes they shared. "You are not one to bury your head in the sand. You will not start now."

Taken aback by her mother's abruptness, Eirlys said, "Maybe they will spare your life if I give them what they want." A gnawing guilt almost made Eirlys take the words back. Lita was never supposed to be here—Eirlys had not planned for her mother to return. And now she would die because of Eirlys's choice, and she didn't know if she could live with the consequences.

Lita shook her head. "You cannot abdicate, and you know it. You will not leave this realm in the hands of that... " Lita breathed out hard through her nose, too angry to even say Aydra's name. "We both know you will not let that happen."

"For your life, I will raze this realm to the ground." Eirlys's voice was fierce, the very flames from which she would light the world on fire to save her mother.

"Let's sit," Lita said. "We don't have much time."

Eirlys did not want to sit. She wanted to rage at her mother for giving up so easily. For thinking her death was inevitable.

Eirlys wasn't sure if she was being childish and stubborn, or if her mother was being a pessimist. But in the end, she sat at the small table by the door.

"Does he know Kestryan?" Lita asked, tilting her head to Price, who they could hear shifting on the other side of the door.

"I doubt it."

"Teach him," Lita said.

Eirlys blinked. This was a woman who may not have fought battles with her hands, but battles of the mind. Battles of words and wit, in shiny ballrooms and at afternoon teas, where a sentence was a dagger and silence a threat.

"I'm listening," Eirlys said.

"Use your allies. Brisa and her guardian, Deryn. They are both on your side. That man out there. He may surprise you. Gain his trust, his loyalty. I know the Ancients"—Eirlys let out a sound of exasperation, but her mother plowed through her interruptions—"most of them are not going to be anything but a hindrance to you. But Iona does believe in true justice, and she will be fair. Ashur may be swayed if the rumors are to be believed. They say he was in love with the first Kestryan Queen."

Eirlys couldn't make heads or tails of who these gods were. She knew Gyda, Cosyn and Olga—the three she had met—but she had no idea who they truly were within the Pantheon.

Eirlys opened her mouth to ask, but Lita waved her off. "Ask Price. He's a proselyte and can give you all the details you need on your new religion."

"It is not my new religion." Eirlys nearly shouted the words, revulsion and searing anger coursing through her veins.

"By all appearances, it must be. You must show the people you are like them. That you are no less because you are Skath."

Evrit's words pierced her thoughts. A traitor to her own

kind, submitting and believing in a religion that doomed Skath children to horrible fates.

"How can I bow to them and honor their religion? The last time I left the castle, I almost died."

"The Ancients wrote their laws, and they will abide by them. Which means once the crown is truly on your head, you will be safe. You must survive until then." Lita tucked a strand of hair behind Eirlys's ear. "But even though you have not been crowned, you are the rightful queen. Act like it."

Eirlys rubbed her face. "I didn't think seeing you again would lead to another lecture."

Lita chuckled. "I wouldn't lecture you so much if you weren't the most stubborn daughter a woman could have. But your stubbornness will come in handy. Play their game, Eirlys. Win it."

Eirlys sat back, stunned into silence.

"I'll take your quiet for acquiescence."

"The only thing I agree with is that this is completely asinine."

Lita leaned forward. "Only if you fail, my daughter. I would never have asked you to do this. I never wanted this for you. But now, you have made your choice, and I cannot help you for long."

Eirlys swallowed. "So, do I have to pretend to be the queen they want me to be until I die? I didn't come here to submit to their will."

"I don't know what you will do during your reign, but it will be unlike anyone else's." Lita gave her a long, sad look, something like regret or fear mixed with the love in her eyes. It made Eirlys ache. "For now, let's make sure you stay alive long enough to get your crown. The rest will follow."

"Without you," Eirlys said, her chest hollow in light of the pain and terror.

Lita walked around the table, pulling Eirlys into her arms and hugging her tightly. "In life or in death, you will never be without me."

After Price escorted Lita back to her room, Eirlys wound up her courage and asked Price to do what he was sent to do. Teach her.

"Have a seat," he said.

She was annoyed at only having one small seating area in a room where she spent all her time.

"Do you know why we call the queen 'Grace'?"

Eirlys went to shake her head and stopped. "No, I don't. I assumed it was like 'Your Majesty' in Kestrya."

"I do not know the religion in Kestrya, but I can guess it is not based on the Ancients."

Eirlys agreed.

"The Council of the Ancient has four Obligations and four Prohibitions. Today we discuss the matter of your queenship and the reason you are still alive today. You should know it is only because of the Ancients and the faith their people believe in that you are alive right now. But not everyone is religious, and not everyone reads the doctrine the same way."

Eirlys swallowed hard. Her life teetered on the edge of a precipice she didn't know how to balance. She stared at Price with rapt attention, realizing this man was her lifeline, her safety net to getting to know Kygemian culture.

Price gave a knowing smile. "The first obligation we will discuss is: 'You are obligated to follow your queen for she acts with our grace.'"

Eirlys mouthed the words again and again. Our grace. The Ancients grace.

"The next one is a Prohibition. 'It is prohibited to attempt to kill the queen for she represents us. As one would not harm a god, one shall not harm her.'"

"Harm a god?"

"And this is a problem. How can our queen be our grace, our mouthpiece for our gods if she is a Skath, a being who in other prohibitions and obligations, we must kill? And told to deny help? Do you see the problem?" Price asked.

Eirlys stiffened. "Yes, I see the problem."

Price sighed. "I wish I could say it will get better, but it most likely will not. My purpose is to keep you alive until your coronation."

Right, all she had to do was stay alive. For now.

"Again," Price said, his thumb and forefinger pressed against the bridge of his nose.

All afternoon, Price had pinched the area dozens of times over Eirlys's imperfect memory. It must be bruised or chafed by now.

"Gyda, Cosyn, Olga, Ashur, Iona, Sarna, Eversil, Pania, Nym and Nyx," Eirlys paused, cursing the gods and their names as she tried to remember the last two. "Walo and Esona?"

"Now in the same order, their epithet."

Eirlys wanted to throw the now cold tea in Price's face. Her head ached, and her brain felt like porridge.

"Reverence, Obedience, Truth, Honor, Justice, Discipline, Intelligence, Benevolence, Perseverance, Vitality, Courage, and Focus."

"There is one more," Price said, leaning forward on his elbows, placing his chin on the back of his entwined fingers, knowing he had stumped her. "Technically, you also missed one more god."

Eirlys's mouth popped open. Had she missed a god? She counted back the twelve gods and their titles. Twelve and twelve. But Kygem also followed the thirteen cycles, thirteen months in a year, thirteen years in an age.

Eirlys smirked; they had butchered the blessed number of thirteen too. "I am the thirteenth god. My title is Nobility."

"Finally," Price said.

"You try memorizing a whole new religion in a few hours," Eirlys snapped, her face heating, feeling extremely ungodlike in that moment.

"I don't have an entire realm to rule; you do. You must learn fast or die," Price said. His thin fingers rubbed his temple. He was more fidgety than normal today, and the healer in her wanted to reach out to him, to help him.

Eirlys went to her balcony door and watched the last rays of sun disappear behind the mountains, turning the sky into shades of lavender, rose, sienna, and gold.

"Are they preparing me for slaughter? A martyr of a Skath trying to redeem herself?"

"No, I don't think so. I can only tell you what they told me. They wanted you to learn your knowledge from... well, not from Brisa."

Eirlys turned away from the painted sky and shook her head. "Of course, the one person who abdicated the throne would not be a fit role model for their polished trophy queen."

Price smirked. "In any case, I'm glad I'm here. You have a sharp mind, a quick tongue, are too bold and honest, but it is refreshing. Royal blood flows through your veins, which cannot be faked."

A thought occurred to her; one she didn't yet know how to deal with. Her biological parents and all they struggled to achieve.

"Are you okay?" Price asked. His voice was a shade deeper than normal and Eirlys felt a familiar tug near her navel. But she pushed that far, far away.

"Price, what was my father's affinity?"

Price's eyes tightened. "He was a Ta."

The knowledge didn't make Eirlys feel better. It made her feel more disconnected from the realm she hoped to rule.

"And my birth mother?"

"A Sa. Her glamours were spectacular."

Eirlys plopped onto the floor, her back to her bed. She and Price had been talking for so long, her throat hurt. But she went silent, lost in her thoughts and doubts.

"My whole life has been a lie," she said, softly, barely able to voice the actual words. "Even Lita, the woman who raised me with what I thought was complete and utter honesty, save the truth about my parents, has kept so much from me."

"She didn't want to hurt you," Price said.

Eirlys practically snarled at him.

He raised his hands in mock surrender. "You once said intentions matter. I know her intent wasn't to harm you in any way. She assumed, and rightfully so, that your birth parents would be around for a long time. Long enough... "

"Long enough for me to live a full life," Eirlys sighed. Despite being irritated, Price was right. That wasn't exactly the issue.

"Her time is running out here. And I feel like I have no time to get to know this new Lita, or the old Lita, I guess."

Price worried at his lip for a moment. "I don't think I should be the one you ask about it."

Eirlys rolled her eyes. "Helpful. Why do I bother having friends if I can't work out my thoughts with them?"

"Oh, are we friends now?" Price asked, amusement lacing his voice.

She searched his cerulean eyes and found in them what she needed. Comfort and familiarity.

After dinner, Eirlys kicked off her heels, wondering why she ever liked them in the first place. Price watched the lights wink on in the city from her balcony door. A clatter of storm clouds flashed with lightning, outlining his body in stark relief.

"But you have Ra, right? So, what happens when they don't just see but they know, when they speak in rhymes and rhythm?" he asked.

He was enthralled with Kestryan religion and customs. He wanted to pick apart all the ways they were similar and different.

Eirlys sat crossed legged on her bed, rubbing her aching feet from learning how to prostrate in heels. "I don't know. It's different from here. A prophecy in Kestrya is only taken seriously by the person listening to it. No one writes it down and puts them in your"—Eirlys searched her mind for the large hall where prophecies were kept—"Progaeneron."

Price nodded at the word, pleased. Then he looked confused and asked, "You mean, you've never had one come true?"

Eirlys sighed. "Not any that have shown me the future. I understand the usefulness of being able to see miles away or into the past, but the future is ever changing. Until I made the choice to come here, no one could have foreseen this. Quite sure if they did, Mom and I would have been discovered much sooner."

Price spun to face Eirlys. "I know about Zoasis. Obviously, everyone here believes she is our founding mother, the woman who gave birth to the four daughters, Xemané, Koana, Briaris, Nelene. The first four elementals. I know you believe Gylena is the goddess of death, but we don't. In any case, Zoasis is not present. She gave the ancients access to the wraith for a reason, to help us and guide us to paradise."

Eirlys pondered this new information. The Ancients were guides in the void. It was a nice thought, Eirlys had to admit, but didn't account for the Naevni that existed elsewhere in the world.

"We believe the void shows you the way to paradise, but it isn't always easy. You will have to face the choices you have made. Sometimes the choices your ancestors have made or even impossible futures. But if you are true to yourself, you will find paradise."

"But to harness that kind of magic, it's powerful," Price protested.

"I agree the void is powerful." She had avoided telling anyone in Kygem about the Naevni in Kestrya. It was one of the most guarded secrets, the Wraiths at August's command. "We can all feel the void, feel our spirits, but even we can use wraith ourselves," Eirlys said.

Price froze. Once again she broke some absurd rule she didn't know. "You can harness wraith?"

Eirlys wasn't surprised the Ancients didn't allow their followers to harness pure Wraith. "Yes, but it requires sacrifice."

"Like killing someone?"

Eirlys nodded. "If someone were truly desperate, then yes, killing someone and using their spirit as pure wraith would work. However, it is considered one of the forbidden powers because for you or me to use it, the spirit must be completely destroyed. Once the wraith is harnessed, they will never walk the void. It essentially destroys them."

She almost mentioned how Lita had escaped the Barrenlands with Eirlys, how she killed a man and destroyed his spirit to save her infant niece. Or how Eirlys had once used the dead to save August, but the way Price was looking at her made her backtrack. She let out a breathy, nervous chuckle.

"Of course, your Ancients can harness wraith because of their access to the void." Like all Naevni could, but Eirlys bit her tongue and continued. "But even something small like a cut, a wound, a mouse, would be okay for small magic and self-sacrifices and animals are acceptable."

"I can show you," she said, trying to stand.

"No!" Price said, and he frantically got up to kneel in front of her. She retreated, hitting her back on the side of her bed, and he placed his hands on her shoulders. Sometimes, he seemed out of control, like he was one spark away from exploding. "Don't. The Ancients are the only ones here who use wraith. They allow us to walk the void if they so choose. They cannot find out that you can harness wraith. Don't, not here. Don't even talk about it."

"Okay, okay," she said. She had no intentions of showing the Ancients any sort of thing, but he needed the confirmation. She touched his arm in reassurance, and she could tell he tried hard not to show any emotion. But it was there; something was wrong every time she touched him. Or very, very right.

She squeezed his bicep. "Why do you love them so much if you are so terrified of them?"

"Eirlys," he said in a warning tone.

Her name on his lips sent a thrill through her. He was so close, his blue eyes intense and fierce. Eirlys could smell him, nearly taste the smoke on her tongue. Imagining the salt and wood flavor in her mouth, her next breath came out shaky and shallow.

His throat bobbed as he swallowed hard. He gently rose,

breaking the contact, and his eyes narrowed in pain. He went to sit by the doorway, ending the conversation.

She didn't move, content to watch him, puzzling over her new friend. He would flinch and shift like he was never comfortable. It was unnerving to know he had something wrong with him. He still refused even a simple examination, though she asked daily.

"Do you want to learn my language? I can teach you," she offered. The spark of flames in his eyes ignited her spirit, sending her heart bounding. Her mind warned her against him, to be wary but seeing him smile made all logic run from her thoughts.

"Yes," he whispered fervently.

And so, they began.

# CHAPTER SEVENTEEN

## PRICE

Over the next few days, Price made sure Lita was brought to her daughter's room often. Eirlys deserved to have some time with her mother. They only spoke in Kestryan, and although Price was learning, he could never fully understand them.

Because Eirlys grew up bilingual, Price felt her continued frustration with him when it came to the Kestryan language. In truth, he saw how the two languages evolved from a shared ancestry across the two continents, but applying that knowledge proved to be more difficult.

Eirlys was currently telling him a story about her life in Kestryan. His eyes narrowed as she talked, slow and deliberate, the silken syllables slipping through the grasp of his mind into an unintelligible knot. Somehow, he ended up focused on this one freckle, brighter and larger than her others, above her left eyebrow.

"Are you listening?" she asked in Kygemian.

Price shook his head and let out a breath. "I zoned out," he said. "Sorry."

She rolled her eyes at him, kicking the side of the bed. She often stood or paced since the only two options for sitting were the small table, the bed, or the stone floor.

"Do you think we could get more furniture for this room?" she asked, still in Kygemish.

"I'm guessing you could ask for anything."

"Except weapons." Her brows furrowed, and she plopped onto the mattress.

He sighed. "That's probably true. But if you could have a weapon, what would you prefer?"

She pursed her lips, her eyes glazing over. "I used to have two curved daggers before some asshole tossed them into the sea. They were folded steel and the metalsmith even worked in a little bit of silver."

While Va favored silver, Ra favored gold, Ta iron, and Sa platinum. If Eirlys was handed an iron sword, she could use it, but silver would make it easier for her because it complemented her magic.

"Who trained you?" he asked.

Eirlys leveled those fierce eyes at him. He couldn't read the expression behind them, and when she finally opened her mouth, he wasn't sure what part of the truth would come out.

"In Kestrya, we have conscription. Every immortal from the age of twenty-one to twenty-three serves in the military, barring special exceptions." She shook her head. "Honestly, I learned more from being in the royal palace than I did from the army. They train their royalty harder than their guards. I ended up training with Prince August most of my life."

Her voice caught on his name. An ex-lover? Once, she had been happy and loved. Now she sat on a throne made of secrets and lies and half-truths.

"Did you pick the daggers?" he asked, attempting to steer the conversation away from the dangerous and immoral direction it had been heading.

She smiled at whatever fond memory played in her mind, settling onto the bed with a sigh. "Sort of. My best friend thought they wouldn't make good weapons. 'Too elaborate, too fancy,' he said. I practiced until I beat him in the ring." She grinned, all teeth and pride. But something in her face fell and she let her eyes drop.

"Eirlys?" Her name was a question, and she shook her head, unable to explain or perhaps not wanting too.

"I'm sorry." Her words were choked and filled with tears.

Gods curse him. He had made her cry. "No, I'm sorry," he said, kneeling in front of the bed.

She laughed then, humorless, and dry. "Why are you sorry?" she asked. "Did you force me to come here? Are you threatening my mother? Did you turn my little sister into a murderous, sadistic bitch?"

He swallowed and placed his glove covered hands on the tops of her knees, thumbs moving back and forth. "No, I didn't." There were other things he needed to atone for though. Other sins against his own religion and against her. "But I belong to the realm who did. The realm where Aydra fits in, and we don't."

He hadn't meant to say that, hadn't meant to voice their connection, to hint at his secret. His mind whirled, and he scrambled to figure out when he'd started to think he and Eirlys were similar. The truth was, no matter how his traitorous heart thrummed in her presence, they were not similar. He was Klara, and she was Skath, no matter his past.

By the Ancients' grace, she made no comment on his slip up. Instead, she muttered something in Kestryan. Though he did not understand the words, he guessed it wasn't for his ears. It was for everyone she had left behind.

"There are days when I think I'm okay. Days when I think I can do this. I have Brisa, and Deryn, and my mother." Eirlys stopped, switching into Kygemish, and raising her head. Their eyes met. She reached tentatively, hand outstretched towards him, hovering over his face. Price froze but did not stop her. He couldn't stop her. She rested her palm on his cheek and every painful nerve quieted, every muscle stopped aching. The world paused for the space of a heartbeat, the hitch of a breath. He was whole. He was hers. "And you."

If she was waiting for a response, Price had none. Though he would give her the sky to keep her hand there, to stay in this perfect peace, there were no words for the cessation of the pain that haunted him every day of his existence. Half her mouth quirked, those brilliant green eyes never leaving his face. She let out an airy snort, caught halfway between a laugh and a huff before continuing.

"Do I have you, Price? I don't know. You say one thing, and your actions... " she trailed off, eyes distant, unfocused. She was no longer staring at him but through him. He wished he could say she saw his spirit, his soul, but the tattered mess of it was buried deep inside him even as she touched his skin.

With a trembling hand, he cupped her fingers against his face, finding the will to speak through the shattering stillness of his body.

"Eirlys, you are not alone," he whispered. Price turned his face to kiss her palm. *Too bold,* but he was drunk on her, on the feeling her touch gave him. She trembled and her inhale of breath made him smile and he buried his cheek into her fingers. "I understand how lonely this all must be, how cold our world must seem to you. But I am here. Brisa and Deryn, they are here with you. We won't let you fall or falter. We will help you stand against those who would tear you down."

She hiccupped and laughed, a small joyous sound as if she had needed to hear that. As if he were her last lifeline. A tear slid free, leaving a wet trail down her cheek. He couldn't help it. He pulled on his magic and dried her tears with gentle flames.

Something in him snapped when the reality of what he was saying, what he was doing barreled into him. He cleared his throat and tenderly removed her touch from his skin. The fire blazed back into his core, and the silence was replaced with the hum of pain he knew so well, the heady peace of her touch faded. He could think again, sober as a soldier preparing for battle. A few steps away gave him more of the clarity he needed before he said void it all and kissed her anyway.

Eirlys merely shook her head and sighed.

"What?" he asked, trying to keep his tone light.

"Do you have a partner, Price? Is someone waiting for you to get home from your assignment? Maybe hoping I die sooner rather than later?" Her tone was bitter and laced with something—not jealousy. No, this was anger, embarrassment, rejection.

He didn't know how to reconcile these growing feelings with his religion, his realm, or his life so he let her pull him in only to force himself away, straining this tenuous thing between them.

Instead, he focused on her question. "No, I don't have a partner at home."

She swallowed. "Do you like women?" she asked, showing all the vulnerability she had in her.

By the gods, Price was an idiot. He had missed the signs that the attraction went both ways. No, not missed them. He blatantly ignored them because it was easier for him to think his attraction was merely caused by her magic. By the relief her touch brought. Not by her—by her smile, by her words. It had always been her.

Honesty then, from here on out. "Yes, I like women, but I usually have a preference toward men. The malady I told you about, well, it's genetic and I don't want to pass it on."

She looked at him then, the lines of her face full of conflicting emotions. "I'm Devoid, Price. I can't pass it on."

Price's stomach dropped, and he floundered for a second, struggling to form words. In a twisted sort of way, he'd made her his perfect woman. But how could he say any of that? She rescued him by continuing. "I figured either you preferred men or perhaps had a partner at home."

"Why would having a partner matter?" he asked.

"I guess—I don't know—maybe Kygemians are monogamous or something."

Price laughed then, finally striding back over to where she sat on the bed. "I guess that's an important distinction since all of the couples we have talked about are, at least for now, monogamous." He sat beside her, not close enough to touch, but close enough to feel her warmth. "My parents were old when they met and lived out in the middle of nowhere. But if my mom were to find another stranded sailor and fall in love, I doubt my father would blink an eye. Your parents were... "

Her eyes lit up with curiosity, then doubt. It was hard for her to want to know about them. About the parents who abandoned her to die.

He continued. "Rose and Caio were different. They fell in love and that was all it was."

"Brisa and Deryn?" Eirlys asked.

Price chuckled. "I don't know about Brisa, but Deryn has their fair share of suitors and lovers while out on assignment.

Brisa has never told me to kick Deryn's ass so I'm assuming she is fine with it."

"And you?" Eirlys asked. She bit her lip but didn't take the question back.

"It seems silly to limit love," he explained. "I don't choose one parent to love, or one friend to love over another. Why should romantic love be any different?"

"You mentioned my parents?" Eirlys said after a moment, picking at the skin around her nails.

"Yes?" Price responded, unsure of where this conversation was headed.

"Lita wanted me to ask you for the chance to say goodbye. She wants to be at the King and Queen's funeral."

Price sighed but promised Eirlys he would try.

He spent the next few days fighting with Aydra and the other proselytes to ensure Lita and Eirlys would be allowed at the funeral. Price used every Axiom he could think of to sway the votes.

Now, he was regretting that decision, watching the throng of people assembled to ascend.

Price looked at the Progaeneron, the High Hall of the Ancients, before gesturing for Eirlys to step onto the platform. She eyed him and the platform, bearing a wary expression.

"Why is a Ra temple only accessible by a Sa platform on top of a cliff?"

Aydra muttered something under her breath, not loud enough for Price to hear it, but Eirlys did. She turned those green eyes to glare at her younger sister. Price stilled his mind and didn't rip the Princess in two, which was a testament to how much he had grown over the last few years. There was once a time where any provocation ended with him in a fight, his volatile, broken magic constantly yearning to be free.

"I won't let anything happen to you, Your Grace."

"Are you going to catch me if I fall?" she retorted, stepping onto the platform.

He smirked at her. "I'd be honored to cushion your landing."

She rolled her eyes at him, but the tension released from her shoulders—until the platform moved. She stared at the cliff face, hands in fists for a few seconds before she closed her eyes and leaned her head into Price's chest, her fingers clenching his jacket. He could feel her breath through his shirt, coming in panicked gasps. He wrapped his arms around her, thankful for the protection between his skin and hers.

"I won't let you go," he whispered. And it was so close to the truth, his throat seized. *Why was it suddenly so hard to breathe?*

How did this woman come into his life and ruin the very core of his being? His beliefs were now shattered into unknowable pieces. Her strength and drive kept him admiring her, and her touch... He had wondered since the first time he took her hand if this was a test of the Gods. If they were watching everything he did, every moment his spirit quieted when her bare skin met his. Even being around her was enough to still the racing thoughts, to quiet the aching pain. With her in his arms, he was undone, unmade, and completely screwed.

He gently pried her hands from his shirt after the platform stopped. Aydra darted off onto the waiting cliff, spitting in the face of tradition and propriety. Brisa hissed under her breath, but a hand from Deryn stopped her. She plastered on an almost genuine smile.

It was going to be a long day.

Every instinct in him warned him to get Eirlys and Lita far away from the nobles. Olena and Ilias Inwood sat far in the back, trying to make themselves as small as possible. The rumors of the attack on the future queen and the deaths of two in line for the throne may have been the only thing stilling the hands of others. But it did not quiet their animosity which radiated hot and heavy in the room during the service.

After the conclusion, the two princesses were the first to say goodbye followed by Lita and Eirlys. Price stayed beside Eirlys the whole time, blocking her from view, taking the brunt of the hostility toward her.

Only because of this did he hear her gasp when she gazed at her father. While Lita and Eirlys might have been mistaken for sisters rather than aunt and niece, all her coloring except for her eyes came from her father. The pale skin, the scattering of freckles over rose colored cheeks, the ashen blonde hair. Would Caio have loved and admired his daughter if he had been given the chance to know her? Price stared at the man who had been king. He wondered why they bothered killing Caio when he stood in no one's way to gain the crown.

He didn't look at Ambrosia, unable to reconcile the kind and gentle woman he had known every summer with the one who abandoned her infant daughter in the Barrenlands, leaving her to rot if Lita hadn't been there. Once he had been willing to spill her blood on that dusty soil but now...

He shuttered, shaking out this new horror and pushed Eirlys along. She didn't argue, walking from the temple to the platform in contemplative silence. This time she closed her eyes and crossed her arms, holding herself instead of him. He yearned to hold her again. He hated himself for that.

Once inside, Deryn took Eirlys upstairs while Price was dragged along by some of his fellow guards to give him reports.

All royals and nobles had been escorted off the castle grounds by his squad.

"Keep the patrols doubled until morning, then regular shifts from then on."

The guardian agreed but asked, "Sir, I don't mean to be presumptuous, but why are we bothering?"

Price couldn't even fault him for his assumption. The biggest truth of this assignment was that Eirlys might die. There might not be anything they could do about it and his life was tied to hers because of the vow he made.

"Because it's our job," was all Price said before heading upstairs.

He rubbed his eyes, hoping Eirlys slept well tonight. Her nightmares left them both exhausted. For guard change, he awoke every two hours sleeping outside her door when he could. He wasn't sure who he trusted less, his fellow guardians, her, or himself.

The guard stationed at the top of the stairs to her tower nodded at him. "Evening. How was the funeral?"

"No one died... " Price cringed at the flatness of his own joke, but the guardian merely smiled.

Price thought Eirlys wasn't in her room when he first went in. The storm-dark sky flashed, and he saw rain drenched blonde hair out on the balcony. He stood at her doorway, hands clenching the doorframe. He needed to go to her; he needed to walk away. He should turn and leave. He should leave this assignment but, no, he couldn't do it. Perhaps his chronic pain had turned him into a true masochist.

She still wore her funeral attire, the dress soaked and clinging to every curve. Her face, turned up into the rain, was contorted in pain or sorrow or a mix of the two. Everything about her screamed vulnerable, lost. And how could she not be? She wasn't naïve—she knew what was happening today.

The world had been sizing up the new Skath queen. She would never be free as a Skath. Not here, not with the crown weighing her down.

He didn't recall trailing to the balcony door. Her name escaped his lips like a prayer he hadn't meant to utter. Her eyes flashed to him, shadowed in the darkness.

She wiped her cheeks like she had been crying.

The rain splattered him as he stood on the edge of a precipice he wasn't sure he could climb back up from.

"Are you okay?" he asked.

"I like water," she said, her voice cracking, betraying the emotion the rain was cleansing away.

It couldn't clean him. He stayed tethered to that edge, where the water touched but did not consume, free from the fury of the storm, of her, of his own deep and never-ending turmoil.

"What is it?" Eirlys asked. She went to reach for him, but her hand strayed, falling back to her side.

He recognized the look in her eyes, the want within her. He was no stranger to it. Most people were rarely shy around him, nor he around them. If... If Eirlys hadn't been... her, he supposed, this would have been as easy as breathing.

"I don't know," he answered.

She sighed deeply before closing her eyes, as if she couldn't bear to look at him. It made it easier for him to step into the rain, to let it pour over him, coating everything, his skin, his thoughts. A flash of lightning and a crash of thunder burst around them. With her eyes still closed, he reached out for her, for the relief her touch would bring. The moment his finger trailed her cheek, it was like waking up from a nightmare, from lifelong torture.

She opened her eyes in surprise, and from so close they

glowed. She placed her hand over his own and whispered the one word that was his undoing.

"Please."

A groan slipped from him before he crashed his lips against hers. His hand gripped the back of her head, keeping her close, their bodies touching. She sunk into him. Her arms wrapped around his neck and her tongue traced his bottom lip, a question, a want. Shame rushed through him, quick as a lightning strike.

He pulled away, breaking the hold she had on him, and backed up until he hit the railing of the balcony. How easy it would be to throw himself off it. To end it now and stop the way he wanted her, he needed her.

Because by his religion, by his beliefs, she was wrong. She was everything wrong and yet, she felt so right.

His feet froze in place by her magic. Whether it was because she thought he was about to fall or about to jump, he didn't know.

An expression of horror stole over her face as her fingers touched her lips. He almost said something, almost took her back in his arms to erase that look of fear. But he didn't. He couldn't.

"I'm sorry," she said, voice shaking. "I don't know why. I didn't mean to force you."

"You didn't," Price said. His head reeled with the memory of her lips against his, the honey of her kiss lingering on his tongue. He wanted more. He wanted to discover if the other parts of her tasted as good as her mouth did. If he said more, if he took her in his arms again, he didn't know if he would be able to stop. "I can't, Eirlys. Not with you." Or only with you, he thought. "Release me, please."

She unfroze the water around his feet. "I don't understand."

Tears pricked his eyes, and the rain covered their path down his face. Eirlys's eyes widened. He strode forward, gripping her hands and bringing them to her chest, pressing their bodies intimately together. His face was so close to hers he could feel her breath against his lips. He savored it. He would not allow her to get this close again. Never again.

"This," he said, squeezing her hands. "It's wrong. You are wrong. Being Skath, it goes against everything. My entire being, my entire life, my religion, it all warns me against you. My feelings for you are wrong, evil. I can't, Eirlys. You tempt me in ways I cannot reconcile within myself."

Eirlys stared at him wide eyed. "Price, I am not wrong. I am no different than you or anyone else in Kygem."

He laughed, cruel and bitter. "Oh, how wrong you are, Your Grace."

His eyes darted to her lips and his mouth parted. He needed to hurt her, hurt her enough that the stubborn woman he was falling in love with would never want him again. "Please, never touch me again. I know you yourself are not evil, but the magic under your skin is vile, and wrong. I cannot stand it."

*Because all I crave is that magic, that touch.*

She jerked away from him, pain creasing her brow.

He took his leave, escaping from her room. He barked at the guard in the hallway to guard her door before finding his way to his small room near the castle. Price opened a vial of liquid obsidian and splashed more than enough to numb his spirit, his thoughts, his heart, into a glass of whiskey and downed it.

The look in her eyes, the pain. She had trusted him— trusted him so thoroughly he had shattered her using only a few words.

Price didn't remember when he plunged from consciousness to his nightmares, but her eyes were there in his dreams. They haunted him until he woke with the rising sun and the knowledge he would have to face her.

# CHAPTER EIGHTEEN

## EIRLYS

I f Brisa hadn't found Eirlys on the balcony, she might have stayed there all night, wrapped in her grief, her humiliation, her horror.

*Your magic is vile. You are wrong. Never touch me again.*

Instead, Brisa helped her into bed, cursing Price's name. Eirlys didn't ask how she knew it was Price, but she accepted the help under the circumstances.

*Please, never touch me again.*

Morning dawned with a fresh perspective and a worse outlook. Eirlys was a fool. To think she was able to turn Price away from his religion. He was a proselyte, named so aptly for their conversion to this newer, horrible religion. Even five thousand years later, they honored the fact that their religion went against the rest of the world.

*Not with you.*

His words kept replaying in her head, repeatedly. Even when Brisa scrubbed the sleep from her eyes having fallen asleep beside Eirlys, she kept reliving the look on his face: revulsion, plain and clear, after their kiss.

*I cannot stand it.*

He might as well have said he could not stand her, because she was her magic. She was Skath and she could not change that. It was foolish to be upset, to be surprised. This cursed realm and their cursed religion could offer Eirlys nothing. And to get involved with a proselyte of their faith. She let out a bitter laugh, and Brisa side eyed her.

"It's nothing," she said. "Worship today?"

Brisa pointed to the end of the bed. "I set everything out and I can help you get dressed."

"That's not your job, Brisa."

Brisa let out a similar bitter laugh. "I have no job anymore, not in this castle. And it's not like I can go back home."

"I'm sorry," Eirlys said but Brisa waved her off.

"Oh, don't be sorry. I didn't mean it like that. It's just... when you abdicate, you are left with little choice. I couldn't stand to work for a realm that continued the way we were."

Brisa bit her lip, but before she could respond, Eirlys blurted, "I'm fine. Really. Let's forget about Price and move on?"

Deryn snorted but didn't move from their post. Eirlys didn't know if the guardian had moved all night.

"Go grab a nap, Deryn. I don't want you to be useless at worship."

Deryn turned their dark eyes back toward the two of them. They opened their mouth before shrugging.

"If I see Price, I'll send him up. We can't afford to lose him."

Knowing this to be true did not help Eirlys feel better about it, but she remained quiet, pondering the clothes in her hands. Leggings, skin colored and skintight, paired with a white gauzy skirt, if one could call it a skirt. The fabric joined together at the waist, but two slits cut into either side would show off her legs from hip bone to toes. The shirt was made up of the same material as the skirt, loose, and only a skin-colored bralette would cover her breasts.

Eirlys would never call herself modest. In the sweltering heat and humidity of Virva, backless dresses, short skirts and shorts, sleeveless blouses, and swimwear showed off every asset she had to offer. It wasn't the faux nudity bothering her, but the vulnerability it showed. Only she would wear the sheer white while her patrons wore gold in a sturdier fabric. Slipping on the outfit, Eirlys glanced at the mirror and frowned at her hair. With such ornate clothing, surely her hair staying down wouldn't be a possibility.

Eirlys let out a frustrated growl.

"Are you okay?" Brisa asked.

"No," Eirlys said. "How in the cursed void am I going to run this kingdom when I don't even know the proper way to wear my hair?"

Brisa stared at her. They both knew this breakdown was not truly about her hair.

"Just help me, please." Eirlys grabbed her sister's hand. "Help me be the queen they want me to be."

A tightening in Brisa's face made Eirlys realize what she had said. "Eirlys, that might not be possible."

"I have to try," was all Eirlys said in return.

Every week Seers would surround her and attempt to See her future. Every Goddess-cursed week. She shuddered and rolled her shoulders.

Thankfully, the Hall of Gyda, the largest public temple in

Alby, was set near the castle grounds, so she did not have to walk through the city. Though smaller halls were found throughout Alby, this was the one to be at today. Since she had not been formally announced, she had no doubt everyone wanted to attend to get a look at their soon-to-be queen.

Outside, after the large ornate doors of the castle shut behind her, her prison seemed more like a sanctuary.

Price fell into step at her side. A wave of anger and deep sadness threatened to overwhelm her. Price gestured for her to go first, and she sidestepped him, exaggerating her movements to ensure she would not accidentally touch him, as requested. But when she did so, the scent of alcohol lingered on him. She assessed him, the deep bruising under his eyes, the pallid skin and slight sweating.

"Are you hungover?" she hissed at him.

"Don't push it," he said.

She gaped at him. "You are my guard. How am I supposed to trust you to protect me now? You can barely walk."

"I've had worse nights, Eirlys, but don't worry. My lapse of judgment will not be repeated."

The pricking of tears stung Eirlys's eyes. She turned away from Price, head high, and walked right past him. She would not cry over this stranger.

"Why don't you just stab her in the back?" Deryn said as they joined Eirlys near the front of their group. They gave Eirlys a reassuring smile, which Eirlys fought hard to return.

The path descended veering to the southwest, the gravel under foot carefully manicured and free of weeds. She caught glimpses of the city of Alby from behind the trees. Eirlys longed to visit the city properly. Her short visit to the Progaeneron showed her eastern parts of the castle grounds, the valleys and hills surrounding the mountain, and the cultivated areas for farming.

The mysterious city of Alby called to her. She longed for people and the sounds of bustling, the yells of merchants, the questions of citizens, the whisper of SaCarriages moving about the streets, and the shouts of children. With a jolt, she realized she had been envisioning Virva and its high humidity and oppressive heat. Eirlys yearned to be back home—Alby, despite all its glory, may only bring her sorrow and yearning. Eirlys forced herself to focus on the path to the Hall of Gyda.

High iron gates blocked the path, and the fence circled the castle to the cliffs on either side of the grounds. One of those cliffs led to the Progaeneron, while the other led to the mountain range to the north. Attendants bowed to her and opened the gates.

The Hall of Gyda mimicked the beautiful facade of the Pendry Castle. The center of the brick red building came up to a steep point with white oak doors and a large stained-glass window set above it. On each side rose two, three story towers. A final tower appeared toward the back, its white glistening stone sides shining in the intense sunlight. The roof was tiled in deep slate shingles.

Inside the stunning temple, the grand circular room plunged down marble steps to the center of the floor. The white marble was banded with brilliant red, as if the goddess had splashed blood onto the stone itself. Twelve matching marble pedestals held massive gold carvings of the Ancients placed on the steps, their stone eyes watching the congregation, all looking toward the sunken dais. The high, arched ceiling glowed gold and hummed with the reverberations of the void's haunting cry. The lowered dais made of pure white marble was gilded in gold icons. Brightening the center, the outer walls were dark gray. The whole place held an otherworldly presence, like the spirits themselves would manifest in the sunken temple.

Opposite of the door stood an ornate pulpit carved of white-gray marble and painted with gold and red. It rose above the ground, supported only by two identical staircases on either side. On top the raised circular pulpit sat a carving of three sisters. The three original Pendry sisters, all pictured in battle stances. Each of the staircases led to a small pedestal hosting another set of carvings. Eirlys did not recognize the figures, but they were carved in the same gold as the Pendry sisters.

Price urged her in, his duty outweighing his feelings. While he walked beside her, she took advantage of his distraction and palmed the dagger from his side, slipping it into her waistband. She wasn't the best pickpocket, but since Price was hungover, she was good enough.

She took her place standing on one of the lower steps under the goddess Iona, the Ancient of Justice.

In Kestrya, adoration was held on every Wednesday and Saturday. The temples were designed for individual prayer, the dais adorned with the likeness of the goddesses. Zoasis, the goddess of life and magic, and Gylena, her lover, the goddess of death and void, plus their four daughters, the very first immortals. Candles of varying colors could be lit. Oracles would guide adorers in prayer, offer insight into the void, talk to spirits, or reveal a prophecy. Eirlys had been devout, going as often as her duties allowed, always bringing an offering of pure magic which she spent every Saturday creating.

Worship, as they called it in Kygem, was a public affair of community and royalty. It would revolve around Eirlys herself. Eirlys rose, back straight, and the city of Alby took their spots on the stairs. Many craned to see Eirlys, whispering into neighbors' ears and pointing. Price tensed while Deryn and Brisa scanned the room. The proselytes shut the doors pushing back the people still waiting to get in. A collective groan from the outside resonated into the chamber.

"Just follow the proselyte," Brisa said, giving Eirlys's fingers a squeeze.

Dread's cold fingers entered her veins and swept through her limbs. Before Eirlys could ask what would happen, the sweet twang of a violin sounded.

Eirlys recognized Alina, the proselyte of the Progaeneron, where the funeral was held, entering from the back of the room directly under the pulpit. She carried a smoking thurible, followed by two younger proselytes carrying smaller versions. The crowd parted as they made their way to the sunken dais. The smell of gardenia, sage, and lilacs filled the air with a hint of cinnamon and ginger. Eirlys continued to breathe though the scent increased to an overwhelming amount, and she teetered on the edge of consciousness.

Then a high, clear voice rang out, beckoning her to remain awake. Alina had reached the center of the dais and spun gracefully. Her voice sang foreign words Eirlys didn't recognize, but somehow felt familiar within her.

The two proselytes placed their thuribles below Eirlys's feet, the cinnamon and ginger taking over, and each offered a hand to her. Eirlys searched for Brisa's face, who smiled in encouragement. Eirlys gently placed her hands in the proselytes', and they led her to Alina. As she took each step, Alina's voice became deeper, the sound emanating from her mouth blooming toward the ceiling, then pulled downward to the center of the pit, filling the room. Power pressed in, and the crowd shifted, adjusting for the pressure. The smoke curled upward and undulated around Eirlys.

As the pressure became too intense, Alina cut off her last note and the silence was deafening, heavy. No one breathed.

"Your Grace, through you, we receive a deeper view into

the void. Through Your Grace, we will become closer to the Ancients whose powers are lent to you in this place. Through my guidance and power, you will See, and we will Hear. Hallowed by the light."

Eirlys knew her line at least. "As foretold through Sight."

Alina dropped the thurible, and into the void it went, casting its smoke around the whole room, dousing the steps in misty darkness until the only light in the room shone on the dais. Tendrils of smoke reached out, each coming from a statue of an Ancient until twelve wispy fingers met between Alina and Eirlys. Alina sang out from deep in her throat, the eerie, other-worldly keening reaching two octaves at once, one high and one deep, the voice of a Ra and the voice of a Naevni. Alina pushed her hands through the smoke and her thumbs closed Eirlys's eyes.

At once, Eirlys became nothing and everything.

Alina's hands disappeared, but Eirlys had no control over her body. Her back bent and her feet left the ground. The void called to her, demanding, pulsating, screaming all at once. She reached out to it and found her arm lifted. She touched the void. A flash of hot wind flooded her as her body stretched out, pain radiating through her core. Her spirit woke with a fury, not in pain but joy. And it saw the vision Eirlys could not have, using her mouth to speak.

"*Three sisters, three lovers, bound together in a flash of time,*
*betrayer and betrayed, amid the dead rising,*
*the bind of golden rings, the blood red seeps through cracks,*
*an immortal, a queen, a guardian,*
*death mars her future and will not let her go,*
*until she enters the void and conquers all.*"

As she finished, Eirlys realized she was not alone in speaking the prophecy. Every Ra in the room spoke out, save for one. She fell to the ground and landed on a bent knee as gracefully as she could manage. Price's blue eyes were a wealth of anguish. Alone, he was the only Ra who did not speak.

Eirlys spun toward Alina, who shook in kind. *What in the ever-living fuck did that mean?*

"Death mars her future and will not let her go," she repeated softly. She clenched the fold of her skirt. Her legs were aching to run away, but she must stay. She almost didn't care if this was only her second appearance in public. She had been completely at the mercy of magic she didn't understand.

An uproar from beside her tore her gaze away from Alina's awestruck face. Something heavy hurled her way. A remembered lesson screamed inside of her not to draw power, so she grabbed Alina and dove to the ground. The boulder crashed on the dais where she'd been standing. Alina's head smacked the ground with a loud crack.

She tried to find her sisters and guardians in the crowd when a loud sound thundered through the room. The ground rumbled and the marble shifted, wrapping a man on the steps above in its grip. Price appeared beside him, sword braced, daring him to draw power and attack Eirlys again.

"If he moves, someone chop off his Ancient-cursed head," Brisa yelled, the power fading from her face.

Deryn and Brisa ran to the dais, forming a semi-circle to surround Eirlys.

"Wait, wait," she protested as they tried to pull her up. She turned back to the proselyte still lying prone on the ground.

"Will you allow me to heal you?" Eirlys asked Alina.

The proselyte nodded, slightly dazed. Eirlys drew on her power and poured her magic into Alina, feeling the fracture in the woman's skull. Using a tiny burst of power, coolness rushed over her, a burst of pain flashed in her temple, and it was done.

"Thank you," Alina said.

"Do me a favor and rest today," Eirlys said.

A howling sound burst through the hall and echoed off the walls. "I don't think that'll happen," Alina said, standing quickly.

Brisa pulled Eirlys to her feet when she saw an Ancient standing on the pulpit. It was a man; he had the same white hair and nearly white eyes as the other gods Eirlys had seen. He was frailer though, like a twig swaying in the wind. She tried to remember the names Price had told her. The Ancient surveyed the scene and Eirlys wished to do the same, but she didn't dare take her eyes from the man. His Kenos stood on his right, her dead eyes glaring at the gathered worshippers. Eirlys was the first to go into the revered bow while the rest of the crowd mingled around for a second before realizing their mistake and falling into position. The man sauntered with deliberate steps off the pulpit directly to where Eirlys sat. She lifted her head.

"My, my, what have we here?" he said. Almost imperceptible, his eyes widened at the sight of the boulder.

"As you were," he said gently. He pulled Eirlys up by both hands. She didn't turn away from him, both frightened and captivated. Here he was, a god, holding her hands and regarding her with enigmatic eyes.

"A shadow queen. What a prophecy—what a response. Are you aware that any attempt on your life is punishable by death?" he said.

He drew on his power, and she expected the roar, but not the shimmer in the air. A vibration before the howling sound nearly deafened her. He stepped into the void, coming out behind the man her sister had captured. The Ancient grabbed Price's sword by the hilt, knocking Price's hand out of the way. He yanked back and blood splattered across Price's face and the surrounding crowd. The severed head rolled down the steps, settling on the sunken dais. The body fell forward, and immortals cried out, moving away the headless corpse.

"Our laws are unyielding," he said. He didn't seem phased at all by the dead man whose blood was staining the stone floor. Price paid little attention to the blood on his face, but when the Ancient handed back his sword, he wiped it clean before placing it in its sheath.

The Ancient walked around, the congregation moving out of his way. When he stepped onto the pulpit, he surveyed the crowd, his eyes resting on Alina.

"Please join me, Alina" he said.

She bowed her head and hurried up the steps. Brisa drew on her power and turned the boulder to dust, then expertly fixed the dais and steps. The god held his hands to Alina. She took them carefully. Her Wraithmark shined brilliantly across her face and fire flashed behind her eyes.

"Tell me what you see, my dear," he said. His voice was gentle, but patronizing, like he was too tired to deal with these immortals and their pesky squabbles.

"You have yet to decide, but the path you are heading down will not end well. Guidance, patience, will lead to what you are looking for."

"And the consequences?" he asked.

Alina gasped and trembled. "I can't," she said breathlessly.

"You must," he insisted, and a blast of power squeezed the air. Eirlys's knees began to buckle. Oh goddess, he had so much power.

"There are too many variables, but please understand that by force, the path you seek will be blocked."

"We have laws which must be followed," he said insistently.

"Yes, the path has been cleared, allow time, allow grief," she said.

The god pulled his hands back. Alina was crying.

He addressed the congregation. "The trials for the traitor and assassin will be tonight, here in this Hall," he said, projecting his voice so all those in the room could hear it. Pity filled the god's face. "We have stalled long enough. I suggest taking these last few hours to say goodbye." He stepped into the void and was gone.

Eirlys stared around wildly, her body going numb. "What? No. Why have a trial if he already thinks my mother will die?"

A confused Brisa grabbed Eirlys by the shoulder, steadying her. "He said our laws are unyielding."

Eirlys stared at her.

"He killed him to show that they will follow their laws... "

And it clicked into place, like a key sliding into a lock. Lita had been right. In order to protect Eirlys, their grace, their queen... they would hold a public execution for the beloved, lost, traitorous princess.

# CHAPTER NINETEEN

## EIRLYS

E irlys sat on the bed of her mother's room, staring at the wall. Her eyes were dry, her mood flipping between an odd, disassociated calm, and sheer, unadulterated panic. She should say something—she should do something. For the first time in her life, she couldn't. She had no plan, no strategy for a rescue. She was useless.

Lita was going to die. And she could not stop it.

Eirlys looked into eyes matching her own, the same hue of green, still holding her hands.

Lita's expression held a restful sorrow. Acceptance. "I'll still always be with you, Eirlys. I'll see you from the void."

Eirlys smiled sadly at the sentiment. "I don't know if I can do this without you."

Lita placed her hand lightly on Eirlys's face. "I raised you to be strong, to be independent."

Eirlys leaned into her. "But not to be alone."

"You are not alone," Lita replied. "You'll find your way. You always do."

Eirlys stared at her mother. "What if I don't want to find a way?"

Lita's face brightened. "You shouldn't want to. Things are not going to be easy. But my darling daughter, you are one of the strongest people I have ever had the pleasure of knowing."

Eirlys blinked in shock. She loved her mother with every fiber of her spirit, but her mother had disapproved of some of the choices she'd made over the years.

"My sister, your mother, was a sweet soul. Perhaps too sweet and too gullible. None of her daughters share that trait, thankfully. Rose cried when she found out her favorite stew was made with the cute little lambs they visited in the countryside and when Mom wouldn't let her use healing crystals for injured animals. It is hard to be queen when you are full of such innocence, such innate trust in the world."

Lita laughed, lighting up every nerve in Eirlys's body. Anger and hatred poured through her at the thought of the mother who had abandoned her—who was too gullible to stand up for her infant daughter. Lita stopped when she saw Eirlys's face.

"Rose wasn't a bad person, Eirlys," Lita said.

Eirlys bit her cheek, a tear escaping to trail down her cheek. She would not fight, not today. Not with her mom.

"I know, Mom," she whispered, conceding.

Lita wiped her own tears away. "Don't give in," she breathed to her daughter. "Don't let them beat you."

Eirlys's hands trembled, but Lita said no more.

Eventually, guardians came to escort Lita to the Hall. As they approached the intimidating marble face of the building, Eirlys clung to her side. On the threshold, guards had to unclench her fist from her mother's shirt. Eirlys couldn't breathe, barely able to follow the party inside. She gripped her dress in lieu of the fabric of Lita's blouse until Brisa placed her hands on her shoulders.

"Your Grace, you need to appear strong. Everyone will be watching."

Through the door, the excited rumbling of the crowd outside echoed in the temple. An execution was entertainment, and good entertainment too, for people like them. She wanted to say fuck them, fuck everything, but no matter what, she was here to do a job... if she managed to live through this horrid day.

Eirlys stood a little straighter, using all her remaining strength to keep her composure. A howling sound emitted from the air, bouncing off the walls and sending a shudder through Eirlys. The Ancients would try Lita and Evrit together, both as traitors.

Proselytes let the crowd in. No one tried to stop them from swarming into every nook and cranny of the temple, and no one bothered to close the doors. Reporters surged forward and their cameras, powered by Sa magic, blinded her. They hovered and buzzed along the periphery of the mass.

When she sat in front of Brisa, Deryn, Aydra, and Price, a hand touched her shoulder for a second, warm and supportive. When she turned around, it was gone, and no one acknowledged it.

When the entire council appeared, Eirlys finally beheld her new gods in the flesh. The Ancients, white haired and white eyed, standing in a circle around the inside of the dais. Each of them held their Kenos in their left hand, the gold translucent, incorporeal bodies rippling and dead haunting eyes staring blankly ahead. Their manacles and chains rattled as they were pulled forward by the Kygemian gods.

Eirlys scanned the Council of the Ancients and her eyes landed on the fifth goddess in the circle. Iona, the goddess of

Justice. Iona exuded calm grace in her pure white robes with red trim. Her wavy white hair spilled over her shoulders in lustrous waves. Her nearly white eyes were large and took in the room, not quite like the other Ancients. She cast her gorgeous smile to Eirlys and studied her, her expression only darkening when it finally settled on Lita.

"Evrit Khan, we call you forth to take the stand and be given a trial by the Council."

The Ancients lifted their hands. Red poured onto their faces, and Evrit knelt in the middle. Instead of reverence, pure exhaustion exuded from him. He lifted his head and his Wraithmark marred his face with shadows. Everyone sucked in air. The crowd muttered and shuffled.

Eirlys's emotions flared to the surface as he sat there, drawing power from the shadows, making the Skath look exactly like Kygem expected them to be. Rage boiled her blood. This man was part of the reason she wasn't in Kestrya. He knelt in his malevolence, the dark Wraithmark prominent on his face.

Everyone wanted to blame Lita, but all she'd done was save Eirlys, allow her to live. Yet this fucked up realm saw them as the same crime, worthy of the same punishment.

His eyes met Eirlys across the room. A grin cracked over his too white teeth. He barked a laugh, and everyone jumped except the stoic Ancients, who glanced her way, their expressions solemn.

The Council of Ancients would ask the Reckoning questions in reverse order. From the Goddess of Focus, Esona, on to each God in turn.

Gyda produced a yellow SaGlass and touched the surface. Evrit's voice boomed throughout the chamber.

"The king and queen are dead. They have a daughter in Kestrya. Your beloved Princess Lita stole her. The king and queen are dead. They have a daughter in Kestrya. Your beloved Princess Lita stole her."

Eirlys flinched at her mother's name, but gawked at the sheer joy in his voice, the laughter ringing through her skull ever after the recording faded. Brisa's hands clenched on her dress while red flames danced in Aydra's lighted eyes.

"What day did you cross our border?"

Evrit stared at her but kept his mouth shut.

Esona smirked, dropping the chain holding her Kenos. It moved so fast, she blurred as she stepped through Evrit. For a moment, nothing happened, then his face crumbled. Agony stretched over it, and he screamed, guttural.

Fear tore through Eirlys at the sound. Goddess, despite what she had endured, she was not prepared to hear that kind of pain. She'd been tortured before, but never had she made a sound so desperate.

Who could lie under such torment, or the threat of it?

Evrit collapsed to the ground. With shaking hands, he lifted his body, leaning back on his heels.

"Answer the question," Esona commanded.

Evrit did, which of course, was Eirlys's birthday.

Walo, the God of Courage, asked, "You say 'we'. Who did you bring with you?"

"My son, Emzelhal."

The crowd murmured as Eirlys shivered.

Goddess Pania stepped forward. "How did you know it was Lita and the princess?"

Evrit's eyes stayed fixed on Eirlys, as if answering her directly. "I didn't at first. I knew it was some stuffy bitch by the way she was dressed. It kept going around, the date of the princess's death, the rumor she was stillborn, the death of the queen's sister on the same day. I put it together in the end."

The God of Intelligence regarded Eirlys, though she spoke to Evrit. "Did you want a Skath on the throne?"

"I thought you all would kill her to be honest, but yes, there were plans in place if she got the crown."

Fuck. Eirlys cursed silently. The way he was talking made it seem like Eirlys knew about the assassination, was aware of her heritage, and staged the whole thing to get the crown.

The twins, Nyx and Nym, stood side by side. Nyx spoke first. "How did you manage to stay in Kygem for so long without being found out?"

"Your citizens aren't all Skath haters, you know. A few realized what I was, but mostly, we didn't use our magic and were treated like regular folk."

"Why didn't you attack sooner? Why wait twenty-seven years?" the twin asked.

"You think it's easy planning a coup? Everything had to be in place, perfect. It almost was. Didn't get the little brat though."

Evrit's eyes finally moved from Eirlys's and flicked to Aydra, who hissed under her breath.

Sarna asked, "What plans do you see for our returned princess?"

Eirlys scowled, her heart racing, blood pounding in her head.

"I hope she tears you down and destroys what you have built," he said, a hint of laughter in his voice.

The sound of his mirth finally broke her carefully built walls. Eirlys sprinted from her seat, plowing through the narrow gap in the Ancient's circle. She drew on her power, an icy hand gripping Evrit's throat.

"Listen carefully, you piece of trash. I plan on living and thriving here. I will not give up; I will not hurt my family. I will not bring more pain and suffering into this world. If you ever thought I would join you, help you, or be pleased that my parents are dead—that you orphaned three women—then you have no idea who I am."

The Council of Ancients murmured.

"Are you going to kill me, Shadow Guard?" he asked, amused. His eyes twinkled in their deep-set bruised sockets. He chuckled and beckoned her closer. "Did Prince August ask you to assassinate me like I assassinated your parents?"

He obviously meant the words to be a blow, and Eirlys did not cover her reaction fast enough.

"Oh. I see. You know." His deep chuckle chilled her to the spirit. "But do your sisters know? Your new gods? What about that adoring little guard of yours? Does he know what kind of men you love? What men will do for you?"

Eirlys's blood ran cold, and pain exploded in her chest. Deep inside her, the urge to protect August, to protect her home, flooded through her. No one must ever know. War would be imminent, if it weren't already, but August would be the target.

She lifted Evrit to his feet, holding him in front of her to block the crowd's view as she retrieved the stolen dagger from her belt.

Eirlys took a deep breath, the cloy of disgust rising within her. "I am nothing like you. If I took a life, it was for someone I loved, someone I protected."

Evrit considered her, his head tilted. "You think I did this for nothing? Not for the love of a realm, the love of every Skath infant buried in the cursed ground? Do you think your beloved means more than an entire realm? I risked my life, my son's life to change the world. What will you do?"

"This."

She placed the dagger in Evrit's hand, his shock not alerting him to what he gripped. Then she pulled herself forward, the knife slicing through the fabric of her clothes and into her stomach.

Eirlys cried out and she stumbled back, leaving the bloody dagger in Evrit's hand.

The Hall exploded. Someone grabbed her, pulling her out of the line of Ancients who swarmed Evrit. His screams cut through the hall, vibrating her skull. She had done this, made his execution brutal and horrifying. When his final scream cut off, Eirlys was being laid on the ground by Deryn.

"Isbeil?" Deryn called, but the healer was already kneeling beside Eirlys.

"How in the void did he get a dagger?" she asked no one in particular. She placed her hand over Eirlys's stomach. "The wound missed all your vital organs, so this should be healed easily."

Eirlys breathed a sigh of relief. She aimed well enough to not maim herself. There was a brief coolness. Her spirit became restless, and Eirlys tamped it down to not interfere. Then the pain fled, the blood whisked away, and she was being helped up.

Price was examining the leftover remains of Evrit's body. He toed the dagger, his face becoming livid. He looked back at her, and she met his gaze, refusing to back off. Let him say something to her in front of everyone. Besides, she had more important things to worry about once they cleared Evrit's body from the sunken floor.

"Lita Pendry, we call you forth to take the stand and be given a trial by the council," Gyda said.

Nothing was going to stop the Ancients from continuing the trial. Not even their queen's near death.

Lita came out from behind the Ancients, and Eirlys eyes brimmed with tears, her breathing unsteady. She swallowed hard. Lita gave Eirlys a small smile and her defeated mood devastated Eirlys.

The Goddess of Focus started again. "Lita, do you regret your decision to take the princess and leave your family?"

Lita smiled at Eirlys. "No," she said.

Question after question fired at her, and her bright eyes held the ones mirrored in Eirlys's face. Her mother's story, her savior's story, coming out for Kygem to hear. The story of a mother—no, not mother, a woman—making the sacrifice to protect a child, becoming a parent and defying her past beliefs.

"How long did it take you to cross the Barrenlands?" Eversil, the God of Intelligence, asked.

"I didn't cross the Barrenlands with her," Lita said, and something in her voice wavered. Eirlys's heart leapt to attention, remembering Price's warning to never use or talk about wraith in front of the Ancients.

Eversil didn't get a follow up question, so Nyx, the goddess of Vitality, had to choose wisely.

"Are you and Eirlys Devoid?" Nyx asked.

The stillness of a room had never felt so chaotic—a silence had never sounded so loud.

Lita could not lie surrounded by Kenos. "I am not. Eirlys became Devoid this past summer," Lita said.

Then the crowd exploded in a cacophony of shouts and the odd soft hiss of too-loud whispers. Lita's eyes darted away for a moment, and Eirlys stole a glance behind her, searching for someone—anyone—to anchor her in this chaos. Without meaning to, it was Price who caught her stare. A quiet desperation stole over him before it faded into resignation. Eirlys swallowed down the bitter truth and forced her attention back to Lita.

Gyda watched the crowd closely and raised a hand. A hush fell over the temple.

Nyx came forward. "How did you think the future for you and Eirlys would turn out?"

Lita eyed the goddess, then turned her gaze to Eirlys. An expression of sorrow fell over her face. "I thought I'd have a century, at least. I thought, hoped, if I crossed the world, if the realm thought her dead, the line would break and move on to another child. I thought for sure Queen Erie's bind on the crown would never fall on a Skath child. I was wrong, and I am so sorry."

The apology didn't exist for anyone but Eirlys, and she needed nothing from it. Eirlys lived twenty-seven wonderful years. She loved and had been loved in return. If twenty-seven years were all she would be given, it was better than the one day her own mother had chosen to give her. And for that, there had never been a way to say sorry. Eirlys needed to tell Lita. Maybe when they read off the punishment, she would ask for one last word, one last chance to say she loved her, and how grateful she was to her.

Sarna glanced between Lita and Eirlys. A cruel expression spoiled the goddess's face. The words coming out of her mouth reached across the chasms of time to fall directly on the perfect moment to make it all go wrong.

"How did you get to Kestrya?" she asked.

Lita gritted her teeth.

"A guard followed me when I grabbed the baby from the Barrenlands. I asked him for a knife, and he thought I meant to kill the child, but I killed him instead—"

A faint rustling and the howling screech proceeded Gyda's movement through the void to stand in front of Lita. She thrust her hand forward in a movement so fast it blurred, then pulled back and held something in her outstretched palm. Eirlys's mother stared at Gyda before looking at the goddess's hand.

Eirlys followed her gaze, her gorge and horror rising in a cresting wave.

Lita's still beating heart lay there, dripping crimson onto the marble.

Eirlys cried out as she dropped to the ground, not even making a sound when her soft body hit the stone floor. The heart toppled from Gyda's bloody hand to land beside Lita. The goddess's bone-white fingers grabbed at the air above the body and Lita's spirit materialized into the world, screaming silently, gold and pulsating, a Kenos with translucent hands beating against the goddess's grip. With one swoop of Gyda's hand, Lita's ghostly eyes burned. From inside came a bright red light, growing until gold suddenly exploded out from her spirit, sending scatters of sparks throughout the temple.

A guttural, spirit-rending scream roared from the depth of Eirlys's being, and before she knew it, she charged out of her chair at the goddess. A wall of fire and earth stopped her as both Brisa and Price grabbed onto her arms. Price's bare palms spasmed against her skin and he pushed Eirlys back.

"Please stop," Brisa said, voice cracking.

The wall vanished and Brisa gasped. Gyda appeared before the three of them.

"We are sorry, but this was necessary."

"But, her spirit," Eirlys choked out through her tears.

Gyda peered at her. "A regrettable need."

Eirlys stared at the ancient one, hatred bubbling under her skin. "Fuck you."

Gyda's eyes widened at her audacity, and Eirlys's mouth snapped shut. The temple went chillingly still. Eirlys bowed her head, and her tears fell to the ground.

Someone announced the end of the trial. Guardians swarmed in to remove citizens, but Eirlys gazed at Lita's hand, deathly still and already marbled with the pallor of death. Eirlys didn't know how long she had been standing there before gentle hands pulled her back. Brisa gripped her shoulders and forced Eirlys to break her stare.

She held onto Eirlys as she crumpled into her arms and cried her heart out, right there in the middle of the temple. The execution of Lita's body was one thing—but her soul, the very spirit would have returned to the void and allowed Eirlys to reunite with her in death—Gyda had destroyed it. Lita would never meet Gylena, the goddess of death, and walk to the Valley. She no longer existed. To destroy the spirit was an unthinkable crime. Kestrya reserved it for the most heinous criminals.

Trying to be helpful, respectful even, Price stepped forward, flicking his hand out to set Lita's body on fire. Eirlys ripped from Brisa's grasp and clawed at Price's face, unchaining the monster roaring under her ribs. He hadn't done anything wrong, not really, but the sight, the smell, and the complete, utter finality of Lita's death broke her. She screamed as Brisa and Deryn pulled her away from Price. She slashed sharp nails across his face again before Price gripped her arms, a strangled sob breaking through her.

Defeated, she slumped to the ground as the flames licked and danced, turning the body to ash with unnatural quickness. She wanted to say sorry to Price, but she couldn't form a coherent thought or the words in the sea of her bleak sorrow.

He apologized instead. "I'm so sorry, Eirlys."

Price held out a small handful of ashes. Brisa created a delicate vial from the marble floor, and Price tipped them into it.

"Since she's been executed as a traitor, we can't bury her, but they don't have to know you still have her with you," Brisa said.

Eirlys reached over and squeezed Brisa's hand. Price pressed his lips to her head while she kneeled on the marble dais of the Temple of Gyda.

Broken.

# CHAPTER TWENTY

## AUGUST

August didn't know what to expect when meeting the son of the man he had sent to assassinate the Kygemian royals, but the man in front of him was not it.

He was handsome, no doubt about it. Light blue eyes, rich, brown wavy hair, about August's height with intense eyes, full lips, and a strong jaw. Everything about the man screamed capable, trustworthy. He strutted through the void at Vara's side and into the small room at the inn.

"Too bad we didn't have access to the Naevni when we crossed," Emzelhal murmured, looking at Vara with something akin to bitterness.

"It took a decade to convince both my mother and the Naevni to even offer their services. No one wanted to incur the Ancients' wrath or notice," August explained.

He took a step forward while Emzelhal studied him. He did not bow or make any gesture. Under normal circumstances, August would have been relieved. He was much too revered everywhere he went. But Emzelhal made it feel like an insult, a calculated action.

"Yes, you seem primed to take your mother's crown soon. Are you ready?"

August wanted to laugh at the idea of being ready for a crown that was never supposed to be his. But Emzelhal didn't need to know that. He needed this man to view him as an authority, as someone from which to take orders.

"When my mother is ready to relieve her duties, I will be there ready to take them on."

"It seems you are ready to take them now," Emzelhal said, motioning to the current state of things.

August took a moment before he said, "My mother still grieves for her lost children and fears for me."

Emzelhal picked at his shirt. "Do you not grieve for them as well, Prince?"

Oh, how his heart still ached for Amalthea's laughter and Lex's need to turn everything into a competition.

"Every day but I refuse to live in their shadows. I can only rise above them."

"By throwing away your life to save one girl?"

August wanted to be angry, but he couldn't deny what he was doing. Sure, he planned to live through this, but that didn't mean he would.

"Two women have had their lives ruined because I wanted to prove to myself and to my people that I will not be a king who does nothing. Us Karakos have done nothing for too long. I will not be like them."

Emzelhal nodded once.

"She lives. The girl, Eirlys."

"You saw her?" August's voice was breathy, a plea and a prayer.

"I did," he said. "Nearly got caught doing it." Emzelhal's words had a strange quality when he spoke. Clipped and odd.

"Was she hurt?" August imagined the worst, her beaten and bloody, being forced to abdicate.

"Nope. Looked pretty fucking good to me. Her guard is quick though. Barely had time to get a peek at her before I was chased off."

"Her guard?" Rory asked, coming up behind August.

Emzelhal flicked his eyes to the other man briefly. "Yep, outside of her door. I had to break the lock on her balcony to get in. Not sure if they are keeping her in or other people out."

"Like whom?"

Emzelhal smiled, but it wasn't pleasant. "You think Kygem is happy they have a Skath princess? They want her dead, Prince. Many of them."

August furrowed his brows and Rory shifted beside him.

"Yeah, but the good news is they are allowing her to be the head of their Spirit Fest or whatever the fuck they call it. That is what took me so long to contact Vara here."

"How long ago did you see her?" August asked.

"A week or so. She is still alive."

"Lita too?"

Emzelhal nodded but sorrow filled his gaze. "Unfortunately, Lita may not have a long time. Rumors have flown about that the gods will use her as an example. Break the law, lose your life. My father will also be executed."

"Can we get them out?" August asked.

Emzelhal considered the prince. "Are you so sure Eirlys wants out? She looked pretty cushy in her queen-sized bed."

August paused, unsure. "No, I don't know. But I know if I can get her mother out to safety, I will."

Emzelhal pulled a sheet from his pocket and laid it onto the table. August, Vara, and his Shadows stared at it.

"This is Pendry Castle. With Vara, we don't have to worry about sneaking in the way we might have otherwise. It'll be easier to create a diversion during the festivities. If you can grab the princess, someone else can grab her mother. She probably won't be there. I heard she isn't allowed out of her room much."

"He's not grabbing anyone," Caden said. "He's not going to Kygem."

August blinked at her. "Excuse me?"

"She's right," Basil said.

They were looking at August like he had grown three heads.

"Curse it, August. Do you think Redna will let any of us live if we let you go to Kygem and get you killed?" Nik asked.

"Then don't let me die," August snapped.

"August—"

"No!" August cut off Caden. "I am going. You can either come or stay behind. Couldn't give a fuck to be honest. I've seen what happens when I leave my plans up to other people." August glanced at Emzelhal. "No offense."

"None taken. My father had all these grand plans, and now I'm left to deal with the fallout. Which is why I want to ask you a favor."

Rory tensed beside him, but August laid a hand on the man's shoulder.

"What would you like?"

Emzelhal jutted his chin in Vara's direction. "Her."

That was not the answer August was expecting. "You don't want to save your father?"

"I have explicit instructions to let his execution go as planned."

Gylena's tits. Who were these men?

"Unfortunately, she is not mine to give."

The man gave August a look. "After this mission, I'll need her help. There are people in Kygem who want to get out. She can help. With her, it won't take me weeks to get messages across the continent."

"I'm not a courier," Vara said, annoyed. "Nor do I want to draw attention to myself from the Ancients."

"It won't. You would be my most prized weapon."

Vara frowned at the words and didn't take her eyes from the assassin's son.

"It is up to her," August said.

Taking a deep breath, Vara bowed her head to August.

"Okay. She's yours, for now."

Emzelhal reached out his hand to her. Smart man. She took it and they shook.

They spent the next hour, despite Caden's constant glare, deciding how to infiltrate Spirit Night. August inspected the castle map, to the tower where Eirlys was being held.

August was coming for them. Just a few more weeks, he thought.

He was coming.

# CHAPTER TWENTY-ONE

## EIRLYS

The passage of time warped into bursts and stretches after Eirlys returned to her room. The world around her spun, and the frame of minutes or hours or days lost all meaning. When she woke to find starlight peeking through her curtains, she didn't know if it was the same night or the next.

She ate little of what they brought to her, picking at her food in her few times of lucidity. When numbness gave way, sorrow took over, wracking her body with aches and a pain in her chest she had never known. Her small, quiet cries of agony echoed through the chamber, intensifying her own loneliness. Guilt rushed through her when she remembered her mother's words.

*Don't let them beat you.*

The phrase pounded into her skull. Reality came in fragments. Deryn and Brisa provided brief moments of relief, followed by intense paranoia. Eirlys wasn't sure she could trust anyone here. Price had made his alliances clear. He pretended to be her friend. What if Brisa and Deryn were doing the same?

What if no one here believed in her? What if she died on the same cold marble as her mother? She almost wished for it until she remembered.

The execution wasn't the hard part. Lita had known she would die—she had made her peace. She had helped Eirlys begin to accept it. But after what Gyda had done... she would never in all eternity see her mother again. Her spirit was scattered into particles like a star into a nebula, never again to be whole, never able to return to the void.

*Don't let them beat you.*

A sob broke from Eirlys as the words whispered across her mind, and she rolled over and shoved her fist into her mouth to control the hysteria welling up. Her whole body shook, so she bit down harder. She didn't stop until she tasted blood. She screamed into her comforter, the tears finally spilling over, and she couldn't control them. She wasn't sure she'd ever function again.

*Don't let them beat you.*

Some unrelenting time later, in a moment that was an island in the ocean of her grief, Eirlys's eyes opened, and a wave of familiarity piqued something in her. The morning sun skimmed the horizon. She rose for the first time in—how many days—her legs unsteady beneath her. Her bare feet pattered over cool stone to the washroom. She heated water in the tub using her magic, adding chamomile and lavender, and washed her body of the days and weeks of sadness and apathy.

Something had changed, as if this sunrise had brought a renewed strength back to her mind and limbs. Her broken heart still ached, and it would never heal, but it wasn't shattered anymore. She ached for Lita's warm hand in hers, but the thought did not crush her. Her mother was gone, every part of her old life over.

209

They had no one left to hold over her. And they would not beat her.

# Chapter Twenty-Two

## Eirlys

While Eirlys grieved, summer had given way to autumn, the coolness creeping in with steady, lingering fingers. The true beginning of the season would be marked by a holiday Eirlys had only read about—Dvasia, or Spirit Night. She had been poked, prodded, and perfectly measured for her dress and spent hours with Deryn learning the role she would play—the role meant for the queen.

Eirlys sat in the dining room, staring at her porridge, her tea empty, when Brisa reached over and touched Eirlys's hand. She jumped, letting out a startled laugh. Deryn and Brisa often ate breakfast with her while Price freshened up for the day.

"Sorry," she murmured.

"It's okay. After our parents died, I didn't get out of bed until they sent us to get you," Brisa said, sympathizing.

Eirlys frowned. "You were saying," she asked, forcing down a bite of porridge.

Brisa smiled. "We need you to attend council meetings. I will be there to transition you in."

She poked at her food. Royal duties, boring council meetings. Eirlys had expected to rage against the system, not join them. She was good with a dagger; her words often led to disaster.

"I know it seems too soon but the sooner it's done... " Brisa didn't finish her sentence, seeming to search for the right words.

"The sooner the gods will stop hating me?" Eirlys guessed.

"Well, that, and it'll give them time to get to know you before you are crowned."

"Is that important?" Eirlys asked.

Brisa's face darkened. "Perhaps a bit too much. They don't know you. Even without being Skath, I think it would be terrifying to hand over such power to a stranger. Though the crown and throne are yours already. Being queen is not just a lineage; it's a magical tie. They might as well call you goddess-blessed with a crown. It'll take *the* goddess herself to break that bond unless you willingly give it up."

"From my cold dead hands," Eirlys said under her breath.

Brisa widened her eyes, but Deryn smiled. "I like you," they said, turning to Brisa. "She's got spunk."

"Well, it's nice to see some fire in those eyes for sure." Brisa shook her head but said nothing else.

The silence went on a bit too long this time. Eirlys noticed instead of being lost in her own thoughts. She turned to her sister.

"What is it?"

Brisa glanced at her lap, avoiding Eirlys's gaze. "Look, I love my younger sister, but since I abdicated the throne, she has been unbearable. The last born, getting a chance for the throne—she took to it with fervor. She tried to do that instead of her apprenticeship, but thankfully our parents forced her into proselytehood."

"She's still training?" Eirlys asked, unsure of how long apprenticeships lasted in Kygem.

"Yes, Alina is her mentor. She only ever takes on royal Seers," Brisa explained. "My point being, Aydra is going to be difficult."

"Tell me what part of this will not be difficult," Eirlys said sarcastically.

Brisa pursed her lips, reminding Eirlys of Lita. She made the same face whenever Eirlys was being difficult. It tore something in Eirlys chest.

The clock chimed—ten in the morning—pulling Eirlys out of her grief, at least for the moment.

"All I meant is you and Aydra should spend time together. Let her get to know the Eirlys I know, not the Skath refugee who stole her crown."

"Is that how you see it?" Eirlys asked.

Brisa ran a finger around the rim of her mug before she said, "Even though you did not intend to, it is what happened."

Eirlys couldn't imagine a world in which she and Aydra would ever be able to talk like civilized people. Without answering Brisa, she rose, her now cold breakfast only half eaten. Frowning, she silently scolded herself—she needed to maintain a healthy weight for her muscle mass to return. She had become soft since coming to live here and the weeks she had spent in bed.

"Would you be willing to spar with me?" Eirlys asked.

Deryn rose and grinned. "Absolutely."

Brisa laughed. "Count me in, too. Deryn goes far too easy on me."

Eirlys didn't want to spend the day inside. Her empty room reminded her of the days she spent mourning and her balcony held the sting of lost kisses.

Deryn and Brisa walked beside Eirlys, who marveled at the

grounds. With the threat of assassination curbed since the brutal execution, she found a new freedom. The sprawling mountain and high meadows were fading into brown. The last of the fruit had been collected, the flowers sheared and plucked. The change of the season, the dying of the earth around them, made Eirlys feel like she was losing the rest of her past. Buried in the sea between the continents, she let the waves flow over it. As the world readied to die, she readied to live.

That newfound resolve followed her after dinner. She and Deryn trudged up the steps, her thighs burning from the mountain inclines. If she ever got the chance to build her own castle, it would be a flat expanse of rooms without a stair in sight.

The chair outside of her door was empty. She glanced at Deryn, but they just shrugged.

"Maybe he's running late."

Eirlys frowned. Her earlier presumption of Deryn and Brisa had been confirmed in the past few weeks. They shared a multitude of stolen kisses and hand holding. Their alone time must be extremely limited by Deryn's newfound role in Eirlys's life, and guilt clawed at her. She tried to give them as much time as possible.

Although she was allowed onto the grounds, her room was constantly guarded between Deryn and Price sharing twelve-hour shifts. For him to expect more from Deryn or from Brisa made her blood boil.

Eirlys paced the room while Deryn sat patiently in one of the pathetic chairs by her door. After an hour she pressed the bell by her door, calling an attendant. Deryn's onyx eyes narrowed.

"Don't," they said. But they were already getting up, pulling the cloak from the hook by the door.

"He doesn't get to shirk his duties because of—" Eirlys paused, trying to think of a way to say anything without insulting herself. "He needs to get over it, or he can leave for all I care."

"Eirlys," Deryn scolded gently. "There aren't enough people to guard you right now. Be easy on him."

"Like he was easy on me?" she snapped back.

Deryn merely fastened their cloak shut.

The attendant opened the door. "Your Grace, how can I help you?"

"Take me to Lord Price's room, please. He and I need to have a chat."

The attendant bowed and gestured for Eirlys to follow him. Deryn trailed behind and Eirlys's thoughts flitted to everything they had told her.

After an illness left her mother with a crippling cough no Va could heal and unable to continue working, Deryn asked to be transferred back to Alby. Ambrosia knew Deryn's mother and insisted Deryn take up a position in the castle as Brisa and Aydra's fighting instructor where Deryn had fallen completely for—at the time—the eldest Pendry.

Although Deryn knew their way around a blade, what Eirlys needed most was not a guard but a friend. And though Brisa and Eirlys were forming the foundations of their own friendship, talking to Deryn was natural. One of those people who Eirlys could talk with for hours and never feel the minutes passing. And yet, Eirlys was still wary of the guardian, unable to trust again.

Price's room was located on the north side of the castle, on an offshoot of the main building bordering the courtyard. Although not as ornate as the actual castle, the addition was lavish compared to the attendant and servant quarters found further down in a detached complex.

The attendant announced Eirlys, and they entered the room together. Deryn stopped outside, their hands tucked behind their back, giving Eirlys and Price a little privacy. Not that he deserved any.

He lived in modest accommodations, holding only a bed, a wardrobe, and a small chair and desk. More than servant quarters, less than visiting guests. Price stared out the window and didn't acknowledge her presence. She normally wouldn't mind, but after tracking him down and making Deryn wait, she was livid. Compounded with the way he acted after her mother's death, the past few weeks he hadn't said a word to her about Lita. No condolences, not a void thing.

"You may leave," Price said.

Eirlys wondered for a minute if Price was referring to her before the attendant's eyes widened and stammered, "Your Grace?"

Price sighed and his head fell against the windowpane with an unnerving thud.

"Just go," Eirlys said. The attendant bowed and left.

"Where the hell were you?" Eirlys asked, crossing her arms.

"I was here, obviously," he said, finally gazing at her.

His blue eyes flamed to life. She took a step back. She didn't draw on any power but wished she had stolen back the dagger from—. She stopped short, refusing to think of the Reckoning, of Evrit's death, of her mother's.

"I just—" Price exhaled, and for once she was grateful for the distraction of this easier, more manageable pain.

"Look, I let my duty slide. I should have been more of a guardian and less of a friend. My job is to protect you and guide you in our faith. If I get close, I may let that interfere with my job."

Eirlys tilted her head in confusion. "Okay, but why didn't you show for your shift?"

216

"You stole a dagger from me because I fucked up. You stabbed yourself in front of me, with my own dagger, and I didn't know. I didn't know it was missing. I cannot let that happen again."

"That doesn't answer my earlier question but since you brought it up. You fucked up by what? Kissing me?"

Price exhaled exuding frustration. "No, it's more about respect. My family is barely royalty; I'm a proselyte who has no Sight, a low ranked guardian and only serving you because… " He closed his mouth and flinched. His arm wrapped around his waist like he couldn't breathe.

Eirlys took a step forward and reached out for him. Any healer worth her salt was empathetic enough to know he was in pain.

*Never touch me again.*

She pulled back at the thought.

"Why were you assigned to me, Price? What makes you so special?" she asked, her words lashing at him like whips. His eyes narrowed in pain for a moment.

"It is not my place to question the Council," he blurted and turned away from her.

He was hiding something, had been since the first day they met. Now she was hurt, and it made it worse. He chose his faith, his gods over her. She wasn't even sure she could blame him, considering her own beliefs were being ripped from her day after day.

She sighed, pinching the bridge of her nose. "Just stay here tonight. Decide if you can handle guarding me or not. I will not run Deryn ragged because you can't handle your emotions. Don't forget, you rejected me. I have the right to be hurt here. Not you."

With that, she pivoted and exited the room, slamming his door in frustration.

Deryn followed her back through the grounds and upstairs into her room.

"You don't have to stay, Deryn. I'll call for another guard."

"I'll leave when they get here but are you alright?" Deryn asked softly.

"No. I'm realizing how alone I am here," she said.

Deryn motioned for Eirlys to turn around and it took her a moment to realize Deryn was going to help her out the corset she sported.

"Brisa can manage it," Eirlys said. Even after the execution, no one was willing to take the job as Eirlys's personal attendant, so the job fell to Brisa most days.

"I want to talk to you without her around, if you don't mind?"

Eirlys frowned but gave Deryn her back. They pulled the corset off and Eirlys fluffed out her underdress, grateful for the ability to breathe again.

"Did you ever wonder why I am here, beyond Brisa?" Deryn said.

"Of course, I have."

Deryn gave a small hmm. They walked to the fireplace, lighting it using the RaGlass. They stared at the fire, talking to it instead of Eirlys, so at odds with the person Eirlys was getting to know.

"I was married once, to a woman I loved dearly. A few years ago, after my fortieth birthday, we decided to have children. Our first child was a TaKlara, like my wife. Relief flooded me the moment her Wraithmark glowed light... I can't even begin to explain the feeling. However, it did not work out as well for our son. He was a Sa like me, but a Skath like you. The pain, the fear that gripped my heart when I saw the darkness steal across his face—it was unbearable."

Deryn's face glistened with tears. Eirlys wanted to tell

them to stop, to beg them to not tell her the horrors of their past. But she didn't. This was the realm she ruled; these were its people. She couldn't ask Deryn to face the brunt of Eirlys's reality if she was not willing to listen to Deryn's reality. Deryn, who grew up in this goddess forsaken realm and suffered more than Eirlys even imagined.

"I froze. I couldn't do anything but hold him in my arms. Somehow my wife didn't notice when the boy's Wraithmark darkened, and I didn't say anything. I thought I could hide it, keep it a secret until I could teach him to never use his magic. But my cursed midwife who I had sworn to secrecy told her. When she found out... well, she was always more devout than me, and it filled her with rage to know I had defied the Ancients and our laws. She was devastated to know the son she loved was an abomination and blamed me for letting her fall in love with the boy when he should have been killed at birth."

She'd heard stories of how her own mother forced Lita to carry Eirlys in those first few hours, not even willing to hold her daughter.

"I begged and pleaded, but she would not listen to me. In her rage, my wife took our son and threw him over a cliff into the northern sea. By the time I found him, his body had been brutalized, battered, and broken against the rocks. He was long gone. I left her afterwards. She took our daughter, though I tried to fight to keep her. My wife must have felt guilty for she never told anyone what we had done. They called it a tragic accident, and I never fully explained why I let my other child go. Her silence on the matter was won by letting her leave with our daughter. But what I learned from all of it—"

Deryn's gaze bore deep into Eirlys. "I saw my son. I held him, laughed with him, and loved him until the day he died. He wasn't evil. He was a child, an innocent being. It taught me the law is wrong. The Ancients are wrong. Skath are not evil; they are people, like everyone else. And if we can show others, if Kygem could have a Skath queen—maybe you'll be the one to change things, Your Grace."

Eirlys stared at Deryn, unsure what to do with the information of their darkest secret. How many Kygemians despised the Skath Law and what did it mean for her reign?

"I am sorry for your loss. And thank you, I will need a lot of support in this realm," Eirlys said.

Deryn smiled at Eirlys. "I know you don't fully trust me. I wouldn't trust anyone either, especially since Price can't pull his head out of the Ancients' asses." They mentioned Price with a fury which surprised Eirlys. "But I will be here to help you and maybe be your confidant."

"I would like to be alone, if you don't mind," Eirlys said, unable to process her thoughts.

"I'll be back in the morning, Your Grace."

Eirlys sat and let out a breath. Deryn's revelation deeply disturbed her. They'd let a woman who threw their infant son over a cliff run away with their daughter. Eirlys wasn't a parent, but she was sure she wouldn't let someone take her child if they could murder an infant. However, she guessed most of the people of Kygem were capable of that since it was expected here.

Her stomach roiled, and she ran to retch. There was barely anything to throw up and she heaved for far longer than she vomited. This realm, her realm; a world where it was legal, and encouraged, to kill an infant. Maybe she couldn't rule this realm after all.

She got up, washed her face, and called for an attendant to bring her a cool rag.

Price stood outside the door, relieving Deryn. He peered in and Eirlys smiled politely. His returning smile was strained.

The attendant came and handed her the cool cloth. Price stared at it for a second, concerned. He opened his mouth to say something, but closed it fast, so Eirlys closed the door. She poured a glass of wine and sat on her balcony until the sun set. Tears streamed down her cheeks as the day turned to night in her lonely room.

"I wish you could hear me," she said softly. "I wish you were there, in the void, watching over me. I don't know why I'm talking out loud. I know you died thinking I could do this. How can I do this when I need you so badly. Mom?"

Only the silence responded.

# CHAPTER TWENTY-THREE

## EIRLYS

The festivities of Spirit Night loomed in the distance as the sun moved lazily across the sky until dipping below the horizon. The rain that had been falling steadily for a few days stopped mid-afternoon, leaving the moon gleaming on the wet earth. SaCarriages floated up with ghosts of footprints appearing and fading from the incoming guests.

Eirlys watched from the balcony, hidden from view. Her lips moved, reciting the words she would speak tonight even though she knew them by heart. Her breath stilted out in small puffs in the chilled air. She wrung her hands together to stop the shaking. All these people were here to watch her take part in their culture, to prove she was one of them.

Deryn placed their hand on Eirlys's shoulder, seeking her attention. She turned to her sisters.

Brisa wore a green dress that reminded Eirlys of Lita's eyes. It was sleek, made of fine silk. The top wrapped around her while the sleeves hung off her shoulders. The bottom fell from her ample waist and pooled at the floor. Her hair flowed around her like a chestnut waterfall. Aydra was dressed in blue satin, the dress bunched at her left hip, and the sleeves were embroidered with tiny crystals catching the light. From the back, a sheer train fell to the ground.

Brisa's small crown was designed to match her dress— green crystals studded the iron band. Aydra's crown, crafted of white and yellow gold, appeared to be aflame as she moved. Eirlys's own crown was made of delicate strands draped over her head. It spilled onto her forehead in waves of silver. Tiny seashells marked every joint and sapphires were studded throughout.

"Ready?" Brisa said, approaching her.

Eirlys briefly nodded, too nervous to speak. She paused in the dressing room so the attendants could adjust her jewelry and the skirt. Her own dress was ivory brocade made to appear as if she wore a swirling vortex of water. Corseted around her torso in a sweetheart neckline, thin straps wrapped around her shoulders. The dress pooled out at her waist into a large intricate skirt. Over the top laid a thin sheer tulle that moved over the dress, creating the illusion her skirt was made of liquid. Her hair was pulled up into a side chignon before spilling into curls over her shoulder like cascading blue rapids. The necklace had been Lita's, silver metal sparkling with crystals and ornate filigree metal work across her chest. Brisa had given it to her. Her sister explained that heirlooms were often gifts during Dvasia after coming of age.

Aydra surprisingly gave her earrings, a beautiful pair of teardrop sapphires, simple but gorgeous. They had been encased in blown glass so healing power could be stored inside. Aydra said since Eirlys was the first in the family to be a healer, she should have the one heirloom designed specifically for her. The young princess might be Eirlys's greatest hurdle, but even Aydra wouldn't defy tradition.

The defining characteristic of every person attending tonight was their gilded skin. Dusted with gold powder, Eirlys and her court appeared to be Kenos in their own right. It was said to make the dead feel more welcome.

Smoothing her dress one last time, she signaled the attendant. All around the castle, servants moved, silently and efficiently like well-oiled cogs, ringing bells in room after room, preparing for the descent of Eirlys and her court. The attendant waited for the last bell to sound and then motioned for Brisa and Aydra. Eirlys waited, breathing in and out five times, simultaneously counting the beats and trying to stop the trembling. A final exhale, then she marched forward, descending the spiral staircase leading to a hidden hall behind the ballroom. Her heart pounded and her head swam. Her vision blurred as tears sprang to her eyes, but she kept them in check with an unsteady breath.

Eirlys glanced back at Deryn standing at the entrance to the stairs, who gave an encouraging smile before she stepped out of the hidden room.

The chatter of guests filled the ballroom. They were positioned by rank within their courts, but many vied for closer spots to the new dais. The castle ballroom had been transformed. A raised dais for Eirlys and her court let her view the room in its entirety. The floor was covered in a deep gray carpet so their footsteps wouldn't offend the Kenos. The drapes covering the windows were sheer black, and behind them spherical lanterns glowed with flittering luminescence, the only form of light in the twilight ballroom.

As hundreds of eyes bore into her, Eirlys was deafened by the sudden silence. Her heart thundered so loudly she was sure everyone could hear it. A trumpet sounded and despite all her training, she jumped. She smiled at her sisters who stood on the makeshift dais, Aydra to her right and Brisa to her left.

As she approached the middle chair seated the highest, she stopped in front of it, facing Brisa, and waited only a second to calm her nerves. Then she spun to face the waiting crowd. Hundreds of her subjects, royals, nobles, guardians, gathered before her.

The High Proselyte Alina approached Eirlys. Although Eirlys did not possess the power of the Ancients, she needed to pretend like she did. The fact that her first act as their future queen would be to lie to them had not been lost on Eirlys. The excuses flowed from her court.

"It's always been done this way."

"It will show that the Ancients have blessed you and accepted you as their mouthpiece, their queen."

"No one will be able to deny your claim to the throne after tonight."

It did nothing to make Eirlys more comfortable with the idea, but she practiced anyway. Every movement, every word.

Alina smiled at Eirlys before she began.

"Crown Princess Eirlys Pendry."

Eirlys tried not to cringe at her new surname. Her other one lost in Kestrya, belonging to a refugee who fought for every scrap of respect and honor she could gain. Now, she was about to lie in front of hundreds to gain the favor of gods she did not believe in.

"You will lead us through the ritual of Dvasia. Spirit Night is our most sacred holiday, where the Kenos of our dead will join us. We bring them into this world, not to mourn them, but to allow them to say goodbye one last time before they journey with the Ancients throughout the next year to deliver them to the Valley."

Were Gylena, her lover, and their four daughters still in the Valley, the paradise in the void they had found to gather their children after their deaths? If they were there, what did they think of the Ancients guiding others to their place of paradise? It was meant to be a place designated for those who had found peace within themselves, peace that was only gained in the void during the journey to the Valley—not by having some Naevni show them the way.

Taking a deep breath, Eirlys purged her mind of such thoughts. Not now. Not when the entire royal family watched her every breath.

"It is now time to bring them forward."

Alina gestured for Eirlys to start. Pretending to draw on the power from the void, Eirlys nearly jumped when she heard it. The howling of the void pierced the ballroom. She had been prepared for this. An Ancient, though she didn't know who, stood behind her. A hand touched the back of her neck, sending Wraith through her. Her Wraithmark appeared scarlet red, and the crowd gasped. Then a murmur, not of people or of the living, but of hundreds of Kenos, whispered in their haunted tones throughout the crowd.

The void sounded once more and Eirlys breathed a sigh of relief. She shook out her hands as the power faded.

"To those who have just arrived, and those who have waited. Welcome to Dvasia. Enjoy the night with those here and gone. This is only a goodbye for now." The words flowed out of Eirlys, not stilted or awkward. In the presence of the dead, and the folly behind her, she felt more relaxed, more present.

Scanning the crowd, her eyes pulled toward two Kenos standing near the dais. She froze. She had only seen these faces in portraits and at their funeral, now buried in the plot near the castle.

Ambrosia stared at her daughter, her golden hand pressed against her chest. Her husband stood beside her; even in his golden state, his hair and beard matched Eirlys's platinum strands. His hand tensed on Ambrosia's shoulder when he caught Eirlys staring back.

Brisa cried out for her parents. She and Aydra sprinted to them. Eirlys didn't watch. She couldn't watch a reunion she would never have.

Lita wasn't coming.

She would never be able to come to Dvasia. Her spirit was destroyed, sent into the void as pure energy. Brisa turned around to look for Eirlys, but before she could utter a word, she sprinted off the dais, losing herself in the crowd of the living and the dead.

For some reason, the idea of this night and Lita's death hadn't occurred to her. It had all seemed so far away, removed from the reality of her world.

A gloved hand caught her arm out of nowhere. The touch was terribly, painfully familiar. She jerked out of Price's grip.

"Are you okay?" he asked.

"Why do you care?" she spat.

He shrank back, face crestfallen, and let her dissolve back into the crowd.

"Your Grace," Deryn called.

She turned to her friend, grateful they were walking toward her. Although the one benefit of the night was that Eirlys was not to be guarded, she still felt safer with Deryn around. It was supposed to be a show of trust to the Kygemian people. Or perhaps the gods were hoping someone would take her out.

"Deryn," she breathed.

"Let me introduce you to some people," Deryn offered.

Anything to get her mind off her grief.

She didn't even have time to think afterwards. Deryn led her to important people, people she smiled at, people she laughed with, people with dead loved ones clinging to them.

But not every Kenos was elated to be there. Did they not see the fear in some of their eyes? The grief in their faces? Kygem was so blind to their faith, they didn't see the horror show in front of their eyes.

She attempted to memorize names, trying desperately to ignore the Kenos clutching onto the arms of many. Her face scrunched hard in concentration until Deryn asked if she was okay. Eirlys waved them off but reminded herself to control her face through the night. She yearned for the night to end, for this macabre nightmare to be over.

It's not as if Eirlys wasn't used to the Kenos. Sometimes the shroud between worlds thinned. The dead who couldn't move on drifted to the world of the living, and sometimes the living journeyed to the dead. To complete her first rite, she'd stepped into the void itself. It wasn't the quickness of a shimmering, which transported the body, but leaving it behind to become a spirit in order to enter.

Tonight, it was the spectacle of it all. Naevni in Kestrya often worked in grief counseling, able to deliver messages or in extreme cases, call a spirit into this world. Private. Personal. Everything about Kygem was public. Their religion, their lives, their dead. All splayed out for the world to see.

"Your Grace," a man said.

If Eirlys hadn't been conscious of her reactions, she might have gasped aloud. His hair was starting to whiten, brilliant streaks of light gray shattering the pure night of the strands like stars. He was possibly older than her old mentor, Teresa, who had been nearing three hundred. She might have assumed him a Kenos if not for his solidness.

He dipped into a curt bow.

Deryn smiled, strained and uncomfortable. "Princess Eirlys, this is the Countess of Frig Hinami, Sumi Esana, her husband Lord Eckard Esana, Lord Price's parents."

She had noticed Price before, but he was always close by guarding her. She didn't think anything of him standing behind the couple until Deryn introduced them. Lord Esana shared his son's dark hair, and that's where the physical similarities stopped. One look at Sumi's facial features left no doubt Price was her son.

His parents had either waited a long time or didn't meet until late in life. One child, one chance, and that pressure landed on Price's shoulders. Whatever they had done to save his life made more sense now, and Eirlys understood Price a little bit better.

They bowed and took their leave, their son trailing behind them.

She glanced at Deryn. "Go find your girl. I think I'm done being paraded around like a show dog."

She began to turn away from the crowd but in the corner of her eye caught something. Copper eyes and brown hair. She stopped, searching again. She had to be mistaken. Caden couldn't be in this crowd. Her mind was making things up, seeing another ballroom, in another place.

She sighed and found an attendant serving drinks.

"Glass of white?" he asked.

"I prefer red," she said, hoping it didn't break some inane rule.

"It's customary for the queen to drink white," the attendant suggested, being carefully articulate with his words.

"I'm not exactly customary, am I?"

To her surprise, the attendant chuckled and handed her a glass of red. She sipped the wine on her way out to the courtyard which bustled with immortals soaking up the pleasantly cool nights before they were completely stolen by the northern winter. Vast RaGlass crystals were placed every few feet on the edge of the courtyard, their pulsating warmth keeping the cold at bay. No one outside had Kenos beside them; the magic only worked in the one room. A few smiled and bowed as she walked past, others raised glasses, or touched the hollow of their necks, a sign of respect and honor. She tipped her glass toward them, taking another sip of wine.

Eirlys thanked the goddess for the clear night. Innis, their beloved moon, was missing a sliver of his glory. His purple face slashed with the brilliant silver of his rings. According to legend, Innis was the only brother of Zoasis, lonely and wandering the earth after Zoasis created her lover. Zoasis birthed Nelene, a Sa with wind in her hair and breeze-colored eyes. Innis fell madly in love and to show his devotion to her for all time, made silver rings to place on their heart fingers. While Nelene became pregnant, a whispering spirit from the void called to Innis and he left Nelene all alone. To punish Innis, Zoasis sent him into the sky where the ring from his hand surrounded him, binding him to the sky, out of reach.

"Your Grace," Price said, startling Eirlys from her reverie.

Only with a burst of power did she manage to not spill her drink.

"I'm sorry, I didn't mean to startle you."

She smiled at him politely and the ebony faded from her eyes. "Quite alright, it's been a long night."

Price leaned on the stone banister, his hair falling across his face while he gazed at the city.

"You don't have anyone you want to see inside?"

"No," he said, short and clipped.

Eirlys pursed her lips and downed her glass of wine. She didn't want to go back inside but she also didn't want to be stuck out here with a man who despised her.

"Can I ask you a question?" Eirlys said.

"Anything, ma'am," he said gently, this time slipping back

into old habits. Teasing, but it stung a little bit, reminiscent of her first days here when he had been her friend.

"What are you hiding from me?" she asked.

He jerked his head toward her, those blue eyes intently watching her. "Eirlys, please believe me when I say that it's better you don't know." His voice was soft, pleading.

She absolutely believed him, but it didn't make her want to know any less. She didn't push Price further.

Stepping up to the balustrade, she followed his gaze to the city. When she snuck a peak at him, he no longer looked at the valley below but at her.

Eirlys smiled at him. Price regarded her, smiling back. But something twitched in the corner of his mouth. His blue eyes glowed in the moonlight and emotions swept behind them: lust, pain, sorrow. He stepped away from her gaze, bowed and went back into the ballroom.

She watched him through the open door when she was sure she saw a signal—a quick gesture, one she recognized from the Shadow Guard. *Clear, move left.* But when she looked closer, she found no one familiar.

Eirlys went to dart inside when Brisa stepped through the doorway, tearing her attention away. She scanned the crowd looking for her parents, but wherever they were, she could not see them.

Brisa leaned against the banister, tilting her head back, sending her hair over the edge of the balcony. She righted herself, grinning and happy.

Small flashes of light burst from the city. Fireworks. The city was filled with laughter, beer, mead, and wine. Another loud bang came from closer to the castle. A cackling of laughter echoed through the canyon. Eirlys couldn't deny the joy brought to her people, to her sister. Caught up in her own anguish, she hadn't truly seen the happiness of those reunited.

"Why did you run earlier?" Brisa asked. "I told them not to follow you, but they wanted to meet you."

She swallowed and hoped the words came out the right way. How did she explain to someone that seeing their dead parents only reminded her that she had none? Her mother was lost, and the ones that were here tonight had tried to kill her.

"There are days when I wished I had been executed too, wished they had ripped my heart out right beside Lita's. Days I wished our mother had succeeded when she left me to die in the Barrenlands. Lita would be alive and I would be safe in the void," she said.

She held up her empty wine and the attendant from earlier grabbed the glass and replaced the drink for her. She needed to find out his name.

Brisa sighed. "You should come in and let Mother explain. She is so grateful that you are still alive, that she failed to kill you. That her sister's life which she thought had been lost, went to a good cause, to saving you," Brisa explained. "I think she missed you all the time."

The information did not bring Eirlys comfort. In fact, it made her yearn more for a time when she didn't know anything. Her own mother hadn't wanted to kill her child. The gods Eirlys were supposed to represent had mandated she do so.

"Everyone is impressed with you," Brisa said, changing the subject.

Eirlys was grateful she was not being forced to go back inside.

"It feels nice to be accepted," she commented after a moment of silence. Brisa said nothing. "Ever since I arrived, I have been treated differently and it's harder than it looks. I was a stain upon the house of Pendry which could not be scrubbed away, so I was primped and prodded to fit a mold instead.

Underneath there is still this blemish, though, a spot that cannot be gotten rid of no matter how many times it is washed."

Eirlys drew on her power for a moment, snowflakes falling delicately from her fingertips. A starless night masked her face. She pointed her palm to the sky and using a burst of power sent snow into the sky, so it flurried around the two of them.

"Eirlys," Brisa breathed, beholding the lightly falling snow around them with wonder.

She breathed out, the darkness retreating from her pale skin.

Eirlys patted her sister on the hand, downed her last drink, and placed it on a tray held by another attendant at the door.

Brisa followed behind her, but when they stepped off the balcony, Deryn snatched her up, twirling with the princess in their arms. Deryn's sleeveless black lace shirt fit over a flowing peasant blouse tucked into black floral brocade pants. When caught in the right light the fabric showed roses, lilies, and honeysuckles. Draped over their shoulders, sheer tulle created a train, and the illusion of a skirt was trimmed in delicate silver starting at their waist. Deryn kissed her before placing Brisa back on her feet, her sister giggling. They lost themselves in the crowd.

Eirlys, her head buzzing with wine, scanned the crowd for Price, wishing to end the night and crawl into her warm bed. She caught Price's eyes before a man stepped in between them.

She caught the scent of a storm on the sea. And yet it was impossible. His gray eyes could not be here. Not in this ballroom, not in the castle, not in this realm.

The sharp, hot edge of anger welled through her, but another emotion followed close, dousing the flames. Because she still loved him for all his foolishness.

He held his hand out to her.

August was in Kygem.

# CHAPTER TWENTY-FOUR

## AUGUST

"You are a hard person to get alone, Your Grace."

He gave her a wink, while his other hand pressed a finger to his lips. He had made sure her two guardians and her sisters were far from where he approached her. Busy, distracted. Hard not to be with the Kenos roaming the place. No one looked at him twice. The living were not the spectacle tonight.

She stared at him, her eyes roaming his face before they darted to the crowd around them. Perhaps checking for her guards before she grabbed his hand. To reassure her, he grinned. She trembled under his grip, although her face betrayed nothing as she granted him a small half smile.

She was alive and here. She was blessedly whole and intact.

"Have you lost all common sense?" she whispered, her lips barely moving.

"Just stay here. Rory is looking for your mother."

Eirlys's eyes widened, before she lost the composure she had carefully kept into place. August's heart sank. He had searched for Lita everywhere, to be sure. When he spotted Eirlys alone—no Kenos by her side—he foolishly hoped Lita was still in the castle.

"No," he said.

Perhaps a bit too loud because Eirlys's eyes widened. When the guests looked at them, she laughed and patted him on the chest.

"I'm not that drunk," she said, slurring her words. Small chuckles escaped from her guests who turned back to their drinks.

"My apologies," August said. "Eirlys, I'm so—"

The look she gave shut him right up.

"Why are you here?" she asked, her drunken facade completely wiped away.

"To save you," he said.

This time, when she threw her head back, the laughter that came out was frightening, bitter, mocking. She locked eyes with him, her stare hard and ruthless.

"Did I ask you to save me?"

"No," he said, shame welling inside him, oily and slick. "But you, your mother. It's my fault."

"Well, it's too late for her," she snapped, and her eyes said it all. She had made her bed and now she would lay in it. No matter what it cost her.

"Eirlys, I'm so sorry."

"Don't you dare," she said.

He flinched away and something in her eyes shifted to a softer version of herself. The one that wanted to give him his way, to shield him from the horrors of the world. Her fierceness amazed him, her strength always guiding him. Without her, he was trying to emulate that.

She reached for him, placing one hand on his cheek. Gylena, take him to the void now, he missed her touch.

"You didn't know. If your guilt drove you here, I absolve you of all it."

"But Lita... "

"My mother was not afraid in the end. She walked to her death as strong as the woman she raised me to be. Neither of us blame you. Nothing about war is fair. Nothing about war is kind."

He really looked at her then. Her dress was beautiful, shimmering like her affinity for water. He had watched her all night, her dress flowing around her. She wore a crown atop her head, something he had wanted to see for so long and could only ever dream of. But it wasn't the crown his wife would wear—it was the crown of his enemy.

She hadn't been dragged out in chains, forced to perform this dreadful rite. She had chosen this.

August was a fool.

"We cannot talk about this here," she insisted. "Go home, August."

"Stop trying to protect me," he said. Anger finally ignited through his confusion and guilt.

Eirlys narrowed her eyes. "Tell the Shadow Guard that I'm disappointed in them. If you were under my watch, you would never have been allowed to come. No person is ever worth your life."

But she was. She was worth his life, worth this risk. He had expected her in chains, bloody and beaten and forced. He should have known better.

And through it all, she was still trying to protect him. And he hated her for it because he wanted to be *her* hero. But Eirlys had never needed saving, not now, not ever. She would do it herself, blades swinging, magic singing in her veins. He had been so caught up in his own guilt that he hadn't considered her.

"Eirlys."

He said her name because there was nothing else left between them.

"Go," she whispered. She pulled away from his arms, turned around, and the loss of her touch on his skin left him a boat unmoored.

Although his world was shattering, everything around them was going to plan. Eirlys froze after only half a step away from him. They were surrounded; August recognized each face and so did she—the Shadow Guard and the assassin's son. She tensed like she was about to fight, muscles bunched, her hands grasping empty air as if searching for a weapon.

"Someone alerted the guardians. We must go. Now," Rory said. Those blue eyes were worried, but they glanced at Eirlys anyway, crinkling in happiness.

"I can get him out of here," Vara said, motioning to August.

Eirlys stared at the woman before recognition dawned on her face.

"No," she said, quickly, quietly. "Do not let Kygem know that we have Naevni. Create a diversion."

She said *we* and August's heart soared, desperately and foolishly. He would never be able to let her go.

"Glady," Emzelhal said, spinning Eirlys into his arms. This time, August's heart dipped, plunging into an ocean of cold fear. This was not part of the plan.

She gasped and snarled, "You!"

She braced to defend herself, but Emzelhal pulled on his power, lifting Eirlys and him into the air. August pulled on his magic, ready to jump in the air, when Nik and Rory grabbed his arms, pinning him. No one was looking at them. Everyone's attention was on the two immortals hovering above them.

Emzelhal grabbed Eirlys and spun her around, pulling her back into his chest. Her eyes went wide with horror.

August struggled against his captors.

"No," Rory said.

"Let me go, Rory!" August snarled. The flash of metal in Emzelhal's hand made him lose all his breath. But Rory ignored him, ignored what was happening above. His purpose was to save the prince, despite what August wanted.

"Vara," Rory cried. The sound of the void was drowned out by someone's scream.

Emzelhal cut Eirlys's throat, blood spilling over her chest, covering her dress. Something ugly, black, and feral twisted in August's chest as Emzelhal dropped her. Before the void swallowed August, he saw the blue-eyed guard catch her, devastation spilling across his face.

Vara shimmered them outside on one of the balconies leading into the ballroom. August rushed to the window, Rory behind him, shoving his head lower to keep them hidden in the shadows. Though no one indoors was even remotely looking at the windows. They were huddled around a prone form. August thought he caught the rise and fall of her chest, but Emzelhal had slit her from ear to ear.

Defying all the odds, Eirlys sat up. She seemed dazed, but otherwise fine. Her throat was covered in blood, not even a scratch where the blade had cut her.

Before August could sigh in relief, the sound of the Naevni pierced the air in the ballroom, its sound rattling the balcony's glass. A man with white hair and nearly white eyes walked toward Eirlys. An Ancient. August had met one before and had no desire to repeat the process.

"That's our cue," Emzelhal said, slipping over the balustrade and onto the balcony. His finely pressed clothes were splattered with his lover's blood.

"Indeed," August said, swallowing back his venomous words.

Vara deposited them back into the inn where they'd been staying. The smell of the ocean and stale alcohol flooded August's senses and he leapt to his feet, shoving Emzelhal back against the ale-stained wood.

"What the fuck is wrong with you?" His forearm pressed against the man's neck, leaving enough room for him to breathe, barely.

The icy steel of a blade pressed into August's throat, but he was beyond pain, beyond reason.

"If you want your prince to live, I suggest someone get a hold of him," Emzelhal said.

August leaned further onto the man. A flash of silver came out of the corner of his eye. Emzelhal hissed, nearly dropping the blade.

"The next one goes through your hand, and the one after that will go through your temple," Caden said, flicking another throwing knife between her fingers.

Emzelhal removed the blade, releasing a spurt of blood across August's collar bone.

"Look, the girl is fine," Emzelhal said.

"How?" August asked. His vision blurred and he teetered.

"Easy there," Rory said, placing his hand over the wound in his neck and healing him.

Holding August up, Rory said, "You have a lot of explaining to do if you want to leave this room alive."

"Look, the girl is not normal. Even as an infant. I witnessed one of the goddesses shoving a dagger through her heart when I was a child. In mere minutes she was crying again."

"Bullshit," Basil said.

Emzelhal raised his hands. "I'm only telling you what I saw. What my father saw, and why we needed her in Kygem."

"Remember that story Eirlys used to hate?" Rory nudged August.

He frowned. "Eirlys and I were on my ship, with a small crew. Out for a pleasure cruise, before I was always surrounded by guards. We ran into trouble. A ship had been scouting the borders of our territory and they shot cannons at us. By the Sa Daughter, I swore she took a cannon straight to the chest. She was blown backwards. I tried to reach her but there was too much chaos and fighting. Then she was up, just like that, nothing more than a bruise on her chest. No broken bones, no internal bleeding."

But before relief could flood through him, unfamiliar anger roared through August, and he nearly lunged for the spy again. "But she is Devoid, you fucker. She can't even heal a papercut."

"Well, she obviously healed from this."

August fumed.

"Vara, get him out of my sight," August demanded. "Please," he added on. Vara hadn't done anything wrong.

Emzelhal sighed and waved his hand saying, "Call if you need anything."

With Vara and Emzelhal gone, August paced the floor. He stroked his stubble, still covered in the gold dust that had coated Eirlys's skin. His heart burned as he glanced at his clothes, his arm, at all the places she'd touched him just hours ago. He ached for her already.

"What now?" Rory asked, placing his hand on August's shoulder.

Rory's touch grounded him, and August was able to find his words. "I guess we go home."

Caden gave August a little nudge with her elbow. He gazed at her. "She'll be okay. If this is her choice, we should respect it. She will be what Kygem needs."

August only stared at the far wall, numbness washing over

him. He wasn't her hero. He was nothing but a middle child trying to prove himself worthy of a crown that never should have been his. He'd go home, face his mother's wrath, and wait.

*It's up to you now, Eirlys. You were always the hero.*

# CHAPTER TWENTY-FIVE

## EIRLYS

"She's coming to," someone yelled.

Eirlys blinked, catching snippets of her world beyond the cool nothingness of her eyelids. A VaKlara pulling water. Price leaning over her. Brisa and Deryn standing together beside Aydra, who stared in disbelief. Eirlys attempted to sit up, but hands held her down.

"Hold on, Your Grace," the VaKlara said, before pulling on water and healing Eirlys.

She clenched her fists as her spirit came to life, eager to help with its meddling, useless magic. Eirlys gritted her teeth and shoved the spirit back into her body where it belonged.

"Where is he?" she asked, glad her larynx was healed. She obviously wasn't in danger anymore since people were milling about. She tried to sit again, but dizziness swept through her. Leaning back, she was thankful when Price's chest caught her.

"No idea. He created a vortex which knocked us back, and he escaped through the crowd. He glamoured his face, and we were all looking at you anyway."

The Va whispered something in Brisa's ear and Brisa knelt. Price's arms tightened around Eirlys.

"Eirlys, did you heal yourself?" Brisa asked.

"You know I can't," Eirlys said. "Self-healing is what I lost when I became Devoid."

Brisa frowned. "Are you sure?"

Everyone stared at Eirlys. Sighing, Eirlys pulled on her power and created an ice dagger.

Gasps pierced the quiet surrounding her. Deryn unsheathed their sword and tension gathered in Price's chest behind her, but she ignored everyone. She sliced her palm, sucking in a breath when the pain slashed through her again. The cut on her neck hadn't been this painful. She held her hand up to show the blood flowing down her wrist.

"Be ready," Eirlys told the Va, who frowned at her.

Eirlys pulled on her power again and her spirit rose from the depths. Her magic swelled within her, soft and cool at first. Then it turned sour, becoming angry and frustrated. Instead of healing, the power turned inward and the small wound on her hand split open further. Bones broke and more blood poured from the wound, her own magic eroding her hand from the inside.

"By the gods," the Va said, rushing over to her hand. He pulled on his power and closed the wound.

The faces around her gaped.

"Told you," Eirlys muttered.

Price gripped her other arm and lifted her too fast. The world spun around her.

"Hold on," she breathed, willing herself not to throw up in front of everyone. Eirlys bent over and put her hands on her knees, breathing as her world tilted. The Va healed her wounds but couldn't replace the blood she'd lost.

"Are you okay?" Price asked, placing his hand on her back.

"Oh, yeah, almost being assassinated feels great," she said sarcastically before rising. "Oh gods, are you okay?!" He looked horrific.

Price laughed, a haunting chuckle that was anything but happy. "It's all yours."

She gaped. He was drenched in blood. *Her blood.* His shirt clung to his body, while his arms were caked with gore, a violent splatter of red streaked across his face.

"I caught you," he added. His eyes stared into hers, a soft sorrow playing behind the blue. "Eirlys, you were dead. I swear it. I know what you said, but when the healers came around and your eyes started to flutter, I thought I was seeing things."

"Price," Eirlys said. He closed his eyes slightly, turning away from her. It seemed like whenever he got too close, felt too deeply, he pushed away from her.

"Can I go shower?" Eirlys asked, facing Deryn as disappointment settled over her. Their eyes were narrowed at Price.

Aydra walked over with Ancient Walo who studied her for a moment and lifted his hand. "I think our sacred night has come to an end."

She heard a sharp intake of breath. Across the room, her mother's Kenos tried to reach for her. Ambrosia's brows were knitted in concern, her mouth opened to call for Eirlys, fraught with longing, but Walo was already pulling on his power, sending the dead back into the void.

Eirlys knew at that moment, Ambrosia would not walk with the Ancient's to the Valley. She would stay and wait. Until next year—until Eirlys was ready to confront the woman who had left her for dead.

Price escorted her upstairs while Deryn ran to work the crowd outside the steps of the castle.

Eirlys began pulling at the intricate dress, ready to have the blood-soaked fabric away from her skin. However, the knots would not budge.

"Shit," she cursed. Price jumped at the sound of her voice. "I can't untie the corset."

Price's eyes widened and he gulped.

"I can figure it out," she said quickly, noticing the startled expression on his face and not wishing to invade more of his time.

"No, it's alright. I can handle a corset."

"Not your first time helping a lady undress, huh?" Eirlys regretted the joke the moment it left her lips. They regarded each other silently for a moment before Price moved.

He walked into her room and followed her into the washroom. His fingers pulled deftly on the ties, but the blood had caked the knots to the point where he couldn't undo them.

"I have to cut this," he said.

"Well, I don't think I can ever wear this again anyway." Eirlys laughed.

Price pulled a small knife from his boot and cut the knots. The dress would have fallen away if it hadn't been for the blood plastering it to her body.

"Thank you," Eirlys said, rounding to face him.

"Your hand?"

She held up the limb. "All better. I'm used to it by now. I kept trying. My friend Rory—" She ignored the way her throat caught on his name after seeing him tonight and barreled on. "He was so mad at me, always having to heal these horrific injuries."

Price grabbed her hand, his blood-soaked gloves long gone.

"But we did this," he said. "We caused the curse, what it did to you, and watching it—"

He let out a long sigh and Eirlys realized just how close they were standing when his breath caressed her cheek.

The desire in his eyes shocked her. His mouth was partly open. Covered in her own blood, nothing about the situation should have been sexual and yet the tension heated the air. A pulse crackled the space between them. Why was this tension here, this heat, after how he'd treated her? He had been distant, in some ways cruel. Eirlys' mind and heart warred with each other at the thought of his hands on her skin.

Eirlys closed her eyes to avoid his intense stare, unwilling to let herself get caught up in him again. The gentlest kiss brushed her cheek, and in it lay all the unspoken words burning the air between them.

# Chapter Twenty-Six

## Eirlys

Yellow, green, and red leaves dotted the trees surrounding the castle. Although the days were unseasonably warm, the autumn air chilled the nights. As the sun rose later and set earlier, this far north there would be days when it would only grace the sky for a few hours. Eirlys wandered on the castle grounds, her hands trailing the lower branches. She was alone, having snuck out early in the morning, telling each person she saw that she would find another guardian soon. She needed time with her own thoughts. And since Dvasia, her security had been increased so tightly, she wondered if she would ever be alone again.

Her own fears about the worship taking place later in the afternoon coursed through her. It had been months since Lita's death and every time she entered the temple, it reminded her that Lita's spirit was gone. Dread hammered her gut, and she was unable to stop the fear from taking over, lancing her bones with slick unease.

The prophecies which poured from her mouth during

worship gave her a headache and the smell of cinnamon and myrrh sent her heart fluttering. She hated every moment of it, now stuck in this constant loop of fear, trepidation, and anger. Another worship today, another pang in her heart as her own religion slipped further and further away.

A clearing emerged and Eirlys stopped when she could make out the headstones: a cemetery with a large crypt door in the center. Her parents would be there if she wanted to visit them someday. Today, she wasn't ready for that. She went to turn around and noticed a small headstone placed near the front of the cemetery.

The words etched upon it were worn after twenty-seven years' worth of weather and elements. Her breath left her body, and her heart raced as she took them in. She lost feeling in her hands.

The headstone read:

EIRLYS PENDRY
BELOVED DAUGHTER
MAY GYDA DELIVER YOU FROM THE VOID

That's all they had to say to her. It was a neutral saying, reserved for all dead Skath infants whose parents murdered them.

Beloved daughter.

It wasn't even a true headstone; if a casket existed below the sun browned grass, it lay empty. A grave dug for no other purpose than to hide her affliction, her Skath nature concealed beneath a story of sorrow. She stood and debated trying to pry the gravestone from the ground when a snapping twig caught her attention.

She whipped around. A man lingered in the shadow of the trees, watching her. His arms were up in surrender. Dark hair, light blue eyes. Familiarity piqued at her though she couldn't make out his features.

"Pretty creepy, seeing your own gravestone. A little macabre for my tastes," he said, tone mocking.

She would never forget that voice. Emzelhal. She pulled on her power, wishing she hadn't insisted on being alone. Emzelhal's Wraithmark deepened to color of the night sky, but he kept his hands up.

"I knew you wouldn't die. I've seen you come back to life before," he said.

Eirlys almost released her magic, surprise gripping inside of her. "Excuse me?"

"Let me explain," Emzelhal said, stepping out of the shadows.

Unease gnawed at her gut. She formed an ice dagger in the palm of her hand.

"Stay where you are," she demanded as he took a step forward. The blade was perfectly balanced, and she threw with deadly accuracy.

"Closer would give you a better chance. I'm an exceptional Sa, as you have noticed," he said, chuckling.

"I've had practice throwing knives into wind vortexes. If you want me to get some more practice, come closer."

"I think your prince would be upset if I died. I *am* his only contact here in Kygem."

"Leave August out of this," she growled.

"Sweetie, he dragged me into it. Did you think I was infiltrating your room for no good reason?"

She shivered. "You mean creepily hovering over my sleeping body. Fairly sure he didn't ask you to do that."

She left out that she would throttle August the next time

she saw him if she ever did. The fool knew she was alive and healthy and still he tried to save her. She wasn't in chains; she was in the shackles of her own morals and beliefs, her own choice to come here. Her own arrogance that she could make things better for an entire realm.

He shrugged and sat, gesturing for her to do the same. Eirlys didn't think she was being given a choice. She chose a bare spot of grass to sit on, avoiding her empty grave.

"How could you have known I wasn't going to die, unless you meant it to be shallow?"

"I nearly cut off your head," he pointed out.

"You must be awful with a blade. The Va who healed me said it was a shallow wound," she explained.

"Has anyone ever told you they thought you were dead, for you to only be superficially wounded?" Emzelhal asked.

Eirlys eyes narrowed, knowing exactly where this conversation was going. "You mean before you tried to kill me?

He sighed. "Yes, obviously."

"People have told me I couldn't possibly have lived through a wound. Once while I trained as a guardian, a rock pierced my chest; everyone said that it hit my heart. But here I am. Around five years of age a large wardrobe fell on me. Everyone thought I was dead underneath, but I was perfectly fine except for a few scrapes. A cannon nearly took me out, but I think it ricocheted off the mast before it hit me. I was only bruised."

Emzelhal shook his head. "And you still never realized. I didn't take you for a fool."

Eirlys bristled. "So, what do you think you know about me that I don't know about myself?"

"We saw you when we crossed into Kygem. My father and I had been skulking around the borders for days, trying to decide the best way to get across without being seen. Suddenly, this woman dressed all fancy came walking in our direction. Father glamoured us and we backed away. She placed a baby on the ground and left. I remember walking up to that babe. This was on her blanket."

Emzelhal reached over and drew on a bare patch of earth the symbol of the Pendry family—a triquetra.

Eirlys stopped breathing for a moment. The truth hit her as she understood what they had done.

"Did you leave me there?" she asked through gritted teeth. The world was full of monsters.

Emzelhal stared at her. "Yes," he said, after a moment.

Eirlys leapt to her feet, her hands shaking.

"Are you seriously upset right now?" Emzelhal asked. "We had bigger concerns than a babe in the Barrenlands. One life was worth sacrificing if we could fix Kygem—if we could stop it from ever happening again."

Eirlys stared at Emzelhal. She herself had sacrificed so much, become *Devoid* to save a stranger's child, and this man had simply walked away from her.

"How exactly do you plan to do that?" Eirlys growled.

"Can I finish my story?"

Eirlys frowned at him and slowly sat again, not liking his tone or his manners, but seeing few other options than to let him finish.

"We were going to Kygem. Queen Redna sent us on an important mission. Infiltrate the north. Give Kestrya an edge. We couldn't take you back."

Then something changed in Emzelhal's face. "I know you won't believe me, but I thought we were done for, my father and I. Gyda, that scary Naevni bitch, stepped through the void. Right to you. She... "

"She stabbed me in the chest," Eirlys said.

Emzelhal blinked at her. "How did you know?"

Eirlys pulled the neck of her shirt down showing the small

starburst shaped scar on her chest. "It was like the first thing Gyda said to me."

"And that didn't make you believe you couldn't die?" Emzelhal sputtered.

"I always thought whoever did this just missed."

Emzelhal threw his hands up. "Anyway, you know the rest. Now, we need someone to make changes in Kygem—and who better than a Skath queen?

"Why the fuck do you think I came here? Before I knew about you and your father's plans, I wanted to change things and protect the Skath. You two were not the only ones who cared. I don't know what you want from me, but you just tried to kill me, and I'm not helping you."

"Why not?" he asked, shocked. "You haven't attacked me yet. You haven't screamed for the guards. Don't tell me it's merely because the prince is working with me. Was working with me, anyway."

It didn't help, but there was a reason Eirlys still sat here— this man was a potential ally. And she was in sore need of allies if she had any hope of making headway against the gods. She'd put up with more than enough scum as a Shadow Guard in Kestrya. Emzelhal would be no different.

Eirlys sat back, crossing her arms. "Fine. I'll listen to what you have to say, and maybe we can find a way to work together. But just remember who's queen here. I have my own goals, have made my own sacrifices and choices that I'm not willing to compromise. I won't be a pawn in your games."

A smile crept onto Emzelhal's face, the kind of grin that sent trepidation and dread skittering down Eirlys's spine.

"Will you be a pawn in theirs?"

At worship, Eirlys sat after her part and listened to Alina discuss the new prophecy. Aydra was supposed to be teaching her how to do this, but both Eirlys and her kept making excuses not to. Price and Deryn fumed at Eirlys all through the service but said nothing about Eirlys ditching her guards earlier.

Their attitudes were still bitter and resentful as they headed up the path. Brisa and Eirlys exchanged a glance as irritation rolled off Deryn and Price in waves.

"For fuck's sake," Eirlys cried out halfway to the castle. "Spit it out. Yeah, I did a stupid thing. Yes, I deceived you. I'm fine, let it go!"

"It's not fine, Your Grace," Deryn said. "If you had died, it could be our heads on the cobblestones."

Eirlys rolled her eyes. "The Ancients would throw you a blessed ball if I happened to get killed accidentally."

"That's not funny," Price said, his voice tight.

"I am more than capable of taking care of myself."

Deryn and Price shared a look, their friendship apparently back on speaking terms. Eirlys fumed.

"Fine, how about this. If both of you beat me in combat, I'll allow you to always be at my side," Eirlys said. She almost took back the words. It had been months since she practiced, and since they tightened security, she and Deryn hadn't had a chance to spar. Doing push-ups in her room only kept her muscles from growing soft.

Price cocked his head at her, smiling slightly. "Deal." He removed the gloves he always wore and unsheathed his sword. He gripped the hilt, fingers adjusting into the groves which perfectly matched his hands after years of use. Deryn stepped forward, palming the hilt of their sword.

"Eirlys, if they hurt you," Brisa said. Deryn put a hand on her shoulder.

"Brisa, a weapon please." Eirlys held her hand out.

Brisa wrinkled her nose but pulled her two axes from their holsters. She extended both to Eirlys. Eirlys only took one, waving away the other, unsure she would be able to fight well with the extra weight. The curves of Brisa's body hid the intense muscle underneath—she would win in a wrestling match any day. Eirlys whirled the ax around the air, getting a feel for the additional heft and too short reach.

"Rules?" Deryn asked, unsheathing their own sword.

"Get your sword on my neck, heart, or spine and I will stop arguing about the extra security," Eirlys said.

"Should Deryn and I attack together?" Price asked.

"You'll need to if you want to beat me." Eirlys grinned. She didn't wait.

As she struck, Deryn raised their sword in time to block. Price launched from their side and Eirlys dropped the ax, ducking and sweeping her hands to catch the weapon before bringing it up to strike. Deryn struck and Eirlys was forced to parry. Price pivoted, pulling his sword up again. Eirlys kicked at his leg and brought her ax toward Deryn, who blocked and stumbled. Eirlys jumped back, watching the two of them circle her.

Price looked pleased, almost proud. They both attacked and Eirlys parried Price's sword, sending it into the earth, and caught Deryn's sword with one iced-over hand. Eirlys grinned and pushed them back. Price moved behind her and Eirlys ducked, pulling the sword with her, sending Deryn sprawling onto their back. Price's sword missed. Eirlys jabbed, and her ax finally caught flesh before Price flashed away. A small chunk of his calf was missing, and the wound seeped blood.

"I'll heal you afterward," Eirlys taunted, smirking.

Deryn coughed; their eye-line glowed. Eirlys jumped from the ground, avoiding the air trying to swirl around her. The ax slowed her down and she had to let it go to avoid getting caught in the attack. Price sprinted toward her and Eirlys pulled on her magic as she ducked. But he caught her arm and pulled her straight into him, chest against chest, sword pressed against her neck.

Cold, sharp steel bit against her hot skin. Eirlys flushed. Price's breathing matched hers and his bright blue eyes flamed in excitement and a hint of relief, like a weight was removed from his shoulders. A million seconds could have gone by as the lines of their bodies met and the small space left between them pulsed with electricity. His breath steamed the steel of the blade at her throat, and the world stilled. His hand squeezed her wrist, more of a spasm, and he stepped back, removing the sword without even scratching her skin.

Price limped away and Eirlys's body followed of its own accord. She gingerly touched his clothed wrist and helped him down while Deryn retrieved their own sword and handed Brisa back her ax. The cool rush poured through Eirlys, followed by the sting of his wound as she healed him. She flung the blood from his clothes and helped him stand.

Back at the castle, Eirlys wound her way up the stairs, Price bringing up the rear. She had lost. Not just lost—she hadn't even lasted as long as she should have.

"Good fight, Your Grace," Price said, sinking into his designated chair outside of her room.

Eirlys rolled her eyes and sighed. "I admit, I'm out of practice."

Brisa snorted. "That was out of practice?" Eirlys faced her sister. "Deryn's a commander and I think you could beat them if it was one on one."

"My word still stands," Eirlys said.

Deryn patted her hand and frowned at Price. When Eirlys turned to him, he was staring at his hands. They were still bare; he hadn't put his gloves on after their fight. The look in his eyes was full of grief, pain, and a forlorn longing that made something prick in Eirlys's stomach. Deryn closed the door and Eirlys stared at it for a moment longer before heading to wash up.

# CHAPTER TWENTY-SEVEN

## EIRLYS

"Your first Council meeting is tonight."

Price barged into her room, ignoring the flabber-gasted attendant who tried to stop him.

"It's alright, Claire, thank you," Eirlys said dismissing the attendant, who bowed and backed out of the room.

Eirlys shot a look at Price. She stood at her new bookcase, placed on an outside facing wall, and was arranging her books in a pleasing manner. Currently going by subject, and then by size within those subjects. She loved the aesthetic, the neat rows of books, the simplicity of a good pattern.

Her room was fully furnished for the first time since she'd arrived in Kygem. A loveseat sat in front of the fire before a beautiful mural rug showing the icecaps of the northern sea. Her dinky chair and table had been replaced with a writing desk, and on it sat a box she had yet to open. It would hold details of her new job, her new queenliness; everyday there would be study material, laws, etiquette, family trees and documents on her role as the religious head.

Price did a double take. Eirlys glanced at her body, wondering if something was amiss. She wore a simple white shift dress, seashells strung together to create the straps. White sandals adorned her feet, and a royal purple shawl with ivory embroidered roses wrapped around her arms. It matched her new hair color, a vivid purple on her tips that faded delicately into her natural hair color.

"I was sent to get you ready," Price said.

His cold demeanor had returned the day after their sparring match, but there was a stiffness to it, an obvious falsehood. Whatever was going on with him was an act—a bad one. But he tried so hard. She went to ask him if she needed to change but couldn't get the words out before an attendant opened the door to announce Brisa and Aydra. They both bowed to her, Aydra with a smirk on her face. Her spoiled attitude had returned once the shock of Lita's death wore off.

"We can take it from here, Price. Thank you," Brisa said.

Price went to exit but Brisa called, "Don't go far. You'll probably be going too."

"Why?" Eirlys and Price asked in unison.

Eirlys bit her lip, annoyed at the man for no good reason.

"I think they will swear you in today," Brisa said to Price.

"What? Now?" Price said.

His nervous energy in turn made her anxious. He was already sworn to protect her—what more could they want?

"You agreed to guard her," Brisa said. "And seem the most comfortable with her."

Price frowned, and Eirlys thought she had to be joking. At first, yes, but now, he could barely stand her...

"I have not agreed to be the queen's Guardian though."

"What is that?" Eirlys said, looking back and forth between the two of them, alarmed by the strain in Price's voice.

Price spoke in a clipped tone. "A guard to the queen, once

sworn in, is hers forever. There hasn't been the need for one in—"

"—centuries," Brisa said, finishing the sentence for him. "During each war there has always been one assigned. Our mother didn't have one though."

"What do you mean mine forever?" Eirlys asked Price.

"I would do whatever you ask of me until the end of your life. I would protect you with my life and would never leave your side."

Eirlys stared at him, then at her sisters. "No. Absolutely not."

She caught the pain flooding Price's face but resisted the urge to take her words back. In no way would she allow this man to sacrifice his life for a future queen he barely respected, barely tolerated.

"Eirlys, you aren't just a queen, you know. You are a part of our faith, a part of our pantheon."

"When I am officially crowned, we can discuss it. Not before."

Brisa pursed her lips but said nothing. Price breathed a sigh of relief.

"Be on call. The council can overrule her," Brisa said to Price.

*Curse it!* Of course, gods overruled future queens.

"Lovely, when does this start?" Eirlys asked, not bothering to hide the bitter bite in the words.

Eirlys held her head in her hands, bent over on her seat at the head of the council table while the voices around her argued and fought. She should have let the conversation about Price go on longer but since she refused to take him on as her personal guard, the Council of the Ancients had moved on to heartier topics.

Her head pounded, the pain boring into her. The bright white of the council room burned her retinas. Her first act as queen would be to make it illegal for rooms to be this bright past midnight.

Twelve gods sat in a circle beside their golden Kenos.

The crescendo of the voices became deafening, so loud she couldn't hear her own thoughts. Her face hurt from controlling her emotions as her expression tried to say what her mouth couldn't. She tried to keep herself in check, from feeling anything, but her mother's name kept coming from the lips of the people who had sentenced her to death. They kept arguing about the best way to uphold their laws about the Skath.

"Can we be quiet for a second?" Eirlys said, her voice mumbled between her hands.

Aydra and Brisa fell silent and glanced at her. No one else stopped.

"Shut up!" Eirlys screamed and jumped from her seat, hands pounding on the table. Like a dark storm, her power flared and streaked across her eyes. The cold filled her veins before bursting out in a tempest of snow and ice, covering the room in glittering frost. A heavy moment of silence followed as her breath puffed out in white clouds from trembling lips. With a wave of her hand, she evaporated her magic while the entire Council stared at her Skath face.

"It's not working," she said into the quiet, which felt like a soothing rag to her irritated mind. "You keep arguing about how to uphold the laws, how to punish people for not obeying them. Instead, you should be looking at the laws themselves."

"Our laws are a part of our religion. We cannot separate the two," Goddess Cosyn said. "This is a theocracy."

"But it's not working," Eirlys said, her teeth clenched.

"How so?" Pania asked.

Eirlys frowned, pulling at her magic. She conjured water and flung it about, tossing a small water ball between her hands. The spectacle did much to show off her shadowed Wraithmark. "I am living proof that your system is broken. Your own beloved princess stole the heir and ran away with her. Something must give. People attacked me on castle grounds and my own heir tried to kill me. Her conclusions from your laws meant my death would have been a kindness, and she wasn't wrong."

Aydra stared at her hands, not at the gathered Ancients. Eirlys had an inkling her attempted assassinations had been council approved. She scanned the room, meeting the eyes of the council. Iona, Ashur and Gyda were the only ones who didn't avoid her gaze.

"As future queen, you expect me to uphold laws I have fought my whole life against. Being raised in Kestrya, I bore witness to the destruction The Skath Treaty has wrought on not only Kestrya but your own people. Those who have looked to the sky and prayed for you to do something, anything, while the curse took hold of their bodies. They still believed in you while they fled your rule. We cannot ignore the fact that something is broken within the system. Your citizens are more afraid for their children than to lose the Ancients' guidance in the void."

Iona's face remained blank, but Eirlys thought she saw a hint of pity before she spoke. "That is why we destroyed your aunt's spirit. As a warning, a reminder of what we are capable of. Of what we can do in the void. We will not abide by traitors, and we are not mere immortals sitting in our high tower while our laws are being broken."

Eirlys gaped. What Iona had said was pure extortion. This was her new government, sitting in this bright tower, with their circular table, deciding how best to control the people.

Everyone focused on their future queen, and she no longer had the words which were building in her moments before. Immediate loss weighed upon her. Eirlys's head pounded, and she sputtered for a moment.

"There has to be another way," Eirlys said in desperation.

Ashur opened his mouth, but Iona shot him a warning look.

"We can think about it," Iona said.

Eirlys eyes darted between Ashur and Iona. While Eirlys was playing a game of survival, the gods were busy running her realm. She scanned the circle, wondering who was beyond her. Gyda, Cosyn and Olga would never side with her. Ashur had come to her rescue in the Hall, but he also started the Reckoning for her mother. Iona possessed an almost human-like quality to her. Not as godly as the others. She knew nothing of the child-like Sarna and preferred to keep it that way. Then there were the twins, Nym, Price's patron goddess, and her sister, Nyx. Eversil and Pania, quiet, almost gentle, gods could be options. Walo, God of Courage and often the patron god for the guardians, might be able to be swayed if Eirlys brought him a good military tactic. She just had to convince him. Eirlys didn't know enough about Esona, the Goddess of Focus.

She took a deep breath. In a gesture of futility, she held her hands up and plopped unceremoniously into the chair as Iona announced the council dismissed. Her head fell into her hands again and she wondered if she could convince someone to run out and get her a stiff drink.

Exhausted by the time they left, Eirlys slept in the SaCarriage on the ride home, only waking when they reached the entrance to the courtyard.

Price helped her out, a package tucked under his arm. Deryn and he talked at Eirlys's door. After Deryn helped her change, Eirlys settled into her personal sitting room which she had discovered on a tour of the castle. She'd just popped open a book when Price entered.

"You okay?" he asked, setting down the package.

"Not really," Eirlys said.

An attendant brought Eirlys the tea she asked for and promptly left. Price passed the fireplace and with a pulse of power, he changed the flames from their customary orange-yellow hue to the soft blues and whites Eirlys preferred to read by. He took a seat beside her and patiently waited for Eirlys to continue.

"I feel like I am screaming into the void for all the good it does me. The Ancients won't listen. They think they can keep forcing their people with violence, with fear, and it's breaking the realm. It's breaking the world."

Price said nothing for a moment, his eyes still soft, thinking. "The world is a harsh place, a harsh reality."

Eirlys laughed, short and bitter. "Well apparently, they agree. I was trying to make them understand that we are all people. Skath, Klara... " Eirlys paused because it felt so natural to include the Naevni.

"I think you do that very well," Price said.

"I don't feel like it. I feel like I'm failing. Like I'm failing both of my peoples, my adopted home, and my birth home. By taking the throne, I'm giving up everything I was."

Price's eyebrows furrowed. He reached for her hands and held them gently. She couldn't help the small gasp that escaped her lips before she realized he was wearing his gloves.

"Eirlys, you were born for this. You have drive, you have need, and you understand the consequences. I think the only thing you lack is confidence in your decisions."

Eirlys laughed again, this time a quick huffing noise of surprise and appreciation.

Price grabbed the package and handed it to Eirlys. She took it with wide eyes.

"I never gave you anything for Dvasia," he said in explanation.

She pulled the ribbon on the box and removed the delicate wrapping paper. Inside were two gleaming circlet daggers.

Eirlys stared at a near replica of the weapons she had lost, still presumably in her bag at the bottom of the sea. The blades curved out of blue ribboned hilts inlaid with sapphires. Eirlys picked one up and pulsed her power through it. The blades were imbued with silver, accepting her magic better than other metals. Her eyes welled up. Weeks ago, Eirlys had talked about her old daggers. She had reminisced about them, about sparring and maintaining her shape. Before the kiss, before her mother—and yet, he remembered.

"Thank you," she whispered.

"Maybe we can give them a try tomorrow," Price said, standing.

Eirlys opened her mouth to tell him not to go but chose to stay quiet.

Price paused. "I can stay if you like."

She wasn't going to ask him but agreed to his suggestion. If she wasn't the one to say it, that made it different, right? She set down her box and opened her book. Just one chapter, she thought, but her mind did not agree. The words were senseless ink on the page, losing all meaning.

She closed her eyes. She didn't open them when Price picked her up but spared the strength to wrap her arms around his neck. How he managed the stairs, she didn't know, but when he laid her in bed, she clung onto his shirt half asleep and not wanting to be alone. He gently pried her off and she gripped the covers instead, sinking back into her dreams.

In the morning, she couldn't remember how she had gotten to bed.

# CHAPTER TWENTY-EIGHT

## EIRLYS

E irlys couldn't tear her eyes from the throne. She rubbed her hands on her dress, feeling the thick linen. The dress featured a full skirt, a wide silver belt, full sleeves, and a plunging neckline where Lita's urn sat nestled on her chest. The ice blue color made her already pale skin glow. On her head rested the crown of the heir. But she hadn't sat on her throne yet.

Her throne. Eirlys took a couple of steps backwards and warm hands braced her.

"Your Grace?" Deryn said.

Eirlys shook her head. She was not ready for this.

"Would you like some wine?" Deryn asked.

Eirlys frowned, eyes never leaving the plush seat. She nodded, too weak to refuse, too weak to speak, too weak to rule the realm.

As an attendant darted out, Eirlys put one foot in front of the other, slow and deliberate, until her hands rested on the throne's arm, her fingertips sliding over the polished finish. She gripped the chair, faced the front of the room, and sat.

The mumbling in the hall stopped. Eirlys wondered if she looked regal, if she looked like a queen. Or did she look like a fraud? This was politics: meeting her people, listening to them, offering advice, and ruling over an entire kingdom. It was a task better set for August, who had the charm and grace to sit and listen. Eirlys had been to dozens of these public sessions and all she could remember was the tightness in her shoulders, the line of her back drawn straight and ready, poised for whatever threat would befall August.

Now, her turn had arrived. Deryn handed her the wine, and she took a larger than normal gulp. She set the gold chalice on the armrest. She peeked at Price, who gave her a strained smile—better than nothing. Brisa and Deryn took their positions on the lower floor to her left. Aydra, who would also sit on the dais, could not attend due to her training.

"Crown Princess Eirlys, future queen of Kygem," the attendant announced but there was a shift in his tone and a smirk on his face before he continued. "Her Dark Grace."

There was a palpable tension in the air as the people around her stiffened. It wasn't a title they had discussed. Eirlys knew an insult when it was thrown at her. Redna was good at those. But the citizens were shuffling in, the old and young alike, the rich and the poor, the lowly and the noble. If they wanted to draw attention to the fact that a Skath sat on the throne, then let them. To save her people, she would become Her Dark Grace.

Eirlys took another sip of wine and motioned for the attendant to bring up the first citizen. A young man spoke about crops in his village doing wonderfully and wanting better prices. Eirlys smiled at the trivial request and a scribe in the corner wrote it down. A couple asked for Her Grace's blessing for their marriage; Eirlys gave it. And on it went. She gulped her wine generously and answered questions the best she could.

When a man with cropped dark hair, light warm brown skin, and bright green eyes approached, Eirlys stiffened.

"His Royal Highness, Count Jasper Inwood," the announcer called out. "And his wife, Lady Basilla Inwood and daughter Lady Terenia."

The family resemblance was there, in the slant of their noses and the quirk of a lip. Eirlys leaned over when Deryn bent to whisper in her ear. "Jasper is eleventh in line for the throne, Teren is twelfth over her older brother. They live on the crescent shore. Basilla's fathers passed away a few days from each other, so they were not able to attend Dvasia."

"Allies?" Eirlys asked.

"Jasper and Price are the only two nobles to join the guardianship. The Count helped Price secure a position despite his... "

Deryn stopped talking. Eirlys wondered if they were about to mention Price's affliction, his inability to See.

"How may I help you, Count Jasper?"

"Greetings, Your Grace," Jasper said, bowing. "We merely want to attend and offer our apologies for not being at Dvasia. If rumors are to be believed, the Gods have granted you their gifts."

Brisa stepped forward, looking back at Eirlys for permission. She waved at her sister to go ahead. If Brisa thought something was important to bring up, it would be good for her people to know she had a court on her side, no matter how small.

"Where is Sidris? I have not seen my cousin in many years."

Eirlys watched Teren's lip twitch and her eyes darted to her

269

father. Such a simple gesture that Eirlys was sure meant, 'I told you so.'

"He is preoccupied," Basilla said.

"Hunting families across the Barrenlands," Deryn muttered.

Eirlys widened her eyes at them and whispered, "Truly?"

Deryn nodded. "He and his corrupt friends like to watch the border. As if they have nothing better to do with their time. I heard they found a commune where Skath infants were being hidden. Ran them out and across the border."

Eirlys's blood ran cold. From her time on the border, she'd seen so many families running, the slaughter of their infants. The screams still haunted her nightmares. How many did her cousin slaughter? Long before her life was uprooted, had she and him ever crossed steel, hurled magic at one another?

*That is why you are here. That is why you must get your crown,* Eirlys reminded herself.

A sharpness took Eirlys's breath away, and her hand wrapped around her stomach as the piercing pain thrummed through her belly. Deryn stepped forward and Price tensed. As quickly as it came it was gone. Eirlys breathed in relief, sitting up straighter and reaching for her chalice.

The pain burst back to life, exploding in her gut, behind her eyes, and in her limbs all at once. It stripped feeling from every nerve in her body, and the chalice fell from the throne's arm, its blood red liquid seeping into the royal purple carpet. Eirlys blinked and tried to stand, unable to find the words to scream for help or the strength to walk forward. She didn't make it far before she fell to her knees in front of the throne. Gloved hands grabbed her. But when Price tried to pull her up, scarlet poured from her mouth, soaking his legs, and splattering around them.

"Help! Someone get help!" Price called.

Eirlys peered at the crowd standing there, shocked. Her bones ached, her muscles screamed, her head pounded, and she shook violently. Poison, it had to be poison. Yet, no one moved. Not one of her citizens, not Jasper or his family, not a single person went to get help. They had accepted her as a queen because their laws required it, but their laws did not require them to stop her from dying.

Brisa and Deryn guarded Eirlys, who fell onto her side. Price's power flared in response to his anger.

"Deryn, go," Price nearly screamed.

Deryn shook their head. "If someone tries to kill her here... she needs as much protection as possible."

"Someone already is," Price said.

Eirlys leaned forward, vomiting again. Their voices sounded distant, as though she were under water. She let her head fall, too tired to hold it up, and the soft warm carpet pressed against her cheek.

Deryn growled and sprinted out of the room, their magic flaring, daring anyone to try and stop them. Eirlys's dull, dying eyes watched them leave when strawberry blonde hair appeared around the corner. Aydra sprinted to the dais.

"No!" she screamed, her hands finding Eirlys's face and lifting her head. "I told them not to." Her voice was weak and defeated.

Any remaining color drained from Eirlys's face, though when she tried to speak blood bubbled from her mouth, spraying Aydra's dress. She tried again, letting rage fill her with strength and bring clarity to her mind.

"Get away from me," Eirlys hissed, slapping her sister across the face. Aydra stumbled back off the dais, landing hard on the floor.

"Get out," Eirlys said, the anger renewing her will to fight. She tried to stand. Price held her up, and she rested all her weight against him. Aydra sat there, gazing in defeat. Eirlys spit in her face with stunning precision. "Get out," she repeated.

Her sister scrambled to her feet and darted out the door, her wailing cries echoing through the hallway.

Eirlys knees buckled and gave way again, her brief strength gone. Price's hands were the only thing keeping her from falling. He lowered her gently, her painted red hands touching the carpet. Her chin and neck were slick with the blood still dripping over and down her pale dress. She tried to call her magic; maybe it would kill her, and the agony would be over. But nothing happened. She pulled and pulled, and nothing came. She couldn't feel anything from the shadows. The darkness which gave her power was leached from her bones, gone from her grasp.

"Obsidian," she whispered.

Price blinked at her before grabbing the chalice and wiping the bottom of the cup. Flecks of black speckled his finger. Horror etched his face as he lifted Eirlys up. Her stomach rolled and she buried her fist into mouth to keep from vomiting again. Price ran down the hallway, carrying her in his arms. Eirlys squeezed her eyes shut, the pain from the movement and lights too much to bear.

"I have a Va," Deryn yelled, sprinting towards them.

"It's obsidian," Price blurted.

Her vision became fuzzy. Eirlys wasn't sure where they took her. Price laid her on a soft surface and someone bent over her, their fingers pressed against her stomach. Eirlys screamed, pain rearing its head again.

She closed her eyes, too tired—too beat—to keep them open. What was the point of fighting? She would never win this battle, this war against her and her magic. It was her, alone, against the rest of Kygem.

"Oh gods." Brisa's voice cut through the fog, bringing Eirlys back to her body, back to the pain.

"Obsidian alone wouldn't do this. My guess is poison in the wine. If she makes it through the night, I can try in the morning to heal her. By then the obsidian should have passed," the Va said. There were no words of comfort, no encouragement, just a Skath queen dying from an assassination. Like everyone wanted.

"It doesn't matter," Eirlys said, her voice raw and weak. She still tasted blood and every swallow burned.

"Shut up," Price said. "You matter."

Eirlys smiled. Price was rarely kind to her nowadays. Her mind wandered, thinking of his closeness after their fight, of the relief and almost wonder in his blue eyes whenever his skin touched hers. Her chest heaved and she bucked against the returned pain, spasms wracking her body. Price's hands were on her, trying to somehow make it better, to stop it.

When the convulsions stopped, Eirlys blinked into the light. "If it wasn't twenty-seven years ago, or five years from now, everyone in this room knows my life was shortened the moment I was born into this goddess forsaken realm."

"No," Price said, his voice wavering, a sob on the precipice of his tone.

Pain ebbed and flowed, coursing through her body and her chest tightened. Then a weight lifted from her, the burden of death giving way to a place of solace as her life drained away. She grabbed Price's hand, and her breath caught, once and twice and again.

She couldn't breathe. Her lungs refused to accept air.

Her heart stuttered.

"She's healed," a voice said, gentle and calm. "I don't know how she made it through the night. There was severe damage in her lungs, heart, and stomach, not to mention her kidneys and liver were destroyed. She will be sore and should be on a bland diet for a few days. But she will live."

"Thank you, Isbeil," Brisa said.

"I left some herbs for her to take. She will know how, so I won't bother you with the instructions. Our future queen is terribly lucky."

The door clicked and someone sighed. Eirlys was afraid to move, afraid to upset the gentle peace of her body.

"I'm going to go tell Aydra, not that she deserves any sympathy right now," Brisa said and Eirlys wondered who she was talking to.

The door clicked again, and a ragged breath sounded nearby. Strong hands touched her face and lips kissed her skin. Tears splashed against her forehead.

"I'm sorry," Price whispered.

Eirlys opened her eyes. He hovered above her, face inches from hers, the worst pain she'd ever seen in his eyes. "For what?" Her voice came out strangled and deep.

He didn't answer, instead standing and backing away. He reached the door and put a steadying hand on the frame, gripping it tightly, as if it were a buoy in a rough sea. He gazed at her for a long moment, then spun to leave, snapping the door shut behind him and leaving Deryn and Eirlys staring after him.

Brisa came back in, a look of sorrow on her face. By the time she reached Eirlys's bedside, it was gone. "They need to know what you want to do with the audience members and guards."

"What do you mean done with them?" Eirlys asked and

then it dawned on her. She propped up into a seated position. "Nothing, let them go."

Two pairs of stunned eyes stared at her.

"Your Grace," Deryn started. "You cannot let this go unpunished."

Eirlys glared at Deryn with such ferocity, the commander flinched back.

"Don't you think I want to kill them? To see them all hung in the gallows for turning their backs on me, for watching me die. But what will that accomplish? Imagine Her Dark Grace killing her subjects after her first audience, passing judgment on them from her bed. I can imagine the riots in the streets. The castle will be invaded by tomorrow morning."

Eirlys gripped the bedsheets as she tried to catch her breath. "Let them go and tax them an extra fifty percent. Every time you go to collect, they will know that I spared their lives."

Deryn cracked a smile.

"You should have them all drawn and quartered," said Brisa. Her face darkened with thoughts of murder.

"Yes, but I am not Klara blessed with the ability to have my faults overlooked."

No one in the room denied the validity of her statement. Her heart lurched and she realized that her reign would be filled with choices which would hang her life in the balance. This would be the first of many times her so-called people would happily stand aside and watch her bleed out before them, in one way or another.

# CHAPTER TWENTY-NINE

## PRICE

"I won't do it," Price said.

He wasn't shocked by the look on his goddess's face. He was more surprised by his own audacity, his convictions that no longer had anything to do with the religion he once preached.

"I cannot watch her die," he said.

The poisoning had pushed him over the edge. He was still covered in her blood. Watching her bleed out, the slick hot liquid rushing over his thigh. It flaked off his skin, her screams still clawing their way in his head. His body still tensed, waiting for her to seize again as her body betrayed her, spasms of pain and shock flooding her. The look in her eyes haunted him, the far off one which said she wasn't here anymore, she was leaving.

By the next morning, she was breathing steadier, easier.

But still, it had been enough. Enough to send him straight to a Hall, to summon his goddess and refuse to do what they wanted.

"We understand," Nym said. "We knew this would be tough for you."

Price blinked. "Oh."

Nym smiled at him. "My dearest proselyte, do you think we would be so cruel as to have you watch her suffer the way you have?"

"What?" Price said.

"If you feel you cannot guide and guard our Grace, we hold nothing against you."

"But you will still alter her?"

Nym paced back and forth. "We cannot crown a Skath. That much is clear. With this latest attempt on her life, it is more urgent than ever. Unfortunately, since the season is about to turn, we will have to wait until spring."

"Spring?" Price said.

"Yes."

Price rubbed his face. "And when are you going to tell her?"

"We are discussing that now. Her recent behavior and her need to change things could be used in our favor. We feel more confident that she will accept."

"I don't accept," Price yelled, anger and fear seething through him.

Nym gazed at him, her head cocked.

"Oh, Price." Her tone was condescending, edging on pity. "You love her."

He stepped back. Nym did not look away. With all the patience of a god, she waited.

"I don't know what I feel for her," he said honestly.

"This changes things."

"How? Why?" He was becoming increasingly erratic.

"We are in a delicate position. Eirlys is no mere immortal. She has a strength we can use, but only if she accepts. Only if she becomes the queen we need her to be."

When Price went to speak, Nym held up her hand.

"If you tell her too early, we could lose her forever. You must swear it to me, that you will not tell her until we are ready."

"It's my past, my pain, my alteration. You don't control that."

Nym made a small humming sound, not agreement, but she wasn't going to argue the point.

"Do you still believe in me, my son?"

"Of course," he said, reflexively.

He had too. He had to believe in his gods, because there was blood on his hands he would never be rid of if that belief failed. If his pain was nothing more than agony wished upon a child for being born different.

"Good," Nym said. "Then do what you must, but trust in us. Trust that we will tell her when she is ready."

He was going to ask Nym about the pain, about her magic and the relief it brought, but he thought better of it now.

"I won't go back. I cannot go back there."

Nym nodded. "Maybe that is for the best. I can take you back to the squad you were with before."

Price shook his head vehemently. "No, thank you. I'll stay at the Hall and find a way to make it work for now."

The goddess stepped forward, placing her hands on either side of his face. She was small, but still the largest presence he had ever been around. "Persevere, my child, until the void takes you."

"Hallowed by the light," he whispered.

"As the hour foretold. Have faith."

Then she shimmered, leaving Price with nothing but Eirlys's blood coating his clothes and every conviction he had shattered on the floor.

It only took him three days to stumble to his barracks, still drunk from the multitude of rounds at the bar. No one stopped him or questioned him.

He reached inside his drawer and took out a bottle of obsidian. It had been years since he took the stuff. Years of dealing with the pain. He glanced at the castle, wondering if she missed him. Of course, she didn't. Despite him trying to repair what little he could of their relationship, she knew what he thought of her.

What he was supposed to think of her. And by the gods, he had said that to her face, told her he despised her magic, the very essence of her being because of his religion. He had broken down a woman he was falling in love with for a faith he had all but lost.

But how could he hate her? He tried to tell himself that her touch was the only reason she called to him, that he needed the relief from the pain. He was a bad liar, even to himself.

Eirlys was so much more than her magic. She was Skath, and that didn't matter. By the Ancients, it should have mattered, but Price no longer cared. And not because of her touch. He went weeks without it until their sparring match. And then, when the obsidian took her magic, he hadn't cared that her touch did nothing to him. He just wanted her to live. And now that option seemed less and less likely. Even if she did live, to imagine her enduring the same amount of pain that he did was torturous.

Price's magic flared at the thought, and he left trails of flames behind him. He opened the bottle of obsidian and downed it, not caring about dosing. He wanted to not feel. How much would it take to make that happen?

He plodded through the castle grounds, unable to leave. Unable to find her. Unable to go to her. If he saw her now, he'd tell her.

Fuck Nym. Fuck the Ancients. How dare they take his magic? Make him this, then act like he shouldn't care about her. When he looked at her, he saw what he should have been. A Skath, perfect and whole. Not broken and pained.

He took a swig from the bottle he had swiped from the bar. The harsh liquor burned now that the obsidian drove his magic away, taking the pain with it. Not like Eirlys did, but a colder, harsher relief from the pain. A dull gray blanketing him, numbing him.

A herd of sheep were grazing a nearby pasture in front of an abandoned farmhouse. He pushed the door open. Used mostly for storage, there was at least an old bed. He tried to clear the dust using his magic and laughed when nothing happened.

He took another drink, a few swallows. He spluttered through some of it, setting the bottle on the floor. Slumping to the bed, he stared at his hands.

He should have touched her one last time, said goodbye, instead of leaving her to think he abandoned her. No, he had abandoned his gods, but it was too late now. Too late to tell her. Too late to make up for everything wrong he had done.

Unlike Eirlys's poisoning, Price had taken obsidian meant for consumption. It wouldn't wreck his insides—the alcohol would do that—but too much and the spirit would leave the body. He would fade into nothing, his spirit leaving for the void, leaving behind nothing. Not even his clothes would remain.

She would never know.

He didn't know when he had decided to die, probably sometime around the third bottle of liquor. If the alcohol didn't do it, the obsidian would. He didn't feel regretful, not enough anyway.

Price owed his gods nothing. They had spat in his face though he dedicated his life to them. His opinion on the alteration meant nothing, despite having gone through it. He'd dealt with the symptoms of someone else's choice every day. He resented them for it—his parents, his gods—masking it in reverence for his whole life. But now, his life was the only thing he had left to control.

So, he was going to take it.

Eirlys was strong. Stronger than him by far. She would think of him every now and then, but only as a memory. She never needed to know what he'd done.

One day, he'd look for her in the void. He only hoped that day would be in centuries.

He lost consciousness with one thought.

*Let her live.*

# CHAPTER THIRTY

## EIRLYS

Eventually, Eirlys recovered her strength. One thing she didn't recover was Price.

He had left and not returned for three days. No one could find him. She tried to pretend like she was okay, tried not to mourn a man who wanted nothing to do with her.

She failed miserably.

One night after dinner, Eirlys was reading in bed when a figure appeared in the door. Aydra.

"Don't," Eirlys said, setting the book down. Deryn moved quickly in front of Eirlys, protecting their queen from the would-be killer.

"I want to explain," Aydra said, not moving from the doorway.

Eirlys barred her teeth, getting up to face her sister. "Explain what? That you are a child? That you have no idea that your words once said are no longer yours. The realm sees you as its true heir, and if you claim to want me dead, they will follow you into the void, Ancients be cursed. That's what happened; you acted on selfish thoughts and childish motives, and I am still healing from your mistake."

Aydra opened her mouth, closed it, and opened it again before setting her lips in a hard line. It reminded her of August. Funny, this selfish, wanton girl could remind her of a kind, patient prince.

Aydra waited a moment, then bowed her head. "You are right," she said. "And I'm sorry."

Aydra left and Eirlys kicked a nearby chair, frustration taking hold of her senses.

"You should try and forgive Aydra," Deryn said quietly.

Eirlys gaped at them, hovering near the fire.

Deryn raised their hands. "Not saying what she did was right, or forgivable, but for your own sake. She's your heir for better or for worse and if something... " Deryn paused. "Eirlys, if you had died, your sister's legacy would've been to have murdered her sister for the crown. We cannot have a queen like that. We need a queen like you, and only you can teach Aydra to pass on that legacy."

Eirlys worried about Deryn's words. If Aydra was successful and they crowned her anyway, it would prove that regicide didn't matter when it came to a Skath. It would have been so easy to overlook, to pin it on the audience members or some attendant.

Aydra's scream sent Deryn and Eirlys hurtling out of the room.

Eirlys's little sister laid on the ground, her back arched toward the sky. Her eyes were filled with flame as her Wraith-mark lit up her face.

Her voice drifted eerily through the air.

"*A raven. Dead.*

*An omen. Death.*
*Shadows all around. Bleeding red.*
*Smoke tinted vision. Burning breath.*
*The absence of a beating heart.*
*Bright blue eyes will soon depart. "*

Aydra screamed again, her voice rattling. Her body launched into the air by whatever magic took hold of her. She choked over the white foam that poured from her mouth. Eirlys ran forward and attempted to pull her down. She recoiled, her palms blistering. Aydra's skin was hotter than fired steel.

"A price to be paid, cold, burning. The abandoned in the abandoned where the white walls loom, casting shadows as safe as her magic," Aydra whispered, detached and remote, before she collapsed.

Eirlys and Deryn caught her, her skin burning up but no longer untouchable. Brisa sprinted up the stairs and Eirlys looked at her other sister, helpless.

Aydra's eyes popped open. "Eirlys, you must find him. He's dying."

"Who is dying?" Eirlys asked, unwilling to even think of his name.

"Go," Aydra said, grabbing her arms. It burned again, searing her flesh.

Eirlys flinched back. Two guards were headed up the stairs.

"Take care of her," she shouted and shouldered her way through them.

She raced towards the barracks, ignoring her burning lungs. Price wasn't there—hadn't been there all week. Footsteps raced behind her, a clattering echo on the stone.

"Aydra?" Eirlys asked when Brisa and Deryn caught up to her.

"The guards are taking her to a healer."

Eirlys bit her lip, trying to remember the details of Aydra's prophecy. If there was ever a time, she wished they were true, it was now. "Search for an abandoned building, below the castle."

Neither of them bothered to ask who they were searching for before they darted off. Without losing another second, Eirlys ran. She didn't know where to go but she wracked her brain for some memory of an abandoned building near the castle. As she mindlessly ran, she prayed to her goddess and for the first time, she prayed to the daughter Xemané, the very first Ra. *Please protect him. He's one of yours.*

The sky began to darken, and the descending sun took with it any warmth left in the day.

Brisa called out for Price. He wasn't going to answer— Aydra's vision wasn't a normal one. With her Sight, she had touched someone who was either in pain or experiencing a malady and taken on their symptoms. Eirlys once witnessed a Ra who tried looking for a missing child with the Sight succumb to drowning while sitting in one of the Guard stations. The child had fallen into the ocean while the Ra focused on them. With the spirits connected, both died. It was one of the few Ra abilities Eirlys trusted. Aydra couldn't fake this: Price was hurt, possibly dying.

"Price," she whispered desperately.

She wheeled around the quarters, the backside of the castle abutting the mountain range and Eirlys's insides gave a haunting lurch. A small barn nestled past the grazing lawn and the bleats of sheep and goats filled air. A gentle flicker, like a dying lantern, shown through the dusty cracked window.

The door creaked when she opened it.

Time slowed as she took in the scene. The room was compact, with only a bed, a table, and an unlit fireplace. A washbasin sat in the corner for bodies and clothes. A door towards the back would lead deeper into the barn. Dust covered most surfaces; the smell of rotten wood and musky animal odor pervaded the air. The lantern flame wavered unsteadily from the table illuminating the mess surrounding it.

Pieces of a shattered liquor bottle covered the stone ground, mingling dust with droplets of amber liquid. Price lay sprawled on the bed, his pallor skin glistening with sweat in the light. His hair stuck to his face and vomit trailed on the pillow from his mouth, foamy and tinged red. He loosely hung onto a small vial seated in the palm of his hand.

Her heart stopped and she raced to him, the numbness giving way to adrenaline. Her aches forgotten, Eirlys fell to her knees at his side and conjured water. She coated him with it, cooling the water slightly so as not to shock him. He burned with fever. With a flick of her wrist, she removed the vomit from him into the washbasin. She touched his neck to feel his pulse; thready, weak, failing. Her wrist brushed over his forehead and a layer of ice appeared on the skin. Nothing in this plane or the next would stop her from using the full strength of her magic right now as the adrenaline coursed through her body.

Eirlys needed to assess his condition before trying to heal him. She grabbed the bottle from his hand and opened the little stopper. When she tried to pull on the liquid inside, a stunted sensation she wished to never feel again overwhelmed her.

Obsidian.

The vial was labeled with Price's name scrawled neatly on the side, obviously given to him by a Va healer.

He had taken obsidian. Had he taken the whole bottle? Why?

She pulled the water over his body to examine him. She

had never examined anyone with obsidian in their system. It appeared heavy and dark to her magic, a vast hole of emptiness. Her hands dropped to her sides and the water soaked him again.

Outside, Brisa called for her. Eirlys covered Price in a cold blanket and refroze the already melted ice on his forehead. She opened the door as Brisa walked up.

"Oh, Ancient Ones, what has he done?"

"Obsidian, combined with alcohol. I don't know how much he took," Eirlys said, tossing the bottle into a basket on the floor.

Leaving Brisa standing in the doorway, she walked back over to Price, grabbed more water, and placed her hands over his abdomen. His heart and lungs were healthy, but the obsidian pulled at her magic and forced it into other places. Although rarely needed, she had used this type of obsidian on some of her own patients. When either out of control with fear, pain or some drug or poison, it kept both the patient and healer safe.

With a shaky hand, she let go of her magic and sighed.

"I can't do anything but treat him physically," Eirlys said.

"Can I help somehow?" Brisa asked.

Eirlys shrugged, deciding not to reject the help. "Yeah, can you grab my earrings from my room that Aydra gave me? Bring me my bag on my altar. It should have the essentials in it."

"And Brisa," Eirlys added as she turned away. "Can you please bring me my daggers?"

Brisa nodded. Her face fell when she took in Price's condition. Steeling herself, she ran towards the castle.

Eirlys worked on Price. With his temperature still high, she kept the blanket cold. She wanted to reduce his fever and the inflammation in his kidneys first, but the obsidian lingered stubbornly. She brushed his face, lifting the matted hair from his skin. Tears flowed down her face.

She stared at him and in the moment, he looked young and relaxed, not in pain. It wasn't often she saw him this way. She took her hand away and nothing changed. Touching her usually ignited some response from him. She stroked his face and stared into his unhardened expression.

Brisa cleared her throat behind her.

"Oh, thank you," she said, her hand darting away from Price's face. She wiped her palms on her skirt guiltily and grabbed her bag from Brisa.

Eirlys went to the fireplace and started a fire with a RaGlass crystal she pulled from the bag's side pocket. She fell into the familiar rhythm of mixing herbs, adding ingredients little by little to a pot over the fire, the things she used to do all the time. It reminded her of the days in the Kestryan Navy.

Once the liquid had cooled, Eirlys struggled to lift Price.

"Want me to hold him?" Brisa asked, still standing in the doorway, unsure of what to do.

"No, no, I'll do it," Eirlys said. "You can stay or go. I've got him. I don't think anyone else should know. Tell them he was found, and he's injured."

"Eirlys." Brisa's voice cracked. "Save him."

Brisa's back disappeared out the door. Somehow, she didn't mean just in this instance. Save him from what? Himself? How was that her job? How was that fair for it to be pinned on her, when she already had so many responsibilities of her own?

She finally got him to drink the liquid and lifted him off her lap. She froze the blanket again along with his forehead and sat with the last remaining whiskey in one of the bottles on the table. She took a swig, knowing her kidneys were not ready for it and not caring. Price didn't get to be the only reckless one.

At least he had good taste, she thought, taking another drink. Price groaned, and Eirlys reached to touch him without a second thought. He calmed. Maybe he would explain that. And the obsidian. No wonder he had recognized it.

Whatever his affliction, his only option was to take the leeching volcanic glass and dull his magic. What could be worse than not having magic?

# CHAPTER THIRTY-ONE

## PRICE

P rice woke searching for her. Her voice called to him, and
he yearned to open his eyes and reach for her. Eirlys's
soft breathing stuttered in and out of sleep, her hand resting
softly on his forearm.

She had obviously noticed her touch did something to him,
but when had she figured out that it helped? The burning in
him, the fire constantly flaring inside, was extinguished now.
His pounding head and aching stomach were another matter,
but compared to his normal level of pain, he felt relieved.

Price's stomach rolled and he heaved into a wastebasket
placed near his head. He wiped his mouth, worried he had
woken her. He stared at her sleeping form, sitting on the floor,
and curled over the side of the bed. Her mouth was partially
open with a small, threadbare blanket over her shoulders. She
must have been exhausted, still recovering from her own near-
death experience.

This woman was the queen, and here she lay beside his bed
like a common healer tending to her patient. But she was far

from common, and far from just the queen. She had seen battle, healed the wounded and the sick. She had told him stories of nights spent on dirt floors and camping in tents pitched on solid rock with only their sacks as pillows. In Kygem alone she had been beaten, spiked, attacked, and poisoned; and yet, here she was. The same stormy spirit coming back again, doing her job, never backing down.

Price remembered the moment, the innocent contact which destroyed his world and rebuilt it again on the touch of one blond-haired woman. The solace within her touch illuminated his bleak existence with bright clarity. The brush of her skin felt like coming home, and its withdrawal was fleeing through a rain of fire and ash.

Not for the first time, Price wondered if his pain was a punishment. Was it the wrath of the goddess herself, her revulsion of his tainted magic?

As if he'd asked for this. As if he'd been given a choice.

Now he faced the consequences of the mutilation done to him—his every day was agony, every night unrelenting pain, all because of the abomination of his magic. Shadows thrust painfully into the light; a Skath changed into a Klara.

He'd had no idea how to begin to tell her. Instead, he spent time with her, got to know her. The way her eyes lit up when she would talk of Kestrya; the way her mouth flattened when he mentioned the Ancients; the way she pleaded that night on the balcony, her eyes still red from her tears, soaked to the bone in summer rain.

There'd been a decision to make: to be with her and forsake his religion, or distance himself and break her even more. Regret filled him when he thought of her face, defeated and broken when he chose the Ancients, choosing to not lead himself down a path of blasphemy. Her magic, that Skath magic inside of her, became his own personal paradise, which did not mesh with any teachings of the Ancients. Skath magic was supposed to be cursed, evil, harmful. And yet, it sang to him, to his spirit, calling to it in a language so ancient and stirring it needed no words.

As hard as he tried, she charmed him anyway. Beyond his need for her touch, he was drawn to her for her strength, her wit, her bravery. Everything about this Skath queen was not what he'd expected. She didn't take any shit from the Ancients or the royals around her. Price chuckled before groaning softly at the pain lancing through his body, and Eirlys gripped his arm harder in her sleep. He glanced at her. She didn't wake, still recovering from her own disaster.

Now, the cracks from that day were beginning to show. The damage of what she could do to him hovered under the surface of the thin ice upon which he found himself.

She was a Skath. How could he tell her? The conflicting needs raged inside him, tearing him in two, warring between his body, his heart, and his mind.

When she found out the truth about him, and what the Ancients wanted to do, she would hate him. And she should. But there was no going back now. He had to tell her, even if it meant losing her, because it had almost cost them both their lives.

His eyes roamed the planes of her face, the bright purple tips of her hair splayed across the pillow like a flower. He wasn't sure when he began to dream again—his dreams were always filled with her anyway.

A light burned bright through Price's eyelids, and his headache burst to life with ferocity.

"Eirlys," he moaned, squinting against the brightness from the window, unable to open his eyes.

Eirlys stood silhouetted against the sun with a mug in her hand. She whirled, surprise on her face.

"Oh!" She grabbed the curtains and pulled them shut. "Sorry, I didn't expect you to wake up."

He groaned again. "Am I dying?"

"Do you want to die?" she asked, a hint of accusation in her voice.

"I don't care one way or the other, but if I'm going to feel like this, please kill me," he said. He closed his eyes and his hands lifted to touch his face. He sucked in a gasp, "Fuck," he hissed out.

Eirlys padded over to him and placed her hand on his bare shoulder. He sighed and breathed slowly.

"Thank you," he said.

"Yeah, any time. You'll have to explain this eventually, you know."

Price sort of chuckled, a breathy noise. "Yeah, I think I don't have a choice at the moment."

"Rest for now," Eirlys soothed. Her thumb began moving back and forth, over and over again, touching his skin, and eventually his breathing slowed, and he fell back to sleep.

By the time Price woke again, the sun had set and the only light in the room came from the fireplace. Eirlys once again stood at the window, her face pinched with worry and exhaustion. When he sat up, she turned around, and the smile which blessed her face tore at him.

"Hey," she said gently.

He smiled and then grimaced.

"Can you eat?" she asked, coming to his bedside.

He shook his head, the thought of food sending his stomach into a panic.

"I'd prefer it if you would try," she said.

"Why bother asking?" he asked, teasing her.

Her eyes crinkled in amusement. "Look, there are some rolls in here, with some water. I'll get you some pain relief tea for your headache."

Price ate a small part of bread while Eirlys ate gingerly beside him. He watched her pick at the bread, tearing the crust off piece-by-piece, leaving a center of crustless mess on the plate.

"Did you go to the castle to get food?"

"Brisa brought the basket. I found it a few hours ago."

Eirlys fixed them both a cup of tea before she boiled a pot of water for him to wash in. Price hesitantly moved around the bed, trying to stand.

"I can leave if you are more comfortable," she said.

"No, I'm trying not to throw up in front of you," he said, more embarrassed about being sick than nakedness.

Price peeled off his sticky clothes and guilt rushed through him when he handed them to Eirlys. She cleaned them in the separate pot along with the sheets she stripped from the bed. Price watched her with fascination, her Wraithmark growing darker, then fading as she swirled and heated the water. She wiped her forehead with the back of her hand.

"What is it?" she asked when she caught him staring.

He smiled. "A queen is cleaning my clothes. I feel like I should stop you."

Eirlys chuckled. "Oh, this is only my millionth load of laundry. I always did the laundry at home, since I can heat, swirl, and dry the laundry quite fast."

For some reason, that little bit of information shocked Price. She was not raised as royalty, and yet, a task as mundane as laundry did not belong to someone as extraordinary as Eirlys.

Price tried to ignore Eirlys's wandering gaze while he finished cleaning the grime from his body, standing stark naked in the middle of a farmhouse. She finished, the water running clear, the smell of soap lingering in the air. She grabbed the clothes and pulled all the water out, tossing them to Price. Eirlys grabbed the pot and dumped it outside as Price dressed, feeling cleaner and better than he had in days. He sat at the table, pouring himself tea of whatever herbal mixture she had concocted for his head. It didn't help the burning in his body, but only one cure existed for that. And she sat across from him much too far away.

"How's your head?" she asked. She warmed up the cold cup of liquid in her hands.

"It's alright. The tea is helping," he said. He looked at her hand and the muscles twitched in his arms, straining with the desire to touch her.

Eirlys smiled, noticing his movement. She reached out and touched his hand. His hand balled into a fist and his jaw clenched as relief washed through him. He shouldn't let her touch him; in mere minutes, she would be storming out the door.

"Am I hurting you?" Eirlys's voice sounded puzzled at his tense expression.

"No, no, it feels good. I... curses. I better start. It's a long story."

Price sighed at the expectant look on her face. Eirlys sipped her tea, patiently. Where in the void should he begin?

"My parents are old, as you saw—my mother just cele-brated her three hundredth birthday, and my father is a few years older. My mother never found anyone to settle down with until she met my father seventy-five years ago. One day, she was out riding and saw a man nearly sinking like a rock in the rough southern seas. She dove off the cliff and dragged my water-logged father onto a small patch of beach. She used her Sa power to get them up the cliff and nursed him back to health."

"He had taken a boat to the southern seas to see the legendary white cliffs and hit rough water. It demolished his boat. They used to joke that he should have Seen it coming, being a Ra and all. They were married within the year. Not long after their wedding her parents faded. My father's parents were killed in the battle of Karavesh. Now the only two members of their families, they decided to start one together by having a child. But as you know, getting pregnant is no easy task for immortals, especially those my parent's age. It took them fifty years to conceive."

Price paused, then grabbed Eirlys's hand and gave it a squeeze.

"After I was named, they performed the ritual, as they do for all infants in Kygem. Like my father, the pure white flame touched my face and showed my Wraithmark. But it was not the light of a Klara blazing across my eyes. It was the shadow of a Skath."

Eirlys stiffened, her face confused.

"My parents were desperate to keep me—I was the product of so many years of hardship and anguish, meant to be a light for them, a new generation of our family. Being so old, they had knowledge lost to many younger immortals. They traveled with me to beg the queen and king for council."

"They'd heard rumors, a few decades before my parents were born, of the Ancient Sarna. She spent a lot of time studying the Skath, more than any other Ancients. During her studies she discovered a way to pull the Skath magic from an immortal and replace it with Klara magic." Eirlys stopped breathing, wide eyed, and her hand twitched beneath his. "She had practiced on any Skath she could catch and tried to perfect the process; but more often than not, the magic rejected the body, and the immortal died. A council meeting was called and Sarna agreed to attempt it on me."

Price paused, trying to swallow through his dry mouth.

"It... well you can see it worked. I am a Klara, but it's all wrong. I have poor control of my magic. I have never Seen—I don't think I've ever detected a smidge of intuition in my life. I'm in pain, everyday; it's like a burning sensation under my skin, like something is constantly trying to get out. My magic knows it doesn't belong in my body. But I survived. To help with the side effects of the alteration, a healer gave me obsidian to help on the worst nights. Alcohol can help dull it as well."

Price continued knowing if he stopped, he'd never finish telling her.

"When they called me to guard you, I wasn't expecting this," he said, lifting their hands. "The moment I entered the room—void, the moment I entered Alby, I could feel the pull; it was like home, like a calling. Your touch was irresistible, but every time you stopped the fire reignited, and my body craved the solace you brought. I couldn't handle it, so I ran. I pushed you away because the lying was killing me. The pain would burn me just thinking about you, and you were getting close to figuring it out."

"After you almost died in my arms... Eirlys, I didn't even think about the pain that day. All I could think about was how close I'd come to losing you, not only because of what your touch does to me, but because of who you are."

He chuckled, dry and humorless.

"I came here and tried to dull everything—my pain, my lies, the way the thought of losing you haunted me. I wanted to die. I would've been better off. Maybe I would have gone into the void so my damaged spirit could be fixed, and my magic could have dissipated into the nether, where I'd never have to feel it again. And yet here you are, with me. You're scared, I can see that, but you're here."

Eirlys trembled. She reached and wiped the tears from his cheeks. "I'm here," she whispered. "I don't know what I can give you, Price. I don't know what to do with this. But I'm willing to try."

Price smiled sadly, shaking his head. "Oh, Eirlys. Brisa said even if we told you, you wouldn't get it."

"Get what?" Eirlys's voice sounded high, worried. A little panicked. "Get what, Price?"

"You are going to hate me," he said, defeated. He pulled his hands away and ran them through his hair, letting out a shaky breath. Without her touch, the pain flared, and he both hated and loved what she could do to him. "They won't coronate you as a Skath. And thanks to the "success" of my alteration, there is a way to change that."

Eirlys stared at him for a minute. "You said that the people they try it on rarely survive."

Price gripped her hands tightly again. "I might as well tell you, so you have all the information; never has there been a successful alteration of an adult. With anyone over two years old, the death rate goes up exponentially."

Eirlys dropped his hands, her face contorting in utter terror as the truth hit her.

# Chapter Thirty-Two

## August

August leaned against the door frame, his hand on his sword and his eyes locked on Rory's. He pulled on his magic, the air answering his call as he listened into the apartment. Someone was whimpering.

August nodded at Rory, readying his magic around his sword.

Rory used that tall, strong frame to break down the door. He entered first with August behind him. The rest of his Shadow Guard followed.

The sound of clashing swords rang through the air. A halberd swung at him, over his head. August pushed the air, sending the halberd flying upward, his sword swinging toward his opponent. Air pushed back at him, and he hurled it away from him. He caught sight of the glowing Wraithmark of the woman he was fighting.

She snarled at him, reaching into her belt. August plunged the butt of his sword into her hand. The bone cracked and she screamed. He brought his sword to her throat. The woman froze, releasing her magic.

"Get out of here," she shouted. Her eyes betrayed her, darting to the door.

"Caden!"

She appeared beside August, her sword touching the other side of the guardian's neck.

August didn't wait, sprinting into another room off to the side.

He had hoped to never face another Ancient again. And yet one stood in his fucking realm, holding one of his own people hostage.

The Ancient was small, with a round face, white ringlets, and a button nose. Adorable. Except for the cruel smile playing across her lips, turning her childish face feral. Despite her small size, a man was fully in her control, his arms tied behind his back, mouth gagged. A small piece of obsidian jutted out of his abdomen.

"Hello, Prince," she said mockingly. "Catch me if you can."

August roared, raising his sword and sprinting toward the Ancient. Recklessness was far behind him now. But the Ancient merely stepped through the void, reality splintering around her and the man before they were gone.

He growled in frustration, swinging his sword at the wall.

"August," Basil said, standing in the doorway.

He turned on his friend, magic exploding from him in a whirlwind of fury he could no longer control. Basil merely held up their hand and redirected the air, keeping it inside the room until August's rage was spent. He collapsed to his knees, pressing his forehead into the wood floor.

"It's not your fault, August," Basil said.

"I'm too late. I'm always too late."

"We still have the Kygemian here. Maybe we can stop her next time."

Yes, next time. The constant prayer he had been chanting for weeks now. Next time they would catch her, next time they would get a good look at her face. Next time, he would kill her for stealing his people. And for what?

To break the treaty over four people was madness. It didn't make sense.

And yet he'd break the world for Eirlys.

August heaved himself off the floor. He pried his sword from the wall, sheathing it hastily.

"Let's go find out what she knows."

The city of Bosfall had a nightlife like no other. The streets were alive with music, the autumn air still warm with summer's shadow. The clatter of musicians and revelers could still be heard through the closed window. Basil pressed their hand to the glass, creating an impenetrable shield of air to keep the sound in.

The Kygemian woman peered at August from the floor.

"I'll never tell you anything," she spat.

August smiled at her, his pleasant smile, the one he wore when talking to advisors or some prattling noble.

"Don't worry. It's not me you'll be screaming your secrets to."

August left Basil to guard the door and Caden to do his dirty work. When he asked where she had learned to torture, she and Rory shared a look. August didn't wonder anymore. Eirlys had kept so much from him, to keep him safe, to keep him in her arms. He'd always known that there were darker and more gruesome tasks his guards must do. But torture, the kind of torture Caden performed-the kind she'd learned from his past lover—was beyond even his imagination.

The large flat they rented was only sparsely furnished, enough places to sit and sleep. August had barely managed to grab the money he kept tucked away before he fled the castle in the dead of night with his Shadow Guard.

When he returned home from the disaster in Kygem, his mother had raged at him, at his guards. She had threatened to dismiss them all until August stepped in, claiming they tried to drag him back but couldn't. For the first time since August was an idiotic teenager, he had been grounded. But his Shadow Guards did not take orders from his mother. They belonged to him.

He didn't have any clue where he was going. He couldn't stay in the castle, doing nothing. He started chasing rumors. Close calls with beings with white hair and deadly powers. Without Vara, they would have never even gotten close. The woman was running herself ragged, darting between Kestrya and Emzelhal in Kygem.

She had gotten them to Bosfall but left shortly after their arrival. They had more to go on now. Every kidnapping was a VaSkath, typically those who lived alone and were on an extended holiday. They wouldn't be missed for a long time. August tracked those in the city who might be targeted and came to the apartment after nightfall.

He had been right, but he had been too late.

An hour later, the door opened.

"August."

He got up and went inside the room.

"Tell him," Caden said.

August did not look at her work, at the damage inflicted on the Kygemian woman.

Her face was splattered with blood, her eyes bloodshot. She still had enough fury to glare at him.

"And you call us monsters." Her voice was ragged.

"Tell him," Caden repeated.

The Kygemian gasped and sucked in a breath. "Fuck you." Then she screamed and when Caden finished, the woman cried, "Fine, fine!"

She locked eyes with August. "That little Skath bitch who is going to take the throne. They plan to make her a Klara."

August flicked his eyes to Caden and Basil. They stared back with carefully blank expressions. He had heard correctly, but it couldn't be right. He focused back on the woman.

"That is impossible."

"It's difficult, but not impossible."

August waited for her to finish. "Why are they stealing Skath?"

"For practice." The woman gave a quick quirk of the mouth. "It's better for them anyway. Even if they die in the process, their magic won't be tainted, evil."

"Die?"

The Kygemian sucked in a breath, like talking hurt, like breathing hurt. "Not everyone makes it. In fact, almost no one does."

"Sa Daughter, save us all."

"No one is coming to save you. Your gods have abandoned you. They do not rule the void or this earth. They are nothing but forgotten Kenos, content to live in their Valley. Content to let the world burn. At least my gods have tried to perfect it."

August blanched. "Rory!"

The man darted into the room. "Heal her and then knock her out. Contact Vara. Have her take this woman to the Barrenlands. She can stay here in Kestrya and pay for her crimes, or she can walk back."

The woman went whiter than she already was. "Kill me."

"No." August sneered. He leaned into Rory, whispering in his ear, "Have Vara reach out to Eirlys. See if she knows."

"And then what?"

"We get them out. Kygem cannot steal our citizens and not suffer the consequences."

Rory placed his hand on August's shoulder. Those soft blue eyes stared into August's gray ones. Reassurance, love, and dedication. These were his people. The ones who would follow him to the edges of the earth and into the void if they must.

"Anything, my prince."

# Chapter Thirty-Three

## EIRLYS

"I'm going to die?"

Eirlys leapt to her feet ready to run; run back to Kestrya, run into the sea, she didn't care. Blood pounded in her ears, deafening her. The world lost focus for a moment before sharpening, red edging her vision.

"Why not kill me now? Why go through the motions? They should have ripped my heart out when they ripped out my mother's! They could have destroyed me with the assassin. Is torture the only thing good enough for them? Let poor Eirlys believe she has a chance, then snatch it away? Break her down and see how she falls?" The words came heavy and tumbling from her mouth, an avalanche she couldn't stop. And she was already so close to sliding over the edge.

Breathing heavily, she bent over to catch her breath. A sob bubbled up, and she crumpled to her knees, sorrow ripping through her body.

Price wrapped his arms around her. She gripped his shirt and settled her face in the crook of his neck. The smell of him brought back the only tether she had to this world. They were going to destroy her. Everything that she was. They would take away her magic, rip apart her spirit. They would sculpt her until there was nothing left of her. She would be bright, shiny, and new, the perfect queen; or she would be dead.

The queen of Kygem could not be Eirlys, not the person crying on the dirt floor, not the one who cared. Because to rule Kygem, Eirlys needed to give up herself. Or die. Through her tears, she laughed, hysterical and almost manic. Price pulled away to look at her, concern etching the lines on his face. Which only made her laugh harder.

"Do you know the one thing I have been doing since I arrived here? Trying to *do* something. To save the Skath. That was my only goal, and too often I had to merely try to survive. Now I've come to find out they were never going to let me have any real power, make any real changes. They have a nice little loophole to kill me anyway."

Price said nothing but wiped her tears away with his thumb. Oh Goddess, would it ever end? Even if she did survive, what would change? Her magic, her ability to heal, was the only goodness she brought to this world. If she lost that, was she nothing more than a killer? Nothing more than a deadly weapon to be wielded by those pulling her strings.

The pain. Price. She had known for a long time that something bothered him, but chronic pain was not what she had been expecting. She was no stranger to it, but no masochist either. Eirlys shuddered.

She tried to think of what she could do, if anything. Going back to Kestrya would put Aydra on the throne early—Deryn's voice screamed in her head. Pass on the legacy. She might have weeks, if she was lucky, months to teach Aydra... what? How to be a good person? In truth, nothing Aydra had done was worse than Eirlys on a good day.

But Aydra cared nothing for the Skath who would continue to die.

"Please talk to me," Price said, pulling her away from her wondering mind.

Eirlys stared at the palms of her hands. Teardrops mingled with sweat, beading in wrinkles threading her skin. 'You are going to hate me,' he had said.

"I don't hate you," she whispered, catching his eyes.

With all the force she had, she kissed him. Price groaned, from need or from relief she didn't know. Her hands wrapped themselves into his hair, holding onto reality as their lips moved together. Eirlys pulled her legs from under her, never breaking their kiss, to wrap them around his waist, setting herself in his lap. His hands reached around to grab her wrists and suddenly he wasn't kissing her, and her arms were above her head locked together with Price's hands.

"Wait," he said. His voice strained, as if stopping dug a knife in his gut.

"Why?" Eirlys asked, feeling the uncomfortable dreads of rejection well through her.

"You might as well be drunk right now," Price said. Still gripping her wrists, he moved her back to the bed, but the action was anything but sexual. He plopped her on the bed with an unceremonious thump where she leaned back on her arms to gaze at him.

"No," she said, her voice small. She cleared it. "No. I'm angry, I'm terrified, but I am thinking straight. If my life is forfeit, I will not spend it wallowing, like some broken girl waiting for her execution. I am not that girl. I will not go gently."

Price smirked as he remained before her, knees almost touching. "I know."

She glared at him. "I know what I want. I will take whatever happiness life gives me. You should do the same."

"And tomorrow, the next day, next week, will you feel the same?"

Sitting fully up, Eirlys crossed her arms. "Between the two of us, Price, I am not the one who ran away. I am not the one who pushed you out."

He flinched, and the guilt on his face cut through her. Eirlys reached for him again, standing and wrapping her arms around his waist, laying her head on his chest, and listening to the thundering beat of his heart. She gently touched his chin, guiding his lips to catch her in a kiss. Soft, almost too sweet, but with need too, powerful and surging.

"Be my escape," she breathed against his mouth.

## CHAPTER THIRTY-FOUR

### PRICE

Her breath caressed his lips. No part of her touched him, and his pain flared, almost gently. As if it was reminding him of all he could gain from this, all he needed from her was a single touch. Her request lodged in his mind and tore through every carefully laid wall he tried to put up. How had this woman so thoroughly imbedded himself into his every waking thought, dug so deeply he could not say no to her?

"Eirlys," he said.

Her eyes shot open. Venom filled them, turning the already green poisonous.

He chuckled and was sure if looks could kill, he would be dead. He reached for her anyway, tracing a finger along her jaw. For a moment, he just reveled in the feel of her. With nothing else to distract him, all he could do was marvel at the softness of her skin, the way her breath caught.

Oh gods, he wasn't sure he could do this. If he let himself

be with her, her magic as dark and sweet as it was now, would he survive when her magic was no longer hers?

Perhaps he was a masochist because of what he said next.

"Not here," he said.

Not in a small one-bedroom quarters where he had tried to end his life.

She nodded and swallowed. "Back to the castle?" A frown creased her brow. How could she walk back into that castle, back into the place that wanted to see her destroyed? No, he would not ask that of her.

He shook his head.

His room in the barracks felt out of the question, too. They were barely private, and there were noises he was dying to hear her make. Which also made any inns in the city out of the question.

An idea struck him, and he was shoving aside barrels to get to a closet. He was grateful to find a few blankets inside. He snagged them, hoping they didn't smell too awful.

"Take it easy. You are still in recovery," Eirlys said, grabbing the blankets from him.

He looked at her, a smirk blooming across his face. "I have no intention of taking it easy on you."

Oh, the way her cheeks flamed. But her eyes grew dark.

"Tell me this place is close by?" Her voice was low and husky.

Need rushed through him, but he tamped it down, so he didn't just take her in the woods, all thoughts of finding a decent spot trying to flee from his mind.

"If I can find it," he teased.

The afternoon sun was barely warming the air, keeping it on this side of comfortable. Though Eirlys didn't feel cold in the same way and Price could stay warm with his magic, he was grateful for the last remnants of heat.

He glanced over at Eirlys, holding a bundle of wood they had taken from the room. She insisted on carrying it, even after his little joke.

"It's just up here," he said, pointing east of their current trajectory.

The sound of falling water finally reached them and over the next rise, the waterfall came into view. It wasn't a grand fall on a river but large enough the water had eroded the limestone from underneath, creating a decent sized cave behind the thundering flow. Eirlys gasped as she took in the clear pool of water beneath them.

"It's beautiful," she said, though a look of confusion crossed her face.

"Follow me."

The bottom of the waterfall spilled out into a vast but comfortable space. It may have been a bit humid, a bit rough, but it was sequestered away. No pesky sisters would bother them, and hopefully no Gods would be rude enough to interrupt. Though maybe they would want to. He wasn't sure how accurate they could be. Could they shimmer into a cave they didn't know about?

"Price?" Eirlys asked, still holding the bundle of the wood.

"There," he pointed to a spot in the middle.

She placed the wood down, not seeming to care that dirt and moss clung to her arms and shirt. Eirlys walked the circumference of the cave, her hands trailing along the walls.

"I love it," she whispered. Maybe for him, maybe not. He smiled anyway.

Price arranged the logs, igniting his magic. Blue flames

flickered to life, holding steady. The logs would hold his magic for as long as they burned. The sounds of Eirlys spreading out blankets filled the cave, just audible over the crackling wood.

He did not turn to look at her. Not yet. Right now, he needed a moment, the calm before a raging storm he never wanted to end. She might end up drowning him, so he'd never breathe again, his only tether to this life held by a woman who so thoroughly wrecked his entire being. But before that, before he committed an act that there was no coming back from, he needed a breath. To pray, maybe for the last time.

He did not reach out to Nym, or Gyda. How could he? What was he supposed to do? Ask his Gods to absolve him of his misdeeds? As if Eirlys was something to be cleansed from, something to regret. The very thought made him recoil. While he knew she had killed, tortured and done many things to ensure her and her loved ones' survival, Eirlys was not the ice-cold shadow queen they thought she was.

Her heart wasn't cold; it burned. With passion, with love, with desire. She wanted with everything she had and gave everything for a cause she believed was right and just. And when that cause was the lives of millions of infants, even if they were Skath, Price could no longer turn his back to their suffering. She had taught him that.

But he did not reach out to Zoasis or Gylena either. He was not sure they would be there for him. Even if Eirlys believed in them, he wasn't sure he had the same faith. Why would they allow this to happen for so long and not intervene? If the Skath were worth the same as Klara to them, where were they? Would they intervene when Eirlys was placed on that table, her magic torn from her spirit?

Staring down at the fire as blue as his eyes, he realized who he wanted to pray to. Who he wanted to worship.

With a determination and tranquility he hadn't felt

perhaps ever, he stood. He unclenched his fist and splayed out his fingers.

Then he turned around.

She was sitting on the ground, her legs crossed in front of her. A piece of blonde hair fanned across her face, the bright purple tip looking almost indigo in his firelight. It took him back to the days when they first met, her hair bright and blue, like his eyes. It was after that kiss when she first changed it. Anything to get him off her mind, he supposed.

Price walked to her, watching those eyes follow him from underneath her eyelashes. He reached down for her, the first time he would allow her to touch him since they left the small rundown shack. To bring him the relief he so desperately sought. How foolish of him to think that he could run from her. He was enamored. So far gone over the edge of her that he no longer saw the lofty heights where his Gods once stood.

She took his hands, and he lifted her to her feet. And he breathed. Each time felt like it was the first time they had touched. Her magic, dark and sweet, bloomed across her face before fading back beneath the freckles. He would not think about when that darkness faded forever, about when the Gods would strip away the last bit of solace he had on this planet. As long as he still had her, in the end, nothing else would matter. As long as she survived.

She stood in front of him, her breathing becoming shallow. Her throat bobbed.

"Are you nervous?" he asked. His voice was gruff, and her eyes widened a bit at the sound.

"Yes," she admitted. "You're looking at me like I am... " She blew out of breath. "Like I'm someone worthy of your devotion."

"Are you not?" One thumb stroked over her knuckles, slow and soft. He lifted his other hand to cup her jaw in his palm.

She leaned into it and whispered, "No."

A wicked smirk played across his face. "I will prove to you just how worthy you are to me."

And like the evil little thing the gods thought she was, she flashed him a smile that promised a dark and naughty night ahead of them.

"Who in the void could say no to you?" she breathed. Her fingertips brushed the stubble along his jaw. "Then revere me, Price. Idolize me until I cannot breathe. Until the only prayer on my lips is your name."

Price crushed his lips against hers, pushing her back against the cave wall. His magic flared, the flames behind them jumping with his pleasure. He groaned against her mouth, the feel of her tongue probing his bottom lip sending him into dizzying spirals. She would be his undoing—and he wanted, so desperately, to be unmade.

He broke off from her mouth, trailing kisses down her neck, nipping at the pulse beneath her skin. One of her hands was clenched in his hair, the other gripped on his shoulder. He could feel her nails through the thin fabric of his shirt, a pleasurable pain he didn't think was possible.

When he got to the collar of her shirt, he made a growl of displeasure. She let out a breathy laugh, ridding herself of the shirt and leaving her body exposed to the firelight. A soft azure glow painted her skin, nearly blending in the freckles along her clavicle. They softly faded from her chest as his eyes veered lower. He nearly sank to his knees then and there, but he wanted to take his time. His mouth found the exposed flesh of the top of her breast. And when his tongue trailed against her nipple, she arched her back into him, moaning his name.

She grabbed onto his shirt. "Off," she begged. And who was he to deny her?

She kept her hands on his chest as he lifted the shirt above his head. Perhaps, she needed the contact too, but some part of him realized that she was probably attuned to his pain. A healer through and through.

"Much better."

"Indeed," he said, admiring her half naked body.

Then his mouth was on hers again, trailing down her neck, stopping for a moment at her breasts before continuing lower. He nipped at the skin just above her waistband. She jumped and threw her head back against the wall.

"Fuck," she whispered when Price began to undress her the rest of the way. "Fuck."

Then he was kneeling in front of her, hands placed on either side of her hips, staring at her naked glory. His Dark Grace spread out before him as he gazed up at her.

Her eyes smoldered, a heat that wound its way into his core. He was not afraid of burning, of being consumed by the flames. Nothing in the entire world could have stopped him from jumping into the fire. Together, they paused in this moment, in this piece of paradise they carved from blasphemy and wickedness. His goddess stood before him, and he mourned the lost time when he could have made this stunning creature his. He should have worshiped her from the moment they touched.

Then his hands moved, one around her body, cupping her ass firmly. The other brushed his thumb against her folds, torturously slow. She sucked in a breath, never taking her eyes off him.

"Don't let me fall, Price," she whispered.

"I'll catch you," he said, because he had already fallen.

Then without warning, his tongue plunged into her. By the gods, she was already so wet, and warm. Her gasp of pleasure turned into a delicious moan as he found her clit. He flicked his tongue over her, gauging her reaction. Each small, fast stroke brought her panting; long, slow licks had her grinding against his mouth, her hips thrusting forward.

His own body responded. Already, he stretched against his pants, aching and yearning for her with a delectable type of pain.

Her fingers were tangled in his hair, keeping his pace exactly as she needed it. He let her lead as she rode his tongue, faster and harder. Her legs began to tremble, and he used his other arm to hold her steady, to keep her standing.

Eirlys moaned his name until, as promised, it was prayer spilling from her lips, over and over again. "Price, Price, Price." Her fingers tightening in his hair was his only warning just before she came. She bucked against him, head thrown against the cave wall, her back arching. Her legs trembled and a string of curse words flew from her mouth. He felt the moment her legs gave out, catching her in his arms.

Price lifted her from the ground, cradling her against his body. Blinking back from semi-unconsciousness, she reached to touch his face and tried to speak. She let out a chuckle, swallowed and tried again after catching her breath.

"Price?" His name was a question on her lips.

"Hmm?" he asked.

"Fuck me," she demanded.

He wanted to call her needy, to tease her a little bit, but he was beyond humor. He laid her against the bedding, kissing her while her hands deftly undid the laces of his pants. Together, they shimmied them off his body, so he was bare, hovering above her. Her fingers were gently tracing patterns across his chest and her eyes were not on his.

"Eirlys. Look at me," he breathed. She glanced up at him. "Good girl."

Then he was pushing into her and though she was wet and oh-so-fucking ready, he took his time while watching her eyes widen, her breath catch. Her hands became wild and erratic as the sensation took over her.

When he was fully buried within her, he paused, to catch his breath and to feel. Just fucking feel the rightness of it all. Sex before always had an edge of pain to it. That never ceasing painful burn, a constant visitor to his pleasure. But with her, here and now, there was just the feel of her around him, warm and slick. There was the pressure of her hand on his chest, the other now thrown over her head. He could focus, be in the moment in a way that had never been possible for him before.

How had he once believed the gods had given him a gift when all they had done was destroy who he should have been?

She watched him with a careful expression on her face.

"What is it?" he asked.

"Don't think about them," she said after a moment. "Let's escape together."

"Yes," he said. He pulled almost completely out of her before sliding back in. "Yes, Eirlys."

He knew he wouldn't last long, not for the first time with someone that could fully erase his pain. But her first orgasm made her more ready, and her body reacted quickly. She was panting in mere minutes, her nails digging into the flesh on his back. Again, there was that perfect sensation of painful pleasure, and he relished in it. His rhythm became stunted, and he cursed, willing himself to hold on just a little bit longer.

She reached up and pulled him in for a kiss, their bodies moving in time, deliciously close to each other. Then she whispered against his mouth the words that were his undoing. "Come for me, Price."

As if he could ever say no to her.

Stars exploded in his vision, hot and bright. She bucked under him as she cried out his name through her own orgasm. Her body tightened around his cock, another round of pleasure

317

threatened to pull him into unconsciousness before he collapsed on top of her body, both slick with sweat.

Price lay there, listening to the thundering heartbeat play in Eirlys's chest beneath his ear.

"Do you worship all of your gods like this?" Eirlys asked, humor alight in her words.

Price's breath hitched because once he had worshiped a goddess like this. Before the thought of Nym's body would leave him breathless. Now, he wanted to wash the memory of her away.

"I only have one goddess now," Price breathed.

Eirlys's chest moved in silent laughter, too spent to laugh wholeheartedly. And although Price was making a joke, he wondered if she knew how true that statement really was.

.

# CHAPTER THIRTY-FIVE

## EIRLYS

E irlys hadn't slept, and lead weighed down her limbs. In the afterglow of sex, she had been content to settle in the nook of Price's arm. Her finger trailed the line of his chest and he dozed. Her mind allowed her to escape for a moment, but now the crushing weight of what had been revealed to her strangled itself in thick knots around her thoughts.

She tried to think through the agony of the revelation. Hate coursed through her but none of it was for Price. He had not chosen to change his magic; he had not chosen to become a chess piece in their games. He nearly took his own life rather than be torn between her and his religion. She knew that feeling deep within her, that sense of needing to prove loyalty to a realm which had saved him.

Her mind and heart battled inside her. Fear drained her desire for change, her certainty that this realm needed her, that it could be changed at all. But his face, so dear to her already, called to her in a way she hadn't expected. Soft as silk, the gentle flame within her sparked to life again. Friendship, loyalty, a camaraderie between two immortals who had been destined to die and somehow lived.

Eirlys tried adjusting, but Price shifted uncomfortably until she placed her hand back on him. It might have been annoying if she weren't so terrified. She never had anyone need her like this. Price had been her first friend here, her first confidant. He wasn't scared of her, and one of the few who treated her like a human.

It was the kiss which had doomed them. She tried to imagine kissing someone who brought so much relief it was intoxicating, but she couldn't. The implications of last night had not been lost on her, to have that pain be completely gone coupled with passion—the thought sent shivers back through her and she had to clear her mind.

If she got up and left, told the council, Price could go back home, away from her—away from his solace. There was another reason he had run from her, and she pieced it together while she lay in his arms. If she went through with this alteration, she'd either be dead, or changed. No longer a Skath to soothe him. The healer inside her knew the answer. No matter the wound, no matter the pain it might cause later, patients focused on the current pain. No matter how much you told a birthing woman that her child would make her forget the agony, she'd curse at you all the same. And even here, in Kygem, these women who tossed their Skath infants to the elements went on to have children again. They moved past the pain, although it never left.

Price woke with a start and Eirlys placed her hand back on his forearm. He smiled sleepily at her.

"Do you want to go back?" he asked. Worry etched his face.

"I'm not in a hurry, to be honest," she admitted.

He nodded and leaned back against the wall of pillows.

"Are you okay?" she asked, scooting near him so she didn't break contact.

"They didn't want me to tell you. I was explicitly forbidden to say anything."

Eirlys sucked in a breath. They often took their rules far too seriously. She didn't want to imagine the punishment which awaited Price.

"Give me your oath," she said in a moment of panic.

Price's eyes widened. "What?"

"If you become my personal guardian, any oath made to them will be null. I will rule you, command you, and I can tell you to break your silence."

Price hopped from the tangle of blankets. She expected him to run from her, but instead he knelt in front of her.

The sight of him kneeling on the floor, naked and baring his loyalty to her, nearly undid her.

"Do you know the words?" Price asked, his face carefully controlled.

Eirlys forced her eyes up, trying to focus anywhere but his sculpted chest. *Fuck.* In her vast amounts of reading, she had memorized the oath at some point. Luckily, it wasn't that different from the one she had given to August all those years ago. She called up the words from her conglomerate of memories.

"Do you solemnly swear your oath and allegiance to me, your queen?"

"I do."

"Will you remain faithful to me, and renounce and abjure all allegiance and fidelity sworn to any other person?"

"I do."

"Do you solemnly swear to protect my life even if you have to lay down your own?"

"I do."

"Will you, guardian, protect me to the end of my natural days under penalty of death or until I release you from your bonds?"

"I will."

Eirlys pulled water from the air and gently tapped a drop on Price's forehead. It glowed brilliant gold then dissipated—the vow complete.

Eirlys sighed and lowered herself back onto the makeshift bed. She patted beside her and Price crawled in.

They lay side-by-side, legs intertwined, one of Price's hands laid gently on Eirlys's bare hip. One set of hands was clasped together between them as Eirlys's finger danced delicately on his shoulder, neck, his face. His eyes were closed, and he breathed in and out gently.

She wondered when they would've told her they planned to rip out her magic and replace it, possibly killing her in the process. That would be lucky for them. They would never have to worry about her. Might as well keep prepping Aydra.

She couldn't think about it any longer. She had to maintain composure. Never had she thought about leaving—not really—until now. A new guilt settled over her, the oily feel of it coating her thoughts. If she abandoned her people now, abandoned the Skath infants, could she live with herself? By Zoasis and her daughters, she didn't know.

Death did not scare her. She'd come too close too often. Pain—well if Price could handle it then so could she. And if she left, the guilt might eat her alive. Neither death nor pain could stop her. She would fight through the pain. If she died, her spirit would fight its way back. She'd haunt the Ancients just to annoy them. Even killing her would not free them of her presence.

Her choice was made the moment her foot left the Kestryan dock. She needed to see it through.

Though she shouldn't, her thoughts turned to Price. The man lying in her arms. Twenty-five years old. A guardian because of his lack of magical control, doing his duty for his country and his religion in the only way he could. His devotion to his religion, which would make her the absolute last person he would want to be with. He must feel like he was being torn in two constantly. She could feel his heart beating underneath her ear, steady and strong. Those blue eyes snapped open, and his gaze lingered on her, warm and intense. Instead of breaking it, she leaned forward and kissed him.

When the kiss broke, Eirlys bit her lip, debating on voicing the thoughts in her head.

"You have questions?" Price guessed.

"Yes, but not the ones you think."

"Ask away. I'm an open book now."

Eirlys furrowed her brow but ignored the implications. "Do you hate your parents?"

Price didn't miss a beat. "Do you hate your parents?"

"I asked you first." Eirlys bit her cheek.

Price sighed and settled closer to her. "At first, I nearly worshiped them. The sacrifice they made for me, what they potentially gave up, the fact that I still lived seemed like a blessing."

Price's fingers convulsed on Eirlys skin. He pulled away and broke all contact. She reached for him, but he held up his hand, then stared at it like it wasn't his own.

"As I got older," he said, his Wraithmark blaring to life. Blue flames licked his hand. "I realized it wasn't their sacrifice but mine. Made for me. The pain of losing a child, is it worse than being in pain all day? Is my life worth it?"

Eirlys wanted to tell him yes, it was worth it. Because without him, where would she be? She couldn't deny Price had been instrumental in her continued existence here, that he had saved her life more than she cared to think about.

Price continued. "I got into it with my dad once, just back from guardian training and about to join my company. He said something I don't remember anymore but it set me off. I told him he should have killed me. I called him a coward, said he did everything so he would avoid his pain, never considering the pain I feel. Mom nearly whipped me when she heard us. I yelled at her, too. Things have never been the same." Price shook his head and extinguished his magic, placing his almost too hot hand back on her hip. "I should hate them. I should hate the Ancients, the council, even in some way your parents, but I don't. I didn't at least. I don't hate my parents, but the sacrifice they chose for me can never be taken back."

Price half smiled, sad and quick. "What about you? Do you hate them? The late queen and king?"

"Do you know I have a gravestone in the cemetery?"

Price shook his head.

"It's... " She waved her hands around looking for the words. "Boring. It's plain, nothing special about it. The queen's first daughter, and they couldn't spare a few extra words for what they did to me. I need to hate them, because if I don't, I don't know what that means. I yearn for a life where I grew up here, and yet I long to go back home to Kestrya. I can't let myself lose sight of what they did, because if I do, if I forget, then what? I'm only alive because my aunt is different from them. I must be different. So, I have to hate them?"

It came out as a question, and Eirlys shut her mouth, teeth clicking together.

"But you don't hate me or Brisa or Deryn?" Price prodded gently.

Eirlys leaned into his touch again. Price's fingertips caressed her cheek, and she opened her eyes, sighing.

"No, I don't. I should, I should hate everyone here. Apart from Aydra, they aren't bad people." Her weak attempt at humor was rewarded with a half grin from Price. "They are people in a tough situation. I've been there, more times than I like to count. I can pretend I'm different, but I'm not. I've done things that make Aydra's weak attempt at assassination look like child's play. Maybe I shouldn't throw daggers at Sa, you know."

Price lowered his head, tucking himself under her chin and placed his head on her chest.

"Throw all the daggers you want, Eirlys. Make them fucking bleed."

# CHAPTER THIRTY-SIX

## EIRLYS

The howling sound and the rushing of the void surrounded them as the council room appeared before her. Eirlys squinted at the brightness in the room, meant for Klara, not for her—not yet at least.

Eirlys fumbled through the morning, the weight of sorrow and regret filling her. Emptiness took over, a deep well of blackness enveloping her spirit. She tried to fight it, but the knowledge of what would be done to her made it difficult. She'd thought her mother's death had shattered her, but now she was a crumpled piece of paper discarded on the floor.

Before, when she'd accepted her role, she'd thought about changes—thought about a little bit of subterfuge to try and charm the council. She'd thought she would have decades, centuries, to rule in Kygem. Now her life might be limited to a few months or weeks. She wasn't sure. It was this unknown, the terror of the future writhing within her, whispering her darkest fears as she stood before her own council and the gods who had voted to change her life.

Eirlys took her place next to Iona. Aydra sat on her left.

The room vibrated with rage and indignation, prickling her skin and setting her teeth on edge. As if they had any reason to be mad. They had not been betrayed, lied to and deceived. Eirlys's own anger flooded her much like it had the first moment she found out. The whole world shifted from a numb calm to a righteous fury.

She wasn't trembling from fear. Today, she was a string held so tightly it began to shake. One more pull and she would snap.

Gyda stood at the head of the table. "Your Grace," she started, her tone almost placating, bordering on condensation. "First of all, we would like to issue an apology for not disclosing the true requirements for your coronation."

Eirlys sat with her hands in her lap, staring at the goddess. She would accept no apology. They weren't sorry. They were pissed they got caught.

Gyda continued, her voice a little more strained. The act must be a hard one to hold up. "We would like to formally inform you that to be crowned, we will require you to be altered. We cannot have a Skath on the throne."

Eirlys nodded, unable to hold on to the anger. She found that the entire realm exhausted her. "I want to know what this all entails. The procedure, the side effects. All of it. The entire truth before I will agree to anything."

"Ancient Sarna, you have the floor," Iona said.

Sarna was small, tiny, and delicate. She had all round features, round eyes, round lips, a button nose, and tight ringlet curls of pure white falling around her face. Sarna, the Ancient that created a terrible, perverse magic.

Eirlys turned her eyes away to keep from staring at her.

Sarna didn't avoid looking at Eirlys. A burst of howls and

wind, a faint shimmer, and Sarna appeared beside Eirlys. Standing, Sarna's form was a head taller than Eirlys sitting.

"Draw on your magic for me, lovely," she crooned. Her voice was like liquored honey, sweet and biting.

Eirlys didn't recall ever hearing her speak before. Now she wished she never had. Shuddering on the inside, she never wanted to be called 'lovely' again. In this bright, horrid room, drawing on her magic was a sluggish pull. Her Wraithmark deepened in the blazing light. Sarna grabbed Eirlys hand.

The goddess took a deep breath, as if she were smelling Eirlys's magic. "Fascinating. A strong magic within you, feisty spirit, too, held in check by that mind of yours. Brilliant but unsure. Fierce and uncontrolled. Hmm. A good candidate, I believe."

"Will she live?" Iona asked.

"Does it matter?" Eirlys snapped, snatching her hand back.

The entire chamber stilled. Not a single immortal breathed.

Iona's eyebrows raised, amused. "Perhaps."

Sarna giggled, light and free, so at odds with tension in the room. "I do believe she has a fair chance. She does have a look of defeat about her though, and the character of the specimen will matter greatly."

"Do you want to live, Eirlys?" Iona asked pointedly.

"Yes. Of course," she said. And she meant it. Laying down her life for a cause was different than lying down and accepting the inevitability of her death. She had fought for her life and the small spirit sitting inside her flared to life. She wanted to live, too.

She sighed. "I think I will be less disappointed if I antici-pate my death though."

Sarna laughed. "Logical, this one." Her giggle was grossly childlike.

Iona shook her head. "That's enough, Sarna."

Sarna bowed to the other ancient and even to Eirlys before practically skipping back to her seat.

"Eirlys, do you have any questions right now?"

"I have a request," Eirlys said. Iona gestured for her to go on. Eirlys pointed at Sarna. "She is to never touch me again. She can have someone else do it—a healer, you, I don't care."

Iona furrowed her brow. "We will see what we can do. Will you deny the alteration if she is involved?"

Her skin crawled with invisible insects at the ghost of Sarna's little girl laughter. "Yes," she said, determined.

"Very well. We will start preparations."

"How soon?" Eirlys asked.

Iona thought for a second. "It must be before your coronation. The alteration requires time, obsidian that has been untouched by sunlight, and glass that has sat under the full moon for five consecutive cycles. I think early summer would be the latest, and we want this to go right, so delaying as long as possible will give us the best chance to prepare everything properly."

Early summer. Eight months to live as herself, or to live at all.

"There's something else," Iona said.

The edge in her voice made Eirlys's eyes narrow at the goddess. What more could they take from her?

Iona reached for Eirlys, and she gripped the goddess's hand with caution. Aydra stepped up and Iona pulled them into the void.

In the brightly lit atrium of a healing station, the crowd of immortals stopped, gasping in shock before dropping into bows. Iona ignored them, heading straight to the receptionist.

"Stay here, I will be back. We might as well tell everyone at once."

Iona came back gripping Price, Brisa, and Deryn. Price did

not look at the goddess, but he clenched his fist together. Eirlys wanted to run to him, to touch him and dispel the look of pain and desperation from his face. But she didn't know what Price had told them, if anything.

"We are going to the basement," Iona told the receptionist gently, touching her forehead.

"Yes, oh Revered One," the woman said and gestured to a door on the left side of the atrium.

The door was unobtrusive. Eirlys hadn't noticed when she'd scanned the room. Heads remained in their astute bows as she walked through the door.

Iona led the way with a brisk sense of purpose. The power rolling off her weighed on Eirlys and when she glanced at Aydra, her normally smooth face glistened with sweat.

"Unfortunately, we were hoping to tell you this in a different way. There is a delicate balance to these sorts of things. Your... " Iona pursed her lips together in a motion so human it took Eirlys aback. Her eyes flicked to Price. "Guardian insisted he come with you."

"Isn't that his job?" Eirlys asked, trying to tamper her rising temper.

"That boy protects you far more than he should. He will need to be dealt with," Iona said.

"That boy took an oath to protect me at all costs. You will not touch him," Eirlys said, grabbing Iona's arm. Aydra gasped.

Iona peered at Eirlys's hand upon her wrist with a calmness which boiled Eirlys's blood. As if she were merely removing a child's grip, she pried her hand away.

"Your Grace needs to watch her tone when speaking to a god."

Iona's power flooded the stairwell, her Wraithmark burned red as immense power crashed down upon Eirlys. The pressure was so forceful Eirlys could barely squeeze breath into her lungs.

"Rattle your cage all you want little Skath girl. But before you begin smashing those bars, remember who we are. I am not yours to command."

Iona let go of Eirlys's hand and Eirlys dropped to the ground to catch herself, inadvertently kneeling. She kept her head bowed even though her power rushed to the surface of her face. Little Skath girl indeed.

"Come and see the fate that awaits you if you are not strong enough to handle the alteration," Iona said, turning in a great sweep of gray cloak.

Aydra tried to help Eirlys to her feet, but Eirlys shoved her out of the way, moving briskly to stay in front of her. She had no power here, but she was not about to let her little sister walk before the future queen.

"Although most alterations do fail—Price being the only true success—there are some Alters who still live."

"What happens to those who survive but aren't 'of use'?" Eirlys asked, spitting the rotten words from her tongue. People weren't meant to be used like tools or toys to be discarded once their purpose had been served.

Iona smirked and pushed the door open. Eirlys, and those following, entered a bright hallway, alight with RaGlass. Two Va bowed to their goddess and their princesses. The looks on their faces were indiscernible as they glanced at each other.

"Access is limited to those who will keep their mouth shut. There is no need to cause panic to the public," Iona said.

Eirlys swallowed. A moan came from somewhere in the distance, and Eirlys turned her attention to the hallway lined with thick, heavy doors containing reinforced glass windows barely bigger than her hand. A woman's face appeared in one. Her hand beat on the door, bloody and raw.

"Curse it," one of the Va said, rushing to the door.

Eirlys followed behind. The Va opened the door with a key and grabbed a hold of the woman. With practiced ease she pinned the bloody patient to the ground. The woman screamed, raged, and even tried to turn around and bite the attendant. Eirlys watched, unbelieving, as the insane woman fought with the healer. The patient's Wraithmark ignited across her features and the room trembled. Her eyes turned animal, feral slits forming in her amber irises and a forked tongue escaping her mouth. Thankfully, the transformation ended there.

"Mei, I told you, you have to keep your spike in. Otherwise, you have to take a dose" the Va said.

"Fuck you, Kalyn," the woman on the ground spat, actual venom searing into the concrete ground.

Eirlys stepped back, shocked.

The Va rolled her eyes as the other healer, a Va man, ran in. They restrained Mei together and shoved obsidian liquid down her throat. Eirlys's chest clenched, remembering the feeling of obsidian within her body, the helplessness and the pain.

As the woman choked and swallowed, her power died, dimming her face as her eyes and tongue returned to normal. Mei mumbled incoherently as Kalyn helped her back onto her bed. Her eyes closed and she drifted into sleep.

"She's insane?" Eirlys asked.

The female Va pursed her lips. "Technically, although the term is frowned upon here. We call them afflicted."

An affliction: a term they used when referring to her being Devoid as well. How similar was the process between crossing the Barrenlands and this alteration?

"I'm Antony and this is Kalyn," the man said.

Kalyn finished bandaging Mei's hand and picked up the bloody spike.

"Follow me, Your Grace," Kalyn said, stepping out of the room.

Eirlys followed her out, watching as she carefully lock the door behind them.

"We have seven afflicted here. They range in age from twenty to twenty-five. Since I have worked here, twenty Skath were brought to us with the help of the Goddess Sarna. When they started dying, we were told not to tell anyone, and we didn't. When parents brought back out of control children—Ta causing earthquakes, Sa that stole breath—we knew something was awry."

"Why only those ages?" Although Eirlys guessed before Kalyn answered.

"It was forbidden after the twenty, well twenty-one, patients didn't do well."

"Out of the twenty-one, one is living, his mind intact. There are seven in here and the others"—Eirlys swallowed— "They died?"

Kalyn stopped in front of another door. "Yes, thirteen dead, the seven who live here were all under a year old when they were altered. The others were between two years and fifteen years of age."

As the knowledge dawned on Eirlys that someone had hidden their Skath child for fifteen years in Kygem, Kalyn opened the door.

"This is Fern. She is one of our more aware residents."

The woman, Fern, sat on a small bed, her hands folded in her lap. A faint whiff of burning hair scented the room. Fern's locks were singed in places, shorter and longer in places, along with some newly healed bald spots.

Fern's eyes darted to meet Eirlys, and she tore her gaze away from the woman's mangled head, embarrassed. The Ra inclined her head in a simple bow. "If I had known I was meeting royalty today, I would have dressed better."

Her hand ran through her hair, trying to ruffle it as she would have if it had been long and thick enough to push out of her face.

"I'm sorry about how I look, Your Majesty. I used to have beautiful hair, but instead of burning Kalyn or Antony, I burn myself."

Someone's quiet gasp came from behind Eirlys. She had completely forgotten about her audience.

"Fern, you don't need to worry about how you look," Eirlys said.

Fern smiled. Her Wraithmark grew bright, and she gasped. Flames flashed in her eyes before she slumped forward, power extinguished.

"Pardon me, Your Grace. My visions are weak, worthless things, but they try to come anyway."

Eirlys braced herself on the side of the door, plastering a fake smile on her face.

"My magic doesn't work right either. You know I'm Va, but I can't even heal myself."

Fern thought about it for a moment. "Can you heal others?"

"Yes, I can."

"If I can be so bold, Your Grace, that's truly all that matters."

Tears pricked at Eirlys's eyes. "Yes, it is."

Eirlys rose, her body aching from the nights spent with Price and her recovery from her poisoning. Eirlys followed Kalyn out and met the other residents of the hospital— another Ra, two Ta, a Sa, and a Va. This last man was only allowed to be glimpsed through the window.

He raged in his room, his Wraithmark brightened to a

blaring hot light, matching the boiling water he sent flying into the walls. He burnt himself and healed, watched the blisters disappear and the skin turn from red to pink. When his eyes met Eirlys's through the window, he lobbed ice against the glass, making Eirlys jump back and draw on her power.

Everything turned quiet. The Va having a fit quieted, someone else murmured softly in her room, and Fern came to stand at the window to watch Eirlys. Eirlys gently released her power and the quiet remained. A small respite for those afflicted.

Then Fern screamed. Flames erupted from the Ra, blasting enough heat through the hallway that it caused the air to wave.

Eirlys turned and tried to walk back toward the girl.

"No, Eirlys, no," Price said, his face going pale. He grabbed her wrist. "You are not going into a room with an insane immortal! She's a Ra. She could torch you in a moment."

Eirlys let him drag her down the hallway. Far enough away that she hoped her words wouldn't be overheard.

"Price, I have to try," Eirlys argued. She raised the arm he was touching. "If I can help her, even for a moment. If it helps your pain, why wouldn't it help her?"

Iona widened her eyes, and Brisa stared between the two of them.

Price ignored them. "Eirlys, when you let her go, her pain will flare back ten times as strong. It might take her over the edge."

Eirlys stopped. The comfort also brought more pain in its absence. Void him.

"Why didn't you tell me?" she snarled back at Price.

Price didn't answer right away. "Because I don't care, but she might."

"I care."

"I'm sorry. I should have told you," Price said.

Eirlys didn't have time for a wordy retort, so she clenched her mouth shut and proceeded back down the hallway.

Kalyn held the key and when Eirlys nodded, she turned the key and backed far away.

Eirlys entered the room.

Fern's eyes shot up and fire flashed towards Eirlys as soon as she crossed the threshold. She drew on power quickly and doused the flames. Price hissed.

"Skath," Fern spat like a curse. Fire dangled from her red, blistered fingertips.

"I'm here to help you," Eirlys said.

"You cannot help me," Fern said.

"I can heal you," Eirlys said, pointing to Fern's hand.

"It doesn't hurt. It helps me," Fern said.

"How does it help, Fern?"

Fern shrugged and paced again.

"Fern, can I touch you?" Eirlys asked.

"Why?" Fern asked, still pacing.

"I think it might help you," Eirlys said. "I have a friend, he's like you. My magic helps him."

Fern's eyes flicked over Eirlys's shoulder to look at Price in the doorway. "He's mad at me."

"No, he's mad at me," Eirlys said.

"Why?"

"He thinks I am putting myself in danger."

"Am I dangerous?" Fern asked.

"I don't know. Not on purpose."

Fern stopped moving. "I don't know what to do anymore. Some days, it feels like I'm okay, some days I think I will get out of here. But some days, the pain becomes one with me and I burn and burn and burn and burn... "

Fern beat her flamed hand onto her head catching her already scorched hair on fire. "... and burn and burn."

Eirlys grabbed her wrist, ignoring the lick of the flames, and Fern stopped. Everything stopped. The light from her face faded, the fire disappeared. Fern's face went slack. The room stilled for one brilliant moment as she relaxed, her pain erased.

"Thank you," she said softly as light started glowing from within her. "I'm free."

Fern's skin broke apart like the earth, revealing the molten golden core of her spirit escaping. The light inside crackled.

"No!" Eirlys cried, reaching to grab her with both hands.

Arms wrapped around her waist, pulling her away. She tried to twist out of Price's hold. She beat on his grip and screamed as he dragged her from the room. The door shut and Price struggled backwards when the explosion hit the door and blew it open. The flames descended on them and Eirlys threw her arms upwards. Ice shielded Price and Brisa, the only two close enough to be in danger, as the inferno tore into the hallway and vanished within moments.

Tears fell to the concrete floor and Eirlys let go of her magic. Glass shards littered the tile, the magic within them building and settling into the fragments. Fern's magic had created RaGlass. Eirlys reached out to grab one, but Brisa's arm shot out to stop her.

"Who knows what magic is concentrated in there."

Eirlys got up on shaking legs. She stepped into the smoldering, black room.

"I tried," she whispered.

No body remained, only the charcoaled remains of a shattered woman who had never experienced a moment of solace. When Eirlys had delivered the first truly sane moment, Fern had taken her life to find peace in the void.

But all Eirlys could think was that this was her future.

Insanity, pain, or death awaited her at the end of this alteration.

# Chapter Thirty-Seven

## Price

P rice kept expecting Eirlys to break down. He watched her on the ride home, her green eyes staring out the window, transfixed on the landscape. Did she see any of it, or was she replaying Fern's demise in her head repeatedly? The Alters, others like him, were so destroyed that their magic spiraled out of control to the point of insanity. Price was truly blessed compared to them.

He walked her to her room. She still hadn't said anything, and he worried about her.

"Eirlys," he said, softly.

She blinked at him as if awakening.

He wanted to ask if she was okay, but of course, she wasn't. No one would be. She didn't say anything, her eyes unfocused.

"Eirlys."

This time he grabbed her hand. The feeling of relief was shadowed by how cold her hands were and how badly they were shaking. He pulled on his magic, heating his palms, and placing her fingers between them.

"Talk to me," he begged.

Maybe he should run out and grab another healer to check on her. He knew the signs of shock, any soldier did. But what could he do when the wound was her own future, her own demise?

"All I have," she started, her lips barely moving, "in the goddess forsaken realm, is me. I am the only thing I can control here. And now they want to take that away. Take away this." She tapped her temple.

Her voice grew stronger as she talked. She raised her free hand and slapped it across the side of her face where her Wraithmark would bloom.

"All I am. All of me. Burned away to become some mutilated version of myself. Kygem has taken so much. A part of my magic, my fertility and I gladly gave it."

Price flinched from the words, but she didn't notice. Or didn't care.

"I can't walk into that alteration, Price," she said. "No matter what I told Iona. The idea of losing my mind, losing my sense of self. I can't. I can't. I can't."

The last word came out in a strangled sob, and she collapsed against him. All the tears and anguish of the day spilled over her cheeks. Her fingers dug into his shirt as her knees finally gave out. He helped her to the floor, gathering her in his arms.

Price's heart ached. He needed to do something, but what power did he have with the gods? He wasn't about to change the mind of five-thousand-year-old beings. But he could get her out.

The thought came to him. So unbelievably simple. *Get her out.*

"Eirlys," he said her name again. "Leave."

She stopped crying. "What?"

She gazed at him, sitting up fully, and wiping her face. "What did you say?"

"Run," he said. "Leave Kygem. Leave the castle. Go back home."

"Price." She rubbed her palms on her thighs in a nervous gesture. "There are people here who need me. Skath infants being born and killed every day."

But her words lacked the strength he expected. The drive that had kept her going for all these months. She said them because it's what she thought she should say. For these few months, those thoughts were the only thing that had kept her going.

"How can you tell me to leave them?" she asked.

Price reached forward and placed his hand on either side of Eirlys's face. "Because this, between my hands, is the only thing in this world that matters to me. This mind, this face, this body. You are all I care about. If this means that you live, that you survive, then I will do what it takes to make sure that happens. I did not forsake my gods to tell you about this, only to watch you die. If you want out, I'll get you out."

She stared at him, her mouth popping open in surprise. What he said sounded awfully like a confession, but he didn't take it back. He meant it.

"Okay," she said. Springing up, she paced back and forth in the room she had furnished. The room she had planned to stay in until her coronation. The room that was once her prison.

Price counted her paces. When he reached a hundred, he stopped her. "Tell me what you are thinking, please."

"Did you truly mean it?" she asked. "That you would do anything to get me out?"

He nodded.

"Follow me," she said.

She grabbed his hand and Price followed Eirlys out the door and nearly out of the castle before he pulled her back.

"Take a cloak," he murmured. "It started to snow on our way back."

She snatched the cloak from the wall and grumbled, "What's the point of having a Ra around if he won't keep me warm?"

Price's eyes widened, but he smiled at her joke, eternally grateful that she had some purpose again. Even if that purpose meant leaving him.

He trailed behind her as she made her way to the cemetery. By the time they reached the clearing, a dusting of snow blanketed the entire graveyard. Price pulled on his power to warm him up.

"Since Elisha Pendry, there have been no Va born in the Pendry line, right, except me?"

"Yes?" Price said it more as a question than a statement, wondering where Eirlys was going with this.

"How many Va were in your company?"

Price furrowed his brow. "Two."

She let out a sharp breath. "Two, in more than a hundred guardians."

"We can barely spare Va for healing the military. Many are needed in their hometown or in the big cities, such as Alby. But why are you asking?"

Eirlys touched the top of a headstone, her fingers dragging through the snow, leaving lines of dark gray behind. "There is no indication that Skath or Klara will be inherited. But I'm wondering if Va are more likely to be Skath. And Ra more likely to Klara."

"I wasn't." Price still found it strange to talk about what

happened to him as a child with Eirlys. He had kept it a secret for so long, and those who knew rarely talked to him about it.

"That is true. And Isbeil and many other healers are Va. It is just a theory anyway."

Price gazed around the cemetery.

"What are we doing here, Eirlys?"

"Waiting," she said. And explained no further.

The sun began to set, the snow coming down harder. The first real snowstorm of the season. Price's face glowed as he kept himself warm and although Eirlys didn't appear cold, she did keep the snow off of them.

Suddenly, she perked up.

"Behave," she said.

Price strained his ears and caught the soft distant sound of footfalls on snow. The whispered crush of steps cautiously approaching.

He wasn't sure why he needed the warning until the man stepped into the clearing.

"You had to bring the proselyte. Surprised he's not sucking on one of his god's cocks," Emzelhal said.

Price saw red. And not just in anger, but in the blood that had spilled down his lover's neck as she plummeted into his arms. He saw this creep floating over her bed, when he had barely known her, and yet would have jumped off that balcony to save her life.

Flame burst from him, a torrential onslaught towards the assassin's son. Emzelhal's Wraithmark crossed his face and with a movement that spoke of boredom, he redirected the inferno into the surrounding trees. Fire cleared the snow as steam evaporated into the air.

"Stop it!" Eirlys screamed, throwing a wall of snow in between Price and Emzelhal with her on the other side.

"Eirlys," he called.

Her voice came to him, angry and annoyed. "I told you to behave."

"You could've warned me," he snarled back at her.

She sighed. "I honestly didn't know how to explain."

He believed that.

"I will put down this wall, if you promise to not roast anyone."

He nodded before realizing she couldn't see him. "Yes, fine."

He swore he could feel her rolling his eyes at him. The wall disappeared as Eirlys doused the snow over the burning trees. It hissed and sputtered against the fire before the flames were snuffed out entirely.

Emzelhal was leaning back against a tree, picking at his nails. "Again, why did you bring him?"

"Did you know?" Eirlys asked, ignoring his question.

Emzelhal looked at Price, dark blue eyes meeting light blue ones. "When he was called, I suspected."

The rage roiling from Eirlys was palpable. Gingerly, Price placed his hand on her shoulder. She tensed but didn't throw him off.

"Why didn't you tell me?"

"Why didn't he?" Emzelhal shot Price a scathing glance. "He knew. I merely assumed."

"You slit my throat for those assumptions. You knew that the death rate was so high, and you think that only I can survive it."

Emzelhal shrugged and Eirlys growled at him, but he merely smiled back at her.

"You will survive."

Eirlys didn't look convinced, and Price was completely lost.

"Can someone catch me up?"

Eirlys shook her head. "In a minute."

"Why bring me?" he muttered, but not quietly enough. Eirlys gave his shin a gentle kick.

"I need to talk to August. I assume you have a way of getting a hold of him."

That overconfident grin appeared on the man's face again. "What a coincidence. He wants to talk to you, too. In fact, we were on our way here already."

"We?" But Eirlys's question was answered as she spoke.

A woman with deep brown skin, a heart shaped face, and black curls stepped from the woods.

"Vara."

Eirlys trembled under his touch.

"It's good to see you again, Eirlys. Although, I had hoped to meet you in less dire circumstances. It seems we are doomed to only pass each other in a crisis."

"As it seems. Caden said you had transitioned before you joined the Wraiths. I was surprised to see your new appearance at Spirit Night. You look good."

A hint of admiration and something a little more laced Eirlys's voice.

Vara nodded her thanks. "I'll get him. He's eager to talk, eager to risk his life these days."

Eirlys frowned at that and reached to grab Price's hand, giving it a small squeeze. Whether she wanted comfort or thought he needed it, Price was happy for the contact.

When Vara's Wraithmark shown brilliant red, from temple to temple, Price nearly fainted.

"A goddess," he murmured, not believing his eyes.

"No," Eirlys said, sighing. "Just a Naevni."

She grabbed his hand and led them a little further away from Emzelhal, who watched them closely.

"There is a lot I must tell you and I don't have a lot of time.

What I showed you could threaten everyone I love back home. I want you to know how much I care for you, to be telling you. Even allowing you to see it. Or him."

"August," Price said, tasting the name of the southern prince on his tongue and liking the flavor. He squeezed her hand in reassurance. "I'm listening."

# CHAPTER THIRTY-EIGHT

## EIRLYS

S omeday Eirlys would sit down and tell Price her whole story. But for now, she stuck to the basics of what he needed to know. About the Naevni and the Wraiths and what truly happened at Dvasia. The look of understanding in his eyes when she told him about Emzelhal's theory. The whole time, Price let her speak, his eyes intent on her, his face rapt.

His eyes flicked up. "I believe he has arrived."

Eirlys turned to watch her beloved prince step through the trees. He looked a little more haggard than she would have liked. A coat that wasn't his own, slightly too big, draped over his shoulders. He didn't belong in this snow coated world. He belonged where the days were long and hot and humid. He belonged on the rail of a ship, on the cliffs near the sea. August was completely at odds with his surroundings.

The Shadow Guard kept their position around August, but it wasn't until their eyes alighted on Price that they pulled on their magic. Eirlys did not let go of Price's hand. She held fast as the five Skath faces deepened. Price stiffened beside her, but he did nothing else.

Eirlys took in her old comrades. Though she still loved them, still grieved for their friendships, they would not let their guard down because they knew her. Pride and admiration swelled within her.

She made a small bow to August which she hadn't done in years.

"Prince August," she said, before lifting her head and giving him a wink.

He relaxed then, although his Shadow Guard did not. As much as she wanted to run to them and fall into their arms, she was glad they were protecting August so fiercely in this enemy land.

"This is my... " she tripped on the word proselyte and settled for, "guardian. Lord Price Esana, meet Prince August Karakos, and his famed Shadow Guard."

Price bowed to him while August glanced between them, their hands intertwined. Eirlys wasn't going to let Price stand there in pain to avoid a little awkwardness. They would get to that part eventually. Besides, they needed to see Price could be trusted.

"Vara said you wanted to see me," August said.

"Same."

They stared at each other. August pushed past Rory and Caden who hissed but allowed it, clearing the distance between in three long strides. He gathered Eirlys in arms, holding her for a moment. She threw one arm around him, breathing in the scent of the sea, the scent of home.

She reached up and kissed his cheek but didn't let go of Price. When they pulled apart, his eyes flickered to their entwined hands, then back to her face. When he smiled, Eirlys didn't need words or signs to know he understood, that he approved.

*Take whatever happiness life gives you.*

August settled in to tell Eirlys the story of what he had been doing for the past few weeks.

A weight of dread fell upon Eirlys, thick as storm clouds. Skath kidnapped by an Ancient. By the same one who used to perform the Alteration. Price was crushing her hand, his anger roiling from him in waves. If he hadn't already forsaken his gods, Eirlys was sure in that moment he would have.

"Did you know?" August asked. "About what they plan to do to you?"

Eirlys swallowed hard. The words came out small and she no longer cared if she sounded weak. "I found out a few days ago. But August, there is more, and it's so much worse than just changing my magic."

By the time Eirlys finished her story, she had leaned into Price, one of his arms wrapping around her shoulders. Rory had made his way to them, but not to protect August. He gathered Eirlys in his arms. Price let her go, and she tried not to think about what it was doing to him. Her friend and lover held her, and she trembled.

"What can we do?" Rory asked.

"Get me out," Eirlys whispered but in the quiet snow-covered graveyard, everyone heard.

"What!" Emzelhal exclaimed.

Eirlys peeked around Rory to glare at him. "Do you have a problem?"

He pushed from the tree. Vara reached out to him, but he brushed her off. Caden angled her body in front of August, subtle enough that only a trained guardian would have noticed. So, her friend didn't trust Emzelhal much either.

Emzelhal ignored all of them, staring directly at Eirlys. "You are running, giving up? I never took you for a coward."

"A coward?" Her voice was shrill. She took a step toward Emzelhal. "You didn't see them, the Alters. They were beyond help. This *realm* is beyond help. Even obsidian did little to calm their fractured minds. Fuck you. Fuck Kygem. Fuck these plans. I came here to change things, but the infection that is the Ancients and this whole goddess-cursed religion are too far gone to be saved."

"Eirlys, the Skath here need you."

Magic exploded from her, her face darkening. Ice shards shot from her skin, scattering through the air. Instantly, blue flames surrounded Eirlys, turning her projectiles into harmless drops of water.

Ignoring the rest of her audience, Eirlys addressed Emzelhal through the fire. "If I die, if I lose my mind, I won't be here for anyone. In Kestrya I could help infants at the border. Imagine the Ancients with a queen who will bow to their every whim."

"That won't be your fate."

"You don't know that!"

"No, but my father died to get you here, a Skath queen. He had fucking plans for you. I have plans for you still. You need to stay and rule. You are the change we need."

Eirlys growled. "Goddess be cursed! I have a way out, a true way out. To go home, to continue to live as who I am now. How can you ask me to give this up?"

"Better than Aydra on the throne, that brat of a sister of yours. Eirlys, you must stay, until your last breath. This realm needs you. I need you! With your mark, I can get rebels lined up to help you."

A blast of wind blew through the fire and Emzelhal reached

for her, grabbing her shoulders. Price moved in a flash to her side, sword singing. Only a quick shake of her head kept Emzelhal from losing his own to Price's sword.

"What is wrong with you? I thought you wanted change as much as I did." Emzelhal shook her as Price's magic flared.

Eirlys knocked his arms off and with one solid push, Emzelhal stepped back. "I *am* fucking trying. At least in Kestrya I did some good. But I have realized staying here does nothing, I will not lose my mind for them. I will not hand the Ancients a powerful weapon."

Her face darkened again but she took a deep breath. "I'm fine, Price."

The blue flames vanished. August and Rory had backed away. Perhaps she was already losing her mind. Emzelhal threw his hands up and paced the clearing.

"There are those I can still help." She sighed and turned to her prince. "You said at least four Skath have been taken. My guess is that they have more. I have until early summer. If I can find them, I will take them with me, plus, the Alters. I must find a way to help them, maybe get them out too."

"Eirlys." Price grabbed her hand again. "What if they decide not to wait?"

"They have to prepare anyway. Iona said as much. I have time."

And yet as she said it, time shrunk to that single moment. Time. How would she be able to leave this realm to their torturous, cruel gods? Then the burned face of Fern, cracking with her own magic filled Eirlys's mind. She shuddered.

"Are you coming with her?" August asked Price.

The man jumped, his eyes going wide. He stared at Eirlys, and regret blanketed his face.

"It's okay," she said. But by the goddess, if she had known

he wasn't going to come with her she would have... But she stopped those thoughts. She couldn't make any other choice. He had suggested she leave, and she agreed.

"I can't, you know. Leave. My parents, I'm all they have and as much as I... want to, I can't leave them behind."

She bit back her words. Parents who were responsible for his pain. Parents who saved the life of their only son.

Price wound his arms around her and held her close.

"We should go," Rory said as the darkness continued to descend.

August dipped his head once. Those gray eyes bore into her.

"Go to him," Price whispered, freeing her from his grasp.

She bounded to August, jumping into his arms. He kissed her. Months without him made her greedy. Her fingers intertwined into his hair, holding him as close as possible. When their kiss broke, he placed his head on her forehead in a gesture so familiar, it cracked her heart.

"Get them out and come back to me," he whispered.

"Okay," she said, not knowing if she would keep her promise. There were so many things broken between them that adding one more didn't bother her. He kissed her gently on the nose.

Suddenly, she was in Rory's arms, who squeezed her tightly, lips pressed to the top of her head. Then the Shadow Guard followed their prince into the forest, disappearing beneath the cloak of darkness.

"Will you help me?" Eirlys asked the still pacing Emzelhal.

"I will free any Skath in this land from the clutches of those cruel gods." He snapped the words at her like a whip, like she wasn't willing to do the same thing. Like she hadn't spent her whole life defending those crossing the border.

"Is there a better place to meet?" she asked. She might not

have felt the cold, but her boots were now soaking through to her feet.

Emzelhal made a noise of acquiescence. "There is a small tavern near the river called The Glistening Branch. Meet me there in three days. Dress less like a royal." He sneered at her clothes before turning away from her and following the slowly fading footsteps of the others.

"I don't like him," Price said.

"I'm pretty sure he doesn't like himself."

"Let's get you out of those wet clothes. You may be a Va, but even you can succumb to sickness."

Back in the warmth of her room, Deryn helped Eirlys undress and took her clothes to be washed and dried. They closed the door on the two of them. A new chest lay at the foot of her bed.

"Yours?" she asked. Price nodded, not having moved from the front of the fire. "Someone was a bit presumptuous," she muttered.

Price let out a breath chuckle. "I can throw it off the balcony, if you prefer."

She rolled her eyes at him, holding out her hand. He walked towards her and into her arms.

"I'm leaving," she said. "And since you won't come with me—"

Price was already shaking his head before she finished her thought. "I'm not giving you up until the very last second."

She stared into those bright blue eyes. "Why are you staying? For your parents? You don't believe anymore. How can you move on here knowing that if you married… "

He pulled her close. "You think I'm going to move on?" He laughed against her hair, but she frowned and stiffened. "I'm joking, Eirlys."

He let out a deep laugh then and kissed her.

She playfully bit his lip, and he swore, deep and low. He grabbed her from the ground, and she let out a small yelp as she was tossed gently onto the bed. She was laughing until she saw the look in his eyes, ravenous lust. She swallowed and let herself get lost in his touch.

# CHAPTER THIRTY-NINE

## EIRLYS

T hick, white snowflakes lazily flew through the air, their twisting, turning dance lulling the sky from the torrential downpour of ice it had unleashed earlier in the day. The castle fires with their base of RaGlass flickered from purple to orange, heating the air. Once the castle burned with new flame, many attendants headed back to their quarters and a quiet hush fell over the castle.

Eirlys retired to her room. She and Price had made their way to the bed, Eirlys thumbing through the most boring book of Kygem history to date. Price snored quietly, his head resting on her thigh, one hand touching the skin of her ankle.

Absent-mindedly, her hand ran through his hair, her book half held in the other. No longer did the attendants or anyone else flinch at her power. In some ways, knowing she was leaving made her more bold, fiercer. In turn, her subjects honored her more because of it. She held audiences, traveled the last weekend of each month to different temples and revealed prophecies to them at worship. Everywhere she went, the longer she stayed and the more they saw her, the better it all became.

But that made it worse for Eirlys. She could never forget what she saw or what her destination would be if she stayed. She didn't forget about the Alters still suffering beneath the healing center. Or the guilt that clung to her every day for abandoning a people who desperately needed her.

Four more months to go before she would have to leave without the stolen Skath. No amount of digging had brought her closer to finding out where they were being held.

What she had done in that time was to learn all she could about the history of her birth realm. If she was going back to Kestrya, she was going armed with knowledge of the enemy.

According to Kygemian historians, the Skath War started with the Twin Kings, sons of the ruler of Keyva—the name of the former realm before the two continents were split between the twins. The Klara king took the reign of Kygem while the Skath King took the reign of Kestrya. Their snipes and feuding eventually lead to the Kestryan king slaughtering Kygem's royal family.

When Queen Ember Karakos, daughter of the Skath king, took the throne of Kestrya, she decreed her royal blood the true line descended from the Twin Kings.

The Pendry's had been warrior sisters, a Va, a Ra, and a Ta, all Klara, who had fought as generals in the Skath War five thousand years ago. With the help of Naevni warriors who became the Ancients, they ascended the Kygem throne. A new bloodline, a new era for Kygem with their shiny new gods.

It would be another hundred years before Kygem started killing Skath infants, but even then, they were not treated well in the north. Ember responded to the news by sending forces into Kygem. Within a few years, Queen Elisha Pendry sent the Skath Treaty to Ember, hoping to find a compromise between the realms. To save the lives of the Skath, Ember agreed. Some-time between the signing of the treaty and the first exodus, the Ancients had managed to curse the Barrenlands.

What no one knew was where or how the Ancients were created. They might use wraith as a power draw, but they were nothing like the Naevni in the south.

Eirlys sat thumbing through page after page of blood and dark deeds.

She shuddered, forcing her mind to move on. She had avoided going back to the Council, allowing Aydra to attend in her stead. Already she was loosening this realm's hold on her, letting the manacles binding her to the throne and her regal duties fade as much as she could. Soon, there would be nothing left of her here, her memory a Kenos in the Pendry castle halls. Better that than a real Kenos, as she would be if she stayed and died or went mad at the hands of the Ancients.

Had it been four months ago that she learned of her fate? She'd handled being queen; she'd avoided assassination, she'd stomached dealing with the blasted prophecies. Losing every-thing, she had endured, but the Ancients were determined to take even more from her. Every last thing that made her, her.

Price stirred beneath Eirlys's hand, and she stayed it, waiting until he settled back down. Price, the other impossible thing she had never expected. Despite his need to touch her, she never felt obligated. He never reached for her out of plain relief, but out of closeness and want. Desire flooded through her. Even after months of near continuous contact, it never ebbed. Eirlys smiled at him.

Finally, her nerves would no longer let her sit still. She gently woke Price.

"I'm going to head to the Healing Center. I haven't been to see the Alters in a while."

He blinked up at her.

"Would you like to go with me?" she asked.

"Sure," he said sitting up, but she caught the look in his eyes. It was instinct now to reach out and touch him.

"It's cold and miserable out there for a Ra. I would not begrudge your company but if you prefer to stay, I understand."

He gripped her hand tightly. "Why don't you go without me? Mei really doesn't like me."

"That's because you hover," Eirlys teased, getting up from the bed. "Do you want me to call up some obsidian for you? We also have that new imported whiskey from Karavesh. I'm going to be there for a while."

Eirlys hadn't been much, if any, help for the Alters but she tried to visit as often as her duties would allow. Only three of them out of the remaining six allowed Eirlys to touch them. More than a dozen times, Eirlys had to be dragged from the floor of their rooms after having fallen asleep with her fingers pressed to their skin.

She didn't mind. It gave her purpose. Something to do that wasn't sitting around waiting for news. August's missives were few and far between as he chased rumors of missing VaSkath throughout his realm. At least he was doing something.

"I might imbibe in a glass or two," Price said, winking at her. "But I'm okay." He flinched again.

She sighed, pulling a thick wool sweater on. She reached over to him and stroked his face. "If I could just leave my arm here, I would."

"Maybe just your magic?" he asked.

It was meant as a joke. But it tore at something in Eirlys's chest. The fact that her magic could be severed like an offending limb was not something they could escape.

"Are you going to sneak Emzelhal in again?"

Price did not approve of letting the man anywhere near the

Alters, but he couldn't deny that having another Skath made it easier to soothe them. Eirlys spent weeks getting them used to her company, enough to be able to touch them. After only a few days, he saw how ragged she was and relented on Emzelhal being allowed to help. Since Eirlys couldn't exactly just waltz into the healing center with another Skath, Vara was nice enough to shimmer Emzelhal inside.

"I doubt he'll be available on such short notice," Eirlys said. She kissed Price goodbye, nodded to the few guards she saw on the way.

Brisa and Deryn were just getting in as she walked into the entrance hall.

"Alters again?" Brisa asked.

"Want to come?" Eirlys snagged her thick fur coat from the rack.

"The snow is waist high out there," Brisa complained. "And my toes are numb."

"You could have just turned into a mink or something. They like the snow."

Brisa rolled her eyes. "Yes, well, mink smell."

"And you don't?"

Brisa threw her wet gloves at Eirlys who dodged them and left the castle before the Ta decided to throw something heavier, like the entire staircase. Her sister's laughter trailed after her into the snowy landscape.

Even with her Va powers, it took Eirlys twice the time to make it to the healing center. She rushed inside, wet and a bit frustrated. Though many people were now used to her magic, she tried not to use it when others were around. Ashur seemed particularly keen on beheading people that attacked Eirlys.

"Your Grace," the receptionist said. She was a Sa with a passion for healing, often helping with triage and stabilization if a Va was not available.

"Helene," Eirlys said, raising her hand. "I'm just going to head down for a couple of hours. If this storm is going to trap me inside, I might as well use it for something good, right?"

"Well, actually," Helene was saying.

"What?" Eirlys asked.

Helene rushed to stand in front of her, blocking Eirlys from her destination.

"Please, Your Grace. The Ancients have asked that you no longer visit the," her voice dropped to a whisper, "Alters."

"Why the fuck not?"

"I... I would never think to even ask. What they decree or why is not for us to question."

Eirlys liked Helene. She really did. One of the few people who didn't mind her shadowed Wraithmark. But right now, Eirlys wanted to punch her. The unwavering faith the Council of Ancients had on Kygem both astounded and frightened Eirlys. In Kestrya, Eirlys knew plenty of non-believers.

"Is there a reason I wasn't told this before today? I walked here in a gods-cursed blizzard."

Twisting her hands, Helene fumbled over her words. "I was just told this morning. Ancient Sarna came by and asked if you were still visiting. She thinks that it will put the wrong idea in the Alters' head and that, well, you won't be able to help them for long."

Sarna. Eirlys fumed. Looks like she was going to have to contact Vara anyway. If the gods didn't want her somewhere, then that place was somewhere she wanted to be.

"I'll be back in half an hour," Vara said as they shimmered right into an empty room.

Or it was supposed to be empty. There were two dozen rooms in the Alter facility, plus a gaming room which was rarely used and a small kitchen and eating area used by the Va's that were on duty.

They never rotated the Alters between rooms. With Fern's old room still in reconstruction due to the magical way it was destroyed, six of the rooms were occupied. Vara and Eirlys always came through this room.

It had never been occupied before.

The woman on the bed stirred, her Wraithmark shining bright like the stars.

"Please no!" she begged, sending a boiling jet of water at Vara.

The Naevni shimmered out of the way. Eirlys was surprised when she stayed in the room. Vara hadn't wanted to remain, not with the mandate from the Ancients in case they were around.

"Don't hurt me again, please."

Eirlys turned back to the woman, and when she saw her face, she desperately tried to swallow down the shock that froze her in place more surely than the storm outside. It was just so impossible that she would be here.

Aliah Saguna, Nik's wife and Ronan's mother, could not be sitting on this bed, her head in her hands, sobbing.

"Aliah?" Eirlys asked, forcing her limbs to move, to take a careful step forward. "Look at me."

"No, no," Aliah cried.

"It's okay, I'm not here to hurt you." But Aliah still flinched away. "Aliah, how did you get here?"

Aliah said nothing, her eyes wet, her magic flickering on her face.

Eirlys went to remove the gloves and Vara caught her hand.

"I don't know if that's a good idea."

"Don't fucking touch me," Eirlys snapped. "She's one of my best friends' wife. She's Kestryan."

"These are the Skath your prince mentioned," she whispered.

"One of them, at least."

"No wonder they didn't want you down here," Vara scoffed.

"I can't leave her here, Vara."

"Eirlys, we can't. If we take her out, you might expose the Naevni."

Eirlys tightened her jaw. She almost wanted to scream that she didn't care. But she did care. The longer they could hold out on the Ancients finding out about the Naevni, the better chance Kestrya had if they declared war.

So, what if she just broke Aliah out? No Naevni, no plot, just Eirlys defying the gods again.

"I need cover, a diversion."

Vara opened her mouth, probably to argue. "It's your head."

"At least unlock the door," Eirlys hissed as the Naevni left the room, shimmering through the void.

The door clicked and she turned back to Aliah. Eirlys ripped off the glove and tucked it away. She grabbed Aliah's hand. Her eyes widened and new tears of relief flooded her eyes as the painfully bright magic faded.

"Eirlys?" Aliah asked, her voice wobbling with relief.

"Hey, stay with me," Eirlys said. "Aliah, how did you get here?"

Aliah blinked. "I was on the way to pick Ronan up from my sister. She's been watching him while Nik is out with August. Someone grabbed me with another VaSkath who works at the clinic with me. Oh goddess. He died. Whatever they did, he screamed and screamed until he died. I thought I was going to die, too," Aliah recounted. "The pain, it's all I can think about every time I use my magic. I can't heal myself—I can't heal anything and I can barely conjure water. My face, it's so bright, and it hurts every time. Oh goddess, what have they done to me?"

"Aliah, Aliah. Please. Tell me where they kept you before this?"

Her brows furrowed. "Kept me?"

"Yes, where did they torture the man? Do you remember?"

"Yes. It was black. Obsidian. Everything was obsidian. No magic, only pain and then... then—light, so bright. I wanted to stay where the magic didn't hurt."

A cold splash of water doused Eirlys from head to toe. She hoped never to return to that place.

"Okay, just stay calm, alright? We're getting out of here."

Aliah appeared to be mostly lucid. She wasn't sure if this was the place where all Alters went or if she was dangerous, but Eirlys didn't care. She almost wanted to open all the doors, to set them free. But she didn't trust this goddess forsaken realm to not just execute them for the ease of it.

Eirlys put Aliah's arm around her shoulders and lifted. Aliah hissed between her teeth but once her legs were under her, she walked steadily. Shouldering open the door, Eirlys peered out into the hall. At least two Va were always stationed at the entrance but with the storm, they may have decided to staff less people. Eirlys could only hope.

"Hello!" Eirlys shouted. "Help!"

She heard the Va's startled exclamation before they were running down the hallway.

He rounded the corner, and his eyes went wide before Eirlys brought a knee into his stomach. He doubled over, that annoying little magic trying to heal him. She didn't let it, grabbing him by the nape and slamming his head into the door, once, twice before his magic sputtered out. He slumped to the floor.

"I forgot how terrifying you are," Aliah said. Her eyes appeared clearer with Eirlys around. If they could get her back to Kestrya, while she'd never be the same again, she might be able to live as well as Price has managed.

"He'll live," Eirlys said. "Come on."

Aliah followed her down the hall. Her fingers curled around Eirlys's wrist, desperate for relief. Then Eirlys cringed. The sound of the Naevni screamed through the hall. Eirlys shoved Aliah into one of the empty rooms.

"Oh goddess," Aliah said, whether from the loss of Eirlys's touch or the Ancient stalking down the hall.

Eirlys hushed her. In the dark room, Eirlys searched for a hiding place. There was a small bathroom, and a closet barely big enough to hold one person.

"If she comes in, hide," Aliah was saying.

"No."

"I'm supposed to be here. I heard them. They think I'm crazy."

"No," Eirlys repeated.

"You don't always have to be the hero," Aliah whispered.

Eirlys would have glared at her if they could see each other. "I'm not trying to be a hero. I'm... "

The Goddess walked by the door. Eirlys grabbed Aliah and pulled her back, as far into the shadows as possible. From the looks of it, it might have been Iona.

"Do not draw on your magic," she breathed. "You are a Klara now."

Aliah nodded through her trembling.

"You have to get home, to your son, to your husband." Nik would never forgive her, the Shadow Guard would never forgive her, if she left Aliah here. She'd never forgive herself.

The building around them shuddered. Eirlys barely held on —Aliah collapsed to her knees. The RaGlass in the hallway started cracking, sputtering out.

Iona cursed softly just outside the door. She didn't shimmer away though. They just heard her heels clicking down the hallway.

Eirlys leaned down to Aliah, barely breathing her instructions: get to the stairwell and escape in the chaos. After listening at the door, Eirlys slid through, holding onto Aliah's hand. She couldn't see but she trailed her fingers against the wall, stepping as gently in her snow boots as possible.

They passed one of the Alter's doors. Ra flames exploded, illuminating Eirlys and Aliah in stark contrast against the night.

Iona, down the hall, gasped. Then she shimmered.

"Run!" Eirlys screamed.

Aliah's magic split across her face, lighting the way back up the stairs, and though she cried out in agony, she kept running. Iona was a shimmer-step behind them, not able to corner them in the winding stairwell. They burst out into the atrium and mayhem greeted them. Healers were crying out orders, trying to calm hysterical patients. Helene was busy wiping the blood from someone's forehead. Eirlys felt a pang of guilt. How many people might have died so she could save her friend?

Then Eirlys remembered this was not her fault. Aliah had been kidnapped from her home, her life, her son, and husband. No rescue would have been necessary if she'd never been here at all.

She grabbed Aliah's hand and sprinted out the door. They were halfway across the plowed sidewalk when Iona shimmered in front of them.

Eirlys pulled on her magic, gathering snow and ice to her. Aliah braced herself into a fighting stance right behind her. She was the wife of a Shadow Guard; she could hold her own. Though the goddess could shimmer away, she could not step closer. A ring of pointed diamond sharp icepicks surrounded them like a shield.

"I just want to talk," she said. Iona dropped her power and looked Aliah up and down. "I don't mean to be rude, but who in the void are you?"

"You don't know?" Eirlys asked, skeptical.

"No, I truly do not. I swear on my godhood."

Eirlys swallowed.

"Can I kill her?" Aliah's voice was strained. Tears streaked down her cheeks. "Do you know what they did to me!?" she yelled. An ice spike shot forward, but Iona shimmered out of the way and back. "They did me last. So, I knew what pain awaited me, what horrors were coming. And all I thought of was that my son needed his mom. I could not leave him. Even when the void called to me." She pushed her magic into the ice again. "I wanted to die."

"I'm so sorry," Iona said when she shimmered back. "You know her?" she guessed.

Eirlys nodded. "She's one of my friends. Your fellow gods have been stealing VaSkath from Kestrya to test the alteration."

Iona, looked distrustful for a moment, then a sort of resignation stole over her features.

"You need to go, Eirlys. I was told to come because Price mentioned you were here. But if the other Ancients went to him... " There was pity in her tone. "Eirlys, he's the only successful Alter ever made."

Eirlys stared at the goddess.

"Go." The goddess shimmered away and did not return.

Eirlys grabbed Aliah's hand, blasting through the snow and ran.

# Chapter Forty

## Price

It took Price a moment to realize that the screaming sound of the void did not mean the Naevni he was becoming increasingly used to. The sound meant one of his Gods; no, not one *his* gods, just one of *the* gods.

Only now could he admit to himself that he no longer claimed them.

He'd fallen asleep after Eirlys left, the pain not letting up for even a second. Sleep brought him a modicum of relief. He sat up straight, feeling every nerve catch fire. Some days he felt as if his skin would blister from the heat searing just below the surface.

Nym stood in the center of Eirlys's room, staring down at Price rumpled in the sheets of his lover's bed.

"It's been a while," she said. "Where is Her Grace?"

"She went to see the Alters," he replied, quickly and sleepily.

Nym narrowed her eyes. "Yes, I guess I should send

someone to check on her." Her Wraithmark flared but what she did or how she communicated, he could not tell.

Price should have moved, gotten up at least but he was too shocked to think clearly, in too much pain to care.

"Did you forget how to prostrate yourself to your patron goddess? Has it been that long?" Nym's voice carried the weight of her power, her Wraithmark flickering bloodred.

"No, of course, not," Price said. "But it has been a bad pain day, Ancient Nym."

The Ancient placed her hands behind her back.

"Do you know what we are doing to help Eirlys? To help her survive?"

Price swallowed. Her Kenos was absent, so he could lie and get away with it. "I don't understand why she needs to be altered. The procedure is dangerous, and I would hope you are trying to keep her alive."

The corner of Nym's mouth lifted and Price felt unbelievably vulnerable, still in bed. Ignoring his pain as he had done a million times, he rose from the sheets, smoothing out his sleep-wrinkled clothes. Unease flashed in his chest as he realized his sword rested against the nightstand on this side of the bed.

His sword. What the fuck was he thinking? Defending himself against a god with a sword?

"When I sent you to her all those months ago, I did so under the impression that you would guide her in our ways. I did not expect for you to be led astray."

"She did not lead me astray; she merely changed the path of my life."

"Towards hedonism," Nym spat.

"If loving her in this life curses me in the void, then I am content to be cursed for eternity."

Nym's lip curled in disgust.

"I do apologize, Ancient Nym. For all the faith you put in me, and all the promises broken. I never took my oaths lightly."

"And yet you broke them without a second though for that Skath whore."

And every muscle in Price's body tensed. Nym could call Eirlys names until she was blue in the face, but her anger frightened him. That sent gooseflesh crawling up his spine, tightening his scalp.

"Prostrate yourself to me, Price, and I might be able to help you."

He would not bow down to this false goddess, not now, not ever again. If he was getting on his knees for anyone, it was for Eirlys. He would worship her until the end of time. Not because he thought her the thirteenth god of the pantheon, but because who else was worth following than the woman who would lay down her life to change the world? Who other than the woman who changed him so irrevocably, opening his mind and heart to new ideas and the abhorrent truth of a religion he had dedicated far too much of his life to?

"I don't want or desire your help, Nym. Ever. I wish for you to never think of me again. Do not worry for my soul. It has found its peace, and it wasn't in you."

Nym's face became enraged. "You were mine," she cried, her power whipping through the room. She shimmered, and in a howling scream, she appeared next to him. With the iron grip of a five-thousand-year-old being, she hurled him onto the stone floor.

"Stay down there until I tell you otherwise," she snarled.

Void, he was hoping to have this encounter without Eirlys knowing. She already wanted to take on the council, like she could withstand the Ancients' wrath. Now, his knees would be bruised, and she would definitely see them.

Price laughed, though, hysterics making him brave. How

long had he wished to rage against the gods? To tell them to shove their grace and their promises, their pardons? Even before Eirlys showed up, he clung to a half-hearted belief because he was their golden child—the one they saved and offered the light to.

Never before had he been so grateful for the darkness.

Her glass staff whipped against his shoulder, sending him reeling back in pain.

"Is that it, then?" he asked, gripping his shoulder. Not dislocated, thankfully. "I chose to not worship you. Not even to worship anything else, just not you, and you'll beat me bloody to comply?"

Nym's white eyes went wide, anger flaring her nostrils.

"We made you," she snarled.

"You ruined me," he shot back. "You couldn't even get this right. Your precious light magic, it is wretched. And you have never been able to do it correctly, have failed again and again. Our Skath spirits will never accept a Klara's magic."

Nym's lip lifted in disgust. "If the Skath cannot be cured, if they can never accept the light, then we were right to scour them from the realm. But I believe in you, Price. I think we can fix you and her."

"You cannot fix her because there is nothing wrong with her," Price growled. On his knees, he glowered up at Nym. He would not submit to her. Not on his knees, not in this lifetime. He struggled to stand. The door opened behind him.

"Price, we have to—"

Eirlys's strangled scream alerted him to the danger... the pain...

But it was a different kind of pain, localized through his chest. Price glanced down. He could have laughed at the irony. How much pain had he endured in his lifetime for him to first register the agony under his skin abating, the fire quelling, before realizing he'd been stabbed through the chest? The jagged, raw obsidian coated with his blood was warm under his touch, the shard protruding grotesquely out in front of him.

Eirlys ran to him, and he reached out to her, but the goddess was not finished. When their fingers brushed, there was no relief, only the slick blood between them as he slid away from her and with the shriek of shimmering, the void swallowed him whole.

# CHAPTER FORTY-ONE

## EIRLYS

A scream bubbled in her throat, and Eirlys pressed her palm to her mouth to silence it, tasting Price's blood on her skin.

They were not moving fast enough. Even with Vara's ability to shimmer, each passing second flew by, like time was mocking Eirlys.

Finally, Vara tugged on Eirlys, hand in hand with Aliah, and the now familiar howling sound surrounded them as wind tore at their clothes. Suddenly, they appeared on the precipice of a cliff. Eirlys yelped as she teetered with Aliah clutched tightly to her. Vara grabbed them both, covering Eirlys's mouth and shimmering them away from the edge. Winds ravaged them, the sea crashing against the shore in a haunting wash of sound. Lightning and the bass of thunder filled the sky as the waves rocked calamitously. Vara's eyes went wide, staring towards the south, and Eirlys gaped.

Night Stone Prison rose before them. Eirlys shivered, and it had nothing to do with the cold. The last time she was here,

Evrit and his wrecked face had made certain the Ancients would never trust her. Not as a Skath. Now, she was back here again, trying to earn her freedom, trying to escape. How ironic that both lay with the prison's guarded obsidian walls.

Vara pulled the bag from her back and handed it to Eirlys.

She dressed, feeling the familiar boots around her toes, the tightness of the leather armor. To feel her magic one more time before she entered that desolate place, she pulled on her power, letting the rush of coolness enter her veins. Pulling her daggers from the bag, their gleaming silver reflected the black of the night. She had planned to sneak around, but without the use of magic, no glamour would work. Now she aimed to kill whoever got in her way. Her people were in there, *Price* was in there, and she would get them out and get them home.

She could not save all the Skath, but she could save these few. Her throat burned, and she pushed down the bile and guilt. It was enough.

It had to be enough.

Her hands found Aliah's shoulders, and she took a second to look into her friend's eyes. "Stay here. You'll be safe this far out. We will come back for you."

Aliah nodded, grasping Eirlys's arms and squeezing tight. "You've saved over half our family now," she whispered. "Thank you."

Eirlys smiled, but there wasn't time to say all the words aching in her chest, so she simply pulled Aliah into a tight embrace. Then she left her friend behind, making her way down the cliff with Vara, towards the shining, onyx gem of the fortress.

"I can try to shimmer us onto one of the walls, or at least above it." Vara gave her a sidelong glance as they neared the building. "Are you sure they brought him here?"

Eirlys wasn't sure, but she'd replayed Iona's words repeatedly in her mind as she raged around her room, in the wake of Price's kidnapping.

*He's the only successful Alter ever made*

Eirlys swallowed hard. "He'll be here." He *had* to be here, or Eirlys might finally break.

Vara nodded, then gripped onto her and Eirlys tucked her daggers into her hip holsters. The air cracked around them.

A gust of wind raged from the sea, spraying them with salt water as they appeared above the black wall. Vara's magic faded from her face, stuttering like a candle in the wind before extinguishing altogether. The wind blew past them as they hurtled to the obsidian floor and landed with a sickening thud.

Pain wracked Eirlys as she coughed, searching for any trace of air in her lungs. Blinking into the night sky, a faint rumbling sound tickled her ears. Rumbling? Eirlys rolled as the sword came down on the spot she had been. The resulting sound of steel on obsidian rattled her brain and she fumbled with her daggers as the guardian came at her again. She got to her feet and sprang away, the guard still charging her. He seemed clumsy without his magic, but Eirlys ached, and her head spun, so maybe she was the clumsy one. She ducked as he swung overhead, and her dagger met its mark in his chest. The guard gasped. She ripped the dagger out, blood spraying red droplets on the slick black surface of the floor.

Someone moved behind her and Eirlys swung on instinct. Vara barely dodged her blow.

Eirlys breathed, and everything ached. She mumbled an apology to the Naevni who waved her off.

"Time is short. Who is top priority?"

"Price," Eirlys said, and nothing in the world could change her mind.

Vara bit her lip and off they went. This was suicidal, but she would tear apart the world before she let them hurt Price.

"Did Aliah have an inkling to where they might be?" Vara asked.

"I think the Skath will be in the center. But with Price, I'm not sure."

"Alright, so maybe the guard tower to the right and the one beyond with the large metal gate in the middle?"

They were the closest, and therefore the easiest to search. With the plan gone awry, Eirlys didn't know who she could count on to help them. She'd sent messages to Emzelhal and August through Vara, but there hadn't been much time for more than a few quick words to alert them that the plan was happening now. Even if they ended up with no back-up, the thought of what they might do to Price with every passing second jolted Eirlys forward.

"Let's go," she said.

The entrance to the tower was a hole in the wall big enough for a body, with no door. They entered the dark hallway with RaGlass embedded into the obsidian, casting the dullest gray light onto the floor.

Gold splashed against the inky stone, and a Kenos stepped around the corner. The woman's long, braided hair laid over one shoulder, her regal dress moving with a wind no one could feel. The gold light emanated from her translucent body. A spirit, brought to this plane or trapped here?

The Kenos startled and a hand flew to her throat in a gesture so human Eirlys wondered how much awareness she had. The woman fled, sprinting past them. Strange.

A small touch on her hand drew Eirlys out of her thoughts and down the hall, where two guardians flanked the gated door. Why hadn't the Kenos warned them? Eirlys motioned Vara forward. They slid with their backs across the wall parallel to the guards.

Ten feet away, a woman's gaze caught on their slinking

forms. Eirlys dashed forward as the guard pulled her sword. She caught the blade with her own dagger, the force ripping a cry from her mouth, and tried to plunge the other into the woman's stomach. Her opponent hooked a knee into Eirlys's ribs, sending her sprawling, then growled.

"Eirlys? Eirlys!" a familiar voice cried, and Eirlys's heart sang.

Price was alive.

Her eyes flew to find him. His hands wrapped around the bars of a cell along the back wall before the guardian gripped Eirlys by the throat in her moment of distraction and lifted her against the wall.

The woman's face twisted in disgust and hate.

Eirlys's toes scrapped the ground for purchase. Finding none, she struggled for one good breath and knowing it would hurt, dropped all her dead weight to the ground. Her throat tore from the woman's hands. Coughing, Eirlys struck out with a low kick, breaking the woman's knee, and sent her down bellowing. Eirlys sprang forward and her dagger found its home in the guard's throat.

"Eirlys," Price cried out again.

Vara rounded the corner, blood staining her chest.

Remembering the small key Olga had used on Evrit's cell, Eirlys rummaged through the pockets of the guard's uniform and found a small glass key. The color inside swirled with black smoke. Vara stared at the key like it was an affront to the goddess herself.

"What kind of magic is that?" Vara asked.

"I don't know. I don't care so long as it works."

She pressed the key to a spot near the bars. It slid in easily. Obsidian bars pulled back into the rock, leaving only a smooth doorway.

Before Price could take more than one limping step, Eirlys

threw herself into his arms. Her hands roamed his chest, still sticky with blood, but no obsidian, no wound remained. She fought back tears of relief. She wound her arms around him and kissed him, pressing herself so no space remained between them.

His scent surrounded her, not the scent of his magic, so fiery like a burning forest. There was only the smell of him, the smell of evenings by the hearth and laughter over cooling tea and the early morning musk of his skin against her sheets. He was not her past, not August or Kestrya, smelling of the sea and sun. He was darkness—quiet and calm, the moon on a sharp winter night. He was her present, her future.

He smelled like home.

"I love you," she whispered when she pulled back, their foreheads still pressed together.

"I love you," he said back, his voice desperate and fervent, like the words were a prayer.

"I'm sorry to interrupt, but we have to go *now*," Vara said, standing by the door to peer into the dark hall.

Though she loathed to leave this moment, to go back to the reality of their situation, Eirlys pulled back, settling for entwining her hand with his. She was not ready to let Price go just yet, but there were other people to save today. "Okay, let's go."

"This way," Vara said, going back out the same door. They headed for the center of the prison.

Barely able to see, they groped their way to the other doorway as Eirlys whispered an explanation to Price about the expedited plan, Aliah, everything. Once inside the next hall, Price tried to use magic, the flickering of his Wraithmark sputtering. He rolled his eyes.

"Get used to being cold," Vara muttered, and she took the lead, disappearing around the corner.

The clang of Vara's ax rang out almost immediately, and Price and Eirlys sprinted to join her. Still holding her stance, Vara's ax met the obsidian wall through the head of a guardian. Eirlys swallowed back bile and circled the stunned Vara.

"It's okay," Eirlys said.

Vara shook her head and pulled the ax away from the wall. Eirlys pretended the sickening, wet thump was nothing more than a noise. Nothing.

"We have to go," Eirlys said.

Vara eyes were glazed over. Fuck, Eirlys thought; she hadn't expected Vara to freeze. Vara, who fought with so much skill, so much vigor. But brains splattered on the wall, and ivory splintered bone dotting the pink, gray goop twisted even her gut.

"There are people who need you," Eirlys pleaded.

Confusion rose in Vara's eyes. "Why is there only one guard here?"

Eirlys frowned. Good question—one would think guarding these Skath would be top priority. A Kenos flashed through the wall, a man this time, and stopped in front of them.

"What are you doing here?" Eirlys asked.

The man shrugged. "I died here."

"Do you guard this place?"

The Kenos laughed and punched through the wall. How? How did the Kenos go through walls made of obsidian?

Eirlys's heart ached as realization dawned on her. The Kenos could not move on from this prison; the spirits without a body were stuck here. They had access to the Void but remained incorporeal and not affected by the obsidian in any other way. The fucking Ancients who were supposed to guide them to the Valley had left them here to wander in this half-life, lost.

"We make poor guards—we can't touch anything. We can sound the alarm, but why bother?"

"Can't you leave? Get out of this place?" Vara asked, making the same connection Eirlys had.

The man shook his head. "I tried to leave once. It felt like an earthquake inside of me, like the shaking would explode out from me and I would cease to be. So, I came back inside. Because here at least, I am whole."

A muffled sound echoed in the hallway, and Eirlys watched the distorted shadows move across the wall. Reinforcements. Kenos dropped through the floor.

"How are you feeling??" Eirlys asked Price.

"Better than ever," Price said and flashed her a grin. "The prison was made for me."

Price had not flinched or reacted to the constant pain. She laughed, and with a smirk threw him a sword she'd picked up from one of the guards. He unsheathed it and swung it once, causing the air to whistle. They each took their stance.

"Your Grace?" came a voice from around the corner.

The line of guardians had stopped before they rounded the corner. Blind on both sides.

"That's me," Eirlys said, not getting out of her stance.

"Your Grace, you need to leave. We were told to subdue and kill anyone who tried to remove these prisoners. They did not make an exception for you."

Eirlys grinned. "Blasphemy, don't you think?"

The guard swore under his breath. In the stillness of the prison, Eirlys heard every sound carried through the walls.

The guards rushed them. Eirlys braced herself and focused on the target in front of her. With a sprint, she darted toward the guard and feinted right, dodging left and then slid into the man's legs, buckling them. His sword clanged against the black icy stone. Eirlys slammed a dagger into his chest and plunged the other one into his skull.

Another guardian swung at her and using the former man's head with her dagger still embedded, she blocked the blow. The man's head exploded as the hammer hit his temple, dislodging her dagger. Eirlys wiped blood and other matter away from her face. The woman who had swung teetered on her feet and Price ran her through with a sword. A guardian nearly took Price in the back, but Eirlys flung her dagger at the man, embedding it to the hilt in his forehead. Vara slid beside Eirlys, and they leaned back-to-back.

"Got an extra dagger?" Eirlys asked.

Vara produced a straight blade, and Eirlys held it in her left hand, keeping her preferred weapon in her right. They braced for the next onslaught. Dodge, duck, swipe and slice, then a sting to the shoulder and a nick to the cheek, shallow and superficial.

Dead, dead, dead—three more down. And her side was clear.

She turned and watched Price fight, his swings practiced, precise. Pain flitted through his eyes, but his opponent had been blocking, and Price stumbled back. Against the black of the floor, a white hilted dagger stabbed into Price's calf. He faltered for a moment, which stretched too long. The sword swung. Eirlys ran, her scream a ragged thing as the blade bit into Price's shoulder.

She tackled the guardian, ripping the sword from Price's body in a sickening squelch of muscle and blood. Pinning the man to the ground, Eirlys's straight dagger plunged into his throat, tearing through trachea and windpipe, leaving a wound of gurgling blood. Her eyes flicked around as the man who had stabbed Price tried to back away, and she flung her dagger at him, taking him in the chest.

Bracing herself, she faced Price, who leaned against the wall with Vara kneeling beside him. He was alive, barely. The guardian had meant to take his head, but the sword came at a bad angle and sliced through the muscle, cutting through to his clavicle and collarbone, carving out a v shaped gouge. His blood-soaked shirt contrasted with the pallor of his skin and sent Eirlys's heart racing.

No, no, no. She couldn't lose him, not like this.

"Get him up," Eirlys commanded, reaching under his wounded shoulder.

"Eirlys." Vara's tone said it was too late.

"Don't argue with a Va. Get him up."

"And go where?" Vara snapped. "You can't heal him in here!"

"I'll throw myself over the cursed wall if I have too."

Vara gritted her teeth, bending to lift Price. The sudden movement sent a chilled cry from Price's lips. *Hold on for a few minutes.* They half dragged Price to the door and Eirlys motioned for Vara to set him down.

Eirlys covered Price in a thin shirt from Vara's bag.

"Go get the other Skath out. Now."

Vara glanced at Price.

"I've got him," Eirlys said. "But you have to go!"

Vara sprinted down the corridor. Eirlys lifted Price and groaned under his weight.

Once outside, a torrential downpour swept over the land, rain pelting down like ice, stinging their skin. Eirlys propped Price on the wall's solid railing. Eirlys peered over the side and immediately regretted it. Pulling back, she leaned against the edge beside Price.

"Did you know I'm afraid of heights?" Eirlys said breathlessly.

"Yes." Price let out a strained chuckle. "You took out"—

Price took a deep breath—"half a dozen guards." He took another breath. "And now you're worried about heights?"

Eirlys frowned. Price's eyes fluttered and she cursed. Not taking the time to look at the distance, she grabbed his good arm and hefted him onto the ledge. She rolled on top of him. Closing her eyes, she launched them over, pulling on her power.

Nothing came. A feeling like a slippery cold blade shot into her stomach. The taste of bile clawed at her throat, grazing her chest with its panicked edge, and she clenched her jaw shut in terror. She pulled on her magic, again and again. Her eyes opened and the earth rose to meet them. Finally magic flooded her and she reached out, not having to conjure water. Pulling from the rain, a swarm of ice-cold water enveloped them, caught them, and gently the earth pressed against her side.

Eirlys flung the water away, briefly drying them as the rain continued. She dragged Price from the side of the wall, worried about the obsidian wrecking her magic. Gathering water in her hands, her Wraithmark darkening, she leaned over Price. The sharp sting of healing hit her, and the coolness rushed through her limbs.

The tip of a dagger met her throat.

"Don't move," Emzelhal said.

# Chapter Forty-Two

## Eirlys

Eirlys raised her hands as the blade pressed in.

"Drop your magic," Emzelhal said.

It took everything within Eirlys to control her magic, her rage. Her vision blurred red and as she breathed out, the water fell from her hands. Her Wraithmark disappeared.

"Get up slowly." Emzelhal shifted the blade, so the pressure allowed her to move.

Eirlys rose, her eyes never leaving Price, who was no longer conscious. The blood had slowed to a trickle. Had she healed him enough, or was she too late?

"Let me—" Eirlys tried to beg, but the dagger nicked her, a sting on her throat.

Following the pressure of the weapon, Eirlys turned. Standing in front of Night Stone was her sister. Her strawberry blonde hair was darkened by the rain, and her bright purple robes looked almost black. Her face twisted with rage.

"Aydra," Eirlys hissed.

"Shut up, Skath!" Aydra shrieked.

Lightning struck behind her, shadowing the irate lines on her face. Eirlys had been so wrong to believe the riotous fury between her and her sister had been extinguished. It had simply smoldered, waiting for the right time to flare up once again. Nothing could ever erase the hate raging in her eyes. Thunder clapped and the bass shuddered through Eirlys's bones. Her own anger bubbled inside her, and the rain poured, heavy and thick. She recognized the feelings—betrayal and shame—and like the rain it weighed down on her. She was ashamed of being so blind, so willing to believe that this world and her sister could change.

Her eyes flicked to Emzelhal. "I see you got my missive. Helping the wrong sister?" she asked. She should be confused, betrayed, but really this was not much of a shock. Deep down, she'd known Emzelhal always had his own plans.

Emzelhal smirked. "Promising Aydra your death was all I had to do to get her on my side, even on such short notice. I thought I'd have a few months, but it seems simply mentioning killing a bunch of Skath, especially you, was enough."

"All I wanted was to save my people and get out," Eirlys cried.

Anger flashed in his eyes. "You belong to me! My father and I made you who you are today. We planned for years to get you back here, to get the crown on your head. You are mine."

"I don't belong to you, and sure as fuck don't belong to them."

Emzelhal scoffed and stepped back, sheathing the knife. "You're coming back with me. After you kill your sister, of course."

Aydra went white with shock, her skin as pale as the Kenos

and as trapped. Eirlys groaned, turning to her sister with indignation in her eyes.

"What do you think he was going to do, you naive, spoiled brat? He's an assassin's son; he can't be trusted. And if you attack me, I will fight for my life, Aydra. I'm done with this game between us."

Aydra sputtered, ignoring Eirlys in favor of spinning to Emzelhal. "We have a deal!"

"You are so thick-skulled!" Eirlys yelled. "Even if you managed to kill me, do you really believe he will let you live?"

Aydra's face twisted in fury. "Don't talk to me like that, Skath. I'll finally kill you and be done with it. Then I'll get the others. We will rid the realm of these stains."

Her mind reeled. Price, Price, Price. He lie dying a few feet from her, and Vara would be out the front doors any minute. And the Skath. And her escape.

Price.

Goddess, all she wanted was for him to live. He wasn't supposed to be here. He should be at the castle, safe and warm, not dying in the rain. Let him live.

Another flash lit the clouds and the thunder crashed around them. The gate opened and Eirlys swore.

Aydra smirked and whipped out a staff, the tips burning so brightly the sheet of rain didn't dampen them. Holding a staff in a storm meant only one thing. As the lightning cracked through the sky, Aydra's grip on the staff clenched. The staff turned white hot, Aydra's hair rising in the static electricity. Before she could attack, her sister's eyes clouded over in a vision, blinding her from the lightning strike as it hit. Following the rivulets of water, the sand melted to glass and the electricity pulled Aydra's power through the ground in a stunning display of purple light. It blew Eirlys off her feet— Price's body flew away. The vision came as the lightning pulsed through Eirlys, like glass entering her veins, sharp and sudden. The future filled her eyes.

*The rain still pounds the earth, and the wind whips it into a fury. Eirlys sees herself stand, and she awaits her own decision. Leave, she thinks. She watches herself run to Price and tries to move him. Vara rushes to help her while Aydra and Emzelhal slaughter the Skath. Leave Price, she thinks and Eirlys watches as she leaves with the Vara and the others and Price dies.*

*The vision shifts and warps. Price alive, kneeling by the throne, guardian armor shimmering in the sun. Aydra, a scarlet red dress hugging her body, smiles with a face like her mother's but with a cruel curve. Eirlys's crown sits on top of her head. A perspective shifts and fields of grain stretch for miles and in the fields, chains rattle. Skath workers' hands blister from the scythes, cutting, cutting, cutting, till they drop to the ground. No one retrieves them. No one helps.*

*A battle appears. Desperate cries fill the air and Eirlys stands beside August—no, not besides, behind him. He is hand in hand with a man, his face masked by the helm he wears, but familiar, like the taste of clean citrus water on a hot summer day. Eirlys fights, her daggers sing. She parries and ducks and Price makes his way to August. Eirlys reaches her hand up, face twisted in agony, and she squeezes her fist shut. Price drops to the muddy ground, dead, but not before his blade takes off August's head. His partner's screams echo through the battlefield and a guardian drags Eirlys to her feet. Head down, the only sound of her demise is the whistle of the blade.*

*"You will die fighting this battle from the outside." The disem-bodied voice rings clear, sharp yet smooth like a blade, and tastes coppery on the back of her tongue.*

The vision faded and coldness seeped through Eirlys as she awoke on the sandy ground.

Emzelhal's gut wrenching scream of rage pierced the air as he flew toward Eirlys. Her measly little dagger was too slow to block. The blade bit home, deep into Eirlys's chest. A heady weight pressed into her limbs, her hands scrambling to reach the hilt, but the beautiful softness of oblivion was taking over, swift and sure, as she fell to the rain drenched soil.

# CHAPTER FORTY-THREE

## PRICE

The first thing Price noticed was the cold. Deep in his bones, weariness weighed on his spirit. He groaned and rolled over. The sand stuck to every bit of his body, the irritating grains grating his skin. He spit water out of his mouth.

He scanned the area, looking for Eirlys. When he spotted her, he would have been shocked if he hadn't watched her die multiple times for the past eight months. She was sprawled on her back, a sword penetrating her chest, staking her to the ground. Her hair was fanned around her like a crown of feathers from a brightly colored bird.

*Get up. Get the fuck up.*

He could barely move, barely breathe. He fought to maintain consciousness. His wounds were threatening to drag him back to the abyss, into the void and away from her. He wasn't about to give in so easily. No minor sword wound was going to take him out—he would leave when he was good and ready, not a moment sooner.

Price sucked in a breath and moved. He crawled, ever so

slowly to Eirlys, one inch at a time. He dug his feet into the ground and pushed, ignoring the pain in his shoulder, the tingling in his arm.

Aydra and Emzelhal clashed in the rain, a torrent of wind and fire, staff and blade. They raged at each other, paying no attention to the man crawling across the bloody sand.

In the background, Vara's face twisted with uncertainty. If he knew August even a little, the main goal would have been Eirlys. Yet, Vara was the only protection for the Skath behind her. If Aydra won, the Skath would be defenseless. Vara was Naevni, but she was not able to be in two places at once.

Price didn't know who had stabbed Eirlys, but he wasn't about to let her die. Not when he could save her. Not when they had come so close to getting her out.

He finally made it to her body and lifted himself over her. A cry spilled out as he pulled the sword out of her chest. A new warmth gushed from his shoulder. He fell backwards, bleeding into the sand. With the sword clutched tightly against his chest, he gave in to oblivion with one thought.

*She would live.*

# CHAPTER FORTY-FOUR

## EIRLYS

Eirlys shot to her feet. Emzelhal was advancing on Aydra's prone body. Free of his blade, Eirlys raised her hand to the sky and pulled on her magic. The rain froze in place. Emzelhal skidded to a stop, turning to face Eirlys.

"Leave her alone," Eirlys growled, and she twisted her hand. The raindrops formed into solid ice, points as sharp as a dagger tip.

"Are you insane? You want to save her? She was going to kill you!"

"You just ran me through with a sword, so you're not exactly in a position to judge." Eirlys smirked. "Don't move," she said and closed her fist slowly. The points of solid ice moved to surround him.

Vara remained at the entrance of the gate, watching Emzelhal with tears in her wide eyes. She had her arms held out, holding back the kidnapped Skath.

"Get them out," Eirlys repeated.

"But you... you'll die."

390

"Not fucking today."

Maybe she did believe in the visions. Maybe Emzelhal had a point. She was needed here. Aydra's lack of understanding, her fierce hatred; as queen, no one would be able to control her. The Skath would suffer more than they already did. A tiny strip of flesh which shone or darkened, magic from the stars or the shadows. The difference meant life or death in Kygem, something that would never change under Aydra's rule.

Emzelhal stood before her with his fierce anger, ever the son of a killer. She had expected more, expected someone who genuinely wanted better for the Skath, but the truth spoke for itself tonight. Emzelhal had always been more Kygemian than Kestryan.

"Vara, go. Get Aliah and go. Tell August"—she swallowed —"Tell him I'm going to make him proud here."

The world had turned a dark and stormy gray, like the sea churned from an abysmal sky.

Kestrya, Kygem.

Virva, Alby.

Realms and cities, all meaningless without the people within them. Night and day, Skath and Klara, light and shadow; just words and labels. Attach people to them—Eirlys, Price, Brisa, Emzelhal, Aydra, Evrit, Lita... and they became the faces of the nouns: lover, sister, mother, friend, traitor, murderer, child.

Eirlys slammed her fist down and the rain spattered around them. Emzelhal blasted the ice away from him. Eirlys ran to Price, listening for the sound of Emzelhal's approach. She managed a quick heal on Price, closing a blood vessel he must have ruptured when he pulled the sword from her, the offending blade still gripped in his hand.

Through the rain, her magic singing in her veins, she heard him approach. She wrapped her hand around the hilt of the weapon and whipped it around, catching the sword coming at her. Emzelhal pushed back and they circled like two predators.

Eirlys tried to focus on Emzelhal, but her attention shifted to the limp form of Aydra's body. *Let her live too,* she thought. *Let her learn. For all the bad in this world, let it not be my sister finding the void today.*

Emzelhal struck and Eirlys blocked instinctively. Her hand swept up and snow exploded in Emzelhal's face. He quickly blasted it away with a gust of wind and reached his hand out. The air Eirlys once drew in left her lungs, and she ached for oxygen. Emzelhal was pulling the air from her lungs, a crime so heinous it was punishable by death even when used in war times. But she possessed her own share of horrors, and the water flowing around him crawled up his neck and into his mouth. He went wide-eyed as he choked, drowning on land. The next moment, Eirlys breathed again, and she released her magic to focus on drawing in a lungful of fresh, rain-soaked air.

Emzelhal rushed at her, and she dodged and swung, driving the blade into his back. Wind pummeled her blade upward and she cursed, trying to adjust her momentum. She was too slow. The sword tip bit into her side, slicing straight through to her ribs. The pain dizzied her. Emzelhal swung again and she reached to block. One icy hand gripped the blade and her own sword swung, stuttering as wind from Emzelhal's power sent him backwards. Eirlys staggered back.

"Are you afraid to kill me, again?" Eirlys taunted.

"I just need you out of the way. I have no problem shoving this sword back into your heart. I'll remove it when I get you back to your throne."

Emzelhal struck out, but the howling sound of the void lifted Eirlys's heart. The Skath were escaping. She parried again, this time knocking the blade from Emzelhal's grip. She let her sword go with it, both weapons sailing into the curtain of rain that poured around them. She grabbed his hands and froze them together, knocking him off balance as she pummeled him into the ground, knees on his chest.

Eirlys reached one ice-clad hand to the man's neck. With her fingers wrapped in diamond hard ice, she ripped out Emzelhal's throat in a gurgling spray of blood and muscle.

Eirlys didn't wait. She searched the air around her. Not with her eyes but with her spirit, the reckless thing living in her body. Only once before had Eirlys betrayed the most forbidden act of magic, using a spirit of the dead to fuel Wraith, to walk through the void. The first time she had been racked with guilt and shame, begging her Goddess to understand. But in the dark night, on a cliff near the sea, Eirlys refused to feel remorse. And she was beyond caring what gods might think of her.

Her spirit sensed it first, the recently departed, so full of energy. Eirlys called out to it and her vision went red as the bridge of her nose-streaked scarlet. The spirit dissolved into pure, usable Wraith.

*Price.* She shimmered beside him, touching him. *Aydra.* Despite their differences, she could not leave her sister to bleed out, and shimmered beside her as well, having taken Price with her.

Finally, Eirlys thought of a city, one whose tall building stretched to the sky and a river flowed along its bank, nestled in a valley covered in a thick blanket of snow. Using the last of the Wraith in her final bout of magic, the three bodies shimmered to the center of Alby's healing station.

Eirlys stood for a moment as the howling sound drew the attention of every immortal who heard it. The red faded from her face and the healers gawked. In reverent bows, they went to their knees. Eirlys didn't care. She begged for someone to heal Price. Getting the three of them out spent the last of her magic, leaving her unable to even remove the water plastered to their skin.

The howling sound of a dozen angry gods filled the air. She could have escaped, with Aydra and Price, into Kestrya. It was so easy to think of Virva and its winding streets, humid days, and sea-kissed nights. Too easy to cling to the idea that visions were useless and what she saw were only glimpses into the possibilities of the future.

Now she'd have to face the wrath of the gods descending upon her.

But she had a rage of her own, boiling just beneath the surface.

# Chapter Forty-Five

## August

One day, August would never step foot near the Barrenlands again. But today, he watched the dark skyline, the wind whipping across the cursed isthmus to run invisible fingers through his auburn hair. His Shadow Guard stood at attention while he paced back and forth under the watchtower by the Kestryan border.

"I'm sure they're on their way," Rory said, trying to comfort him.

August shook his head. If Eirlys's message was to be believed, they should have been here by now. He couldn't stay still. He wasn't going to sleep until Eirlys was back in his arms and his people were safe again. It was almost a relief for the plan to be happening so soon—it saved him four more months of void-cursed waiting.

The air was frigid despite being so near the sea. This winter had been harsh, and August pulled his jacket around him tighter.

Then the familiar sound of the Naevni pierced the thin air, reverberating off the tower walls.

"Something must have gone wrong," August said.

He darted toward the sound, the curse of his comrades coming from behind. They bounded after him.

Vara was stepping through the void, followed by the five stolen Skath. Aliah stumbled out last, and a strangled sound ripped from behind him as Nik rushed forward and caught her, shock scouring his face.

"No," August breathed, taking in the scene. And as much of a surprise as seeing Aliah was, gaunt and sobbing as she collapsed into Nik's arms, there was something much worse.

Eirlys was not here.

"She's alive. Or she was when I left."

"Go back." He stalked towards the Naevni, anger and fear surging through him.

"I can't. The princess, the other one, was there. If she was there, the Ancients won't be far behind."

"They'll kill her!" he roared.

"She will be fine. She made her choice. She's staying in Kygem."

August stopped. His heart sank into his stomach, and the wave of sorrow threatened to crush him. By the Sa Daughter, she had chosen to stay after all this time. What had changed her mind? August looked helplessly toward the north. Toward her.

That was when he saw the approaching figure.

Reality shattered around her as she stepped through the void, scanning the terrified Skath. Aliah rose, pushing Nik behind her even as he scrambled to do the same.

A wicked smile crept onto the goddess's face. "You must be Prince August. I am Esona."

August swallowed. He did not protest when his guards

formed around him, Nik dragging Aliah alongside him, refusing to break contact with her.

Esona's eyes flicked back to Vara and the Skath.

"Now, how did you manage this feat?"

Vara stood with her hands ready. She nodded at August.

"Keep her busy," Vara said. If she could get far enough away, they might not be able to track her.

Vara's blood red Wraithmark shot across her face. Esona's eyes went wide, first with fear and then rage.

"I will destroy you," she snarled, advancing on the Naevni.

"I won't let you," August said.

The Ancient grinned at him. "Please, boy. You cannot beat me."

"I don't have to," August said.

Vara spared him one last look. "Don't die."

He didn't plan on it. Vara and the Skath disappeared, all except for Aliah.

The Ancient pulled on her magic, ready to follow Vara into the void, but while she was concentrating on Vara, August readied his own power.

He threw a knife, pushed by his wind, the black blade landing true. He doubted anything would kill a five-thousand-year-old goddess, but he hadn't been trying. He needed to keep her here.

She gasped as the obsidian drained her power.

"You test my patience today, Prince."

He raised his sword and pointed it at her. He had no hope of winning this fight. Still, he would go down swinging. If Eirlys taught him anything, it was that the fight wasn't over if he had the strength to stand. And he would stand for every Skath he had freed, every infant they had murdered, every Devoid they made. He would stand between them as long as he could.

Esona moved. She shimmered and ended up between Basil and August. August turned but Basil was already in front of him. They braced against Esona's sword, but the Ancient's blade went through Basil, slashing August's chest as it exited through their back.

"Fuck," Rory swore.

He swung out with curved swords, but not to slice. Boiling water shot through the air. Esona backed into the void. August looked around for where she would come out. His only sign was the noise before the world shattered. Caden screamed as the sword pierced her stomach.

"No!" August cried.

Nik pushed Aliah away from the fight and sprinted to his prince, along with the remaining Shadow Guard. Rory, Nik, and Galen pressed their backs to August. Circling him, protecting him with the last of their strength.

They would die around him. They were all going to die.

Esona's blade came for Nik's throat, but August pushed the wind towards the cloud clogged sky, sending the sword upwards. The Ancient spun and sliced through Nik's thigh, directly through his femoral artery. Aliah cried out, rushing to his side despite the danger, trying to heal him. It was as if time froze when she pulled on her magic, and instead of the dark ink of her Skath mark, blaring Klara light scattered across her temples. She screamed as Nik bled out at her feet and she wrestled with her magic, agony embedded deep in her features.

"What did you do to her?" August spun to the Ancient, rage roiling through him. Without thinking, he blasted his magic around them, sending Rory and Galen upwards with him. Curling a gust of wind around Rory, August caught him in midair and set him next to Nik and Aliah. "Heal him," August commanded.

Rory started to sprint to August but stopped as his eyes went wide.

August felt her presence behind him. He turned and it was as if the Ancient stared through him, directly into his spirit. He was amazed at how small she was and yet how large she loomed in his vision, in his bones. He could barely breathe. The pressure of leagues and leagues of ocean weighed on his heart.

"Leave them alone," he begged, squeezing the words from his chest.

"Don't worry, I'm only after you."

She grabbed his arm, and they were through the void. He plummeted into the still soft grass. She yanked him up by his arm, forcing him to stand facing the Barrenlands. With one swift kick of her boot, she shoved him over the line.

# Chapter Forty-Six

## Eirlys

During a storm, the castle's dungeon leaked.

The constant drip, drip, drip, set Eirlys's teeth on edge. No matter how hard she tried, drawing on her magic did nothing. The familiar weight of the obsidian in her hand sent her reeling back to another time, when they held her prisoner in a nice comfortable room.

Three days had passed since the incident at Night Stone. Price lived, or so they told her. Aydra, too. Though no one even thanked her for that. Well, she wasn't dead. Yet. But they had staked her with obsidian and thrown her in the dungeon.

Eirlys groaned and sat up, needing to stretch her sore muscles. The wound on her cheek had scabbed nicely, while the one on her arm liked to open and seep as she slept. The slash across her ribs dripped steadily, soaking through the rag-like blanket they threw her.

A guard served her food once a day and refilled her water. Unfortunately, her chamber pot had not been emptied. In the age of indoor plumbing, this infuriated her. The guards rotated often, but she recognized none of them.

Weak and sore, she leaned on her bad side and regretted it. Instead, she laid on her back on the cot, trying to ignore the throbbing and the constant drip, drip, drip.

She might have preferred to have been kept in Night Stone.

"Get the fuck out of my way!" Price's voice reverberated off the dungeon walls.

Eirlys sprang up, the pain in her ribs sharpening as she sucked in a breath to avoid screaming. Nothing was going to keep her from getting to the cell bars.

Price! Her heart swelled. She didn't want to believe he had died, but also couldn't trust he lived without proof. There was the sound of scuffling and a satisfying thump, followed by a groan and footsteps, leading to Price appearing at her cell door.

"Hey," she whispered.

"Hey," he said back, his fingers wrapping around the bars. She covered his hands with hers.

Eirlys dreamt of Night Stone every night, and the prophecy and deaths of everyone and everything she loved, including herself. The finality of her choices solidified in visions she didn't believe in, but oh Goddess, how real they seemed. Her heart broke under the images. Her magic—her hands—killing Price. When she opened her eyes, she still saw it, burned into the back of her retinas.

"Why did you bring us back here?" he asked. His jaw tightened, the muscles straining in his neck.

Eirlys had been asking herself that for days now. She should have gone to Kestrya as planned. Before it felt like escaping; now, it felt like running. And Eirlys was so tired of running.

Eirlys stuttered for a moment before she spit out, "Because

we both know that I cannot leave here with a clean conscience."

Price's fingers tightened under her grip. "Nothing has changed. Eirlys, you might still die here, or"—Price swallowed —"I can handle it if you leave, knowing you will live a happy and long life. I don't know if I am strong enough to handle your death."

Her throat tightened. She fought back a sob as she gripped his hands. "I cannot walk into that alteration knowing if I don't make it out, neither will you. That isn't fair to put on me."

"Then go. I will come with you. If that's what it will take."

A tear slid down his cheek. Eirlys reached between the bars to wipe it away. "Don't worry. I'm just stubborn enough to make it through this. Then, when I am their perfect little Queen, we will make them pay for what they have done to us."

The door opened down the hall, and Brisa appeared. "Well, you look like shit," she said, making her way over, venom lacing her words.

Eirlys cringed and waited.

"Were you just going to leave like that? Not tell me or Deryn? Who, by the way, is so mad at you right now, they refused to come."

Price opened his mouth, but Eirlys shook her head. It was nothing she didn't deserve.

"I... I wanted to tell you and Deryn. I just never found the right time. Then Price was taken, and I found Aliah... "

"Yeah, Price filled me in." Brisa walked up to the bars. "I thought you trusted me."

"I was working with the man who killed your parents, Brisa. I didn't even know how to begin justifying that to you."

"That didn't stop Aydra from working with him, huh?"

Brisa fiddled with the hem of her shirt. "Why did you save her?"

Eirlys bit her lip. Her decision to save Aydra hadn't been planned, not like her escape, but a choice. To be as cruel as the gods were, or to be as kind as she could muster.

She didn't get a chance to explain before more sets of footsteps descended to her cell.

"We couldn't have spread out these visits," Eirlys sniped.

Ancient Gyda rounded the corner with Aydra by her side. Deryn trailed behind them. She eyed Brisa and Price. Brisa took one look at Deryn and dread clouded her features. As if someone shoved her stomach into her throat, Eirlys waited. Nothing good could come of this.

"Open the cell," Gyda commanded, though she could have easily shimmered in. A guard rushed forward and unlocked the door. "We have somewhere to be, Your Grace."

Eirlys limped forward. "Why the rush?" she asked. Price closed his eyes, frustration leaking from him.

Then Eirlys caught sight of her sister's hand.

"Do you recognize this?" Aydra asked, a smirk spreading across her face.

She held a brooch, adorned with emerald, rimmed in silver. The Karakos crest peeked through the grime and blood dotting the front.

The color drained from Eirlys's face, and her breath came in spurts, but she choked out, "That belongs to the Karakos royal family."

Gyda gazed at everyone Eirlys loved in one horrifying sweep of the room. "It's not only you we can hurt, little girl."

Gyda grabbed her arm. The void was beginning to feel like home as they passed through. All at once she breathed fresh air, salty and humid with a hint of dust and dryness belonging nowhere near the sea. Though she had been on this side of the line only twice in her entire life, she would never mistake where they now stood.

The Barrenlands.

# Chapter Forty-Seven

## Eirlys

The dreary light of the Barrenlands cast warped shadows on the dusty ground, the sun yearning to penetrate the clouds. A chill in the air bit Eirlys's skin, and the sound of waves crashing roared over the earth like a distant cry.

A circle of twelve Ancients and one perpetually pissed off princess appeared around her. Someone gasped, but she didn't know who. Another voice came from her right. Deryn's, then Brisa's. She wondered if the Ancients were going to force her conspirators to cross, all while she watched. The formation of Ancients parted, giving her a clear view.

The demarcation line lay a few feet from Eirlys. On one side, dried, dead grass not quite outside of winter's grasp blew in a strong breeze. Past the boundary were boulders, dust and packed earth, nothing daring to grow in the cursed soil.

Comprehension dawned slow in Eirlys's sluggish mind. A man huddled on the other side of the line, his curly brown hair matted—the blood caked to his right temple was nearly the same color. His eyes, so similar in shade to the gray world around them, were bloodshot. His bottom lip swelled around a bleeding cut, and he held his arm tight across his body.

August's eyes widened in surprise as Eirlys came into view.

Air escaped her. Her lungs, chest, everything ceased to work, and the world promptly spiraled out of control. Her knees shook and tried to buckle, but she clenched every muscle tight and took a gulping breath. The tears betrayed her.

"Abdicate," Aydra snarled. "Or we force him to cross. And send him back to his country Devoid."

"No." Price's voice came from behind her.

She didn't look at him. Her eyes couldn't stray from August's face. There was the sound of feet scraping dirt, the thumps and groans of individuals fighting each other. When she heard the ring of a sword being pulled, she screamed, "Stop!"

"I'm fine," she continued, hoping her voice carried. "Brisa, don't let Price do anything stupid."

Eirlys ignored the watching Ancients and walked to the demarcation line. Spongy earth squished under her feet, ending at the line where dust and rock lay barren.

"What did he do?" Eirlys demanded. "What sort of punishment is this? This isn't a war crime."

"It is not his punishment," Gyda replied. "Abdicate."

Evading Gyda's request, Eirlys spoke to August, her voice soft and gentle. "How did they get you?"

"Followed Vara," August said, his voice hoarse and raw. "Caught up to her and the Skath. She took them and ran. They had Aliah?"

Eirlys nodded. "That's why I needed to get them out sooner. I couldn't leave her."

August's face hardened in pain. "We were attacked and—I don't know if Nik made it."

His words were like a punch to the gut. Eirlys had just

managed to get Aliah out. And now, Nik might be dead. What if she never again saw Nik's face crinkle in laughter, which he so rarely showed? He would never be able to watch his son grow up. If he died—no, not even if he died—just for threatening his life, Eirlys swore to make the Ancients bleed at least once.

"What's going on, Eirlys?" August asked. "I expected death, not... "

He tried gesturing, and a hiss came out of his mouth. He cradled his arm again. Eirlys started to reach for him, but the sound of nocking arrows caused her to freeze. She raised her hands cautiously.

Someone pulled her away from August, and she let them, stumbling backward.

"Abdicate now, or we will make him cross. Then we will turn our attention to others."

Eirlys finally turned away from August to Price and Brisa, arrows pointed at them. Deryn was directly behind her. They grinned, manic.

"Deryn's a Sa, you know," Eirlys said as the archer shuffled, nervous.

"Abdicate!" Aydra screamed.

Eirlys faced her. "No."

A hollow wind echoed through the land.

"Abdicate," Gyda's voice said from a distance. She appeared behind August, ready to launch him over the line.

"Or what? You'll hurt him? You'll punish me? Do you remember what happened the last time you pushed me to the edge? You will eventually run out of people I love to kill."

"This is your final warning, Your Grace. Abdicate," Gyda said.

Eirlys didn't bother acknowledging the goddess. At this moment, Gyda meant little to her. August, broken and battered, hadn't given up, although he had been beaten. Tears burned in her eyes. Those gray eyes pierced hers, searching. How much did their love mean? Not enough. There was not an entire realm's worth of love between them. August shook his head, and she closed her eyes.

Eirlys had become Devoid to save one infant—August would become Devoid to give her the chance to save them all.

"No," she said again.

Gyda shoved August, sending him flying over the line. Eirlys ran, stumbled, and caught him by his good shoulder, taking the brunt of the hit. Together, they fell to the earth. Her own wounds screamed in protest, but no pain could take her away from August. She cradled him in her lap. A wracking sob escaped from his throat as Eirlys sensed the curse in the land course through his body. It passed like the last breath of the dying as he pressed his face into her stomach and silently cried. And she held him for all it was worth.

"Get her away from him," Gyda commanded.

As the guardians moved, Deryn spoke up. "Leave them the fuck alone."

Eirlys watched Deryn's power grow and create a small bubble of space around the three of them. They poured the energy out into a windstorm.

"You've made your point," Deryn said, standing.

Price's sword rasped as he unsheathed it and stood between Eirlys and August and the archers.

Aydra cried out, and Eirlys whipped around to see Brisa holding a clawed hand to Aydra's throat, the nails digging in hard enough to draw blood.

"Leave," Brisa told the Ancients.

"You'll be dead the moment she is," Gyda said.

"She will still be dead." One of the Ancients moved, and

Brisa squeezed harder. Aydra coughed and sputtered. "One hint of that hideous sound and I'll rip out her throat."

Deryn's eyes flicked between Eirlys and Brisa. They raced over to their lover as if they expected arrows in their back.

"How dare you?" Gyda spat at Brisa.

"Goddess, are you blind?" Eirlys glowered.

She touched Price's hand and moved him to cradle the passed-out August against his side. Eirlys rose.

"Look!" Eirlys shouted and pointed at Brisa. "Price, Brisa, Deryn, and who knows how many countless others are turning away from you. They are denouncing you. They are disobeying you. One of your own princesses stole me and fled. Your followers, your precious patrons are leaving. They are done; done killing their children, done hating themselves, done believing you.

"Leave," she said. "Leave us be. I'll complete your cursed alteration, but I'll do it on my terms. I'll be your queen. Brisa, drop her."

Brisa shot Eirlys a glare but dropped their sister. Tears sprang to Aydra's eyes.

"Take the child with you. I don't want anyone else losing their temper around her," Eirlys said.

"Brisa... " Aydra's voice was laced with thick tears. "Not you. I can't lose you, too."

"You lost me long before this, Aydra," Brisa said.

Brisa went to stand near Deryn, and they strode to Eirlys.

"You do not dismiss us," Olga said, but Gyda shook her head. The hatred on Gyda's face made Eirlys's skin crawl.

"I would watch your back, Your Grace. Once I can figure out a way to kill you, I will make it happen. But if I hear of any infraction of your little companions here—"

Eirlys cut her off. "You'll only make us martyrs, so I dare you."

Gyda cleared the space between her and Eirlys in a heartbeat. Her overwhelming power crashed down on Eirlys, but this time, her own enraged fury kept Eirlys upright. She stared the goddess in the face. One hit, one punch would be so gratifying. For her mother, she thought, as her fist closed. Then the twelve gods and a sobbing Aydra disappeared.

"Get back to guarding the cursed tower," Eirlys snapped.

The guardians who had been pointing arrows at her contemplated each other.

"Do you realize what they would have done if you shot me? Committed regicide? Deicide? They would have executed you and told the world you were traitors. I need a SaCarriage for me and"—Eirlys glanced at August—"a guest."

"We aren't —" the guard started.

"Fucking do what she tells you!" Deryn shouted. "I will talk to your commander. I swear to the goddess herself; I will make sure you work at Night Stone for the rest of your life."

Guardians snapped to attention.

"Sorry," Deryn addressed Eirlys. "I figured right now we needed things immediately."

Eirlys walked to August. "Can you lay him down, please?"

"Should you be healing?" Price asked.

Eirlys shrugged and Price did as requested. Eirlys healed August's wounds, but she could not help the ones on the inside. When his body was mended, she conjured water, floating a flat oval plane of liquid over August. She drove her power into him, seeking his spirit. Something she'd normally never try without permission. It was harder to manage this; the spirit didn't regenerate like the body.

Her life in Kestrya had taught her where the curse lay within the spirit. She sensed the warm golden glow of his own. It glimmered in the water, faint. Someone gasped. Tangled near the middle was a gnarled, red knot, tumultuous and pulsing. She pushed her magic into it, but it fought back. The inky devoid consumed her magic, pulling her deeper. It no longer fought her power; it rejected the magic entirely and forced Eirlys out with an energy that sent her reeling backwards. She collapsed, weak with exhaustion, as the water soaked them. She growled in frustration.

"Are you okay?" Brisa asked.

Eirlys nodded anyway.

"The red? The Devoid Curse?" Deryn asked.

"Yes, I've never tried to heal it before," Eirlys explained.

"Your Grace?" a guardian said. "Private Tennen Vern. We have a SaCarriage ready for you. And if you would like, I am a Va. I can heal your wounds."

Eirlys thanked the goddess.

"Yes, if you don't mind."

Tennen bent over her, pulling on his magic. "I don't care who you are or what you have done. No one should have to suffer."

Eirlys let the young healer treat her. Instantly, she felt more like herself. All she needed was a shower.

"Where is the closest city?" Deryn asked the private.

"My parents' estate is a few miles from here," Price said.

Better than nothing, and she needed to get August cleaned up, anyhow. Price loaded August into the SaCarriage as Eirlys rounded the vehicle. A thud and crash sent her running. August's Wraithmark shined on his wild face. Price sprawled fifteen feet away from the car, grumbling.

"Hey!" Eirlys caught August by the arm, and he pushed wind towards her in his signature move but she swung his own body into it, sending him smashing into the side of the SaCarriage. Goddess, at least that part of his magic still worked. "I just healed you, jerk. Stop trying to fight everything!"

August blinked. "Eirlys!"

She rolled her eyes. "Get in the carriage," she said before stomping away.

When the carriage was ready, Deryn and Brisa took the front seats while Eirlys sat between Price and August.

Exhaustion tugged at Eirlys, and she put her face in her hands. Price's fingers traced up and down her back and she collapsed to the side. She fell into a half dream state, her head resting on Price's thigh.

Minutes later, when she was just on the edge of sleep, Price spoke.

"She's told me a lot about you."

August stiffened.

"Not—" Price blew out a breath. "I'm on her side, okay? Trust me, I tried not to be, almost died trying to not be close to her. She saved my life."

"She does that a lot," August said. "She was once my guardian, and I hope she is still my lover, my best friend. She's saved me a thousand times in a thousand ways. But she was always meant for so much more than a life as my wife, even if that's what I wanted, even if I'm not sure we could have had that. I always said I wanted to change things, to help Kygem. She's the one who will actually do it."

August said nothing further and Eirlys drifted off to sleep.

Price shook Eirlys awake. Rubbing the sleep from her eyes, she glanced at the open door. Brisa and Deryn, and even August, stared at her. No one went through it.

"Eirlys, you should go first," Price said.

Mumbling 'I know' under her breath, an estate servant helped her down from the carriage.

"Your Grace," they said.

Trepidation remained in their eyes, dread. How long had it been since the attendants at the castle feared her? August went next and the terror became palpable in the air.

"Show them your power," Eirlys suggested.

August pulled on his magic and his Wraithmark streaked brighter than the dim sun through fog. They still didn't know what part of his magic the curse might have taken, and right now it didn't matter. It would, eventually, but the important thing right now was that they were safe and together, no matter how broken.

The attendants visibly relaxed. Eirlys wanted to pretend she wasn't hurt. She tried to be okay with the fact that even the Prince of Kestrya was welcome here because he was Klara. But it bit into wounds in her heart. She didn't wait. She found the pathway to the house and made her way up the slight incline.

The house's uniqueness could not be denied. Wide, sweeping walkways curved and led to the front door, which was tucked into the alcove of the building. Multicolored stones coated the walls, each a different shape and color, from squares to rectangles and oblong circles to jagged pyramids. Their patterns and textures varied: sea blue, moss green, deep gray granite, white marble. The slope of the roof jutted over the sides, held with red wood beams which created a small awning. An amalgamation of Northern architecture with the southern flair for sharp edges, surrounded by soft curves, made it the most eclectic house she had ever seen.

When she reached the top of the hill, she caught her breath. A smooth grassy hillside ended in a drop off to the sea. The mansion sat on one of the highest points, nestled in the back of a small cove. The tall cliffs encircling the bay were pure white, topped with soft green crowns. The sounds of the waves rolling made Eirlys think of home, and the seawater smelled stronger here. Light mist rose from the cliffs, coating her skin.

A quiet snort and a slight whinny drew Eirlys's attention to a herd of horses dotting the clifftop. The horses were dappled gray or black, their manes either free or braided into woven knots. They stood tall, proud, and ready for any war. Eirlys hoped she'd never ride one into battle, and yet yearned to feel the powerful muscles beneath her legs.

Price came up behind her as she admired the view and wrapped his arms around her. "It's beautiful here, I know. If you stay long enough, there are steps down the cliffs I can show you."

Eirlys desired nothing more than to lean back into his arms, close her eyes, and love him for the rest of her days. Flashes of him crossed her mind, on the bed nearly dead in that farmhouse, the obsidian through his chest, and the shock of pain on his face. Never again, she wanted to promise him. Never again.

Eirlys pulled away and trudged to the house. But when she opened the doors, it was as if she also opened the gates where she'd shoved all the pain and panic she hadn't had time to feel. The events of the last few hours crashed over her head, fogging her brain and tightening her chest. When she stepped inside, she couldn't make out any details: the walls were plain and blurred, the furniture a haze of vague color. A front room appeared before her and the floor to ceiling windows showed the view of the cliffs, but the world was fading. Panic swelled around her, but she couldn't break down yet. August still needed her.

"Can you direct me to a shower?" Eirlys asked, forcing the words through her closing throat.

The attendant pointed the way. Brisa and Deryn were

settled with August in the sitting room further down, and Eirlys motioned for August to follow. She ignored the look of alarm on Brisa's face and walked with him to the bathroom.

"Get in," Eirlys said, reaching in to turn on the shower.

"I'm fine, Eirlys," August said.

"Wash up, please," she commanded. "I will find a way to get you home."

"I can go ba—"

"Absolutely not," Eirlys cried, power bursting forth from her, snow covering the bathroom. *Void it!*

August reached for her, and before they touched, he stopped. The warmth of his skin still struck her, and he dropped his hand.

"Thank you," she whispered. Gratitude that he understood how vulnerable she was washed over her. She fled the room.

Entering the living room, Price stood with his back to her, staring out at the landscape. His shoulders were tense and strained, but he didn't turn to her.

"I told the attendants to get rooms ready," Deryn said.

"No. You're going home," Eirlys commanded.

Brisa gaped.

"I will get August a ship out, or maybe I can contact Vara, Ancients be cursed. Then I'm going home alone. Price can stay here."

Price started. "I'm not leaving you."

"Yes, you are. You will remain here or take a job elsewhere. They will kill you if you return to Alby. Get far away from me. Everyone should."

Price pivoted, taking three large strides, and grabbed her shoulders. "Don't do this."

"Go away, Price," Eirlys said, trying to back up.

"Gods, Eirlys, I swore to protect you." Price's Wraithmark glowed.

Eirlys pulled on her own magic, hands freezing over as they formed fists. "Don't make me do this."

"Do what? Hurt me? Too fucking late! I've been imprisoned and stabbed and yet here I am, by your side."

"Trust me, you should get as far away from me as you can. All of you."

"No," Price said, his tone defiant, but his voice broke.

Eirlys rolled her shoulders and stepped towards him. She went for an undercut, aiming for his stomach. He grabbed her wrist, twisting. Eirlys flipped but landed on her feet. Brisa yelped in surprise.

"What is wrong with you?" Price yelled at her. He tensed, braced and ready.

"I will hurt you to keep you away from me. None of you should want anything to do with me. You support me, but I am nothing but a killer, willing to do what it takes. I'm no better than the Ancients."

"Don't you dare compare yourself to them," Price snarled.

"I'm not a good person!" Eirlys yelled, her power exploding out from her in waves of snow and ice and frigid cold.

Price released his magic and stood there in flaming glory, his Wraithmark as bright as the noon sun, powerful and beautiful.

"What are you talking about?" Price said. "Over the last few months, I have watched you sacrifice your safety, your sleep, and your health just for the sake of bringing comfort to a few people. A bad person does not leave her home for enemy territory to make their world a better place."

Eirlys said nothing, still wrapped in her anger and grief.

"Do you think I'm a good person?" Price asked. "Do you know who I was before you freed me from the Ancients' tyranny? How many people I have preached to, who I led to kill their own children? Goddess, Eirlys, there was once a time where I considered striking you down with an infant in your arms just to rid the world of what I once considered evil. It was you who showed me how wrong I was and because of that, I love you."

"Don't," Eirlys said. Her voice came out harder than she intended.

"Why?"

"I don't deserve it. Look at what I've done, at those I've hurt."

Eirlys closed her eyes. The truth bore down on her like a weight from the endless skies. She had fought so long, pretending to be noble, to be loyal. When push came to shove, she was not only a coward, but frighteningly ready to take life and spirits for her own gain. She'd been ready to leave the hope of all the Skath behind just so she could go home. That she did it to protect those she loved mattered to no one. In a world of gray, she was a stain. Dark as ink, as her own power. Skath, shadow, evil. Did every Skath, when forced to choose, travel down the same path? Did the rock tear at their feet, warning them of danger as they plunged over a cliff, their death brought upon them by their own hand?

A small brush of wind touched her, and she opened her eyes. Gray eyes met hers and his hands caressed her face, gentle and loving. August brushed the tears from her cheeks, leaning in to kiss her. At the smallest touch, a trace of his lips, her power faded. She remained ever still as August rested his head on her forehead. Even freshly clean, the never-ending smell of the sea lingered on his skin, and she breathed it in. Home. Goddess, he smelled like home.

"The choices we must make as sovereigns will always put the ones we love at risk. Merely being born meant me and my siblings were targets. You'll face terrible odds but trust me when I say, to love someone is worth it."

Eirlys shook her head, but August stopped her.

"I will never regret loving you. I will never regret fighting for you. I will never regret helping you."

"But they used you."

"No," August murmured. "They tried, but you wouldn't let them. You won that fight. Trust me. We lose it all only when you no longer care about anything, because then you rule with nothing in your heart. Eirlys, your spirit burns as bright as molten steel. Don't let them harden it into something immovable."

Warm, large hands wrapped themselves around hers. Price held onto her as Brisa and Deryn surrounded her on both sides.

"We aren't leaving you, Eirlys," Brisa said. "I didn't threaten to rip out my baby sister's throat for you to refuse my help. Deryn might lose their position for protecting me."

"Exactly. Look what I have made you do," Eirlys said, but her words lacked conviction.

Within the arms of those she loved, she broke down. Sobs wracked against her chest, stealing her breath. Her knees gave out, but four pairs of hands guided her, slow and steady, and together they held her as she cried.

# CHAPTER FORTY-EIGHT

## EIRLYS

E irlys finally made her way to the shower. The hot water
washed off days of grime and blood. By the time she
turned off the water, the room was clouded in a humid mist.
She waved her hand, dissipating the steam—her shadow-
stained face stared back at her in the mirror. With a strange
gentleness, she reached for her scars, barely missing the tiny
starburst scar from infancy, a raised still pink scar lined her
chest from where Emzelhal stabbed her through with the
sword. Another raised line, with more jagged edges from the
constant reopening, lay across her ribs.

Her marred skin did not represent the scars on her heart,
nor the damage done to her soul. Her spirit was a ragged mess
of a thing, bloody and bruised. And it would not be the last
time she would be torn and changed.

She wrapped a towel around herself but didn't have the
courage to open the door. She sunk onto the bathroom floor,
staring at nothing, until someone knocked.

"Come in," she said.

August opened the door and leaned against the frame. Eirlys studied his muscles as he crossed his arms, lean and taut. Despite the events of the day, Eirlys's breath stilled, and her mouth went a little dry.

But those gray eyes, normally so attuned to her moods, were like haunted, dark clouds. Not the promise of summer rain but the devastation of a storm. He was on the verge of breaking. The too quiet house with strangers he didn't know, and she'd been locked in the bathroom feeling sorry for herself.

Instead of asking if he was alright, because the answer would be no, she rose and walked to him. She didn't reach out to touch him, just let the line of their bodies nearly meet. He was warm and safe... and hurt. All her life, the only thing she ever wanted to do was keep that look off his face, protect him at all costs. For her, for the rest of the Shadow Guard, their duty did not stop at his physical health. They protected his well-being to keep their ever-smiling prince the shining star, even on the darkest of nights.

"You do not have to wallow in sorrow and grief," she whispered to him. Finally, she reached up and touched the side of his face with the back of her knuckles, the stubble from his long journey rough against her skin.

"I'm trying," he said, voice breaking. He swallowed.

"Can I try?" she asked and let every intention, every plan, every goddess-cursed dirty thought going through her mind leak onto her face.

This time when his eyes darkened, it was a promise of carnality. His deliciously wicked grin ignited the dull embers in her heart, and she was pressed against him in an instant. The towel fell to the floor in a hush of fabric. She kissed him, wrapping her arms around his neck. His hands and fingers stroked her back and she moaned, desperately wanting him, needing him.

Without breaking their kiss, Eirlys pushed him into the bedroom until the back of his knees hit the mattress. She pushed him onto his back, gazing at him and lingering on every feature she loved—every part of him she wanted to touch. The large window covering the eastern wall revealed the setting sun casting shadows across the bay, tinting the purple sky with brilliant orange and pink clouds. The golden light gilded her skin with color and illuminated the side of August's face.

There was a knock on the door, but it opened immediately. It was his bedroom after all. Price stepped in and froze, the door still half ajar beside him. Something flitted in his eyes that Eirlys didn't quite catch before lust took over all other emotions. Was it the sight of her standing naked in the light of a dying sunset or the way August was sprawled beneath her?

"Oh," he stammered out, a tightness in his voice, a falter in the look in his eyes. "I'll find somewhere else to be," he said, starting to turn away.

"Stay," Eirlys blurted out, taking a step toward him.

She was tired of the sadness lingering in everyone's eyes. Tired of the way it was all so fucking awkward when, if the world had been a better place in a gentler time, maybe the three of them would have found each other long ago.

Price paused in the doorway. The lighting in the room deepened the shadows across his face. His hand gripped the wood tightly. He glanced at August, who was propped onto his elbows, and the two of them silently stared at each other. Not sizing each other up; appraising, wondering, musing on the idea.

"All of us, together?" Eirlys asked. Her voice wavered

because even in her wildest dreams, she never considered this a possibility. Not truly.

She reached for Price's hand, an invitation. He swallowed and took it. Standing on her tiptoes, she kissed him gently on the cheek. Then he captured her lips with his own and she melted into him. She held out one hand behind her, for the prince now standing at her back. He stepped into her touch, her fingers grazing the top of his hip. She broke the kiss, stepping back enough to gauge their reactions.

The promise of something hungry lingered in Price's eyes, in the corners of his upturned lips. It was stomach-churning good; butterflies-filling-her-entire-body good. It was August they turned to, a question in their gaze.

But instead of his face lighting up with lust or desire, a deep sorrow spread from him like a plague, those gray eyes watching them intently. Wrapping his arms around himself, he turned away and stared out at the sunset.

Eirlys went to August's side. He had been there for her, all day, not once giving into his own doubts, his own losses. And today, he had lost more than she had, and yet she was the one who needed comfort without thinking of him. She fled from him earlier today, too terrified to be stable for anyone. But she was not alone and did not need to carry the burdens of the day by herself. Neither should August.

Price moved up beside Eirlys.

"I don't have to be here," Price said.

August's lips twitched. "That's not a problem for me. I just... watching the two of you. It's like I'm seeing a future that can never be. We can never be. Not you"—he touched Eirlys's cheek—"or you." He faced Price, a halo of the shimmering pure light surrounding his silhouette. "All I can think of is what I'll miss if I let this continue."

He voiced Eirlys's very own thoughts and fears. Price

stole a glance at Eirlys. They were both thinking about it, how unsteady the future was for all of them. Her lingering Alteration, and the rule that waited for her afterward.

"The future is fickle for all of us," Price said. "If the worst happens—" His throat bobbed, hard. Eirlys's hands went numb at thought of her looming death.

"I don't want to miss out on this," Eirlys said. "But if I die —" Both August and Price whipped their heads at her, as if saying the words made them truer.

She barreled on needing to get the words out. "I don't want to leave you two more broken than before. So, nothing has to happen. But I promised to take whatever happiness life gives me. And in this cruel bitter realm, I never thought I would find it in the two of you."

August's eyes widened at the words they used to say to each other in Kestrya. Then his expression lightened, the turmoil fading into surety. "Thank you for reminding me that even if I can't have you forever, I can have you for now." The corner of his mouth raised into a smirk and breathlessly he said, "Both of you."

Then those stormy eyes flashed with the missing heat— and lust and desire—and not all of it was for Eirlys. August stepped into Price, a finger trailing along the taller man's jaw. Price caught his hand, holding it against his face before kissing August's palm.

"Come to bed, Prince. "

They steered back towards the bed, Price undoing each button of August's shirt torturously slow before sliding it off his back. Eirlys climbed onto the bed, her hands trailing up Price's back and removing his shirt as well. She met August's gaze over Price's shoulder. She wondered if her own pupils were blown as wide.

When his breath caught, Eirlys leaned forward and whispered into Price's ear, "Ask him."

Price trembled underneath her hands. But he obeyed. "Can I kiss you?" he asked August.

The prince smiled, soft and almost unsure. "Yes."

Price started slowly, a soft kiss to his cheek, trailing over to his mouth. When their lips met everything soft became fire. A burning heat practically blazed between them. Eirlys flushed, hot and red, her lips parted.

Price flipped them around with ease, pushing August onto the bed beside Eirlys, crawling on top of him. He kissed him, August's hands strong and tight on his hips. When Price left his mouth, Eirlys leaned in to claim it for herself.

"Are you okay?" she asked, checking in.

"Yes," he groaned out. "I want... I need... " He swallowed. Price had stopped his descent, his hands hovering over the waistband of August's pants. "Don't stop," he begged. Seeing August completely undone sent sweet flames of desire through Eirlys.

Then August was reaching for Eirlys, guiding her to straddle his face. She went wide eyed, but he merely breathed in her scent, the whisper of air tickling her.

Then August groaned, tossing his head back. Eirlys peeked over her shoulder to see Price taking August into this mouth, those blue eyes so fucking intense. She was enraptured by the sight until she felt August lick her from her entrance to her clit. She bucked into him. He chuckled against her, and it turned into a moan, the vibration driving her mad with pleasure.

Every single ounce of heat was pooling between her thighs, thrumming as August's tongue circled her, again and again. She tried to stay completely off him, but eventually the pleasure drove all sense of logic from her mind. Between August's moans, the way his fingers tightened against her hips and his hot tongue, she found herself flung over the edge. Pleasure poured through her, her head tossed back, and she rode August's mouth until she couldn't take it anymore.

She collapsed to the side, trying to catch her breath. She blinked blearily as Price stood up and removed his pants. He was hard, his length stretched out in front of him. He walked over and pulled a vial from the bedside table. The oil caught the fading sunlight.

Then August was pulling Eirlys towards the edge of the bed, kissing her deeply, his hands roving her breasts. She tasted herself on him, and she moaned into his mouth.

"You sure?" Price asked.

Eirlys must have missed some discussion while she was learning how to be in her own body again.

"Absolutely," August said.

August's cock was pressed up against Eirlys, the tip of him touching the most sensitive place on her right now. She jerked, leaning her head into his shoulder. He adjusted her just a little and slid in. She cried out into his skin.

"Just—don't move for a second," August said, trying to maintain whatever composure he had left. With her face pressed into his shoulder, she had a lovely view of Price's warm hands rubbing oil over August's backside. She felt and heard him moan as Price's gentle fingers teased and stretched him out.

"Fuck," August said, his head falling into Eirlys's neck when Price finally entered him. Eirlys grazed her teeth against August's shoulder but other than that, no one moved for a second.

Holding onto August, Eirlys felt Price's finger trail over her own gripped onto August's shoulder. Her boys, she thought. And though both would die for her—both almost had—she knew in this moment, that she would destroy the void for them. She'd fight the Goddesses or burn the realms to see them safe. She would let them shatter her, grateful for every shard. And if she let love break her, there would be nothing left for the gods to destroy.

Finally, August's ragged breaths became steadier, and he said, "I'm good."

He gave a small thrust into Eirlys, which made Price groan and Eirlys cry out. August rocked into her, moving Price into him. That sound alone might've undone her again, but the boys found a rhythm and left Eirlys barely holding on. Not just to the man in front of her, or the pleasure building, but the intensity of it all as they joined together as one. Something she dreamed about but could never put into words because before this it was an impossibility.

August's hand gripped Eirlys's jaw, the other digging onto Price's hand on his hip. His cock twitched inside of her, making her lose all focus on moving her hips or her wandering thoughts. And Goddess, the noises coming from him, nearly mewling at the pleasure, pressed up against Eirlys's skin.

With August becoming frantic between them, Eirlys became enthralled by Price, his breathing heavy, sweat glistening on his skin. She watched him, his concentration on the man in front of him, bringing August to the edge. Then that intense gaze noticed her, his mouth parted, and his rhythm stuttered like he was caught off guard. With no gentleness, he grabbed for her over August's body and kissed her. Eirlys was thankful he was tall enough to lean over as tongues and teeth and lips clashed, August pressed between them, his hands tightening on her, hard enough to bruise. Price back bent, head tossed back, eyes closed, and mouth parted.

Her Wraithmark darkened at the sight and her two lovers shone bright, taking her breath away. The scents of sea and brine, woodsmoke and the tangy smell of rain on a parched desert mingled in the darkening room as the sun gave up its journey.

August trembled. He was trying to hold on, trying to not orgasm, to make this moment last, but Eirlys didn't want his restraint. She wanted his pleasure, his release. She wanted him to cry out their names, begging and pleading. To take the wastelands of their hearts and drown them in rapture and love and every part of herself that she could give.

"August," she breathed into his ear. "Look at yourself."

She turned his head so that he was staring into the window but with the dark night, it reflected the picture of the three of them in perfect clarity. August's flushed cheeks, Eirlys's parted lips, Price's lips pressed into August's shoulder.

Those gray eyes opened wide as he took them all in. Then he bucked wildly, holding onto her, Price holding onto him. Every part of him clenched, his teeth grabbing onto the soft part of Eirlys's shoulder, breaking the tender skin. The air around them burst into a whirlwind and the RaGlass on the wall blared with light, replacing the now fading sun so they were captured in this glorious moment.

August cried out their names into her flesh before it melted into soft cries while he finished, his body going loose. Price lifted his head, his pupils blown wide. He pulled out of August, evidence of his own orgasm slick on his cock.

The RaGlass dimmed to a faint orange glow. For a moment, the only sound was their hushed breaths in the twilight tinted room.

"You didn't come," Price said, brushing her hair out of his face.

Eirlys, trying as gently to remove herself from August, said, "I was a bit caught up. You two are delightfully distracting."

August spasmed against her, and he said something she didn't catch. "What?" she asked.

"Not fair," he uttered.

She laughed them off. "I came plenty on your mouth," she said, giving August a playful slap against his arm.

But August and Price didn't accept her excuses. August grabbed Eirlys by the waist, pulling her onto her back. He pressed himself into her side, sliding an arm around her. August kissed her, one hand holding her in place as the other caressed her nipple. She arched into his touch. Then Price was on the other side, his hands sliding into her warmth. He graciously avoided her oversensitive clit, plunging two fingers inside of her with no warning. She was ready anyway, so wet and wanting.

It didn't take her long, with August's mouth on hers, his hands on her breasts and Price's fingers thrusting into her, for her to succumb to the pleasure all over again. She came over Price's fingers, feeling a new warm wetness slide down her leg as she cried out into August's mouth.

Sweat glistened on Price's chest, and Eirlys breathed deeply, too comfortable to move if her limbs would even work. August curled around her back, his palm a whisper on her bare hip. She caught movement out of the side of her eye and saw Price reach for August's hand and together they held her down in this world, kept her grounded.

"I love you," purred through the room, too quiet to make out who said it.

"I love you both," she whispered, eyes closed. They trapped her body between a raging forest fire and a wind-swept sea. And yet, she had never felt safer.

Eirlys sat at the kitchen table sipping a cup of tea while

Price and August fumbled around, trying to make breakfast. They had sent the attendants out after one girl screamed when Eirlys accidentally touched her. Price promised the poor girl wouldn't be dismissed, but she didn't need to be in the same house.

Brisa and Deryn left for Alby after the first night. Eirlys had cooked breakfast the last two mornings, but today Price and August were trying. She tried hard not to laugh at them. Two noble men trying to cook for themselves. Price fried eggs and August made porridge, though neither appeared edible.

Price somehow set the eggs on fire, and Eirlys doubled over in laughter watching a Ra and Sa attempt to put out the flames. When she caught her breath, she took pity on them and doused it with a flick of her hand.

"Can I cook now?" she asked, looking at the burnt eggs and cemented porridge.

The men nodded, looking ashamed, but August caught Price's arm and kissed him in a moment of surprise. Eirlys ignored sweet waves of pleasure, knowing they needed sustenance over sex. And they'd had days and days of both already. She sliced apples, one of her favorite fruits, and spread them on the bottom of the pan. She topped them with cream, sugar, and cinnamon. Then she made the dough with leftover eggs and flour sprinkled on top, setting it in the oven.

The boys lounged at the table, watching her clean up their mess and chatting absently. Eirlys turned, wiping a little sweat from her brow, and paused, taking in the scene. A moment of peace—a glimpse of the normalcy they might have had. If August were not a prince, and she not a queen, and if the very realm in which they stood had not hated Price so much they'd broken him and called it a gift. If they were just people; Skath and Skath and Klara—darkness and the light that brightened their days. If they were born in a world without hatred and horror.

Lita should be here, and the Shadow Guard, and Brisa and Deryn. But despite the missing pieces, it was all still so beautiful.

Eirlys didn't move, afraid to shatter the bubble that buoyed her up, the spirit in her body singing with her love for these two men, this small sliver of a moment that wasn't real, could never truly be real. It was a gift all the same.

Life was giving her happiness, and she intended to take it and hold on tight for as long as she could.

"What would the perfect world look like to you?" Price asked.

A heavy downpour had scoured the land, trapping the trio inside for days, until they couldn't stand it anymore and braved the cold, misty air to sit on the seaside cliff under steely clouds. The ocean was a turmoil of blue-grays and the whites of cresting waves which crashed far below where they sat. Eirlys leaned halfway onto August's lap, feet tucked up. Price curled behind her where his hand intertwined with August's on her hip.

She glanced up just in time to see August's brow furrowed. "Beyond the obvious?" August said.

"Yes. Let's assume we are all whole and as we should be," Price said.

"I'd want to see a world where the Ancients don't exist. Where people get to make their own choices, and not because an old batty goddess told them too. A realm where choices were based on morals and not religion."

Eirlys and Price shared a look but disclosed nothing. Although August believed in the Goddesses and their four daughters, he never worshiped them the way Eirlys did. They had saved her life, given her a realm to grow up in. Their religion gave the Skath asylum and peace, and yet, she felt abandoned by them in this cursed realm. Price's own struggles with his faith had nearly cost him his life. They were both searching for religion, for purpose.

"What about you?" August said, lifting Price's hand.

"A world without suffering, where pain is a thing of the past. Physical pain at least."

They both looked at Eirlys, who gazed out at the sea and didn't know how to answer. Because the truth was, she hadn't been thinking about the big picture during their time at the estate. Her perfect world was here, on this cliffside. Or on an island off the coast of Kestrya, where the breeze warmed the soul and the ocean never chilled. Where the children she would never have learned to swim as they learned to walk, and one had blonde hair and curls and the other jet-black hair with piercing green eyes. Where her boys loved her for all eternity, and they quietly raised their children, and the world never witnessed the bloodshed she had inflicted upon it. Where her spirit laid in tranquil contentment.

The vision faded as her lovers' words crowded in, only leaving room for the reason she'd come here to begin with. She would change Kygem, even if she must break it to do so.

Now was not the time to talk of shattering worlds. So, she answered instead, "I want to see children, free and unencumbered, their parents not struggling to conceive. I want to see the path between our realms open and free, where families aren't split and torn apart. Where babies aren't murdered, and dreams aren't crushed."

Quiet fell between them, the sound of the rain pattering the already damp grass.

"When I leave tomorrow, I'll hold us to these. That we see these dream worlds made, that we help orchestrate them." August caressed Eirlys's cheek, and she closed her eyes at the sweetness of his touch.

They all agreed. She wanted to take this rare moment of happiness life had given her and bottle it, to spread it, to change the realm with it. To not simply burn the world to the ground, but to grow something in the ashes.

# CHAPTER FORTY-NINE

## AUGUST

"Will you let me know?" August asked.

The three of them stood on the cliff as Vara waited a little way off, giving them privacy. A week of wonder in the house on the shore was coming to an end.

Eirlys smirked darkly at him. "I'm sure you'll hear about it. Either Aydra or I will be crowned."

"That's not funny. Look, Eirlys. Live. Spite them and live for him," he said, gesturing beyond her shoulder.

Price stayed close behind her.

"I love you, still, after it all. I do love you." Eirlys was crying again. He yearned for the days when he hardly ever saw her cry, when death and pain and goodbyes were rare.

He smiled at her. "And I love you."

She leaned forward and kissed him. It had been the most amazing week. For as long as he lived, she would never forget it.

Price approached, and without speaking, they both reached for each other, pulling into a tight embrace. He wasn't surprised a lover Eirlys chose would be so suited for her and in turn for him. Not for the first time that week, August wished they had both escaped to Kestrya. That they would still come with him. Although he still wanted Kygem to burn, Eirlys was a raging storm ready to cleanse the north. She deserved the chance to try, and he'd support her in any way that he could.

They pulled apart and Price leaned his head against August's forehead.

"I'm glad I got to know you," Price said.

Though he only knew Price for a few days, knowing him through Eirlys made him feel closer, safer to the man who loved the same woman. In some ways, he wished he never stayed here for this beautiful week, never pictured the three of them together. It was a dream that could never be and yet one he relished in.

But he'd known his whole life that being with Eirlys forever was just that—a dream. She was never really his, and now she belonged to something bigger than all of them.

The few steps he took away from Eirlys, from Price, were the hardest he'd ever taken in his life. Harder than those anguished moments pounding across the rough slats of the dock as he watched Eirlys sail away from him all those months ago; harder than stumbling across the demarcation line and becoming Devoid. This time it was not a curse that crackled beneath his skin or ruptured through his chest; it was his heart, breaking.

He wondered if he would ever see her again.

Vara was waiting, hand outstretched, and when he took it, he didn't look back. Not until the void closed behind him, and they were back on the familiar palace grounds, and everywhere he looked, Eirlys was not there.

He didn't have to go far to find comfort. One moment he

felt more alone in the world than ever before—the next, a small brown-haired woman slammed herself into August.

"Caden," he breathed.

Rory poked his head out of the nearby door to the barracks. He called back and ran to meet them. He hugged August, crushing the air from his lungs before kissing him breathless. August was crying now. When Galen and Basil came out, they rushed toward him. Then Nik. He hobbled on crutches, but he was alive. Aliah and Ronan followed, still there, still supporting him after he'd nearly torn the small family apart.

They were alive. Wonderfully and shockingly alive.

Both of his mothers cried, from happiness and sorrow.

Redna held her son, while Nyala cursed Eirlys, cursed Kygem, and threatened war. August merely asked for patience, to let Eirlys figure out this new role. Let her survive the alteration. There would be time later to take revenge if there was a need for it. If Eirlys could change Kygem, if she could convince the gods, she might save both of their realms.

August left his mothers with each other and walked through the open hallways. The air was just on this side of warm, comfortable at high noon. He'd been back for a bit now but avoided the places that reminded him of her most. He sighed, knowing he couldn't put this off forever. So, he turned and with tortured steps, made his way to her house.

It sat empty, as it had for all these months. Who else would want to live in the old servant's quarters? It was barely more than a shack compared to the palace's grandeur. He smiled, but it was tinged with bitterness—Eirlys hated it when he called it that. The one story, two-bedroom house was so much less than she deserved. She had an entire castle of her own now, he remembered.

He opened the door. The front room was stuffed with couches, cushions, and various chairs they'd brought in as the group grew. So many late nights were spent here, sprawled out over each other like a pile of puppies, laughter so loud and raucous the walls sometimes shook.

Lita's kitchen, where she taught Eirlys to cook, stood cold and emotionless. No fire lit the stove, the constant smell of baking bread gone with the person who used to cook like it was therapy. He remembered how she would laugh from the kitchen at one of his jokes when the rest of them just rolled their eyes. Or how she smacked away grabby hands, desperate for a taste of whatever she was preparing.

Finally, he made her way to *her* room. He sat on her bed, hands trailing over the rough comforter. They had spent so many nights hidden under these covers, exploring their bodies for the first time and countless times after, whispering secrets to each other.

Unable to hold on any longer, August pulled the ring from his pocket—the one he bought to welcome Eirlys home. He placed it on the bed, nestled on the pillow. It still smelled like her after all these months.

He didn't care that his mother wouldn't have approved, that she would have surely said he couldn't marry Eirlys. It was a battle he'd been willing to fight, something he wouldn't have let anyone take from him. None of that mattered now because she was gone—to do great things, to save the Skath and change the world. And voids-curse him, it only made him love her more, and made her that much harder to let go.

He pulled out a RaGlass. Not the kind used for light, but the kind used to start fires. When he tossed it onto the bed, it exploded in brilliant blue flames, reminding him of Price's eyes. He hoped she gazed into them every day for the rest of their lives. That she loved him, and that he loved her as deeply as he could. For both of them.

Walking out of the house, the fire quickly spread thanks to August's wind. His magic flared and he fueled the fire with oxygen drawn in on a warm ocean breeze. It was only when the entire place had gone up in a blaze that Rory sprinted toward him.

"Help me put it out," he screamed, pulling on his magic, and darting toward the raging inferno.

August grabbed his hand. "Let it go, Rory."

Rory stopped and stared back at him. He looked from the burning building back to August. He frowned but remained beside his prince as they watched the house of their friend descend into ash.

And they let her go.

# Chapter Fifty

## Eirlys

Eirlys trembled as she sat on the obsidian slab. She tried to stop it. Brisa held her hand and they locked eyes; a forest floor meeting a gleaming meadow. Eirlys squeezed tightly. From the corner of her eye, she saw Aydra avert her eyes. Only by decree of the council itself did Aydra manage an invitation to Eirlys's Alteration. Deryn guarded the outside of the door.

Price was—Eirlys closed her eyes leaning her head on Brisa's hands. Price. He begged her to let him join, to be there. Adamant, she refused. Not only had they performed this procedure on him, but if she died, she didn't want that to be his last memory of her.

She pleaded to let their final moments of the night before be filled with love, to remember him happy and at peace one more time. She yearned to watch the thrills of ecstasy cross his face again and inhale the smoky scent of his skin lingering on hers as she breathed. August's absence pressed between them, and in the early hours of the night when she curled into the circle of Price's arms, it was as if she could feel him there, a comforting presence to guide her into sleep.

When she left that morning, Price had pretended not to see the tears on her cheeks, and she'd pretended not to notice the bottle of obsidian on the table. She thanked the goddess for his oblivion.

Eirlys tried to drag out her last few days for as long as possible but the anxiety of the wait, of the unknown, became too much. And there was still so much for her to do, so much for her to accomplish. Every day she went without her crown was another day an infant died, another family torn apart.

There was a knock on the door, and Isbeil entered with a group of Va.

Eirlys's heart thumped in her chest, getting out as many final beats as possible, at the sight of the healer. Adrenaline surged through her veins, and a small spark in the back of her mind caught fire.

If she did die today, the Ancients had some explaining to do. In a press conference in the square of Alby, Eirlys had announced her intention to go forth with the Alteration. One sweet, well-meaning soul had asked about the success rates.

"As I am ascended to the godliness of our beloved Ancients," she had said, "their strength, our strength, and my own grace should protect me. I am no mere immortal."

If Eirlys died, she would go down swinging, taking one last proverbial punch to the Ancients and their vehement rule. And if she lived, she had the long life of an immortal to see if they bled.

"Lay back, Eirlys," Isbeil said. "Princess Brisa, stand with your sister."

Brisa kissed the back of Eirlys's hand and let go. The space between Brisa and Aydra fluttered in turmoil. Underneath a heavy layer of makeup, Aydra's throat sported still healing bruises from Brisa's assault. Aydra's eyes met Eirlys's, and something like panic shown in them. Surely not for her. Eirlys laid back, ignoring questions she didn't have time to ask or answer.

The glass roof brought the sun glaring into Eirlys's eyes. The cold obsidian slab beneath her seemed to mold to her body, accepting her into a cocoon of nothingness. The clank of a metal table jolted her, and she jumped despite herself. Healers appeared on either side of her prone form. She noted only faces and not the instruments in their hands.

"Are you ready?"

She had accomplished what she had set out to do. The Kestryan Skath were home and Vara had managed to escape the wrath of Ancients. August—she sighed. His Devoidness would always be her one regret, but nothing she could have done would have saved him from that fate.

He lived. They lived. But as she stared up into the glaring light, she knew her time may have come. Death, it seemed, had finally made its way to her, and she smiled, knowing it skipped so many others she loved.

"I'm ready," she said.

Despite trying not to look, she caught sight of one instrument poised above the hollow in her throat, thin and black. Obsidian.

Five healers stood around her and together, they lowered the instruments. One entered at the base of her throat, two on each side of her chest and two below her last ribs, a five-pointed star. The rods were long and angled upwards to meet a hand's length above the center of her chest. Pain drove away questions, although not the worst she had experienced. The sharpness and slowness of the instrument's descent into her body had her gritting her teeth. She tried to stay still, her toes clenching and hands curling into fists. They sat there inside of her as her spirit twisted away, trying to escape the invasion. Though she'd hoped she could stay quiet, the panic of her spirit sent agony rippling up her body, and she finally shrieked. Eirlys almost bucked, muscles so tense her back popped with strain. A ripping sensation tore through her as the healers connected the five points in the middle. The rods scraped the inside of her being, raking through every ounce of magic. She screamed again, short and vulgar, and clenched her fists, tightening every muscle so as not to move.

This was more than uncomfortable, as she'd been told the procedure would be. Uncomfortable was sitting on a chair of nails, or broken glass, or even breaking a bone. Torture had been easier than the sensation rocking through her now. And then it eased, not stopped, but faded to a soft throb.

A small glass crystal sat waiting atop of the five rods. Something akin to cosmic dust like the trail of a comet appeared in the rods, flowing up to the glass. When it entered, Eirlys watched her magic with an awe that ascended the strange tearing sensation in her body. The glass filled and inside it, the galaxy of her power danced in an endless black void: golds, purples, greens, blues, the brightest of whites and glints of red. Her magic, spread across its Skath background, showed every color.

"Wow," breathed Brisa from a corner.

Isbeil removed the glass from the contraption. "We will destroy this on the Summer Solstice."

Despite Eirlys begging for the magic to be used to help the Alters, it was decided that no Skath magic could exist in Kygem.

The rods disappeared and Eirlys raised a hand to study it. No magic filled it yet, though a vast nothingness tugged at her, called to her from the void as she closed her eyes. Her dazed spirit leaned toward it, yearned to go, and Eirlys wondered what would happen if she pulled on the vast space beyond her reach, past her senses. As much as she wanted the antithesis of pain in the empty chasm, her mind rebelled, fighting every impulse to leave this world behind.

"Your Grace?" Isbeil said.

Eirlys blinked, frowned, but stilled on the table. She could not leave now, not after all she'd done. All she still had left to do.

Glass rods had replaced the obsidian ones, and she closed her eyes as they traveled through the same holes, a slight sting over the rawness of the first entry. A flash of light reddened her eyelids, and she peeked. The glass crystal holding her new magic glowed like a tiny sun, so bright she closed her eyes again.

The smallest jolt of the glass placed on top the rods warned her of the pain to come. It was not enough. Her spirit reacted, pounding inside Eirlys's body, every kick and silent scream clawing in her mind. The pain seared, a million burns, a million scrapes, like hitting a stone wall repeatedly. Raw and coated in phantom blood from the violence happening inside her spirit, she jerked, unable to stay still. Hands gripped her tightly, forced her back against the slab. She tasted iron and the meaty mess of her cheek, but no other pain made it through the one inside her. Tears squeezed from her closed eyelids, and beyond the pain a voice spoke words she could not understand.

"What did she say?" Aydra sounded panicked, talking too fast and too high.

Brisa's response came out as a growl, low, deep, and angrier than a welt. "She said she's sorry."

"For what?" Aydra asked.

"For being born?" Brisa guessed.

And she wasn't wrong. As the pain whirled around her, the

glass rods pushing in the foreign magic, Eirlys knew if she'd had the Sight before she had chosen her path, nothing in the world, not Price, or August, or Brisa, or all the Skath in Kygem would have made her choose this. In that moment, which stretched to the farthest reaches of the universe, she was nothing but pain.

Slowly, it dulled.

The brightness of the room dimmed, and she opened her eyes as the last slivers of fading light entered her body.

Stars burst before her eyes before the true agony came. The stars multiplied into billions of pin pricks against her pupils. They scattered across the deep black sky, and for a moment, beauty radiated from it all. The sky crashed down upon her and thousands of stars with their sharp points tore into her. A billion cuts drove themselves against her being until the pain encapsulated her. She was nothing, nothing but a writhing, charred version of her former self.

The anguish buried her, shoving her into the ground with each pound of her heart, deeper and deeper. The darkness overtook her, and she couldn't breathe. The pressure was too great, bearing down on her, the entire world crushing her. White-hot pain melted into panic as each breath became shallow, and gulping for air, her lungs seared.

With one final desperate plea to let it end, she flailed for the empty chasm of the void. Anything to find peace, to escape from pain. She grasped the edges of the void and plunged into it, fighting to claw her way through. Suddenly, the pain left, the void appeared, and blissfully, she felt nothing.

# CHAPTER FIFTY-ONE

## EIRLYS

I n Kestrya, they placed altars inside temples and piled them with offerings to the goddess. In the center of each room, hung a masterfully twisted piece of glass. The glass, if one ventured into the middle, showed the swirling void. How the glass was created or when they first arrived, no one knew.

Eirlys remembered the first time the void appeared, as white or light gray, a shifting, undulating space. In the void, the reality of the past, present, and future shifted and merged. If a believer maintained the goddess's ways and abided by her word, later in the void, they should see the good, the best times, sometimes atone for the wrongs they did. Once they found peace within themselves, they journeyed to find Zoasis in the Valley, who would grant her followers paradise. Some spirits never left, too ravaged by their fears and heinous acts committed in life.

Whatever Eirlys had done, she didn't know what to make of the Void. Was this a punishment? A reward? Was this paradise already?

The white, gray, and deepest black undulated around her, steadily moving, shifting, and changing. A hint of a floor appeared, like the stone pattern in the house she shared with her mother, Lita—Eirlys stopped, everything stopped, and she nearly fell to her knees.

Lita stood before her.

She appeared complete and whole—utterly perfect. Her chestnut hair was pulled back in her signature crown braid, her bright green eyes matching Eirlys's. She wore a plain white dress with simple sandals. She smiled, but gently, like she sensed Eirlys was having trouble with taking it all in. How could she not be? The hope of seeing her mother again had been shattered months ago, so how could she be standing here? Waiting for her?

"Mom? How are you here? Am I dead?" They weren't the first words Eirlys meant to say, but they came out anyway.

"What is dead, truly?" Lita said. Her voice carried a strange lilt, a note just a breath off from the tone Eirlys knew in her bones.

"When you stop living?" Eirlys answered warily.

"And what is living?" Lita tilted her head. Eirlys startled, the movement foreign to her mother's mannerisms.

"Sorry." Lita's tone changed, and she seemed more like her mother.

"You aren't my mother." In the depths of her spirit, she realized this was not Lita standing before her.

Lita paused. "I thought this might be a better way for me to see you, talk to you. Offer you some peace."

Eirlys smiled, wistful and reticent. It might have worked with anyone else. Eirlys had adored Lita, worshiped her.

"So, am I dead?" Eirlys asked again.

"Right now, your heart does not beat, your lungs do not

breathe. But that magic inside you, that spirit inside you, she's a fighter."

"Isn't she me?" Eirlys asked. Wasn't it her spirit who traveled the void when she died?

The walls of the kitchen began to form; cabinets were being outlined and as Lita reached for a whistling kettle, the stove appeared.

"The spirit is a conglomeration of wraith inside your body. It is bound by your physical form, but it does not belong there, at least not permanently. It is an entity which absorbs your experiences, your thoughts and reactions and becomes a part of you. When your body dies, and the spirit enters the void again, you have changed it permanently by the life you have lived."

"So, I am her?" Eirlys asked.

"Not quite. As you are not quite dead either."

"Where is she?"

"She is hiding. What you have done to your magic, to her, is beyond her ability to comprehend. You have a bright mind, a deep heart. You are one who doesn't let their spirit guide them, but you are rational, intelligent, and strong. I made you this way."

Eirlys didn't know if she meant Lita raised her like that, or if she—Eirlys stared at the false Lita, who proffered her a cup of tea. She would have preferred something stronger. "Are you —?" She cut the question off. The thought was preposterous, but possible.

Lita smiled. "I know you miss her."

Eirlys took a sip of tea, surprised to find it hotter than she expected.

Lita laughed. "You never could wait for your tea to cool. The void is not a dream, but the reality of all magic and all time and all things."

"Can you bring her back?" Eirlys asked, gesturing to the form of Lita.

Lita frowned. "I can... after some more time." Lita gestured to the tea which Eirlys drank from, and the temperature was now perfect. "I am not as strong as I once was. To gather all the flecks of your mother's spirit and converge them into a being again would take everything I have."

"You *are* the goddess," Eirlys breathed.

Lita smiled, or more accurately, Zoasis smiled through Lita's face. "I am. I was. I have faded into bits and pieces as my children grew and prospered and all was well. It's taken me five thousand years to gather this form, to perform simple parlor tricks. I used to be able to spin the void into my making. Change reality with a snap."

Zoasis snapped Lita's fingers, and the world transformed; the void changed to the hallway outside the kitchen.

"These are happy memories?" Eirlys asked.

Zoasis shrugged Lita's shoulders. "They are places you desire to be, but not all are good."

Silhouettes appeared, drifting in like mist, and solidified into people. A small Eirlys, blonde hair cropped chin length, peeked around the corner as Lita and Camilla screamed at each other. Eirlys hadn't understood the conversation then. But she made out the words now. Eirlys, princess, stolen, Kygem. The woman had been Lita's lover, a second mother to Eirlys in their five-year relationship.

The scene shifted into her old bedroom. If Eirlys had blood in her cheeks, she would have blushed. She saw herself wrapped in August's arms, so young and so naive she almost didn't recognize the girl cuddling beside the prince. But she knew this moment and the thousand others like it as well as she knew her own mind. She didn't need a recap of all she'd sacrificed.

"Stop," Eirlys begged.

Zoasis peered at Eirlys through jade eyes.

"Are you punishing me?"

"Do you deserve to be punished?" Zoasis asked.

"Yes."

The answer never changed. Maybe before when Eirlys had guarded August, she had a paper-thin excuse. But how did she explain to her goddess that she drove her daggers into August's brother's chest over and over again, that she sliced and diced men so easily for love and for revenge? Her choice to reign in Kygem, the infants she'd stolen from the border—those choices made with good intentions could not stem all the blood she'd spilled into sand and snow and dust.

"Do you not feel the existence I have set upon you is punishment enough?" Zoasis asked.

The scene shifted again. A sitting room, Eirlys's favorite in the Pendry Castle, where Price and she had spent many days.

"The life you gave me?" Eirlys asked. Horror dawned on her and although she had no heart in this place, she felt it break.

"I have limited power and what little I have is still growing. I had a choice. I could wait another five thousand years to gain a few more ounces of my power back, or I could set a plan in motion. A rebel princess, a beautiful daughter, and the rest is your realm's history. Took me a few tries to get it right."

"How many tries?" Eirlys asked.

The look of indignation across Lita's face had never appeared there before. "Nine before you," Zoasis said. "Each time, the queen took their baby daughter, their Skath infant, and did what they thought was required of them."

Eirlys closed her eyes. Nine Skath Pendry infants died because Zoasis had become powerless.

"I'm sorry, Eirlys, but I must ask more of you."

Eirlys's eyes shot open. "More of me? What else can I do? I am at my limit I am *dead*. Do I not deserve to rest now?"

Zoasis waved her off. "You seem to enjoy dying. Happens to you a lot."

"Apparently, all thanks to you."

"I had nothing to do with that. You cannot die because of Gyda."

Eirlys blinked. "What the fuck are you talking about?" At least Eirlys talked to all gods like this. The Ancients weren't as special as they liked to believe.

"When Gyda took your life with her own hands in the Barrenlands, something cracked from her spirit. A piece of the very void in her veins entered you, a newborn vessel still open to change. Cursed land, cursed crowns; the Ancients should know better than to fracture the spirit whether of the land or of a body. There are far reaching consequences to what they have done."

Eirlys's hands flew to her chest, but in the void, her scar was gone. Her skin was smooth and perfect.

"You must go back. You need to stop this. My children—your people—are being slaughtered, and I am powerless. I have put all my hope into you, and you have chosen to follow this path. You chose to return to Kygem and heal it from within. You must not fail."

Rage spurred in Eirlys. "This is not how this is supposed to work. *I* chose this path—not you! I am not a pawn for them, and I am not a pawn for you. That's not what faith is."

Tears came, which she couldn't cry. Nothing worked like it should here.

"You cannot cry because your body is healing. If you were here, you would be almost living, more than a mere shade of yourself. For we are immortals, and we never truly die."

"Tell that to my mother," Eirlys spat. She was in for a good smite if Zoasis ever got her power back.

"I don't pretend what I ask is easy. What I have done was for the greater good but not good for you. But Eirlys, I need you more than I ever have before. And I'm so sorry, but it will hurt."

Eirlys groaned, a coppery taste and pulpy rawness in her mouth, cracks in her lips. There was the delicate, cool touch of tears drying on her face. Hurried, whispered voices fluttered in her ear. It was still too bright through her eyelids but past all of that, or before all of it, was pain. If one could call agony gentle, the pain in her was a light burn followed by an ache under her skin. She blinked, then breathed and wished she hadn't. Like gulping fire, the air stung on its way down, expanding her lungs, pressing against her ribs, and tearing through her.

The shadow of the spirit inside her tried to flee from the monstrous pain, and in a panicked moment, she almost slipped away. But pain or not, Eirlys's strength did not waver. She shoved her spirit back where it belonged, where its slender, phantom hand placed its palm on the outline of the body it was trapped.

Someone helped her up and she held in her whimpers at the touch. Brisa and Aydra stared at her, but she watched her hands. They weren't on fire, though they should have been. She moved her fingers, and the pain followed, each creak of her knuckles burned. Something festered underneath her skin, bright and agonizing.

A light which had burned away the peaceful dark.

# Chapter Fifty-Two

## Price

P rice watched her sleep. For hours. He didn't take his eyes off her. Supposedly, she was perfectly healthy. She had survived; by some goddess cursed miracle, she had survived. And yet, he hadn't had the courage to touch her yet. To know because he could feel that she was different. Her soothing magic no longer called to him.

He was grateful to know that the pull of her love was still strong enough that he could not leave her side. Not until she woke.

She began to stir, and Price leapt from the bed.

"Hey," he said.

Eirlys flinched as she tried to move, scanning the room, looking for him. Something in her eyes flared. Pain, fear, and a hint of desperation. Those faded away when she caught sight of him, replaced by relief.

"Hey," she said, climbing out of bed.

She shuffled towards him as if every step hurt. Price backed away, two quick steps, his palms braced against the back of the loveseat. Eirlys stopped, confusion written on her face. She didn't ask but Price answered anyway.

"What if I"—Price clenched his hands against the fabric, and a slight burning smell emitted as his power flashed—"what if all I ever felt was because of your magic?"

Eirlys smiled, her eyes crinkling with fear, a tinge of bitterness. "We tried this already, with obsidian."

"It's not that. You seem... different. With obsidian, it was an absence to be returned, and now it's truly changed," Price said.

"Yeah, it has, but that's what love is, right?" she asked. "Change, growth. Together."

"Together," he whispered.

And he bolted toward her, his hands desperate for her skin and his lips hungry for hers. He drank her in like she was the last bit of water in a parched desert. The feel of her was so distractingly different now. He didn't get a chance to push her away. She shoved at him, tears falling from her eyes, arms wrapping around herself.

"Fuck, fuck, fuck," she cried.

Price's hands reached for her as he stepped forward. "Sorry," he whispered.

"Is it this bad for you?" Her arms released her body.

Price shook his head. "No, but it used to be. My mom said she couldn't hold me for long when I was a child. But I have twenty-five years of practice of it being normal."

Eirlys swallowed. "I don't think I can do this."

By the gods, Price felt that. How many times had he tried to give up? To end it all because the pain was constant. The touch of obsidian helped, but only if he didn't want to feel at all. He never wanted this for her. He had been so close to setting her free, and now the cage of fire would burn her every time she moved or breathed.

"Eirlys." Price's eyes swam, tears silver against his skin.

"Stop, please," she said.

Eirlys stumbled back, reaching for the bottle Price kept by her bed. She missed, as if she were already drunk, and knocked over the RaGlass there. She reached for it, catching it by the tip of her finger and sending it tumbling to the stone floor. It shattered and Price was too slow to catch her before she fell into it.

They both watched her arm. A Klara's Wraithmark streaked across her face, and she backed away from it, squinting her eyes. Price scented her magic on the air, dust and rain and hope. The wound knitted itself together. She healed herself.

"No!" she cried. "They... it fixed me?"

Price smiled sadly, and he leaned over the glass and scooped Eirlys up, arms strong and gentle. She gasped as he settled her back on the bed. He left the mess of glass there and laid beside her.

"They can't fix a broken bottle by throwing more glass at it," he said. "I don't know what parts of your powers will work, but we have time to figure that out. Just because they twisted your magic into a shape of their choosing does not mean they are right. So maybe they did help a bit, but at what cost? They cured you of a brokenness their curse gave you in the first place."

Eirlys reached up to him and touched his cheek.

"Yes, terribly different." The guilt lacing her voice killed him. He didn't want her feeling sorry that she was now as fucked up as he was. It was bad enough that he went through this, and now he must watch his lover experience the same thing.

"I saw... " Eirlys stopped and scrunched her nose. "Is this worth it? Being near me, knowing how it used to be between us?"

Price reached out and with the gentlest of touches, traced her jawbone, her lips, down to the hollow of her neck where a tiny starburst scar lay. One of the many her wretched life had given her.

"I don't care about how I feel. I care about you, and what you need. I'll be fine. I lived with this before you, and I'll live with this with you, no matter what state you're in."

Eirlys leaned forward and kissed Price. He treated her skin like it was thin, made of cracked glass, every touch splintering.

"How do we get past this?" she whispered. Her lips pressed to his cheek.

He smiled, his cheek raising beneath her mouth. "By taking whatever happiness life gives us."

## CHAPTER FIFTY-THREE

### EIRLYS

"**D**o you, Eirlys Pendry, agree to take this oath and secure the crown?"

"I agree," she said. She had not endured all this pain to back down now.

"Will you swear to the Ancients and our beloved goddess to rule and govern the lands known as Kygem according to their laws and customs?"

"I swear." Because she would change those laws.

"Will you revere and worship the Ancients as mightily as our beloved goddess, and maintain their testaments in your faith?"

"I swear." Because her faith in the Goddess was as shattered as her spirit.

"And so Eirlys Resier Pendry hereby swears as your queen to perform her duties, which have been laid out as thus."

Alina placed a thick, heavy crown on Eirlys's head. Her birth mother's crown—a conglomeration of glass and obsidian crystals intertwined with silver, representing her affinity's metal. They had recast it for the first time in five thousand years to fit a Va. Eirlys smiled inside for a moment—the black obsidian in the crown now matched the tips of her hair, as dark and deep as her Wraithmark used to be.

Aydra, acting as an acolyte, handed her a glass staff. When Eirlys's hand touched the staff, her power flared, but instead of seeking shadows and night, she used the bright sunlight streaming through the windows into the throne room. The glaring light streaking her face nearly blinded her with agony, but she stood resolute. She would not let them see.

"I present to you Queen Eirlys Resier Pendry, the Queen of Kygem."

She was the fucking Queen, and she was done with running, cowering, bending. They would not break her—she would break them.

"May the Queen be immortal," the crowd intoned as one.

Eirlys gazed out from the top of the dais at the rumbling people below her, and as the fire burned under her skin, she wondered if any one of them saw the fire in her eyes.

T he whiskey's sharp burning passed over Eirlys's chapped lips, highlighting every crack, a bitter piercing pain. It scorched her throat and seared its way through her body, yet it barely made a dent in her own internal agony.

Buried beneath the fire of her skin lived remorse, dull and aching. A thousand regrets pounded the inside of her skull, and she drank again, downing the cup before it thunked hollow onto the wooden table. The tip of the bottle clanked against her glass as Brisa poured her another couple of fingers. The bar, a small dingy place on the supposedly bad side of town, was now one of her few havens since her coronation.

The tavern had closed three hours prior, but the bartender whose name Eirlys still didn't know left them with a few bottles, the keys to get more if needed, and a wink. No bowing, no 'Your Grace'; just whiskey and a quiet reprieve where, if most people looked twice, they expeditiously avoided her gaze. The Queen did not belong here, but claiming she visited such establishments was a swift way for the gossiper to find the business end of a sword.

Tonight, she didn't drink alone. Deryn sat to her left, staring at their empty glass, and Brisa reached over and poured a drink on Deryn's other side. Her sister's lover lifted their hand and drained it, returning to the same posture. Brisa had a glazed look in her eyes, only becoming focused when Deryn caught her attention. Price's hand rested softly Eirlys's thigh, the line of his body vibrating against her. He swirled his glass around, watching the legs of the whiskey run down the sides. The aforementioned sword lay on the table, and Price placed his hand on it whenever anyone recognized Eirlys.

When Brisa, Deryn and Price walked into the bar, she didn't bother asking how her court knew where she would be. She didn't try telling them to leave. In a way, her people had won. They had gotten her crowned, kept her alive, with all her mental faculties intact. But what victory felt like this, like complete and utter devastation? What did it mean when a victory felt like losing? Because here she was, alive, mostly healthy, and even her magic cooperated well enough as far she had been willing to test it. Yet she had lost so much, been drug further down than she had ever been.

Now with a crown on her head and a throne as her seat, she still had no way to guarantee the safety of those she loved. How was it that she felt no closer to saving the Skath, to freeing Kygem, to protecting Kestrya, than when she first arrived?

She'd promised to break them, bleed them, but in reality? She had no idea how to accomplish such a feat.

Eirlys's fist pounded the table, but only Deryn jumped.

"Fuck it, screw them. What do we do?"

Brisa glanced up. "We can't go back to being complacent."

"Agreed, but how do we beat them? Being outright rebellious made August Devoid, with a clear death threat on your heads."

Price smiled. "Play it smart. The Council may have the power, but you are still Queen. I must admit, since becoming Klara, the people have turned to you."

Deryn and Brisa agreed with clinking glasses.

Eirlys grinned, too drunk and in too much pain for it not to appear manic. "Play the crowd, the courts." She was never good with words, could barely get through a conversation with the Ancients without at least one curse, and the thought of not being able to just stab her way through this problem made her queasy. Or maybe that was the whiskey.

"It's a start," Brisa said, grabbing Eirlys's hand. "We cannot change the world tomorrow, but we can work towards it."

Deryn groaned. "Maybe not tomorrow though either," they said, rubbing their temples.

Eirlys's insides twisted, nausea bubbling in her chest. The never-ending pain flared with her emotional anguish. No, Price could not take them on. Brisa and Deryn, all risking their lives. She couldn't let it happen.

"Don't say it," Brisa warned.

"Say what?" Eirlys said, feigning interest in the cuticles on her left hand.

"That we don't get to fight. That you will protect us with whatever half thought out plan you have. We are not yours to protect—we own ourselves, and can choose how and when we die, what we die for. We get to choose the manner of our deaths. No one else."

Everyone concurred, and Eirlys threw her hands up. "Ungrateful bastards," Eirlys muttered, and her court smiled.

"So how do we plan on dying this time?" Deryn asked, a familiar, ever playful smile on their face.

"Tomorrow we can talk more," Price said, nudging Eirlys.

"If I don't get her back to the castle, they'll send people after us."

Eirlys sighed and rose, teetering on her feet as the room tilted for a moment before righting itself.

"Yeah, take her home," Deryn said, grabbing the bottle of whiskey and pushing Brisa out the door.

The pair wandered off somewhere, probably to find a nice little inn or their own bed in the little flat above the smithy.

Eirlys pulled Price to her, laying her head on his chest, and listening to his heartbeat. How precious the sound had become to her, how devastating if she lost it. Maybe she shouldn't have fallen in love, should have kept her distance. Because she loved him, and that made him a weapon, a tool to be used against her—her own personal torture device wrapped up in the man she adored.

"I'm not going anywhere, Eirlys. Even if they kill me, I will not leave you," he said, kissing the top of her head.

"Promise?" she whispered. Her voice cracked, the effect of the alcohol obliterating what little control she had left.

"I swear it, my love."

Eirlys sighed and brushed away her tears before pulling back. Price kissed her, his breath as intoxicating as the whiskey, and she drank him. Even as agony burned under her skin, flames of desire and a kind of joy erupted in her chest, fierce and bright, not relieving her discomfort but making it bearable. As they kissed it became a mere annoyance rather than a hindrance.

Yet, it wasn't the pain of being altered stuttering her heart; it was the pain of loss, of losing the man she held in her arms, of one more slice of her soul stripped away, leaving a bleeding mess of cuts and scars in a ruined shell.

Far off in the distance, over the hills of Alby's sleeping twilight, a flicker of dawn broke through the darkness. For now, she had this moment, this kiss, this man, and this happiness life was willing to give her.

She had tomorrow, and for now, that was enough.

*End of Book One*

# ACKNOWLEDGMENTS

Where do I even begin? I guess at the beginning. Thank you to my parents. To my dad, who encouraged me every step of the way to pursue this dream and who sent me a bottle of whiskey for every milestone. To my mom, who always lets her children make their own choices and supports them through everything, from me and my siblings, we cannot say thank you enough. To my bonus moms, S and E, I would not be the same person without you. Your enthusiasm and bragging gives me life.

To my partners. There are not enough words in the world to tell you how much I appreciate you... For bringing me water and snacks when I'm at my desk, for not seeing me for a week because I'm out trying to write, for always, always being accommodating. I don't deserve any of you. So thank you for staying and loving me.

To those early beta readers who read Her Dark Grace in its earliest iterations. You all provided me with the feedback I needed to make this book what it is today. You encouraged me to not hold back, to not be subtle and the book and I thank you for it.

To Lake County Press and Brittany Weisrock. No acknowledgement will ever be enough to thank you for taking a chance on a book with a lackluster beginning because you saw something great in it and helped me bring out the greatness of a book so close to my heart. Thank you for loving Her Dark Grace as much as I do!

To Ann H Fox, my fellow book sibling, my best friend. Six

years ago, we sat down in a restaurant, barely even friends, and I told you this story. You said you were Team Price and the rest, as they say, is history. You have jumped on late night discord calls, gone over edits in days of this chunky book baby, held me while I cried, and cheered with me while we celebrated. Your name should be right by mine on the cover page. It is in my heart. Thank you.

Finally, to every one of my readers, both new and old. If you have made it this far, then do not fear. Eirlys's story is not over. I hope to see you in the next one.

Rae Valtera grew up in the 90's playing way too much 'pretend' with her friends or her stuffed animals. She wrote her first book in the 2nd grade about Santa Claus and the Easter bunny switching their sacks on vacation and the chaos that ensued. As a teenager, she wrote a lot of fanfiction, some of it decent, most of it embarrassing.

Rae lives in colorful Colorado with her partners, three cats, and an ever-growing TBR pile. If she's not writing about brutal, beautiful fantasy worlds, she is reading about them. Rae will never pass up the offer to pet a dog, listen to a Taylor Swift album, or enjoy a glass of whiskey.

www.ingramcontent.com/pod-product-compliance
Lightning Source LLC
Chambersburg PA
CBHW022027120726
47901CB00006BA/1464